HARD BATTLES

The lead Interceptor rolled to port and cut down past the curve of the Frigate's hull. Corran caught a flash of red on one of the Interceptor's wings and nodded. "Looks like he was once part of the One Eighty-first Imperial Fighter Group."

Whistler blatted harshly at him.

"Yes, I'll be careful. Neither one of us wants to know what Mirax will do to the survivor if we die." Corran winked at the holograph of his wife fixed to a side panel in his cockpit, then rolled his X-wing and cruised down after the squint. He threaded a path through the turbolaser blasts the Frigate was pumping out, then swept past the ship out near its engines.

Even before Whistler could hoot a warning, the hiss of lasers splashing themselves over his aft shields caught Corran's full attention. His secondary monitor showed the Interceptor dropping in on his tail. *Must have throttled back and hovered near the engines, waiting. This guy is good.*

Don't miss these other
exciting *Star Wars*® books:

X-WING
by Michael A. Stackpole
#1: ROGUE SQUADRON
#2: WEDGE'S GAMBLE
#3: THE KRYTOS TRAP
#4: THE BACTA WAR
by Aaron Allston
#5: WRAITH SQUADRON
#6: IRON FIST
#7: SOLO COMMAND

THE BLACK FLEET CRISIS
by Michael P. Kube-McDowell
#1: BEFORE THE STORM
#2: SHIELD OF LIES
#3: TYRANT'S TEST

THE CRYSTAL STAR
by Vonda N. McIntyre

TALES FROM THE MOS EISLEY CANTINA
edited by Kevin J. Anderson

TALES FROM JABBA'S PALACE
edited by Kevin J. Anderson

TALES OF THE BOUNTY HUNTERS
edited by Kevin J. Anderson

THE BOUNTY HUNTER WARS
by K. W. Jeter
#1: THE MANDALORIAN ARMOR
#2: SLAVE SHIP

CHILDREN OF THE JEDI
by Barbara Hambly

DARKSABER
by Kevin J. Anderson

THE ILLUSTRATED STAR WARS UNIVERSE
by Ralph McQuarrie
and Kevin J. Anderson

SHADOWS OF THE EMPIRE
by Steve Perry

THE NEW REBELLION
by Kristine Kathryn Rusch

I, JEDI
by Michael A. Stackpole

THE HAND OF THRAWN
by Timothy Zahn
SPECTER OF THE PAST
VISION OF THE FUTURE

STAR WARS

X - W I N G

BOOK EIGHT

ISARD'S REVENGE

Michael A. Stackpole

BANTAM BOOKS
New York Toronto London Sydney Auckland

STAR WARS: ISARD'S REVENGE
A Bantam Spectra Book / April 1999

SPECTRA and the portrayal of a boxed "s" are trademarks
of Bantam Books, a division of Random House, Inc.

ISBN-0-553-57093-7

Published simultaneously in the United States and Canada

Bantam Books are published by Bantam Books, a division of Random
House, Inc. Its trademark, consisting of the words "Bantam Books"
and the portrayal of a rooster, is Registered in U.S. Patent and Trademark
Office and in other countries. Marca Registrada. Bantam Books,
1540 Broadway, New York, New York 10036.

PRINTED IN THE UNITED STATES OF AMERICA

OPM   10   9   8   7   6   5   4   3   2   1

To Peet Janes and Peter Schweighofer

Thanks for providing me the opportunity to play in this universe in new and wondrous ways.

ACKNOWLEDGMENTS

The author would like to thank the following people for their various contributions to this book:

Janna Silverstein, Tom Dupree, Pat LoBrutto, and Ricia Mainhard for getting me into this mess.

Sue Rostoni, Allan Kausch, and Lucy Autrey Wilson for continuing to let me work in the *Star Wars* universe.

Peter Schweighofer, Peet Janes, Bill Slavicsek, Patty Jackson, Dan Wallace, and Steve Sansweet for material they created, ideas they encouraged, and advice they offered.

Aaron Allston and Timothy Zahn for letting me play with characters they created.

Paul Youll for another stunning cover.

Lawrence Holland and Edward Kilham for the X-Wing and TIE Fighter computer games.

Chris Taylor for pointing out to me the ship in which Tycho was flying in *Star Wars VI: Return of the Jedi*. (It was the 2nd A-wing that flew out of the Death Star to lead off some pursuit.)

My parents, Jim and Janet; my sister, Kerin; my brother, Patrick; his wife, Joy; and Faith, my niece; for their encouragement and support.

Jennifer Roberson and especially Elizabeth T. Danforth for listening to bits of this story as it was being written and enduring such abuse with infinite patience and grace.

Dramatis Personae

The Rogues

Commander Wedge Antilles (human male from Corellia)

Captain Tycho Celchu (human male from Alderaan)

Flight Officer Lyyr Zatoq (Quarren female from Mon Calamari)

Lieutenant Derek "Hobbie" Klivian (human male from Ralltiir)

Lieutenant Wes Janson (human male from Taanab)

Lieutenant Gavin Darklighter (human male from Tatooine)

Lieutenant Myn Donos (human male from Corellia)

Lieutenant Khe-Jeen Slee (Issori male from Issor)

Lieutenant Corran Horn (human male from Corellia)

Lieutenant Ooryl Qyrgg (Gand male from Gand)

Lieutenant Asyr Sei'lar (Bothan female from Bothawui)

Flight Officer Inyri Forge (human female from Kessel)

Lieutenant Nawara Ven (Twi'lek male from Ryloth)

Support Personnel

Gate (Wedge's R5 unit)

Whistler (Corran's R2 unit)

New Republic Military

Admiral Ackbar (Mon Calamari male from Mon Calamari)
Colonel Kapp Dendo (Devaronian male from Devaron)
Captain Page (human male from Corulag)

New Republic Intelligence

General Airen Cracken (human male from Contruum)
Iella Wessiri (human female from Corellia)

Ciutric Hegemony Forces

Prince-Admiral Delak Krennel (human male from Corulag)
Ysanne Isard (human female from Coruscant)

Crew of the *Errant Venture*
Booster Terrik (human male from Corellia)

Crew of the *Pulsar Skate*
Mirax Terrik (human female from Corellia)

1

Sithspawn! When his X-wing reverted to realspace before the countdown timer had reached zero, Corran Horn knew Thrawn had somehow managed to outguess the New Republic yet one more time. The Rogues had helped create the deception that the New Republic would be going after the Tangrene Ubiqtorate Base, but Thrawn clearly hadn't taken the bait.

The man's incredible. I'd like to meet him, shake his hand. Corran smiled. *And then kill him, of course.*

Two seconds into realspace and the depth of Thrawn's brilliance became undeniable. The New Republic's forces had been brought out of hyperspace by two Interdictor cruisers, which even now started to fade back toward the Imperial lines. This left the New Republic's ships well shy of the Bilbringi shipyards and facing an Imperial fleet arrayed for battle. The two Interdictors that had dragged them from hyperspace were a small part of a larger force scattered around to make sure the New Republic's ships were not going to be able to retreat.

"Battle alert!" Captain Tycho Celchu's voice crackled over the comm unit. "TIE Interceptors coming in—bearing two-nine-three, mark twenty."

Corran keyed his comm unit. "Three Flight, on me. Hold it together and nail some squints."

The cant-winged Interceptors rolled in and down on the Rogues. Corran kicked his X-wing up on its port S-foil and flicked his lasers over to quad-fire mode. While that would slow his rate of fire, each burst had a better chance of killing a squint outright. *And there are plenty that need killing here.*

Corran nudged his stick right and dropped the crosshairs onto an Interceptor making a run at Admiral Ackbar's flagship. He hit the firing switch, sending four red laser bolts burning out at the target. They hit on the starboard side, with two of them piercing the cockpit and the other two vaporizing the strut supporting the right wing. The bent hexagonal wing sheered off in a shower of sparks, while the rest of the craft started a long, lazy spiral toward the outer edges of the system.

"Break port, Nine."

As the Gand's high-pitched voice poured through the comm unit, Corran snaprolled his X-wing to the left, then chopped his throttle back and hauled hard on the stick to take him into a loop. An Interceptor flashed through where he had been, and Ooryl Qyrgg's X-wing came fast on its tail. Ooryl's lasers blazed in sequence, stippling the Interceptor with red energy darts. One hit each wing, melting great furrows through them, while the other two lanced through the cockpit right above the twin ion engines. The engines themselves tore free of their support structure and blew out through the front of the squint, then exploded in a silver fireball that consumed the rest of the Imperial fighter.

"Thanks, Ten."

"My pleasure, Nine."

Whistler, the green and white R2 unit slotted in behind Corran, hooted, and data started pouring up over the fighter's main monitor. It told him in exact detail what he was seeing unfold in space around him. The New Republic's forces had come into the system in the standard conical formation that allowed them to maximize firepower.

Thrawn had arrayed his forces in more of a bowl shape, with Interdictor cruisers ringing the outer edge, preventing retreat and promoting containment. The Imperial forces also appeared to have very specific fire missions and were working over the smaller support ships in Ackbar's fleet.

Corran shivered. *And even if we were to punch through the Imp formation, we'd still have to deal with the Golan Space Defense Stations protecting the Imperial shipyards.* Thrawn, genius that he had proved himself to be, had set a perfect ambush for the New Republic. The Bilbringi shipyards were crucial to the Imperial war effort since they were a major supplier of ships, and their loss would strike a major blow against Thrawn's effort to destroy the New Republic.

Of course, Thrawn figured that out himself and knew we'd be here. Until Thrawn slithered in from the Unknown Regions and began his drive to reestablish the Empire, Corran had allowed himself to believe the tough battles had already been won, and all the New Republic had left to do was to mop up the last of the Imperials. *Now it seems the hard battles are here and waiting to be lost.*

With a flick of his thumb, Corran evened his shields out fore and aft, then throttled back up and slashed in at a pair of Interceptors making a run on a New Republic Assault Frigate. He slid his crosshairs over on the trailing Interceptor as it began its shallow glide along the Frigate's hull. His quad burst caught most of the port wing, liquefying it in an instant. The molten metal froze in a long black tangle of ribbonlike shards trailing after the damaged fighter. The pilot juked his ship to the right to escape Corran, but that flew him straight into a burst from one of the Frigate's turbolasers, vaporizing the squint in an eyeblink.

The lead Interceptor rolled to port and cut down past the curve of the Frigate's hull. Corran caught a flash of red on one of the Interceptor's wings and nodded. "Looks like he was once part of the One Eighty-first Imperial Fighter Group. They used to be feared. Maybe I ought to see why."

Whistler sounded a mournful tone.

"Yes, I know what I'm doing."

The droid blatted harshly at him.

"Yes, I'll be careful. Neither one of us wants to know what Mirax will do to the survivor if we die." Corran winked at the holograph of his wife fixed to a side panel in his cockpit, then rolled his X-wing and cruised down after the squint. He threaded a path through the turbolaser blasts the Frigate was pumping out, then swept past the ship out near its engines

Even before Whistler could hoot a warning, the hiss of lasers splashing themselves over his aft shields caught Corran's full attention. His secondary monitor showed the Interceptor dropping in on his tail. *Must have throttled back and hovered near the engines, waiting. This guy is good.*

Pumping more energy into his shields, Corran rolled the X-wing right, up onto the S-foil. He pulled back on the stick to start a loop and held it for three seconds, then cut his throttle back and inverted. Pulling back harder on the stick, he completed a fast loop, then throttled up through the end of it and rolled out right.

As his fighter's nose came to point at the Interceptor, the Imp pilot rolled his craft and dove away from Corran. The Corellian pilot started down after him, but cut back to 75 percent of his speed. As he anticipated, the Imp cut his speed as well, hoping Corran would race past him. Instead Corran triggered one quick burst of fire that hit high on the Imp's port wing, burning a black hole through the red stripe. He then stood on his right rudder pedal, keeping his guns on the squint, and poured another quad burst of laserfire into the Interceptor.

All four ruby darts drilled through the port wing, then stabbed deep into the cockpit. A bright light flashed through the hole the lasers had opened, and Corran expected the ship to explode, but it didn't. Instead it began to come apart, with bits and pieces of it whirling away as if the bright flash had disintegrated all the rivets and welds used in its manufacture.

Corran looped his X-wing away from the dying squint, but before he could vector in on another Interceptor, he heard Commander Wedge Antilles coming through on the squadron's tactical channel. "All Rogues, come about on a heading of one-two-five, mark one-seven. That Golan Space Defense Station is designated Green One. It's ours."

"Ours, Commander?" The same surprise Corran felt in his chest came flooding through Gavin Darklighter's voice. "That's a pretty tough target."

"We'll just have to be tougher than it is, won't we, Six?" Wedge's reply came loaded with grim irony. "If we can get into the shipyard, the Imps will have to think about more than just pounding our fleet. Besides, we have friends coming out. One Flight is on me. Five, you have Two Flight. Nine, you have Three."

"As ordered, Lead." Corran brought his fighter around on the appropriate heading and locked the target into his computer. "Estimated time of arrival at missile range is forty seconds. Let's move, Three Flight."

Ooryl pulled his X-wing up on Corran's starboard wing. Inyri Forge brought Rogue Twelve up on Corran's port wing and Asyr Sei'lar, in Rogue Eleven, hung back off Inyri's port wing. Corran goosed his ship a bit forward and shifted his attention toward their target, trusting the others to keep him informed if Imps were vectoring in on them from behind.

Not likely, though, since they've got plenty to keep them busy. Throughout the bowl into which the New Republic's fleet moved, massive salvos of energy shot up and down and side to side, filling the area with a dazzling light show. Corran would have been more than content to watch the turbolaser bursts flow back and forth, but the fact that they were lethal was more than enough to keep him from finding much beauty in them. Behind the squadron, Y-wings, A-wings, and B-wings mixed it up with Interceptors, TIE fighters, and Bombers, punctuating the light show with brilliant explosions.

The larger ships, when hit hard, didn't explode as quickly. Instead their fire-blackened bulks drifted through the battlefield, atmosphere burning off as it leaked out of broken hulls. Some turbolaser blasts were enough to peel back armor plates and reduce them to floating metal globules that hardened in the vacuum of space. In other places the shots holed the ships through and through or vaporized things that should have been there, like superstructures or a bow.

The Golan Space Defense Station loomed larger. Lights blinked placidly at the various corners, almost inviting inspection. Over two kilometers long, about half as wide and tall, it bristled with turbolaser batteries, proton torpedo launchers, and tractor beam stations. It massed more than an Imperial Star Destroyer and, while it wasn't as heavily armed, the proton torpedo launchers gave it the ability to inflict serious damage in a hurry. It could easily put down any of the New Republic ships that made it through the Imperial formation.

Corran flicked his weapons-control over to proton torpedoes and linked fire so two would go with a single pull of his trigger. Whistler brought up the heads-up targeting display and the HUD fixed a green box around the space platform. The droid began to beep insistently as it tried to get a target lock; then the HUD went red and Whistler's tone became constant.

"Nine has a firing solution, transmitting now. On my mark, Three Flight. Three, two, one, mark!"

All four of the X-wings fired their proton torpedoes at one time, using Whistler's targeting solution to guide them. A battle station like the Golan sported very powerful shields and individually fired proton torpedoes would have been unable to pierce it. Eight torpedoes coming in at the same time, aiming for the same point, would overstress the shields, draining them of energy. This would create a critical time window in which the shields would be weakened, or would totally fail, and have to be regenerated.

Whistler sounded another long, strong tone. "Three Flight, second salvo. On my mark. Three, two, one, mark."

Eight more proton torpedoes streaked out from the incoming fighters before the first set had hit. The first eight torpedoes detonated against the station's top-port shield. The shield itself went opaque, taking on a milky-white hue as it attempted to dissipate the torpedoes' energy. But sparks shot from the shield projectors rimming the station's middle and a roiling ball of plasma bounced across the hull, scorching gray paint as it went.

The next eight missiles hit in a ragged sequence and exploded brilliantly along the station's middle. Flames vomited into space as a blast opened a hole three decks deep and vented atmosphere. Armor plates whirled into space, half melted and twisted. Turbolaser batteries split apart, leaving blackened holes and warped metal where they had once been grafted to the station.

Corran juked his fighter up and away from the station, then inverted and watched turbolaser fire shoot beneath his canopy. For a half second he thought the Golan's gunners were terribly shaken by the squadron's attack, hence their misses, then he glanced at his rear sensor display. He smiled and keyed his comm unit. "We softened them up for you . . ."

"Appreciated, Rogues, now let us do our jobs."

Two New Republic Assault Frigates, the *Tyrant's Bane* and *Liberty Star*, cruised in toward the Golan station. Though each ship was less than a third as long as the station, they bristled with fifty laser cannons and poured terajoules of coherent light into the Golan. Scarlet bolts lanced through the station's collapsed shields and bubbled up chunks of the metal hull. Stanchions wavered and wilted beneath the blistering assault. As they collapsed, turbolaser batteries sagged and dipped, then melted into slag.

The troops aboard the Golan fought back valiantly, but found themselves at a gross disadvantage. Proton torpedoes exploded, shaking the station. The troops fired in vain at the fighters, then concentrated their fire on the Frigates. While the larger ships made for better targets, their intact shields provided them with protection the station lacked. With each salvo fewer and fewer of the Golan's weapons fired back. A brilliant flare flashed on the station's port side, then it went black.

Power couplings must be down. That half of the station is dead. Corran keyed his comlink. "Three Flight, with me, we're past the station and in on the shipyard. Now the Imps have to move to catch us."

Corran tried to force confidence into his voice. Racing a starfighter through a shipyard, shooting up targets of opportunity, would be fairly easy, but he didn't want to kid himself about the chances that such an assault would force the Empire to break off its attack on the Rebel fleet. *Thrawn might not like what the Rogues are doing, but he can deal with us later, when he's killed all the other ships.*

Tycho's voice poured through the comm unit. "Lead, Two here. I show the Imperial formation breaking up."

"What?" Corran stabbed a button and shifted the display on his primary monitor over to a system-wide scan. The Imperial bowl, which had been contracting around the Rebel cone, was beginning to come apart. The *Stormhawk* and the *Nemesis* were moving to secure an outbound vector for the fleet, while Thrawn's flagship, the *Chimaera*, swung about to discourage pursuit of the fleet's smaller ships.

Disbelief threaded through Wedge's voice. "Be careful, Rogues. Thrawn's got something up his sleeve."

Janson laughed lightly. "Looks like a full-fledged retreat, Lead. They're recovering their fighters."

Corran studied his readout. The Rebel cone began to blossom from the widest end, coming forward to the tip. The New Republic's ships kept a respectful distance from the Imperial ships and moved to begin recovery operations. The Imp pull-back left a couple of their own stricken ships still hanging in space. *And it leaves the Bilbringi shipyards to us, which Thrawn never would have wanted.*

A shiver ran up Corran's spine. "What happened here, Lead?"

"I don't know, Nine." Wedge's voice came through solemn and with a hint of hesitation. "Just got a recall order from Admiral Ackbar. We're to rendezvous with *Home One.*"

"And then he'll tell us what happened?"

"Could be, Corran, but I doubt it." Wedge's X-wing looped out in front of the other Rogues and began the trip back toward the fleet. "For now, let's just be glad that, for whatever reason, Thrawn discovered he had better things to do, and let's be ready for when he decides to come back at us again."

2

As tired as he was, Wedge Antilles found it a major effort to open his eyes when Admiral Ackbar cleared his voice. The pilot had been seated in the waiting area outside the Admiral's office and hadn't heard the hatch open. He started to spring to his feet, but tight muscles slowed him, only allowing him to unfurl his body like a heavy flag in a weak breeze.

"Forgive me, Admiral." Wedge sheepishly looked back at where he'd been sitting. "I didn't mean to . . ."

Ackbar's barabels quivered as his mouth opened in an approximation of a human grin. "No need for forgiveness. I kept you waiting too long. Reviewing Thrawn's tactics is fascinating, and other information also demanded attention. The tide of data washed away the time."

"Understandable, Admiral." Wedge followed the Mon Calamari into his office. As with any cabin on a starship, space was limited but the large viewports helped alleviate any sense of closeness. A globe of water hung suspended in the corner in a gravity-nullifying field and flashed with a rainbow of fish swimming through it. The water also contributed to the elevated humidity in the room, but Wedge didn't mind it too much. *After all these years of dealing with the Admiral, it doesn't feel that oppressive.*

Ackbar waved a flipper-fingered hand at a chair before his desk, then sat with his back to the black expanse of space. "I want to commend you and your people on the run at the Golan station. While the Assault Frigates finished it off, your people put the first cracks in its shell and otherwise hurt it. You should have your techs get ready to paint a Golan on your fighters."

Wedge smiled and ran his fingers back through his brown hair. "I'm sure that'll make the Rogues happy. I'm just pleased you gave us the release to make that run."

"It was a gamble we needed to make at the time."

"And it seemed to work." Wedge's brown eyes narrowed. "I can't believe, though, that our assault was what frightened Thrawn off."

The Mon Calamari sat back and swiveled his chair around to face toward the fish-globe. "It wasn't—which is not meant to diminish what you and your people did. Part of the delay here was dealing with coded messages from Wayland."

"Wayland?"

"Apparently it is a world where the Emperor had hidden a cloning facility. Thrawn was using it to produce troops. He was also using a clone of a Jedi Master to help coordinate his military efforts, and this clone was based on Wayland. Luke and Leia were there to deal with him. Leia also has managed to establish a rapport with the Noghri. They are an alien species the Empire had tricked into serving as agents and assassins. The Noghri worked for Thrawn, but when they discovered the Imperial deception, they used one of the Noghri close to Thrawn to kill him."

Wedge sat forward, the last vestiges of fatigue burned away. "Thrawn, dead? Are you sure?"

Ackbar shrugged uneasily. "There is no way of knowing for certain, since the Noghri assassin has not reported back to his superiors. In fact, they assume he was killed trying to escape from the *Chimaera*. While it is possible that Thrawn was just injured and a subordinate officer issued orders in his stead, causing the retreat, the fact is that the Noghri have been spectacularly successful assassins. This

Ruhk had the same sort of access to Thrawn that Chewbacca has to Han Solo, and if the Wookiee were of a mind to kill Han, I do not doubt he would succeed."

The Corellian pilot exhaled slowly as he sank back into the chair. "Thrawn, dead. That pretty much breaks the back of the Empire's remnants, doesn't it?"

"It certainly hurts them, yes. There are still warlords out there—Teradoc, Harssk, Krennel—and some ex-Imperials who have gone feral and are leading pirate bands. There are also clusters of loyal Imperial systems that are fairly self-sufficient, but they don't seem to be much of a threat to the New Republic. We will have to continue battling the warlords, and I have no doubt there are more Imperial weapons of mass destruction lurking out there to catch us like a riptide, but we have gotten past a stretch of rough water."

Wedge blinked, then shook his head. "It's been eight or nine years now that I've been fighting against the Empire. There were times I didn't think I was going to live another moment. I don't think I ever let myself *dream* I might survive this long, to see this sort of victory. This was always a goal, but now that it's here . . ."

He fell silent as a host of emotions exploded in his chest. An incredible sensation of relief washed over him. *I'm alive, actually alive.* Pleasure at the number of his comrades who had also survived followed quickly on its heels, chased by the melancholy of remembering those who had died. *Biggs, Dack, Ibtisam, Riv, the Admiral's niece Jesmin, Grinder, Castin Donn, Peshk, Jek Porkins—too many, far too many.*

Yet even as memories of the dead tried to weigh him down, his spirits soared. The Rebellion had actually done it, had actually defeated the Empire and liberated trillions of subjugated people. Oppression had been exchanged for hope, misery for freedom. It had been an act of sheer will by so many that allowed for the Rebellion's success, and Wedge took great joy in his contribution to that effort.

He looked up at Ackbar. "I never really dared let myself look beyond the next battle, and now, it seems, there might truly be an end to the warfare. I don't know what I'll do with myself."

Ackbar's lip-fringes twitched. "Said like a man contemplating retirement."

"Retirement? I'm not even thirty."

"Warfare is an occupation from which one can never retire too young, Commander."

"Good point, Admiral." Wedge smiled. "Maybe I could retire—not immediately, mind you. I literally *don't* know what I would do with myself if I did. Maybe write my memoirs or get some education. I always wanted to be an architect, and peace could mean a lot of building."

Ackbar nodded. "Find yourself a mate, raise a small school of children?"

Wedge wrinkled his nose. "I don't know about a *school* of children, but a couple, sure. However, that's further down the line, I think."

"True." Ackbar turned to face him and rested his forearms on his desk. "There is a more immediate problem I need you to deal with."

"Yes?"

"I want you to accept immediate promotion to the rank of General."

Wedge shook his head. "Hey, I won that Wraith Squadron bet."

"Yes, you did, and very adroitly." Ackbar pressed his hands together. "Commander, we have played this shell game, you and I, for years. You don't want a promotion because you don't want to move out of an X-wing cockpit. I certainly can appreciate your desires. I can sympathize with them, but I also know you are capable of handling greater responsibilities than you have been. This promotion would address those responsibilities."

"Address how? I'm at my best planning small-unit tactical operations."

"Ah, so the conquest of Thyferra was a small-unit tactical operation?"

Wedge hesitated. "Well, yes, sort of."

Ackbar shook his head. "I allowed you to deflect me with the whole Wraith Squadron concept, and I value you enough to seriously consider letting you remain in command of a fighter unit."

"Rogue Squadron? Or am I going to have to command a full wing the way General Salm does?"

"Rogue Squadron will be sufficient for now."

The Corellian arched an eyebrow at his superior. "If you're willing to leave me in charge of Rogue Squadron, I guess I don't need a promotion, then."

The Mon Calamari leaned forward, his eyes half shut. "But you do, Commander, you need a promotion and you need one very quickly."

"Why?"

Ackbar sighed. "Because your people in the squadron are refusing their own promotions. They're following in your wake, which is a grand testament to your leadership and their feelings for you, but not really fair to them at all. Captain Celchu should be at least a Colonel—that was the job he was performing in leading the Rogues while you were with the Wraiths. Hobbie and Janson should be Majors, Horn should be a Captain at the very least, Darklighter as well, and the rest of your Rogues should be something other than Flight Officers."

Wedge sat there, his mouth open ever so slightly. "I never really gave it that much thought, I guess."

"There wasn't that much time for thinking, given all you and the Rogues have been through." Ackbar spread his hands. "The liberation of Thyferra made it difficult for us to insist on promotions lest it look as though we were rewarding you for toppling a government. That sort of thing could have encouraged other units to try similar actions on other worlds. Your involvement with the Wraiths further insulated you because of the bet we had. Then Thrawn arrived and promotions became less important than otherwise. Now, with his threat ended, we have old injustices to take care of."

"Right. I'm sure the Bothans would like to see Asyr made at least a Captain."

"And they would like her back flying for them."

"Not hard to believe." Wedge shook his head. *How could I have been so blind? My people have all been great, and certainly more deserving of rank and honors than a lot of folks who've been promoted beyond them. I've been so worried about not letting the Rebellion down that I've let them down.* "I guess I need to prepare reports so they can be considered for promotion, yes?"

Ackbar punched a button on the holoprojector pad built into his desk. Above it little holographic images of each of the squadron's pilots burned to life. The Admiral reached up and touched Tycho's image and it blossomed into a full datafile. "Emtrey managed to take care of filing routine reports for you, including performance evaluations and the like. Appending your comments to each file would not hurt, especially if the reporting officer is *General* Antilles."

Wedge nodded slowly, then smiled. "How long ago did you figure out that using my people against me would work? I mean, none of them complained, did they?"

"No, none of them did." Ackbar's mouth opened in a smile. "In fact, I think they took perverse delight in their situation. As for when I knew how to get you to accept this change, it occurred to me during your time at Thyferra. You're as loyal to your people as they are to you."

"Fair enough." Wedge's eyes narrowed. "Now that you've gotten me to agree to the promotion, it's time you let me in on what else is happening."

Ackbar hesitated for a moment, then bowed his head. "Very good, General. How did you know the tide was still rising?"

"I know you well enough, Admiral, to know you wouldn't have pushed me to accept a rank unless it was important for me to do so. If getting my people to accept rank was the problem, you'd just have me talk to them. You want me to be a General, and I guess I figure that if I have rank, it's because I'm going to need to pull it."

"Excellent reasoning, which confirms your suitability to what I need you for." The Mon Calamari pressed his hands flat against the desk. "Thrawn's assault really was the last effort by a united Empire to destroy the Rebellion. There are, however, many warlords who hold sway over collections of star systems. We're going to need to liberate those systems and worlds. Right now, Rogue Squadron is pretty much the only unit in the New Republic with any sort of experience with that kind of operation."

"Because of what we learned at Thyferra."

"Exactly."

Wedge nodded. "System liberation will be a delicate operation. If we go in with too much matériel we'll appear to be as nasty a force as the Empire. If we make a half-hearted effort and are defeated, it will cost us lives and undermine our credibility with the New Republic's member states. If we do it just right, we give other warlords something to think about, which might make them more open to peaceful negotiations."

"You've distilled four hours of Provisional Council discussions down to the key points. We're going to have to go after the warlords, and the first one has to fall in relatively short order."

"Haste never makes for good warfare." Wedge frowned. "Just picking a target will be tough. The criteria for that choice alone will take hours of debate."

"Already done." Ackbar hit another button on the holoprojector and a new image replaced Tycho's. The man had close-cropped white hair and piercing blue eyes that seemed to project a cold cruelty. Below the image of the man's head and shoulders hung a smaller computer window display showing a prosthetic right hand. A list of specifications for the hand scrolled out below. "You've dealt with this man before."

"Admiral Delak Krennel." Wedge felt the flesh on his arms pucker. "He ordered TIE fighter attacks on the civilians on Axxila and opposed our rescue of Sate Pestage from Ciutric."

"Yes. He murdered Sate Pestage and took over his holdings—the Ciutric Hegemony. It made him the leader of a dozen worlds and gave him a fair amount of material resources. He didn't join Thrawn per se, but seems to have given him monetary support. He rules from Ciutric and has a fleet of a dozen or so capital ships, including his *Reckoning*."

Wedge smiled. "Got it all repaired, did he?"

"So it seems."

"He's been rather quiet—not at all like Teradoc. How can you justify going after him . . . ?" Wedge frowned for a moment, then barked a little laugh. "We're going to bring him to justice for Pestage's murder?"

"That, and the murder of Pestage's family. When Krennel took over, he killed every one of them he could find. Over a hundred people perished in that purge alone, and there have been other purges to keep him in power. His murder sprees give us all the excuse we need to target him."

"And the fact that he took the holdings of an Imperial officer and converted them to himself means that by going after him, we're suggesting to anyone else who might be adventurous out there that what once belonged to the Empire is ours. Interfere with us and you'll lose everything."

Ackbar turned his head and stared at Wedge with one big amber eye. "Political analysis, Wedge? Had I known you'd take to being a General so easily, I'd have demanded the promotion sooner."

"Being aware of politics, Admiral, is light-years away from liking it or being good at it. Still, the lessons concerning Thyferra and how ticklish that all was haven't been lost upon me. Do things right, and we might avoid prolonged battles in the future." Wedge stood and saluted the Admiral. "I guess a General has to keep the big picture in mind. I get *that* right and I keep my people alive. No matter what my rank, that's the duty I hold most dear."

3

Corran Horn hit the canopy release on his X-wing and freed himself of the restraining harness even before Whistler completed the fighter's shutdown procedure. The pilot pulled off his helmet and set it on the spacefighter's nose, then clambered out of the cockpit and jumped down to the hangar deck. He came up from his crouch quickly and turned toward Whistler. The droid was piping shrilly.

"I know you want down. I'll find a tech to do that."

He turned toward the flight operations center and raised a hand to signal for a tech, but a woman slipped her fingers through his, then bumped him bodily back a step beneath the X-wing. She covered his mouth with hers and Corran enfolded her in a fierce hug. He clung tightly to her, drinking in the spicy scent of her hair and perfume as they kissed.

Eventually, reluctantly, he freed his mouth from hers and looked up into her smoldering brown eyes. "Damn, I have missed you so much, Mirax. I . . ."

She kissed him again. "You're here, I'm here. The missing part is over, my love."

Corran reached a hand up and stroked her cheek, brushing away a single tear. "Of happiness, I hope."

"Very much so." She pulled her face back a couple of centimeters and arched a black eyebrow at him. "No tears of joy from you?"

He shrugged. "You'd have a flood, but it's bad for the pilot image thing, you know?"

Whistler's harsh blatting from above them stole any need for Mirax to reply.

She jerked a thumb in the droid's direction. "He's right; you pilots take this image thing much too seriously." Mirax flicked a finger up under his chin. "Then again, guys who weep never have done much for me."

"You love me for my stoic attitude then?"

"No, dear, it's the lightsaber." She swung around on his left, slipping her right arm around his waist. "Do you need to report for debriefing, or can I steal you away?"

Corran frowned. "I think we covered everything on the trip back from Bilbringi."

"So you want to just go home and fall into bed?"

He shook his head as they threaded their way through the chaos the squadron's return had created. "I got plenty of rack time on *Home One* during the trip."

"Not the question I asked, husband."

Corran blinked. "I guess I *have* been away too long."

"I'm sure Mirax will think of ways for you to make up for lost time, Lieutenant." Wedge Antilles smiled broadly. "I hear she's very inventive."

"Wedge!" Mirax launched herself into his arms and gave him a big hug. "I knew Thrawn wouldn't get you."

Wedge smiled and brushed Mirax's black hair back off her shoulders. "Well, someone had to keep Corran alive. I didn't want to have to come back to Coruscant here and tell you he'd died."

"Not a worry, not once." Mirax brushed a hand across the rank insignia on the chest of Wedge's orange flight suit. The round-cornered rectangle contained five dots in a cross pattern. "A General? Oh, Wedge, your folks would have been so proud." Leaning forward, she kissed him on the cheek.

"Thanks." Wedge slipped from her embrace and glanced

down. His face reddened slightly, then he looked up with a smile. "Not really what I planned for a life, but I've heard it said that life is what happens while you wait for plans to work."

"I've heard that, too." Mirax stepped back to Corran's side and slid the fingers of her right hand through those of his left. "New rank and new responsibilities for you, I guess."

"True." Wedge frowned and looked around the hangar. "And I'd be remiss if I didn't ask how you knew when to meet us and how you got in here. This is supposed to be a secure area."

Mirax shot Corran a hard glance. "Been giving him suspicion lessons?"

Corran shook his head. "Not me. And I know the Terriks better than to ask such a question."

"Good point, Corran." Wedge nodded sheepishly. "I guess I should be thankful Booster hasn't parked his *Errant Venture* here."

Mirax laughed. "He would have, but he's not fully trusting the story that Thrawn is gone. He thinks it's a rumor meant to get him to bring his Star Destroyer out of hiding so Thrawn can add it to his fleet."

Corran tapped a finger against his chin. "Booster versus Thrawn. Now there's a match I'd pay money to see."

"Just wait. Eventually Booster will decide that his jumping the *EV* around produced enough stories of an Impstar Deuce running around behind Thrawn's lines that *he* was the reason Thrawn was distracted enough to die at Bilbringi." Wedge smiled broadly. "Five years from now we'll find we were flying with the *Venture* when we took out that Golan station."

Mirax pressed fingers to Corran's lips and gave him a glare that forestalled any comment about her father. "To answer your earlier question, General Antilles, your arrival was anticipated because Admiral Ackbar requested a party to welcome the squadron back. Emtrey, being efficient and interested in good value, communicated to me the needs for this celebration."

Corran gently pulled Mirax's fingers from his lips. "We're having a welcome-home party catered by a droid?"

His wife smiled. "I gave him a choice: his budget or his selections. Things will kick off in your base recreation center about eight."

Wedge nodded. "You making a *ryshcate*?"

"That's my intention. I pretty much have everything I need at home." Mirax glanced at Corran. "Save, perhaps, an assistant."

Corran pointed back to where a tech was using a crane to pull Whistler out of his green and white X-wing. "Whistler will be available in just a second."

Her grip on his hand tightened. "Not quite the assistant I had in mind."

Corran felt a burst of heat rush up his body, then his face reddened. He looked over at Wedge. "If you don't mind, General, I guess I have some cooking to do."

Whistler's diligent timing of the baking *ryshcate* and his promise of a shrill alarm when it was done enabled Corran and Mirax to spend time outside the kitchen of their small apartment. The kitchen itself, while boasting some of the best appliances available, felt as cramped as an X-wing cockpit when all three of them tried to crowd in there. They retreated to a small living room, which was built side-by-side with the smaller of the apartment's two bedrooms. Mirax used that room as an office for her import-export business, which meant it remained crammed with all manner of odd things. Corran didn't mind that, though, since the clutter made it difficult to offer the room to Mirax's father as a place to stay on his visits to Coruscant.

Mirax had redecorated the master bedroom while Corran was off with Rogue Squadron chasing Grand Admiral Thrawn. Redecorating while a war raged may have seemed frivolous, but Corran could understand it. He knew Mirax had not been idle during the Thrawn crisis. She had spent a great deal of time rescuing refugees from worlds Thrawn had threatened and running supplies to those who needed them. When she returned to their apartment in Coruscant, the empty bedroom she had shared with him emphasized the fact that he wasn't there. *By changing it around, by rearranging it into something she would show me when I returned, she worked toward making a future as opposed to worrying about an uncertain present.*

Once the baking process had been turned over to Whistler, Mirax gladly and anxiously showed him all the changes she had made. He found the new bed very comfortable, the carpet woven of Ottegan silk very soft, and the nerf-wool towels decidedly greedy in drinking up the water left behind after a hot, steamy stint in the refresher station. Mirax had even made changes in his wardrobe, having added a couple of suits that were stylishly cut—though the bright colors did seem a tad harsh on his eyes.

Mirax snorted at his protests about the color of the outfit she wanted him to wear. "That vibrant green in slacks and tunic, with an ivory banded-collar shirt beneath, that's the style now, Corran. The Empire made its last attempt to destroy the New Republic. Wearing dour Imperial colors, or the drab sort of things folks wore when fighting them, is out. Those clothes served to hide one away, but no longer."

"It's one thing to not be hiding away, but another to make yourself a target." He smiled as he watched Mirax settle little dangling earrings in her lobes. The jewelry had a silvery sheen to it, much like the highlight and accent color of her gown. Corran couldn't quite figure out how the long black dress, which had been cut low in the front and lower in the back, managed to get silver highlights—*perhaps, it uses some weirdly shaped thread in the weave that reflects from certain angles*—but it clearly made Mirax into a target. "Very impressive gown."

"Why, thank you. You got it for me for our anniversary."

Corran started to speak, then hesitated and frowned. He saw Mirax watching him in the mirror, so he just winced. "I didn't forget the day, you know."

"I know. I got the message you sent. I knew this was the sort of thing you'd get if you were here, so I just helped you out." She turned and kissed him on the lips. "You know, even though we've had to spend a fair amount of time apart, I am very happy to be married to you."

"As I am to you." Corran stroked the bare flesh over her spine as he kissed her. "The next Imp or warlord or pirate that decides to keep us apart is dead, just clean dead."

"My thoughts exactly, my dear." She kissed his nose, then turned him and steered him toward the door. "Perhaps the Rogues should issue a communiqué to that effect and peace will reign from now on."

Despite a personal preference for remaining at home with Mirax and getting caught up with her life, Corran did enjoy the party his wife had arranged. In the almost three years he had spent in the squadron, he had gotten to know his fellow pilots well. He'd spent an incredible amount of time with them, usually under conditions that would most generously be described as adverse. They'd all become very close, and seeing them without the pressure of combat let Corran realize just how much he cared for them.

He smiled as he watched Gavin Darklighter dancing with Asyr Sei'lar. Corran remembered Gavin when he came into the squadron as a tall kid, just past that gawky phase but not by much. His light brown hair and brown eyes combined with a soft-spoken, easygoing personality that instantly inspired trust and friendship. Through the years Gavin had matured—with the goatee and mustache he now sported an external sign of the growing-up he had done. *The war transformed him from a desert-world farmboy to an ace pilot and a man who thinks before he acts.*

Asyr Sei'lar, the Bothan female with whom Gavin had built a relationship, had a playful light burning in her violet eyes. While she might have been described as petite, and her black and white fur did give her a kittenish appearance, she moved with a fluid grace that hinted at a lot of power in her frame. Corran respected her as a pilot and because of choices she had made. *She stuck with the squadron in defiance of the wishes of her Bothan superiors, and she's continued to see Gavin despite disapproval as well.* Bucking authority, especially for a Bothan, took serious steel in the spine, but Asyr had plenty.

Ooryl Qyrgg, Corran's long-time Gand wingman, came walking over to him, bearing a small plate covered with a rainbow of long, glistening, protoplasmic strips. He plucked one from the plate in a three-fingered hand, then delicately sucked it into his mouth, letting his mandibles click shut as it disappeared. A clear membrane nictitated over Ooryl's compound eyes and the Gand hissed in what Corran had long ago learned to recognize as Ooryl's approximation of a self-satisfied sigh.

"Tasty, are they?"

"Yes, Corran, very much so." His mandibles spread apart in the best grin Ooryl could muster. "But an acquired taste. On Gand there are some races that cannot eat these *uumlourti*—they will actually die if they do. I do not think you would like them."

Corran patted his friend on the gray-green exoskeleton over his left shoulder. "Truth be told, I've never been much for food that rates high on the slimy scale. And risking death to find out just isn't something I want to do right now. But, don't let me stop you."

"I have no intention of that, Corran."

The Corellian pilot shook his head. "There was a time, though, when you would have."

"Ooryl does not quite understand that comment."

"Looking at Gavin, I was thinking back to when I joined the squadron. Back then you had not been made *janwuine*, so you always referred to yourself as Ooryl or Qyrgg. You were not so forthright, but more cautious. Then you grew in your confidence and your skill, and it was—*is*—great."

Ooryl gave him a sidelong glance. "The Ooryl you describe would have probably pointed out that he learned much from you during his time with the squadron."

"Probably."

"*I*, on the other hand, would not inflate your ego that way." His mouthparts snapped open and closed sharply. "I am kidding you, yes?"

"I got it, Ooryl. You really *have* learned."

"Yes. I have learned to appreciate my friends." Ooryl gestured at another couple on the dance floor. "Captain Celchu remained focused on fighting the Empire despite being under suspicion of being a spy. Winter remained supportive of him despite the charges the New Republic laid against him. We were all happy when he was proved innocent, but Tycho never showed signs of being bitter."

"True, he took his vindication in stride." Corran looked around the room at the other squadron members. Hobbie and Janson were off in a corner chatting up a couple of Bothans. Inyri Forge, Nawara Ven and his wife, Rhysati Ynr—who Corran had seen only occasionally since she resigned from the squadron to start a family with Nawara—sat at a table listening to an old man tell tales of his days in a cockpit. Myn Donos had joined Wedge in speaking with General Salm, while the Quarren female, Lyyr Zatoq, and the male Issori, Khe-Jeen Slee, both appeared to be deep in conversation with Koyi Komad, a Twi'lek who had once served with Rogue Squadron as the chief mechanic.

"We're all so different, but united because of our experiences in the squadron. That we were able to come together gives me some hope for the New Republic."

"Yes, I have hope in that, too." Ooryl slurped another *uumlourti*. "It is good to see all of our friends here."

"True. I'd forgotten we had so many." Corran smiled and nodded at a tall, bearded man who worked his way through the crowd toward him. Corran knew he had met the man in the past, but he couldn't place him. Then the man raised his right hand in an abortive wave and Corran saw he was missing the last two fingers of his right hand. *"Sithspawn!"*

Ooryl looked over at Corran. "What?"

"That man, coming toward us, he was a prisoner on the *Lusankya* with me. He's one of the men who was missing." Corran started forward, opening his arms. Complete disbelief slacked his jaw. "Emperor's Black Bones, what are you doing here?"

The man stopped and hesitated, the recognition and confidence gone from his eyes and expression. "I have a message for you, Corran Horn." He raised his hands to his temples and winced. "I'm sorry. I know I know you, but . . ." Anguish entered his voice. "I don't know who I am."

Corran pulled up short of the man and let his hands drop by his sides. "You were on the *Lusankya* with me, you served as General Jan Dodonna's aide. Your name is Urlor Sette."

"Yes, Urlor Sette." For the barest of seconds Corran saw relief in the man's brown eyes and felt it roll off him in one strong pulse. Then those brown eyes rolled up into his head, and blood began to stream from his eyes and nose. The man screamed once, sharply, spraying a bloody mist from his mouth. His back bowed and his bones cracked, then he pitched over backward and lay in a slowly expanding pool of blood as the crowd retreated from him.

Corran knelt by his side and reached out to feel his throat for a pulse, but stopped because he could see he wouldn't find one. Though he had never spent much time working with the latent Jedi abilities to which he was heir, he knew beyond a shadow of a doubt the man was dead.

Wedge crouched across the body from him. "What happened?"

Corran shivered. "Urlor Sette was on the *Lusankya*. He said he had a message for me." Corran reached up and closed the man's eyes. "I got it, and given the method of its delivery, there's only one person who could have sent it."

4

Prince-Admiral Delak Krennel strode silently through the darkened hallways of his palace on Ciutric. Though tall and possessed of a solid build with broad shoulders and narrow waist and hips, Krennel had always prided himself on his ability to move quickly and quietly. In his days at the Imperial Academy at Prefsbelt IV he had been an intramural unarmed-combat champion and was pleased that over the years he'd kept himself in fighting trim. *I am yet every gram the fighter I was in those days*.

He glanced down at the naked metal construct that replaced his right hand and forearm. The fingers flexed and collapsed into a fist noiselessly, with only a hint of a reddish glow from deep inside to define the metal plates and pins that made up the artificial limb. *Actually, I am even more a fighter than I was, but this is good. Today I must be*.

He stalked toward his office, his close-cropped hair having been raked into a rough semblance of order with his fingers. His white tunic with red trim still gaped open and he would have been concerned about his appearance save for the hour and the fact that he'd been awakened from a sound sleep for momentous news. The abbreviated message, delivered by a protocol droid, had brought him instantly awake and sent him out to his office to confirm what he had heard.

His blue eyes narrowed. He had a hard time believing Grand Admiral Thrawn was dead—in fact he'd not wanted to believe the news because he had hoped to kill Thrawn himself one day. Krennel had been dispatched by the Imperial Navy to the Unknown Regions and found himself serving under Thrawn. He had bristled at being ordered about by an alien, and while he did acknowledge that Thrawn was a genius, Krennel had also found him fatally flawed.

He recalled how Thrawn would study the artwork of a culture, seeking clues to how the species thought and functioned. Thrawn claimed such study provided him with keys that unlocked the doorway to victory against many alien species. Krennel thought it also inspired in Thrawn a certain respect for these species—*all of which were subhuman*—and weakened his ability to be effective. Krennel had shown Thrawn how ruthless conduct could be even more effective than artistic study, but Thrawn's reaction to the lesson Krennel taught came all out of proportion to the lesson itself.

Krennel's cheeks still burned when he thought of Thrawn sending him and his ship, *Reckoning*, back in the Core worlds. Krennel returned in disgrace and was certain the Emperor himself—with whom Thrawn seemed to have an inordinate amount of influence—would have destroyed Krennel's career. Luckily for Krennel, the Emperor died at Endor, allowing Krennel to escape punishment.

"And forever barring me from vindication." Krennel's deep voice carried through the dark corridor even though he barely hissed the words. His metal hand tightened into a fist again. "Forever leaving my reputation tainted."

He had rejoined the Imperial Navy, resisting his initial urge to become a warlord, but within six months of the Emperor's death, circumstances conspired to offer him an opportunity to fashion his own destiny. Sate Pestage, the Emperor's Grand Vizier, had assumed control of Imperial Center upon the Emperor's death. As the man's position eroded he tried to strike a deal with the New Republic. Pestage had offered Imperial Center and other key worlds in return for the promise of his own well-being and retention of his own holdings. The military tribunal that replaced Pestage after he fled to Ciutric charged Krennel with bringing Pestage to justice. Krennel came to Ciutric, found Pestage, and usurped his holdings and authority. He created for himself the post of Prince-Admiral and succeeded in holding the dozen worlds of the Ciutric Hegemony together through the turbulent times that followed as the New Republic took Imperial Center and even crushed Warlord Zsinj.

Then Thrawn came back. Thrawn claimed authority over Imperial assets upon his return. Krennel had found it expedient to offer Thrawn some support—munitions, personnel, some basic resources—but he never acknowledged Thrawn as any sort of superior. Krennel had dreaded the idea that Thrawn might come after him and his little realm, but he had allowed himself to believe that he could have held his own against Thrawn.

Krennel reached the door to his office and passed his metal hand over the lockplate. He took a step forward, banging his right shoulder into the door, but it failed to budge. He ran his hand over the lockplate again, more slowly this time, allowing the sensor in the door to pick up the signature from the circuitry imbedded in the hand.

Again, it did not open.

Krennel snarled and punched a combination into the keypad below the lockplate. The lock clicked and Krennel shouldered the door open. He took two steps into the darkened room, then felt something cold and slender brush against his throat. He was a half step further on when it began to constrict. Krennel swept his metal hand up and around, grasping the slender metal filament. He yanked, and the wire parted, leaving a garland of garrote wire hanging around his neck.

The lonely, sharp sound of a single pair of hands applauding echoed loudly through his office. Ignoring its source, Krennel stiffly legged his way to his desk and reached for the glowplate switch on the wall. He hesitated, his left hand hovering just above it, then slowly turned his head in the direction of the applause.

"If you wanted me dead, the garrote would have gotten me. Will providing us some illumination kill me?"

Silence answered him.

Krennel looked over at his left hand and hit the switch. The tall room's lighting came from a bank of glow panels built in nearly three meters off the floor. They cast their light up at the domed ceiling, which then reflected it back down. The whole room, which had been decorated in grays, tans, and browns, glowed warmly. Krennel let the light build, then pulled himself up to his full height and slowly turned toward his visitor. He knew he would make an impression, and given the situation, that impression would be important.

And yet, as it turned out, it would be trivial compared to the one made by his visitor.

He'd not seen her in years—save for disturbing dreams from time to time. Barely shorter than he was, she wore her long black hair unbound. Two white sidelocks framed a face that would have made the woman the toast of any number of planets. Her high forehead, strong jaw, sharp cheekbones, and straight nose all combined to make her a rare beauty, but two other elements spoiled the effect.

One element was her eyes. The left one smoldered a molten red, as if the iris were radioactively bloodshot. The pale blue of the other eye seemed colder than frozen methane, and her stare sent a shiver down Krennel's spine. She exuded power, and Krennel found it very seductive, but he also knew she would consume him if she found a way to destroy him.

The other thing that spoiled her beauty was a network of raised scars radiating out from a small puckered crater below her right temple. Krennel studied her closely for a second and thought he saw enough asymmetry in her face to suppose those scars were a sign of massive trauma that had been surgically repaired. He recalled that Rogue Squadron had claimed to have killed her when they ousted her from Thyferra, but her presence in his office put the lie to that story.

Krennel slowly removed the twisted garrote wire and

tossed it on the floor between them. "You had a point you wished to make with this, Ysanne Isard?"

The woman smiled coldly. "I could have killed you here, in your office. Your people would have awakened tomorrow morning with me in your place. It is important that you know I could have taken over for you in the blink of an eye, so you will believe me when I tell you that doing so is not my intention."

Her words came evenly and calmly, and Krennel allowed himself to mull them over before replying. He searched them for her true agenda, not wanting to accept that she was being truthful with him. *The second I allow myself to even imagine she does not have another plan working here, I am dead.* Still, knowing how perilous a judgment it was, he couldn't find her deception. *Yet.*

"You do have a purpose here, then?"

"The same purpose as always: the preservation of my master's Empire."

Krennel allowed himself to laugh, then seated himself on the edge of his broad desk. "Your injuries might have cost you a painful memory or two: such as the loss of Imperial Center and the Emperor's death."

Isard's expression sharpened. "I remember those things very well. I carry the pain of those memories in my heart."

You have a heart? Krennel kept his expression bland. "Then you must also know the best hope of reestablishing the Empire is now dead."

"Really? You think Thrawn was that hope?"

He arched an eyebrow at her. "You don't?"

She pressed her hands together, fingertip to fingertip. "Thrawn was brilliant, there was no taking that away from him. But he lacked the vision he needed. He was stunning when fulfilling the missions he'd been given. You and he clashed over conduct in the Unknown Region, out there in the wilds of the galaxy, but I doubt anyone else could have been as effective as Thrawn at pacifying those areas. And against the New Republic he proved very adept. But he never quite grasped the idea that there are times when the use of overwhelming firepower can produce a wave of terror which is a weapon with far-reaching and devastating effects."

Krennel's metal hand tightened on the edge of his desk. "I had noticed that flaw in his character before."

"A flaw commonly found in nonhumans." The corner of Isard's mouth lazily curled into a grin. "They seek to be treated as our *equals*, whereas we act as their *superiors*. They hold themselves back from accessing the tools power gives them, and therefore can never wrest from us the respect we would give equals. They seek to cloak themselves in nobility, aping all we are and have, yet do not see that if they are not resolved to do what it takes to maintain power, they are never fit to wield it."

Krennel could hear his pulse beginning to pound in his ears. What Isard said, coming in husky, low tones barely above a whisper, quickened his heart. She'd spoken a credo he'd accepted in his heart when, as a child, he'd helped his father burn alien homes so an agro-combine could turn their land into productive fields. The way she spoke, the conviction in her voice, the disdain in her words, resonated inside him. She knew his mind and knew she could bare her heart without fear of rebuke.

He forced himself to exhale slowly through his nose. "So you agree, then, that Mon Mothma's mongrel Republic is an affront to humanity?"

"An 'affront'? You are far too kind to her, Prince-Admiral." Isard began to slowly pace along a curved path that never brought her closer to him than three meters. "It is an abomination that cannot survive. During the Thrawn crisis Bothans were set against the Mon Calamari—and these are two of the more reasonable species in the New Republic. There are others who, even now, are beginning to arm themselves in the hopes that someday—next week, next year, in the next decade—they will be able to create their own empires, or redress ancient wrongs and renew ancient rivalries."

She laughed aloud. "Can you imagine, Prince-Admiral, the discord sown if the identity of those who destroyed the

Caamasi is ever uncovered? Planetary genocide is a crime that will have everyone howling for blood and lots of it, especially since the Caamasi have become even more pacifistic, more beatific in the wake of their near-extermination a generation ago. There are pressures lurking, building, in the New Republic. Much energy is being deflected into creating a government, but once the structures are in place to allow for the exercise and abuse of power, these pressures will flood through it and tear it apart."

Krennel brushed his left hand over the stubble on his jaw. "Astute if not terribly surprising observations, Isard." He made a snap decision to keep her off-balance. "With such understanding, you could easily see a way to create your own Empire. Wait, you tried that, didn't you? And the Rebels killed you for it?"

Her eyes flashed for a second, and her right hand brushed itself over her scars. "They tried to kill me. They did not succeed."

Krennel noticed her words came without confidence. *She doesn't remember how they almost got her—amnesia's no surprise with such massive head trauma. Perhaps she thinks she's lost some of her edge, which is why she's come to me.* "Are you giving me all this political analysis so I can sit back and watch the galaxy fall into legions of civil wars?"

"No, I tell you this so you can recognize the opportunity you have to rebuild the Empire and become Emperor." She pointed an unwavering finger at him. "You will recall I offered you this opportunity before, but you decided to take Pestage's realm instead of bringing him to me. I would have made you Emperor, and now I shall again."

The Prince-Admiral plucked a comlink from the desk. "Shall we call Mon Mothma now and tell her to hand over the reins of power?"

"Not directly, no. She'll hand them to us all on her own."

"What do you mean?"

A brief smile flashed over Isard's face. "It will not surprise you to learn that sources on Coruscant have reported to me that you have been the subject of discussions in the Provisional Council. The Rebels feel they need to make an example of an Imperial warlord, but they want to pick one and deal with him in such a way that they do not so frighten the others that there is no chance of peaceful settlements later. You are going to be their target."

"Me? That makes no sense." Krennel frowned. "I've spent the last five years building up defenses, making sure no one can prey upon my worlds. I'm hardly the easiest target they could pick on."

"True, but you are the one who murdered the Imperial Grand Vizier and so blatantly profited by your act. They think if they wage war on you beneath the pretext of bringing you to trial, the other warlords won't be threatened by what they do to you."

He crossed his arms over his chest. "Transparent political motivations won't turn lasers or shield ships."

Isard nodded slowly. "True, but politics can play a leading role in how power shifts in the universe. Think, for a moment. As the New Republic strives to redress some of the ills of the Empire, who will be discomfitted?"

"Humans. They benefited the most under the Empire, so any moves to create equality will result in greater stress on their resources. Humans will have to make do with less so aliens can have more."

"Very good. And who, *now,* possesses and controls these resources that will have to be shared."

Krennel smiled. "Humans do. And even the most liberal of them, the most alien-loving among them, the ones who want to do the most, will feel their nerf is being gored when they are forced to give up more than they want to in order to help others."

"Exactly. Those who want to preserve their own wealth and power will slow the pace of change, while those who seek power and wealth will want to accelerate it." Isard opened her hands. "This provides you with an opportunity, Prince-Admiral. You declare your Ciutric Hegemony to be human-friendly. You will provide a haven for anyone who feels he or she is being abused by the New Republic.

And you will stress that the Hegemony is open to enterprising individuals of any species—that success here is based on individual effort and the merit of one's contribution, not based on genetic makeup. The only 'entitlement' you recognize is the one of all creatures to be free to make the best life possible for themselves and their families."

Krennel slowly nodded. "When the New Republic moves against me, it will look as though the aliens have enough influence in the Council to use armed force against someone merely protecting the rights of his own species. That should spike fear among humans and even make some of the other warlords willing to band together so they won't be made targets."

"Splendid. And as for the murder charge, you will point out that you merely did to Pestage what the New Republic intended to do all along. In fact, as I recall, Pestage fled from the Rebel forces here on Ciutric and sought sanctuary with you. Could it be he feared they meant to spirit him away and try him for Imperial crimes?"

The Prince-Admiral tapped a metal finger against his chin. "It could be I recall him saying something to that effect before he died."

"Good, more dissent to be sown."

Krennel watched Isard closely. "So, you come here, you tell me what the New Republic has in store for me, and you provide me with a political program that will thwart them. Why?"

"To preserve what little is left of the Empire."

"You said that before. I believe it, but there must be more. There must be something you want, that you want for yourself."

"There is, and you will give it to me." Isard reached up with her right hand and touched the scars on the side of her face. "Rogue Squadron managed to defy me in the past and I cannot let that transgression go unpunished. In the course of what will happen, I will lay a trap for Rogue Squadron and you will give me the resources I need to destroy them."

Krennel snorted lightly. "I have no love for Rogue Squadron, either. You do not ask for much, but your goal may be unattainable. Rogue Squadron has led a charmed life when it comes to traps."

"That's all in the past, Prince-Admiral." Isard's arctic eye sparkled. "I've sent them a message, one that will confuse and distract them. It is bait and, as they follow it, they will move into my trap. You'll see, you'll see I'm right. And, when the time comes, your score with them will be settled as well."

5

Wedge Antilles shivered, and he knew it wasn't just because the morgue was kept cool. Beyond the big transparisteel viewport that separated him from the stainless steel and tile room where droids performed autopsies, Wedge saw row upon row of little doors behind which the dead waited for someone to have the sad duty of claiming them. Two droids, a Two-Onebee and an Emdee-One, slid Urlor Sette's shrouded form into one of the refrigerated drawers and shut the door with a faintly audible *click*.

Wedge turned away from the viewport and looked at the other two of the room's occupants. Corran Horn sat hunched over on a chair with his hands covering his face. Blood droplets stained his jacket front and a small crescent of blood decorated each cuff, as well as the knee on which he had knelt next to the body. Corran's reaction to Sette's death didn't strike Wedge as at all wrong—the death had been shocking and the loss of a friend was never pleasant.

He also knew Corran well enough to know there was more to it than just shock. *Sette's death is a defeat for him. Before Thrawn, before we freed Thyferra, Corran gave his word that he would free the people who had been imprisoned on the* Lusankya *with him. Sette's death is a failure,*

*and opens up for him the possibility that he might continue
to fail in this quest.*

The woman sitting next to Corran rubbed her right
hand along his curved back. She wore her light brown hair
up and had on a cerulean dress with a short black jacket
over it. She'd been at the party, too, and had immediately
taken charge of the situation. Wedge marveled at her calm
strength in the midst of such an incident, but that sort of
strength was something he had come to expect and admire
in Iella Wessiri.

"Corran," she said softly, "there is no way you can
accept responsibility for this man's death. You didn't kill
him."

Corran looked up with red-rimmed eyes. "That's not
what the droids said." He pointed at the small box-and-
wire device that the Emdee-One that had performed the au-
topsy had deposited on the room's stainless steel table.
"The second I said his name, I doomed him. I might as well
have put a blaster to his head and pulled the trigger."

"Listen to me, Corran Horn, you know that's non-
sense." Iella's voice developed an edge and anger sparked in
her brown eyes. "The person who put that device together,
the person who implanted it into your friend, *that* person
killed him."

Corran's green eyes narrowed. "I know that in my
head, Iella, but my heart . . ." He tapped his chest with a fist.
"My heart still feels the guilt. If we'd moved faster to find
them and free them, maybe—"

Wedge shook his head. "Listen to yourself, Corran.
You know as well as I do that we've devoted a lot of time
and energy to locating the *Lusankya* prisoners. While I was
off with Wraith Squadron, you Rogues worked hard on
that problem. You had Iella and a lot of New Republic Intelligence resources working with you. You did all you
could, the best you could."

"But we didn't find them."

"No, you didn't find what, two hundred, maybe three
hundred individuals in a galaxy with thousands and thou-

sands of planets to each one of them? The New Republic barely communicates with three-quarters of the Empire's old worlds, and you know as well as I do that much of those communications are hollow formalities. When Isard scattered the prisoners, she did so because she knew we wanted them, and she was sharp enough to take steps to make sure we never found them."

Wedge frowned. "The secret of where she placed them died when you and Tycho blew up her shuttle at Thyferra. You didn't know that she'd hidden the prisoners, so you couldn't have anticipated the result."

Iella nodded in agreement. "And, Corran, there was no way you could have let her live, let her run. That kind of evil had to be stopped, and you know everyone who was on the *Lusankya* would have agreed with you."

Wedge felt a lump rise in his throat as she spoke. Iella's husband, Diric, had once been a prisoner on the *Lusankya*, though no one had known it until after his death. Ysanne Isard had broken Diric and turned him into one of her agents. She sent him after an Imperial official who was defecting to the New Republic, a prisoner Iella was guarding. Iella had been forced to kill her own husband. *Forced much in the same way as Corran was forced to trigger the death of his friend.*

Corran took Iella's left hand in his own and gave it a squeeze. "You're right, of course. Both of you. I know that. Still, this knot in my gut isn't going away until we find the other prisoners." His voice sank slightly. "Or find out what happened to them."

Iella got up and walked over to the table. She picked up the small box-and-wire device and turned it over in her hands. "Well, we have a good place to start with this. It's a nasty little piece of work, and a fairly specialized one. Most of it is made up of off-the-shelf components, but there are some custom pieces in here, too. Whoever put it together knew what he was doing."

Wedge frowned. "I know that's what killed Sette, but how did it work?"

Iella flipped open the box—which was no bigger than a deck of sabacc cards. Inside, Wedge saw a couple of computer chips, two energy cells, some electronic components, a small motor, a metal cylinder with holes drilled into it every centimeter or so, and a rainbow of wires. Iella hit a small button, and the twenty-centimeter-long cylinder flipped upright.

"Preliminary analysis indicates this cylinder housed a thin-walled glass capsule that contained two powerful drugs—well, one was a drug, the other was a naturally occurring venom, but one seldom found in the quantities used here. The venom is hemotoxic—it acts like acid, eating away at capillary walls, which caused the hemorrhaging from the eyes, nose, and mouth you saw. The drug spiked Sette's blood pressure, pumping the toxin through him in seconds. He died of a massive stroke as the toxin ruptured every blood vessel in his brain."

Wedge shifted his shoulders uneasily. "The box was attached to his circulatory system somehow?"

Iella showed him the bottom of the box, right below the bottom of the cylinder. "They used a venous graft to connect it to his aorta. The second the mix hit his bloodstream, the poison was all through him."

Corran rose from his chair and came over to lean heavily on the table. "The wires came from a nerve graft—the kind they use in cybernetic replacements. The machine hooked into Urlor's aural nerves, picking up what he heard. When the chip matched the voiceprint of my saying Urlor's name to the voiceprint it had stored, the motor turned a gear that spun another one that depressed a plunger down through the cylinder and pumped the kill-juice into him."

Wedge nodded slowly. "You think the voiceprint came from your time in the *Lusankya*?"

"Maybe. Probably not." Corran shrugged sluggishly. "We didn't use names much there. If we used names we could have provided the Imps with clues to what might be happening. I suspect they got it from any of a variety of reports I gave about my time in the *Lusankya*."

General Antilles felt ice trickle through his guts. "Those reports are still classified, aren't they?"

"As nearly as I know."

Iella nodded. "They are, which means whoever did this has access to some of our classified material. That's not really a surprise, though, is it?"

Wedge raised an eyebrow. "It isn't?"

"Think about it, General. Urlor Sette arrives at a party being thrown in the honor of Rogue Squadron—a party you didn't know about until this afternoon. Word was not that widespread about it, but whoever it was managed to get him in."

Iella set the poison injector down. "We have to figure that whoever Isard entrusted with hiding the prisoners was fairly high up in her intelligence operation. While Kirtan Loor's information did turn over to us a good portion of the intel ops Isard had running on Coruscant, recent events during the Thrawn crisis showed we didn't get *everything*, so it's safe to assume we still have secrets leaking to the enemy."

Wedge sighed, then nodded to her. "Good analysis. I hadn't thought that hard."

"You're not trained to do analysis, Wedge. You *provide* intel, or act on plans formulated because of it. You don't have to do interp and analysis." Iella gave him a warm smile. "At least you didn't have to before you won your decade of dots, *General*."

"Save the General stuff, Iella. I'm still Wedge to you." He glanced down. "At least, I assume such familiarity is okay."

"Sure." She winked at him. "I didn't think you'd let your rank go to your head."

"No, but it looks as if I'll be having to apply my brains more than before."

"Just in different ways, Wedge." Iella turned and rested her right hand on Corran's left shoulder. "Corran, you should get out of here. Wedge can take you back home. There's nothing more you can do here. It will be hours before the droids come back with their final analysis of the toxin and the device components."

Wedge nodded. "Be glad to do it, Corran. You look more exhausted than a Hutt-wrestler."

"Yeah, and I feel like one who's lost a bunch of matches, too." Corran heaved himself up from the edge of the table. "I don't need transport, though. I want to walk for a bit."

Wedge inclined his head toward the door. "I could stretch my legs, too."

"No, if it's the same to you, I'd like to be alone." Corran smiled sheepishly. "Look, you're both very good friends and I appreciate your concern, but right now I need to think some things through."

Wedge started to say something, but a slight shake of Iella's head stopped him. He folded his arms across his chest. "Look, you know how to reach me by comlink if you need to talk, find you're lost, want to tear up a swoop-jockey haunt, you name it."

"And I don't want to be left out, either, if you're going to be picking on swoopies." Iella drew Corran into a hug. "Go home, get some rest. We'll have what you need to know to find out who did this by noon tomorrow."

"Thanks, Iella." Corran gave her a kiss on the cheek, then turned and threw a hasty salute at Wedge. "I'll report in tomorrow, General."

"Just let Emtrey know where you are and that will be fine." Wedge returned the salute and gave him a smile. "I don't imagine Mirax would be all that pleased with me requiring you to actually come to the base. Good night."

Wedge watched in silence as Corran left the examining room, then he turned and looked at Iella. "You really think you'll have enough data to let us start tracking the person behind this by tomorrow?"

"We'll have some leads." She tapped the box with a finger. "The common components here are fairly low tech, which means they were probably manufactured on the world where the device was put together. Given what it costs to haul manufactured items between planets, low-ticket trinkets like this aren't worth shipping. The custom components—the chips and the graft wire—might have come from elsewhere, but they were modified during manufacture. The mods aren't that difficult to do, but they require technical expertise and suitable facilities. Once we have a world, we can begin a survey of people and places that could work."

Wedge ran a hand along the edge of his jaw. "What about the toxin?"

"Could have been shipped in from elsewhere, milked from creatures that were shipped in, or manufactured. We'll rule out synthetics first—they're never quite the same as the naturally produced stuff. The easiest thing for us to track would be if it was milked from exotics on a planet where the creatures are not native. Most worlds require the registering of exotic xenobiologicals, so we can vector in that way."

"Sounds like a lot of work." Wedge shook his head. "Where do we begin?"

"*We?*"

"Hey, you said these ten little pips I sport now mean I've got to start using my head in different ways. Might as well start now."

Iella watched him through half-closed eyes, then slowly smiled. "Well, the droids are going to take time for the analysis, and the computers will start chunking out lists, cross-indexing them, and probably come up with a couple thousand likely candidates. When they get that list pared down, *then* we go through it. We refine the parameters of our search, pull up auxiliary data, and narrow the field further."

"So, nothing to do until the list is finished?"

"Oh my, you clearly haven't done anything in the way of detective work, have you?"

Wedge reddened slightly. "Ah, you and Corran were the ones trained by CorSec, not me."

"And Corran has clearly neglected your training." Iella came around the table and slipped her arm through Wedge's.

"The start of any good investigation involves hunting up a reliable source of caf—the kind that can keep you awake through an Ithorian production of a Gamorrean opera."

"Isn't that kind of caf considered a controlled substance within the New Republic?"

She laughed. "I think someone tried to pass a regulation like that, but the Senate staffers live on that kind of caf, so the proposal vanished."

"Data-card probably just fell into a pot of the stuff." Wedge smiled. "Probably improved the taste, too."

"Well, we'll have to see if we can find a place that makes its caf hot, strong, and to your liking, then. And, once we do that, we buy several liters, come back here, and go to work."

Wedge nodded and took one last look at the device that killed Urlor Sette. "You want to know what scares me the most about that device and this whole murder?"

"What?"

"The way it was done, so boldly and obviously, it means whoever did it wants us to come after them."

Iella's eyes narrowed. "Calling Rogue Squadron down upon yourself would be ruled 'suicide' by most coroners."

"Right, which means whoever did this thinks they can handle us, is crazy enough to think they can handle us, or just has one colossal hate on for us."

"Not a pretty holograph." Iella tugged Wedge toward the door. "Let's get that caf. We'll save a little and when we learn who it is we're after, we'll use it to melt them clean away."

6

Corran slipped into his darkened apartment and let the door close quietly behind him. A couple of lights blinked, then a softly rising tone greeted him.

"It's me, Whistler. Keep it down." Corran peeled off his jacket and dropped it beside the door. "Is Mirax asleep?"

The R2 unit tootled affirmatively, but a glow panel clicked on in the bedroom. "Corran, is that you?"

He kept back from the slender bar of light streaming through the narrow crack between doorjamb and door. "Yes, it's me. Don't get up, I'll be with you in a moment."

"Are you okay? Corran?"

And I'm supposed to be the one with latent Jedi skills. "I'll be fine." He pushed open the door to the bedroom with his right foot, then leaned against the jamb with his left shoulder. Looking at his wife as she lay there on her side, her black hair up, wearing a light blue nightgown, he smiled.

Smiled as much as his split lip would let him.

Mirax sat bolt upright in bed. "What happened to you?"

"It was nothing."

"Nothing? Your lip is split, your right eye is almost

swollen shut." She threw back the covers and padded over to the refresher station. Corran heard water running, then Mirax returned bearing a wet washcloth. She raised it to dab at the blood on his chin, but he caught her hand.

"Mirax, I'll be fine." He took the washcloth from her and scrubbed away at the blood. "I decided I needed to get my head clear, so I walked from the morgue. I ran into a little trouble."

Mirax planted balled fists on her hips. "A little trouble? You came out of the *Lusankya* looking better."

He snorted a laugh and followed it with a smile that tugged at the split in his lip. "Well, these are more *Lusankya*-based injuries. I can't get the image of Urlor dying like that out of my head. Wedge and Iella have already told me it's not my fault that he died, but the fact that he wasn't free yet is the reason he died. I promised to free him, and I've failed."

She canted her head slightly. "So you went looking for trouble and let someone beat you up?"

Corran brought his chin up. "Trouble found me all by itself, I didn't have to go looking. It was a little gang of kids. A Rodian was leading them. I wasn't paying attention, so they decided to take me."

Mirax took his right hand in hers and led him over to the edge of the bed. She made him sit there, then she knelt at his feet and started to unbutton his tunic. "I think I can get the blood out of the shirt. Where's the jacket?"

"By the door. Most of it, anyway. One of the little glit-biters made off with a sleeve." Corran pressed the wet cloth to his swollen right eye. "The Rodian swung a pretty good left. He came up on my right side from behind and clouted me. Spun me around, then he split my lip. Another of them grabbed my sleeve and for a second, I thought it was all over."

He shook his head. "I started to feel sorry for myself, then I saw Urlor lying there in the morgue and I realized that as bad as I felt, at least I could *feel*. I thought of you, and of Jan Dodonna, and the other *Lusankya* prisoners, and whoever it was that sent Urlor here to Coruscant. I realized I had more important things to be doing than worrying about myself and that's when things began to get a bit weird."

Mirax tugged Corran's shirt off his left arm, then unbuttoned the right cuff and quickly slipped it past the wet cloth in his right hand. "What do you mean?"

"Well, I'd felt it before, a couple of times, flying with the squadron or when I was with CorSec. Everything slowed down, I knew what the Rodian was going to do, what the others were going to do. I could just feel them there. I knew which way to move to avoid their punches. It felt as if they were puppets going through a series of highly choreographed moves, and I just slipped in and out between them. I didn't have to hit anyone or anything. I just got away."

Mirax tossed his shirt to the floor and pulled off his right boot. "Sounds very Jedi to me."

"Yeah, maybe it was a Force thing. I don't know." He shrugged. "Doesn't matter, though. What does is this: I need to focus on finding Jan Dodonna. Somehow, with Thrawn running loose and everything, it was easy to get distracted. No longer."

Corran's left hand curled down into a fist and Mirax quickly took it in her hands. "Corran, I know you're disappointed in yourself for not having kept your word to General Dodonna about coming back to the *Lusankya* to free him, but you have to remember that you *did* do that. Your resignation from Rogue Squadron is what led everyone to go after Ysanne Isard and bring her down. You did get to the *Lusankya*, just as you said you would."

"Sure, but they weren't there."

"No, they weren't, but I think you need to stop seeing them as complete victims." She reached up and tapped a finger against his temple. "I remember what you told me about Jan Dodonna, how he followed you and stopped Derricote from killing you. He was a smart man, and you have to know that he was fully capable of interpreting the

move from the *Lusankya*. Isard's moving him and everyon
else out of there told them that you were succeeding. If yo
weren't, if you weren't going to make good on your prom
ise, Iceheart never would have moved them. They knov
that."

She let her hand come down to stroke the left side of hi
face. "If I were ever to go missing, I'd have no fear. I knov
you'd turn this galaxy inside out to find me. You'd do what
ever you had to do to find me."

Corran's left eye narrowed. "No question, whatever i
took."

"Jan Dodonna knows you're a man of your word. H
also knows the move will have complicated things, but he'
not going to doubt that you'll keep your promise."

He lay back on the bed and closed his eyes. The convic
tion in Mirax's voice pierced the veil of self-doubt that ha
sprung from his feeling that he'd failed Urlor. He knev
Wedge and Iella had been right in pointing out that th
death was not his fault, even though his voiceprint had been
used as the trigger. Even so, he knew he couldn't duck ful
responsibility for it, because Urlor had been chosen as
weapon to get at him. Had he never escaped from the *Lu
sankya*, Urlor never would have been sent to him. By doin
what he had done, Corran had made an enemy, and tha
enemy clearly felt no compunction about using whateve
tools were at hand to make a point.

*But making a point and attaining a goal are two differ
ent things.* Using Urlor's death to taunt him and point ou
that he'd failed to keep his promise was one thing. Tha
couldn't be the only desired result of that move, howeve
because it was far too modest an outcome for the expendi
ture. *Clearly the person wanted to hurt me. To distract me
keep me from focusing, but focusing on what?*

"Mirax, see if this scans for you. Killing Urlor at tha
party, in that way, pretty much guarantees Rogue Squadro
has its honor bounded up in freeing the prisoners, right?"

He felt her lie down on the bed beside him. "The firs
jump of your course seems well plotted."

"Okay, so then it would seem that our enemy expects us to be thinking a bit more with our emotions than our brains. The enemy has made a move, now we will react to it." He opened his left eye and turned his head to look at her. "Urlor is bait for a trap meant to destroy Rogue Squadron."

"That also seems to follow." She pursed her lips for a moment. "You'll have to assume a trap is waiting for you no matter what you decide to do. You'll have to plan in some safeguards."

"So, tell me, am I just being egotistical by assuming this enemy wants a piece of me and Rogue Squadron?"

"Corran, you're a pilot who used to be a member of CorSec. Ego gets issued with the uniforms." Mirax gave him a quick smile. "In this case, though, I don't think you're wrong. Whoever is behind this is cruel and evil—and there's a list of ex-Imperial leaders we could run down and find plenty of candidates who fit that description."

"This person isn't going to be on that list." Corran frowned. "We're dealing with someone who was close to Isard, who sees Rogue Squadron as the folks who destroyed Isard. They're focused on retribution. I don't think they'll win, in the long run, but I am afraid lots more people will die, as did Urlor, before they're stopped."

Gavin Darklighter swirled the golden Corellian brandy in the small tumbler, then tossed it off. He felt a small bead of brandy leak from the corner of his mouth and work its way down through his goatee. The rest of the fiery liquid burned its way down his throat, but none of its warmth radiated out to dispel the chill that had settled over him.

He idly swiped at the droplet with his left hand, then sighed and shook his head. "The way that man died tonight, it took me back to when we were helping the victims of the Krytos virus here on Coruscant. They bled, too, bled and died."

Asyr Sei'lar nodded mutely from the chair opposite

him. After coming back to their apartment from the party,
she'd changed into a purple silk dressing gown. Sitting in
the blocky chair, she had drawn her feet up so they disappeared into the robe. Of her body he could only see her
white-furred hands and her head, with the diagonal blaze of
white fur that ran from her forehead down over her left eye
and across her cheek. Her markings made her somewhat
unique among Bothans—as did her attitude.

Gavin set his glass down on the arm of his chair. "I
guess I was hoping, with Thrawn gone, that things would
begin to settle down. I mean, I know I'm not even twenty
years old, but there are times I feel positively ancient."

Asyr gave him a half smile. "Battles and death act as
force-multipliers when it comes to time. Always having to
be alert and ready to deal with violence wears you down.
It's wearing me down, too."

Gavin's head came up. "Really?"

"That surprises you?"

"Well, yes, I guess it does." He hesitated a moment,
letting his thoughts order themselves. "You graduated
from the Bothan Martial Academy, so I would have thought
you would have training in how to handle this sort of
thing."

Asyr barked a little laugh. "Gavin, military schools and
training are long on teaching you how to destroy things, but
they don't much deal with the aftermath of that destruction. Everyone assumes that if you win you'll feel good and
if you lose you'll be dead, so how you feel doesn't matter. By
the time war begins to grind you down, it's pretty much had
that same effect on everyone, so the war slows down and
stops."

"Or you get rolled over and killed and your feelings
don't matter."

"Right." She turned her head and looked at him with
her violet eyes. "Are you saying you want to resign from the
squadron, start a family, do something else?"

Gavin frowned. "The squadron *is* my family, you're
my family. I don't want to walk away from that. We both

know that someone is going to have to do something about the guy who died, and Wedge and Corran will push for it to be Rogue Squadron. I don't want to sound silly, but that death was a shot taken at us, and showing the person who took it that they were wrong seems to be the right thing to do."

"Agreed."

He sat forward in his chair, resting his elbows on his knees. "As for the other stuff, like starting a family, I think I'd like that. I'd like to start a family with you. We could get married, make this permanent, and bring children into our lives."

Asyr froze for a second and Gavin feared he'd somehow insulted her. Bothans were a proud species and very much tied into complex relationships involving kin and clans. Despite having been Asyr's companion for the past two years and joining her at a number of social functions, he'd yet to meet another human-Bothan couple. *And I know there are plenty of Bothans who don't like the fact that we've managed to stay together as long as we have.*

She glanced down at the hem of her gown and picked a piece of lint from it. "I like the idea of being married to you, Gavin, but there's a lot to consider. You *do* know that it is impossible for us to have children together."

Gavin nodded. "Yeah, both friends and enemies have clued me into that situation. Strikes me, though, that there are plenty of children who need adopting. I mean, we have those two little brothers who live in the alley near the squadron's hangar. They're just one example. Adopting would give us a chance to help heal some of the damage the Empire has done, you know?"

She looked up and nodded solemnly. "I agree. There is something else you have to know: If we adopt, I want us to adopt at least one Bothan child."

"Sure, no problem."

Asyr held up a furred hand to stop him. "Listen to me, Gavin, because it won't be that easy. You know we Bothans set great store by our families. Political power flows from the networks we build up with alliances and everything. My family sees me as a disappointment because, while I have garnered acclaim in service with Rogue Squadron, I have not presented them with children. Those children would be well loved, but they would also be fodder for future alliances. I've managed to amass what Bothans recognize as a certain amount of power. I'm a political battery in that sense, and my family is disappointed that I've not provided them with a means to bleed some of that power off."

"So you're saying that if we adopt a Bothan child, your family will want to exert some control."

Asyr laughed aloud. "How can you have lived with a Bothan for so long and yet be so polite when referring to our possessiveness?"

Gavin smiled. "Your possessiveness isn't that bad from my perspective. Look, this would be *our* child. I wouldn't be looking to interfere with the child's assumption of his heritage. I wouldn't want to try to substitute a human culture for Bothan culture, but I would want to provide some balance. I'd want to show him that different doesn't mean bad. And I'd hope any other children we adopted—be they human or Rodian or Ithorian, whatever—would get that same message."

Asyr blinked and Gavin saw a single glistening tear roll from her left eye. "How could I have taken you for an anti-alien bigot when we first met?"

"You didn't know me." He got up out of his chair and crossed over to where she sat, then knelt beside her. He reached out and held her left hand, stroking the fur. "Look, I know this won't be easy, but I want to try to do something positive for the galaxy. Sure, flying off, stopping some Grand Admiral from reestablishing the Empire is noble and positive, but the way we rebuild the galaxy is by making lives better one at a time. We can do this, you and I. I want to do it with you."

She leaned down and kissed him on the forehead, then rested her chin on the crown of his head. "You realize, if the adoption goes through, one of us will have to leave the squadron. It wouldn't be fair for both of us to risk our lives and leave some child orphaned again."

"I know." Gavin let his head rest against her breast-bone. "That's a decision we can make down the line. Neither one of us wants to leave, I know, but if that's what it takes to make the galaxy better, it's a sacrifice I'm willing to make."

7

Corran Horn hated waiting for the go/no go signal for the mission. On the long journey from Coruscant to Commenor he and the other Rogues had studied the intelligence gathered about their target. He knew it was less comprehensive than he normally would have preferred, but everyone involved in the operation agreed that Urlor Sette's arrival at the Rogues' party meant their enemy had access to intelligence sources within the New Republic, so the operation was running outside normal channels. The intel they got was enough to plan the mission, but not enough to guarantee success.

Not that success can ever be guaranteed in a military op, and especially one counting on surprise to be effective.

Iella and Wedge had managed to trace the material components of the device that killed Urlor to Commenor. Wedge had been to the planet before, and many of the other Rogues had trained on a covert base on Folor, the largest of Commenor's moons. An Imperial raid later hammered the base, but Corran felt little nostalgia for it. *Training there was a long time ago. Lifetimes ago.*

Tracing the components to Commenor had involved good solid detective work, but locating the site on Commenor where the implantation had happened involved some good fortune. Commenor's medical system contained a fair number of facilities that could have done the implantation, but an analysis of records failed to turn up anything that suggested the operation had taken place there. Wedge located a couple of places where some exotic xenobiological creatures had been kept, and as he concentrated on them as a possible source of the venom that killed Urlor, he noticed that one facility boasted a full veterinary surgical suite, complete with droids. That facility had gone out of business roughly two years earlier, about the same time Isard had fled to Thyferra. The place had been built in a remote rural district in anticipation of further growth, but the collapse of the Empire had cooled Commenor's economy enough that such expansion didn't take place.

The target facility, called "the old Xenovet place" by locals, consisted of a fairly modern central building that served as the main animal hospital. Outlying buildings provided housing for commercial animals recovering from illness or being kept there for breeding and birthing purposes. One of the Xenovet's final programs was an attempt to start a captive breeding program of exotic animals that were endangered on other worlds, but the rebuilding of worlds in the wake of the Empire's collapse took precedence over the rebuilding of creature populations, dooming that effort as well.

On the face of it, the place looked like an easy target. Weather satellite data and other more covert methods of surveillance indicated no weapons systems in place to defend the site. Utility records indicated fairly low power and water use for a place that size, suggesting that no more than thirty individuals lived on the site—anywhere between a third and a sixth of the total prisoners estimated to have been on the *Lusankya*. Shipments of supplies came in through local stores and likewise were not that extensive. As nearly as the local residents knew, the folks at the XV facility were caretakers waiting for some bankruptcy trustee to find a buyer for the place.

Two problems cropped up to make the target harder

than anyone expected. The first was simply logistical. The Rogues could sweep in, pound the place, and reduce it to rubble, but that wouldn't do anything for the prisoners being held there. From his CorSec experience, Corran also knew that destroying the building would destroy any clues as to who owned it, who was running it, and where other prisoners might be. The site itself was a valuable link in the chain that would take them to all the prisoners.

To get the prisoners out would require a commando strike. The New Republic assigned their two top units to the raid: Team One, led by Colonel Kapp Dendo, a Devaronian who'd worked with the Rogues in the past, and the Katarn Commandos, led by Captain Page. Page and his people had worked with the Rogues on their mission to Borleias to liberate that planet from Imperial hands. Both teams had been covertly inserted onto Commenor and had worked their way to the district around the XV site.

The second problem concerning the mission proved more frustrating than any possible defense the Imperials could have raised. Commenor had declared itself independent of the Empire and the New Republic, much as Corellia had done. Since Commenor was a key world on trading routes, it was able to maintain its independence by courting each and every political faction in the galaxy. An attack on an Imperial facility by a New Republic strike team could create an incident that would cause Commenor's officials to bar New Republic trade, impose stiff tariffs, or even cause the planet to align itself with a warlord like Krennel.

Leia Organa Solo managed to convince Commenorian officials that they should sanction the coming operation. She pointed out that when General Jan Dodonna retired, he did so to the Commenorian moon, Brelor—a small moon the Emperor had given him as a reward for his service to the Empire. She suggested that the Empire's subsequent attempted assassination of Dodonna on Brelor was a violation of Commenorian law. Allowing the New Republic to rescue him, or comrades of his, from the XV facility would be a step toward making things right again. Having the New Republic stage the raid would also insulate Commenor from any Imperial reprisals, which was an aspect of the deal the Commenorians liked a lot.

Rogue Squadron's X-wings—painted black for the operation—and astromech droids had been shipped to Commenor under cover as training vehicles for the local militia. The members of Rogue Squadron arrived on a variety of commercial transports and all rendezvoused in Munto, the largest city near the XV site. At the warehouse that served as a hangar for the X-wings, Wedge ran over a briefing with the latest intelligence. Then the pilots mounted up and waited.

Wedge's voice crackled through the headset built into Corran's helmet. "Rogues, we are good to go. Light your engines, but keep the S-foils in transit position until we are out of Munto."

"Finally!" Corran turned to glance back at Whistler. "Now we make good on the promise."

Whistler warbled encouragingly as Corran brought the engines up. He shunted power to the repulsorlift coils and let the X-wing hover there. He retracted the landing gear, then smiled when the ship didn't dip at all. He nudged the throttle forward, then applied a little etheric rudder via his foot pedals and swung the X-wing's nose around to starboard. Corran trailed out after Slee's X-wing, then slid his X-wing more to starboard, swinging wide onto the open ferrocrete slab where another warehouse had once stood.

All around the Rogues most of Munto lay sleeping. Houses had been built up on terraces all around the valley in which the town lay, but most of them were dark save for a safety glow panel here and there. Some airspeeder traffic moved down in the more central part of the valley, and beyond it a roadway carried landspeeder traffic heading up to the town of Kliffen, but otherwise the city seemed all but dead.

One Flight took off first, heading out slowly in a very loose formation. It started off toward the northeast and then would course correct for the target well beyond prying eyes. Two Flight followed with Wes Janson in command. Corran smiled as he remembered Wes proudly sporting the trio of pips that marked his elevation to the rank of Major. Corran had asked Wes if he'd ever thought he'd live long enough to wear three pips, but before Wes could answer, Hobbie quipped, "He never thought he'd live long enough to count to three pips."

Two Flight headed out to the northwest and Corran brought his flight along to the launching point. "Heading two-seven-five degrees, ten percent power. Let's fly."

The X-wings took off easily and headed down into the Munto valley, then hooked north along the roadway. They followed it for a couple of kilometers, and then, when it cut west again for the run to Kliffen, the X-wings pulled up and flew over the ridgeline and out of the valley. They continued on, flying fairly close to the roll of the terrain and over another line of hills before they locked their S-foils into attack positions.

Corran glanced at the chronometer built into his command console. "Time to target is fifteen minutes."

"Nine, this is Twelve. I've got trace readings on my tail."

"Whistler, give me a fine-grade sensor scan of our backtrail."

The droid complied and Corran caught a flash of something moving back there. Whatever it was, it managed to use terrain features to mask itself fairly well. A shiver ran down Corran's spine. *Even though this mission is off all screens back in the New Republic, is it possible we've been betrayed?*

Corran keyed his comm unit. "Okay, Rogues, throttle up. We're going to half power and going to bounce over that ridge. Ten and Eleven, keep going to the target. Twelve, we reverse throttle on the other side, drop to ground, and watch to see what's coming after us. We'll burn it if we need to."

"As ordered, Nine."

The quartet of fighters picked up speed and climbed up the far ridgeline and then over. Corran chopped his thrust back, then reversed it and killed his forward momentum. The X-wing began to drop from the sky, so he cut in his repulsor-lift coils and bounced to a stop a meter and a half above the ground. He nudged the fighter over into a small gully and saw Inyri's fighter go to ground about twenty meters to his port side. In the distance he saw Ooryl and Asyr cruising along and down into a pass that would take them north.

Then, from back over the ridgeline, came four TIE Interceptors. They screamed past nearly fifteen meters overhead, correcting to follow the two X-wings into the pass. Corran saw no markings on them, and the scanner data didn't identify them as hostile. *For all I know those are a bunch of kids out flying around in surplus Interceptors.*

Then one of the Interceptors burned a green laser bolt through the air at Ooryl's vanishing X-wing.

I guess that settles that.

Corran immediately dropped his crosshairs on one of the Interceptors and thumbed his weapons-control over to proton torpedoes. On the heads-up display a green box surrounded the Interceptor, then it went yellow. Whistler's piping picked up speed as the droid sought a targeting solution for the torpedo. When he finally got it his tone became constant and the box went red.

Corran goosed the throttle forward, brought up the fighter's nose, and launched a proton torpedo. The missile leaped up, riding a brilliant blue flame that scorched a Fijisi tree as it went past. The torpedo spiraled up into the air, then curled down as the Interceptor tried to evade it. The pilot's efforts proved partially successful: The torpedo did not hit it, but overshot and exploded when proximity sensors reported it had missed.

The force of the missile blast crumpled the Interceptor's port wing and tore most of it away from the stubby stanchion that connected the wing to the ship's ball cockpit. Shrapnel from the missile itself blew through the transparisteel viewport. Lethal shards of the transparent metal whirled through the cockpit, stabbing deep into equipment and slicing clean through the pilot. Spinning wildly, the Interceptor slammed into the ground and exploded in a golden fireball.

Inyri likewise shot a proton torpedo at one of the Interceptors. Her missile hit dead on target, lancing up through the bottom of the ball cockpit and out through the starboard side before exploding. The torpedo's impact did enough structural damage to the ship that the twin ion engines ripped free and blasted out through the front of the ship, then arced down to smash into the ground. The missile's detonation shredded the rest of the Interceptor, sparking a hot metal rain that started a constellation of small fires burning across the landscape.

Corran keyed his comm unit. "Rogue Nine to Lead, we have engaged four squints, two down. We may be compromised."

"I copy, Nine."

Corran punched his throttle forward and pulled the X-wing's nose up as the remaining two Interceptors turned back around to engage them. He allowed his fighter to go vertical, then he brought it over the top and rolled out to port. That gave the squints a clean line at his back, so he snapped the X-wing up on the port S-foil and pulled back on the stick, taking him out on a turn to the left.

The Interceptors started to adjust their course to come after him and Corran smiled. Behind them, Inyri's X-wing took to the air at full throttle. In seconds she cruised up behind the trailing Interceptor and laced it full of coherent light. Red bolts burned through the ion engine shielding, exploding the engines. Trailing gold fire, the Interceptor somersaulted through the air and finally bounced its way across the ground, sowing patches of fire in its wake.

The pilot coming in on Corran's tail kept a light hand on the yoke and juked his fighter around to spoil Inyri's aim. Corran likewise bounced his X-wing around, making his ship hard to hit. He shunted all shield power to the aft shields, so whenever one of the Interceptor's bolts did finally hit, it just struck sparks.

He's good, he's very good. The Interceptor should have been at a maneuvering disadvantage in atmosphere, but even with the low altitude of the fight and the constraints of battling in a valley, the Interceptor proved very agile. *I can't exploit my advantage and he's not about to fly straight enough for Inyri to nail him. Unless.*

"Twelve, stay with him, but give him space. Aim high."

"As ordered, Nine."

Corran rolled his X-wing out to port, then took it down to the deck. He came up on the starboard S-foil ever so slightly and began a long, gentle turn toward the pass heading north. As the X-wing lined up with it, he cut his throttle back but kept the fighter slipping left and right. Glancing at his rear sensor screen, Corran watched as the range between him and the Interceptor began to scroll down. Looking forward he saw the pass's narrow opening looming closer.

Whistler tootled a warning.

"Yes, I know how close we are. Trust me."

At the two-hundred-meter mark, Corran cut thrust to zero, rolled onto the starboard S-foil, and shunted full engine power to the repulsorlift coils. He stomped on the starboard rudder pedal, swinging the fighter's aft to the right. In a heartbeat the fighter went from being level and headed north to having its nose pointed at the sky, its right S-foil pointed north, and momentum still carrying it in toward the pass.

Corran slammed the throttle up to full and snaprolled the fighter to the left. The X-wing leaped toward the sky, with the repulsorlift coils creating a gravity cushion that bounced the fighter back from the rocks at the mouth of the pass. The fighter rode a rocket of thrust toward the stars above.

The Interceptor pilot following him, as Inyri's gun holocam data would show later, had a split-second decision to make. At the speed he was traveling he could move into the pass, but that would bracket him and Inyri would blast him from the sky. His other choice was to try to execute the same maneuver Corran had, which he elected to do.

He only had two problems.

He started a second later than Corran had, which, at his speed, brought him closer still to the pass's narrow mouth.

And the Interceptor's design gave it serious yaw problems. The pilot succeeded in rolling up onto the starboard wing, but as he tried to rudder around to vertical, air caught on the inside of the port wing. This kicked the Interceptor into a flat spin that brought it all the way around so the front end was pointing back along the path it had been traveling.

The aft end slammed into the rocks beside the pass's mouth. The Interceptor vanished in a scintillating ball of sparks, debris, and smoke as the engines exploded. A crumpled bit of the cockpit rolled back toward the south, trailing smoke, while fire flashed up the pass wall and ignited small plants.

Inyri's X-wing pulled parallel with Corran's as he rolled out to port and pointed his ship north. "Nice kill, Nine."

"Not mine, Twelve, you were the one shooting him."

"He got himself."

"Works for me." Corran brought the X-wing back down to the deck. "Let's move, and hope we're not too late to help out if they need it."

8

"I copy, Nine. Four squints blinded." Wedge Antilles glanced at his rear sensors. "Gate, do we have anything else back there?"

Gate, Wedge's R5 astromech droid, swiveled its flower-pot head around, then tootled negatively. The scopes showed nothing but the rest of the squadron following him. Wedge glanced at the chronometer on the command console. "Heads up, Rogues. Estimated time of arrival is thirty seconds. First pass, shoot at what shoots at us. One Flight will draw fire. Two, you lace them."

"As ordered, Lead," came Janson's terse reply.

Pulling back on his X-wing's stick, Wedge brought the nose up to crest the last line of hills between him and the target. The XV facility had been built on a small rise in the heart of a wide valley. In the distance Wedge could see a number of small communities, and scattered even further around were dimly lit homesteads in the middle of farmland. The Xenovet compound had been situated equidistant between client communities, which made the Rogues' mission much easier by cutting down the chances of collateral damage.

Wedge cruised his fighter down into the valley and began

a low run at the site. He beefed up his forward shields and directed his fighter to overfly the large barn in the middle of the property. He saw nothing as he made his pass. Once beyond the barn, he rolled up on his starboard S-foil, cut his throttle, and pulled into a tight turn.

"Three is taking fire from the barn."

Janson confirmed the report. "E-web in the loft. Don't have a clean shot."

Wedge leveled the X-wing and hit some rudder. "Lead is on it."

As his X-wing came about, he killed the thrust and cut in his repulsorlift coils. The X-wing glided down to twenty meters of altitude and sideslipped left to give Wedge a good look at the pair of soldiers operating the heavy blaster. Standing in the barn's loft, firing out of a feed-loading door, they were spraying green blaster bolts into the air, occasionally hitting shields on a passing fighter.

"Infantry weapons never work well on spacefighter targets." Wedge shook his head and swung his crosshairs on their outline. "The reverse is not true."

The X-wing's lasers fired in sequence, peppering the barn's upper story with coherent light. Bolts burned through the thin metal walls and lanced out the far side. Two red energy darts drilled through the heavy blaster itself, even as the gunner tried to shift his aim and shoot back at Wedge. The weapon exploded, killing the gunner instantly and pitching the other man out of the barn to the ground below.

The man got up and started to limp toward the main building, but he never got very far. From the shadow of a smaller building a blue ion bolt flashed out and caught him in the chest. He pitched down, then two figures in black converged to check him. Others, looking more like shadows than people, moved further in. One group closed in on the main building while a smaller knot moved toward the barn.

A small explosion flashed at the door to the barn, then the doors cartwheeled aside. Two shadows moved forward, threw something, then two more sharp explosions lit the barn's interior, casting light out through windows and the loft. Shadows sprinted into the interior and more blue strobes of ion blast light filled the darkness.

A similar series of explosions lit up the main building. Wedge saw a figure climb out of a second-story window and run along the terrace. The figure looked over and saw the X-wing, then raised a blaster and triggered off two shots. Both of them hissed and sparked against the fighter's forward shield, prompting a smile from Wedge. "Nice shooting."

The figure ducked down behind the low wall that edged the terrace. Wedge dropped his crosshairs onto the wall and popped off a quick burst of laserfire. The quartet of shots blasted into the brick and mortar, chewing great holes in it. He saw his quarry get up and start running, but bricks blown from the wall cut the figure's legs out from under him, and the running man went down hard.

Wedge switched his comm unit over to the ground tactical frequency. "Katarn leader, Rogue leader here. I have one man down on the main building's second floor."

"Anything left of him, Wedge?"

"Seems all in one piece, Page. I was gentle."

"I copy. I'll send someone up. Kapp reports the barn is clear, so the ground situation is stable. I'm calling in our pick-up crews. You might want to get down here, too."

"Got it. Incoming." Wedge flicked his comm unit back to the squadron's frequency. "Two, I'm going down there. Assign us some air cover and send Two Flight back to guide the transport in."

"As ordered, Lead."

Wedge guided his X-wing down to the midway point between barn and main building. He set it down gently and let the X-wing's landing gear sink a bit into the soft soil before popping the hatch and shutting the fighter down. He doffed his helmet, then crawled out onto the edge of the cockpit and leaped down. He headed toward the main building, but a man dressed in black intercepted him.

"I can show you that stuff later, General." Captain

Page gave Wedge a grim smile and took his elbow to steer him around in the other direction. "Kapp suggested you'd want to look in the barn first."

"I've seen what an X-wing can do to an E-web, thanks."

"I know, but that's not what you'll be looking at."

The two men jogged across the compound to the barn and between the Ithorian and the Sullustan standing guard at the doorway. A little smoke from smoldering straw filled the air with a sour scent. Beyond that, Wedge caught a whiff of burned flesh. Someone had tossed a ragged blanket over a human outline that Wedge assumed was the E-web gunner.

Once deeper into the room, he realized why Kapp Dendo had wanted him to visit the barn first. The Devaronian, wearing blackened stormtrooper scout armor and a helmet cut to allow his horns to stick up through it, crouched beside the skeletal figure of a man. Wedge saw the rest of the commando team working in stalls meant for housing nerfs, freeing the people who had been shackled in the small enclosures. As gently as possible, the commandos were carrying the people to the barn's main floor.

The stench that came from the stalls nearly overwhelmed Wedge. *These people have been forced to live in their own filth.* The wrists of the man near Kapp were raw from where his manacles had cut into his flesh. The man's long nails were caked with dirt, as were the lines on his face. Bending down, Wedge thought he saw something moving in the man's gray beard and hair, but he didn't pull back.

A Twi'lek commando standing by a water spigot held up a small vial and swirled it around. The clear liquid turned blue. "Seems potable."

Kapp nodded. "Good. Fill me a flask and bring it over here. Get water to the rest of them." He glanced down at the man before him. "You'll be okay now."

The man reached out and clutched weakly at Wedge's flight-suit leg. "Am I dreaming? I know you."

Wedge crouched beside the man and patted his hand. "Could be. You were with the Rebellion?"

"Ground support. They got me at Hoth. I am Lag Mettier."

Wedge frowned. The name sounded familiar, but he couldn't quite place it. It was possible he knew the man from Hoth, but the picture that was coming up in his mind was of a much younger man, blond, with a booming laugh. "You knew Dack Ralter, right?"

"Dack, I knew Dack." Lag let Kapp ease him into a sitting position and accepted the flask of water the commando offered.

Kapp looked past him and addressed Wedge. "You know him?"

"Possibly. If so, he didn't look like this at the time."

The Devaronian nodded as he looked around at the people moaning and staggering in the barn. "They've all been sorely used here. I'm guessing they've not been cared for at all in the past couple of days. Maybe a week. We had minimal resistance."

Page dropped to his haunches and nodded in agreement. "The main house looks pretty well cleaned out. We have a forensics team coming in to get whatever there is to be gotten."

Lag lowered the flask, water dripping silver from his beard. "It won't do any good. She'll have seen to that."

Wedge frowned. "What are you talking about?"

Lag let the flask slowly settle to his lap, as if he was too weak to hold it up to his mouth. "She said you'd eventually find this place, and she wanted to make sure it would be a dead end." A gray tongue played over cracked lips. "They took the others out of here and left us. She wanted you to find us dead. She told us that."

Wedge helped Lag raise the flask to his lips again. "This woman you speak of, who is she?"

Lag swallowed, then shivered. "Iceheart."

Wedge's blood ran cold. "Ysanne Isard was here?"

"A week ago, maybe two."

"Are you sure?" Wedge dropped a hand to the man's shoulder. "We killed her on Thyferra almost two years ago."

"If you did, you didn't do a very good job." Lag cracked a smile. "She looked more alive than I do, and a whole bunch more deadly."

Prince-Admiral Krennel stalked into the darkened cavern of a room where Isard *laired*. Krennel knew that word was not really exact enough, but he couldn't think of Isard as *living* within the warrens described by the various computers and arcane equipment. Glow panels hanging down from the roof barely lit the canyons of fiberplast crates, making negotiation of the labyrinth all but impossible.

He rounded a corner and found Isard seated in a huge chair at the heart of a small arena. Around her, monitors and holoprojectors danced with countless images. Her fingers flashed over keypads built into the chair's arms. With each keystroke another image changed, or the volume on one vignette rose to drown out all the others. She spun in the chair and the images were altered by the wave of her gaze sweeping past.

She came around to Krennel and stopped. His appearance seemed to surprise her, but then a casual grin curled her lips and she drew her legs up, shifting into a more comfortable position in her chair. Her gaze flicked to the datacard Krennel clutched in his artificial right hand. "I see you got my report."

Anger surged in Krennel, but he kept it in check. He casually tossed the datacard into the space between them, then clasped his hands behind his back. "I got the report. I have read it. I do not approve of it. You cannot put your plan into effect."

Isard snorted a little laugh, then punched a button on one of the keypads. The holoprojector to Krennel's right showed the image of a compound with several buildings, an X-wing parked amid them, and a number of individuals walking back and forth between the main buildings. The figures and the X-wing were rendered in reds and yellows, and Krennel assumed he was looking at an infrared cam feed.

"You've allowed them to hit your facility on Commenor."

Isard nodded. "This feed is six hours old. I had expected them to arrive in a week or so, not quite this soon. Chances are some of the prisoners I left there are still alive. Pity, but they were useless to me anyway. They know nothing of value—nothing beyond what I want them to know."

Krennel nodded his head once, curtly. "What they know could lead the New Republic to suspect that one of my worlds is the location of more of your *Lusankya* prisoners. That will be enough to bring the New Republic down on my neck."

"Oh, I expect so." Isard's smile broadened.

"This is unacceptable. I will not tolerate the loss of even one world of mine!" Krennel narrowed his eyes. "You have been here for two weeks, have requisitioned a fortune in equipment, have authorized payment to agents all over, and so far have only succeeded in losing personnel and turning prisoners over to the New Republic. This is no way to deal with our enemies."

Isard slowly shook her head. "I would have thought the lesson Grand Admiral Thrawn learned so recently would not have been lost upon you, Prince-Admiral."

The low, slow delivery of her comment sliced through his anger. "Meaning?"

"Thrawn died because it was inconceivable to him that anyone could defeat him. While his string of victories made this attitude warranted, this belief also hampered him." She pressed her hands together. "Look at the New Republic. They killed the Emperor. They took Imperial Center. They destroyed Thrawn. Now they believe they are invincible. The fact is, we will defeat them because they have this weakness."

Krennel snarled. "I have never believed in lulling an enemy into a false sense of security."

"Then believe this, Prince-Admiral: You *will* lose a world to the New Republic." Isard's voice took on an icy tone. "I know your strengths and I know their strengths. You cannot stop them, you can only force them to expend more resources than they want to take the world. Now the world I have chosen is a small one, a simple one, one of no value aside from being one bauble in the diadem you wear as Prince-Admiral. In choosing the battlefield, I can choose how the battle will go, and how we will make the New Republic pay for their victory."

"You are wrong, Isard." Krennel turned away from the scene on Commenor and met her stare evenly. "Only by standing up to them in an even fight will I be able to convince them I am too much trouble to take. I can and shall do that."

Isard shrugged. "I suspected that might be your reaction, and I have planned accordingly. You will still indulge me, however, in our political pursuits, yes?"

Krennel hesitated for a moment, then nodded. "Yes. Have your envoy meet with the leaders of the Alderaanian expatriates. I can see giving them a new home."

"And you would issue a statement of conciliation and apology for the destruction of Alderaan?"

He shifted his shoulders uneasily. "If it were necessary, yes."

"Good. What we shall do, then, is this: We will have our negotiations going on, but we will not specify a world. We say we want to learn what the Alderaanians want in a world, and we will pick one to match. We will hint that our generosity is an overture for peace between your realm and the New Republic—perhaps even suggesting that you might like to join the New Republic. Then, when the New Republic attacks, we will note that the world they take from you would have been the one you were going to give to the Alderaanians. This should anger them and weaken their support for the New Republic. After all, the people who have suffered so much now have to suffer even more."

"That ought to work." Krennel nodded slowly, then gave Isard a wry grin. "You are very good at the political manipulation of people—almost as good as I am at killing them. If you confine yourself to what you are good at, I will as well, and our partnership will have a long future."

"I will be happy to limit what I do, Prince-Admiral, if you will agree to a request."

"And that is?"

"If Rogue Squadron survives its next encounter with you," she smiled frostily, "you will leave their destruction entirely in my hands."

Krennel smiled carefully back. "And if they do not?"

"Why then, Prince-Admiral, I will just find you bigger and better targets." Isard bowed her head in his direction. "If you do manage to kill them, clearly nothing else will be able to stop you."

9

Wedge Antilles started to seat himself halfway down the left side of the lozenge-shaped briefing table when a red-fleshed Mon Calamari directed him to a chair several places closer to the head of the table. "This will be fine, Captain Jhemiti. I'll sit here."

The Mon Cal kept his voice low. "Ah, General, these seats are for *junior* officers. Staff officers sit over there."

Wedge hesitated for a second, feeling his cheeks burn with a blush. "Thank you for correcting me."

"Not correcting, General, *informing*."

Wedge suppressed a shiver as he moved to the chair Captain Jhemiti had pointed to. The Mon Cal nodded as Wedge slid it out from the table. Wedge seated himself and scooted the chair forward, then stared down at the keypad and monitor, water bottle and glass, comlink holder and personal datapad recharge jack built into his place at the table. He glanced down at the place where he'd meant to sit and saw none of that stuff.

Hmmmm, rank isn't all bad. He smiled, then killed the smile as the other senior officers began to filter into the room. General Horton Salm took a seat across from Wedge. The balding, mustached pilot gave him a quick nod, then turned to speak with the tall, blue-skinned Duros Admiral coming to the table beside him. Wedge himself offered a hand to the redheaded woman seating herself on his left.

"I'm Wedge Antilles."

"I've heard of you, General Antilles, but what Corellian hasn't." She smiled easily at him. "I'm Admiral Areta Bell, also of Corellia."

Wedge smiled. "We actually met on Hoth, didn't we? You were the navigator on the transport Tarrin flew, the one that Luke and I took out through the Imp fleet."

"That's right, the *Dutyfree*." Her blue eyes sparkled. "I'm surprised you remembered."

"How could I forget. You plotted a great course that got us through in a spot the Imps thought no one could go." He swiveled his chair toward her. "What do they have you flying now?"

"I command the *Swift Liberty*. It's an old Victory Deuce, but it's functional. We're often paired on ops with Admiral Kir Vantai's *Moonshadow*."

Wedge glanced at the Duros Admiral for a moment, then back to Areta. "That's an Impstar Deuce, right?"

The answer came from behind him as a hand fell on his shoulder. "Yes, an Impstar Deuce, the same as my *Freedom*."

Wedge spun around and offered his hand to a tall, slender, black-haired man whose goatee had been grown into a full beard and was now shot with white in stripes leading down from the corners of his mouth. "Commander Sair Yonka, good to see you again."

"And good to see you as well. When last we met, I think my ship was still being refitted at Sluis Van."

"Right, but Thrawn's mole-miners didn't get to it, so you actually managed to do some fighting against Thrawn. You were at Bilbringi, as I recall."

"We were." Yonka's blue eyes focused a bit distantly for a moment. "The *Freedom* didn't get hit, but I lost a freighter that served as a supply ship for me. Had Thrawn not died, I suspect we all would have been hit much harder."

Admiral Ackbar passed behind Salm and Vantai to take

his place at the head of the table. "The fact is, Commander Yonka, Thrawn did die. This puts us in a very interesting position. Please, be seated, all of you, and I will begin the briefing."

While Ackbar waited for everyone to be seated, Captain Jhemiti closed the doors to the briefing room, activated the antisensor fields, then dimmed the lights. The Mon Calamari Admiral hit a couple of buttons on the keypad at the head of the table and Krennel's image burned to life above the holoprojector plate set in the middle of the briefing table.

"As you have all been informed, Prince-Admiral Delak Krennel will be the target of a series of operations. The method by which we go after him is going to have to be very skillful. It is not common knowledge, but the war against Thrawn taxed our military resources rather heavily. We are still more than capable of maintaining a defensive posture that would make any attack against us punishing, but our ability to launch offensive operations is limited. General Garm Bel Iblis's return to the New Republic has supplemented our forces and has many of our enemies guessing what we will be doing next. It is our hope that while his presence keeps our enemies guessing, this operation against Krennel will convince them that they do not want to become our next target."

Ackbar opened his hands. "Krennel is not an idiot, but he is in a difficult position. He has roughly a dozen capital ships: a mix of Imperial Star Destroyers and *Victory*-class Destroyers. He has a dozen worlds to protect. With the *Freedom*, *Swift Liberty*, and *Moonshadow*, we have a taskforce that can destroy any *one* of his ships in a running battle, and can fight any patrol taskforce he's likely to put together. If he concentrates his ships enough to hammer us, we attack the worlds he leaves open."

The Duros Admiral raised a finger. "The force we have is significant, but I wonder if the *Lusankya* will be refit in time to use it against Krennel?"

Wedge's jaw dropped open. "You've rebuilt the *Lusankya*?"

Ackbar nodded. "We have, and it's gone to Bilbringi for final refits. It won't be ready for the start of this operation, but if Krennel does not fall early, we could employ it against him."

Wedge closed his mouth and shook his head. He well remembered the toll taken when Rogue Squadron assembled a fleet of ships to destroy the *Lusankya*. Because it was a Super Star Destroyer it took a lot of killing and yet an ample amount of ship had been left over. *Enough to salvage. This time it can be put to good use.*

Admiral Ackbar hit more keys and a spherical representation of Krennel's realm replaced his image. A dozen worlds were linked by glowing gold lines that marked transit routes. Navigational hazards like stars, black holes, and planets tended to make certain pathways much easier to fly and Ciutric, Krennel's capital world, served as a hub for trade routes with all the other worlds he claimed as his own.

"Ciutric is Krennel's capital and, for that reason, is well defended. It's the most industrialized of his worlds and has a shipyard capable of keeping his fleet in repair. It cannot build new Star Destroyers, though an expansion project now under way might give it that capability in a year or so."

Another world on the display grew up to displace the image of the realm. "This is Liinade Three. Its development was begun in the last days of the Old Republic and continued during the Empire. Much of it is given over to agricultural combines and light industry producing consumer products like comlinks and caf synthesizers. There is nothing about it that is vital, but taking it away from Krennel would result in noticeable, though minor, shortages of goods in the rest of his realm."

Salm nodded. "It would get his people thinking that the stability he's offering is not likely to last very long."

Admiral Bell leaned forward in her chair. "Are you saying that higher prices on comlinks will provoke a revolt?"

Salm shook his head. "Not exactly. You've seen reports coming out of Ciutric. Krennel is offering his realm as a safe, peaceful, and stable place where anyone is welcome to make a home and prosper. Taking Liinade Three will make the Hegemony a little less prosperous and will take away one of his more attractive worlds."

Wedge reached out and tapped the golden trio of trade routes connected to Liinade's blue-green ball. The name of each of the worlds to which the routes were connected flashed up in a little box. "Sure, Ciutric might seem like a nice place to go, but Vrosynri Eight or Corvis Minor? Before reading the briefing files on Krennel's realm, I never even heard of them, and what I've read doesn't make them seem like the sorts of places I'd want to retire to."

"I agree, General Antilles, but once we've cut those worlds off from the main part of the Hegemony, they will be vulnerable. The fear of our coming and taking them might provoke revolts that preclude the need for invasion."

Ackbar held his hands up. "Your points are well taken, everyone. The shortages will be difficult for Krennel to conceal if he is determined to use mass media to make his people believe Liinade Three has not fallen. Washing away one of his worlds will provide the biggest shock for his people, while shortages will become a constant reminder of it."

Salm brushed a hand over his mustache. "And while Wedge is a bit disdainful of Corvis Minor and Vrosynri Eight, those two worlds have tight trading ties to Liinade Three. By taking it, we make the two of them more likely to fall."

The Duros Admiral nodded slowly. "Neither of those worlds is very stable and could be taken with a small force, *if* Krennel decides not to defend them."

Wedge sat back in his chair. "How much do we know about Krennel's intelligence operations in the New Republic? I may be overly concerned because of breaches concerning Rogue Squadron . . ."

Salm nodded. "If it is true that Ysanne Isard still lives, she could be activating hidden intelligence agents. Nothing we do is safe."

Ackbar pressed his hands to the tabletop and leaned forward. "Concern for security is important. As of yet, we have no evidence linking this supposed sighting of Isard with Krennel, but we do know they had a limited history together concerning Sate Pestage's murder. We would be foolish to suppose they have no way of communicating with each other, or that they would not be willing to work together for their mutual benefit. Our operation will be planned with the tightest security we can manage, of course, but we have to accept that it might be compromised. We will hit hard and establish acceptable loss parameters to judge our success or lack thereof."

Ackbar's words sent a shiver down Wedge's spine. Intellectually, he understood exactly what the Admiral was saying. In any military operation the strategists had to decide how much expenditure of hardware and supplies and personnel was justified in attaining their goal. With material and munitions, the costing could be done on a credit basis: by comparing the industries on the world to be taken with how much it would cost to get them, they could determine if taking a world was feasible in an economic sense. The New Republic would either gain from the operation, or at the very least deny credits and resources to Krennel, which was also a positive benefit.

When it came to people, though, cost-accounting didn't work. Acceptable losses were more of a political point. The losses the Rebellion suffered in destroying the first Death Star were hideous, but considered well worth it when compared to what the Death Star would do to other worlds. The Death Star's threat meant that any level of sacrifice, any body count, was acceptable, and no one, not even Wedge, doubted for a second the wisdom of going after it.

When it came to Liinade III, however, there was no visible threat to the New Republic. In fact, Krennel's opening of his realm to anyone who wanted haven made him seem almost benign. Humans would wonder why the New Republic was spending lives to take a world that Krennel had all but opened to them. Nonhumans might wonder why the New Republic was willing to be blinded by so clear a deception. If nonhumans took a larger proportion of losses than humans did in the assault and it failed, nonhumans could even suggest that the New Republic was spending nonhuman lives while winking at Krennel and tacitly supporting him.

For Wedge, *any* losses were unacceptable. He'd certainly ordered men and women, humans and aliens, into situations where their survival was severely in doubt, and he'd gone into those situations himself on countless occasions. He never sent anyone into anything where he knew they would die, but he had often wondered if he would see his people together again at the end of a battle.

Ackbar sat down in his chair. "The New Republic is weary of war, but people, somehow, are never weary of victory. We sustained considerable losses in the Thrawn campaign: ten percent of our forces killed, thirty percent wounded—but those are just averages. On the worlds Thrawn actually hit, the devastation was significant. This operation will need to be clean and crisp. I believe we can sustain a thirty percent casualty rate and still consider the cost justified. I want it to be much lower."

Wedge nodded and called to mind the pilots in his squadron. *A third, gone—one whole flight. Probably two killed, two wounded. Who can I lose? The new people, Slee and Zatoq? Or will it be Hobbie and Janson? Will their number be up?*

Ackbar hit another button on his keypad. "Flooding into your datapads is the preliminary operational plan for the assault on Liinade Three. It calls for *Swift Liberty* and *Moonshadow* to enter a close orbit, while *Freedom* remains at the edge of the system. We expect that Krennel will spring any surprises, like bringing other ships in from other systems, with the initial engagement. Which is when *Freedom* will jump in at a point where we will have tactical advantage.

"*Moonshadow* will serve as the base for General Salm's B-wing Assault Group; *Swift Liberty* will carry Rogue Squadron. *Freedom* will be home to the assault shuttles we'll be sending down. Our capital ships will kill or drive off Krennel's capital ships, then we deploy ground troops to take key factories, energy production centers, mass media delivery centers, and the capital. Once troops are on the ground, we will bring in rising tide reinforcements and supplies. I believe pacification of Liinade Three should take little more than two weeks if Krennel does not launch a counterassault."

Admiral Bell chewed on a fingernail for a moment, then nodded. "Sending our ships out on different patrols, then having us meet up for the run in at Liinade Three should work to keep our assault secret, but gathering the reinforcements and keeping them hidden is going to be tough. Krennel has to know something is up, and Liinade Three is one of his most vulnerable targets."

"We plan to preoccupy him." Ackbar's lip-fringes twitched as his mouth opened in a smile. "One lesson we learned about Krennel from the last time Rogue Squadron dealt with him was that he believes in his own importance. We plan to have General Garm Bel Iblis conduct a planetary assault exercise on Borleias. That world bears a remarkable resemblance to Ciutric in terms of geography, size, atmosphere, and the like. The reinforcements we'll devote to you will be staging there for that operation. Bel Iblis will also make a series of speeches to various groups here on Coruscant and elsewhere that will indicate our intention of coming after Krennel, and will suggest that when the head is struck from a rancor, the body dies very quickly. Krennel will interpret all that, we think, as a coming strike on Ciutric, and will defend his capital world appropriately."

Wedge smiled. "And if Krennel rushes ships from Ciutric to defend Liinade Three, Bel Iblis can always hit Ciutric."

The Mon Cal Admiral nodded. "When you have to assume your enemy knows your plans, providing him two distasteful alternatives often promotes conservative thinking."

Even as Ackbar spoke, Wedge knew there was something being left unsaid. It occurred to him that if the New Republic had enough force to be able to hit Liinade III *and* threaten Ciutric, then it would need to appear to have enough power to hit Ciutric and do exactly what Bel Iblis would be threatening to do. *This means Bel Iblis will be working with a fake force at Borleias—skeleton-crewed ships probably operating with droids to simulate a full staff.*

*We'll be on our own and in trouble if Krennel has gotte_
any smarter over the years.*

Ackbar opened his hands. "So, if you will all please ca]
up the first file, we'll begin going through the plan step b
step and see what holes we need to plug so it does not sin]
without a trace."

10

Iella Wessiri sat back in her chair and closed her eyes in spite of the sandpaper feeling of lids sliding down over eyeballs. She rolled her shoulders and let her head droop back a bit. She slowly worked her head to the right and left, loosening the muscles of her neck, then took in a deep breath, held it, and slowly exhaled.

With the next deep breath she caught the scent of hot and strong caf. Her eyes snapped open and she spun her chair toward the doorway. "Wedge?"

Mirax smiled sheepishly and extended a steaming mug toward her. "Sorry to disappoint you, Iella, but I figured you could use this when you called and canceled dinner this evening."

"Thanks, I *can* use it." She accepted the mug from Mirax and inhaled the steam. "Where'd you get this caf? I haven't smelled anything this strong since . . . since I left Corellia."

Mirax stepped in from the doorway and Whistler warbled triumphantly as he rolled into Iella's office. His head turned in a circle, and he stopped and extended toward her a small bag clutched in his pincer. A tone ran from low to high, and Iella accepted the bag with a gracious bow of her head.

Mirax smiled. "Whistler seems to recall the settings you CorSec folks used on your caf distiller back on Corellia. I don't allow him to make it that strong at home, but I gather he still brews it that way at the squadron. I found a caf shop that let him play with the controls in return for some exotic blends I managed to get my hands on. The result is in your mug."

Iella took a sip, then set the mug down on the desk. She opened the bag and peeked inside. "And the pastries, they were your idea, Whistler?"

The droid trumpeted triumphantly.

Mirax sighed. "I tried to convince him that something a bit more substantial would be better for you, but he seems to think all CorSec officers function on strong caf and foods full of fat and sugar and gluten."

"Well, it couldn't hurt at the moment." Iella narrowed her eyes. "Um, how did you get in here, anyway?"

Mirax fished a security datacard from the pocket of her nerf-hide jacket. "General Cracken and I have an understanding. He uses me to keep tabs on my father's *Errant Venture*. I pass on rumors that I hear while trading, offer opinions."

"Cracken doesn't worry too much when your cargo manifests don't actually square with what arrives?"

"He knows he can trust me not to do anything harmful, and I did have a little to do with *rylca* production on Borleias, so it's an easy détente." Mirax smiled. "Neither Corran nor my father know of my arrangement with Cracken, and I'd just as soon keep it that way." She reached out with a foot and tapped Whistler's barrel body with a toe. "You got that, Whistler?"

The droid warbled emphatically.

Iella raised an eyebrow. "Whistler keeping secrets from Corran? How did that happen?"

Mirax winked. "When he retires, Whistler wants to be the navigator on the *Pulsar Skate*. We have an understanding, which is good, because he's been on the *Skate* enough that he could run it all by himself. He probably knows more about it and my business than I do."

"Whistler used to be that way with our caseloads in CorSec, too." Iella laughed out loud. For years Whistler had helped Corran fight smugglers in and around Corellia. *And now he wants to work with Mirax and her "exotics" trade. Interesting.* She pondered this change of heart on Whistler's part, but then decided it wasn't that radical a shift. *If Corran could fall in love with Mirax, there's no reason why Whistler couldn't do the same.*

"Well, I think Whistler will be great at his new career. He was wired to be an overachiever." Iella drank a bit more of the caf. "This is really good. I'm sorry to have canceled dinner with you, but analyzing the data from the prisoners' debriefings is taking forever."

Mirax tucked a dark strand of hair behind her right ear. "Don't worry about dinner, we'll do it another time. Corran got called back to squadron headquarters for briefings anyway. Looks like something big is going down."

Iella looked up at her friend. "So then I cancel and you're all alone."

Whistler cheeped.

Mirax patted the droid on the head. "No slight against you, Whistler, but I can't force you to order a dessert, then eat half of it."

Iella offered up half a pastry. "I'll split one with you."

"It's a deal." Mirax cleared some datacards off the small office's other chair and sat down. "Anything to clarify the report that Isard is alive?"

Iella chewed a mouthful of pastry, then washed the sticky sweetness from her mouth with caf before answering. "Corran shouldn't have told you that."

"True. But since he figures she's the one who sent Urlor and murdered him, Corran also figures I'm a target, so he wants me to be careful. Give it up, Iella. You know I'm not going to tell anyone."

The intelligence officer sighed. "Several prisoners said they saw her and heard her, but they're in pretty bad shape. I can't give their identifications too much weight since some of them are in the grips of dementia. It seems pretty clear that whoever put those people there wanted them to starve to death, and they were pretty close. If we'd waited another week, we'd just have corpses."

"And dead men tell no tales."

"Not true. Urlor's body led us to these guys."

"Do these guys lead you to Isard?"

Iella sighed. "Not directly." She waved a hand at the datapad monitor on her desk. "I've been going over the reports we all made at the time of Thyferra's liberation and a couple of details don't seem to mesh well."

Mirax licked sugar residue from her fingers. "Like what?"

"Well, first off, I've not been able to find any indication in any record or anecdote or anything that Isard was capable of piloting a *Lambda*-class shuttle. She wasn't a pilot before she went to Thyferra, and no one there knows anything about her being able to fly."

Mirax nodded. "That makes it less likely that she was in the shuttle that Tycho blew up. Still, didn't Corran have sensor readings indicating someone was on board?"

Whistler tootled positively.

"I've pulled the sensor-trace data records and that's right. I also noted something else: There were two comm frequencies being used by the shuttle. Isard conversed with Corran over one, but I don't have any record of what sort of data was flowing over the other."

"So you think Isard was having the shuttle flown remotely from Thyferra to make the Rogues think she was escaping." Mirax's brown eyes narrowed. "If it got destroyed, or if it jumped out, either way no one would be looking for her on Thyferra itself. She smuggles herself out with the Xucphra refugees and she's clear."

"Isard certainly would have had the resources to fake documentation that would get her clear." Iella held the caf mug in her hands and let the warmth bleed into them. "I very much want to believe that Tycho's proton torpedo converted her into free-floating hydrogen, but this little kink in the facts that we overlooked before is a problem."

"Still, it doesn't mean she's back in action." Mirax frowned. "Why would she lay low during the whole Thrawn thing?"

"Isard help an alien Grand Admiral? I don't think so."
Iella tapped a stack of datacards on the desk. "Imperial
records concerning Thrawn might as well not exist, but I
can't believe Isard didn't know about him and his existence
out in the Unknown Regions. She didn't ask him back to
help her when she was running the Empire, and I can't
imagine she wanted to help him reestablish it with *him* as
the new Emperor. She probably just crawled into some tiny
hole and licked her wounds, hoping Thrawn and the New
Republic would kill each other."

"Yeah, and she did have some wounds to lick. She lost
Coruscant, she lost Thyferra, she lost her own private Super
Star Destroyer, *Lusankya*. Getting away with her life and
the location of the prisoners was the only up side for her."
Mirax leaned forward, resting her elbows on her knees.
"How many more facilities like the one on Commenor does
she have for stashing prisoners?"

Iella shook her head. "No way to tell. In fact, I'm not
sure the Xenovet facility was much more than a blind."

"I don't understand. You found the prisoners there.
Your forensics team must have found clues and everything."

"They did, plenty of evidence of records being destroyed, shallow graves for some of the dead, everything we
need to piece together a circumstantial case that points to
the prisoners having been there a while."

Mirax's black hair brushed down past her shoulders as
she lifted her head. "The problem is?"

"The problem is that the evidence would have been
perfect had the prisoners all been dead. From them, however, we have details that make me wonder. For example,
they remember huge, long hyperspace flights, but they were
locked in little cells at the time. According to them, they
were bounced from planet to planet, and they've been in the
current facility for years."

"Corran thought he'd been on a long space journey
taking him from Coruscant to *Lusankya*, but Isard just
faked it all along."

Iella nodded emphatically. "Exactly. Using drugs on the
prisoners, she could have warped their sense of time, or

even had them totally unconscious as she moved them from one place to another. As long as their cells looked the same, the staff was the same, and the food was the same, the prisoners would have no clue where they had been."

"You're basing a lot of this on the idea that someone as smart as Isard was doing all this."

"Probably, but what if it's an individual just following Isard's instructions? Isard would have had to trust this person implicitly to turn the prisoners over to them."

"Okay, if not Isard, someone she trusted to do what she told them to do. Someone who's now making his own play at power." Mirax nodded solemnly. "Someone who has Isard's resources and contacts in the New Republic, giving him the information he needed to plant Urlor Sette here at the party."

"Exactly."

"Okay, you're suspicious of the situation at Commenor, but what's the purpose of faking that facility? I mean, the clues from Urlor led there, so we went. The Interceptors might have been an ambush, but a pretty poor one. What did Isard's agent want to have happen there?"

"I think it was bait." Iella smiled grimly. "We backtracked the trail to Commenor and there's more trail to follow. The bodies pulled from the graves could only have been there a couple of years, but they show more decay on the bones than we'd expect from the soil in that area on Commenor. I think they were buried somewhere else, disinterred, and moved to Commenor. Once we figure out where they came from, we'll go to that new world and find more bait."

"Or a trap."

"Right." She shrugged and sipped her caf. "We get so happy at having broken through the puzzle this person is laying out for us that we allow ourselves to think it was never meant to be broken. We figure we have the upper hand, but we're just following the trail they've laid."

"Interesting hypothesis. How do you test it?"

Iella winced. "There's the problem. The obvious way to test it is to have teams go back to Commenor and look around for clues that indicate the site was faked. If it *is* a fake, then there ought to be redundant clues that will point this out. The bodies that I mentioned would have been missed except I saw them described as being in an 'advanced' state of decay. I checked with the forensic tech to find out what that meant and he walked me through it. I checked with the guys who took soil samples, and I was able to pull together a picture that looks like the bodies weren't always there. That was a tough way to get at the fake data and I'm willing to bet there are easier ones."

Mirax sat back and crossed her legs at her booted ankles. "Of course, if you send teams back, you'll tip the enemy to the fact that you've found the deception and will be following it up."

"You never want the Hutt you're after to know you're following his slime trail. Plus, we don't know how much of our planning and intelligence is getting to the other side."

Corran's wife smiled slyly. "Why not just go there 'off duty?' Corran said you used to do that back when you were with CorSec. We can go without telling anyone. They'll never know. If we find something, we know you're right, and if we don't, that's a step forward, too."

Iella sipped at the caf and nodded. "It could work. We'd have to go in very covertly, since the political situation is a bit touchy in the aftermath of the raid."

Mirax winked at her. "I think I know a thing or two about getting into and out of spaceports without attracting too much official attention. You can leave those details to me. You just get together the gear you'll need and we'll be good to go."

Iella thought for a moment, then nodded. "It'll take me about three weeks to clear up things here."

"Perfect. I can get some vaguely legit business set up on Commenor in that time." Mirax smiled happily. "It'll just be you and me on a girls' night out."

"So you're not going to tell Corran?"

"Wedge and squadron business are what he's focusing on at the moment. I see no reason to distract him."

"He's *your* husband."

Mirax laughed. "He was *your* partner. Would you handle him differently?"

"Hmmmm, good point." Iella fed a datacard into her datapad. "I'll prep a report and entrust it to Whistler here. If anything goes amiss with us, he can turn it over to Corran."

"It's a plan."

"And a workable one, I think." Iella raised her mug of caf in a salute. "If we can confirm that we're being played, we stand a chance of turning the tables on our enemy, and that's definitely a position I want us to be in."

11

Corran Horn looked over from his conversation with the Issori pilot, Khe-Jeen Slee, and smiled at Gavin Darklighter, who stood next to the table's open seat. "Sure, Gavin, sit down. We're just telling stories."

The Issori's dark green scaled flesh lightened slightly in hue as Gavin off-loaded his tray. "We are pleased to have you join me and Corran."

"I don't want to interrupt, but I did have a question for Corran."

Khe-Jeen waved a hand toward Corran. "Please, ask it."

Corran looked at Gavin and rolled his eyes. "Sure, what is it?"

Gavin glanced down at his food and his voice barely rose above the din in the crowded base commissary. "Have you ever wanted to be a father?"

The question rocked Corran back in his chair and he noted that Khe-Jeen watched his reaction with the pure intent of a predator tracking prey. "I haven't thought that much about it. Mirax has said we should talk about it, but we've been kind of busy with Thrawn and all. Is this something you're thinking about?"

The younger pilot smiled and nodded. "You met my family back on Tatooine."

"Right, lots of brothers, sisters, cousins, and all." Corran fingered a round brown biscuit, spinning it as he ran his finger along the edge. "Are you getting the itch to have a family?"

"I think so, yes."

Corran frowned. "Ah, not meaning to pry here, but are you and Asyr, um, capable of doing that? I mean, I thought Bothan-human matings didn't work."

Gavin gave him a goofy grin. "Well, the parts line up fine as far as I'm concerned, but things don't connect that well on a cellular level, I guess. We want to get married, then we're going to adopt. We've filled out the preliminary datafiles and we need to gather all the other stuff they'll want—the officials, I mean."

"That's great, Gavin." Corran slapped him on the arm. "You'll make a great father. You're compassionate and intelligent. You have a great sense of humor, and you're pretty good at feeling out the moods folks are in."

"Thanks, Corran, that means a lot."

Khe-Jeen Slee sucked the meat off a small bone, then began to crunch cartilage. "We are pleased for you, Gavin, and your willingness to accept responsibility for younglings not your own. We have noted a nobility about you which is impressive." The Issori swallowed hard and a big bulge started to work its way down his throat. "On Issor, you would never face the choices you do here."

Gavin looked up, a brown, gooey bean mixture dripping from the spoon he'd raised halfway to his mouth. "You don't allow adoptions on Issor?"

"There is no need for them." Khe-Jeen nibbled the end off the bone and crushed it between his teeth. "We Issori are oviparous. The females of the species produce eggs which are tended and hatch, provided they have been fertilized. The males produce a packet of the fertilizing agent . . ." The Issori unzipped his sleeveless flight suit and began to slip a clawed hand down toward his abdomen.

Corran reached out and grabbed his arm. "We'll take your word for it, you don't have to show us."

A clear membrane flashed up over Khe-Jeen's amber eyes. He slowly withdrew his hand, bringing with it a sheaf of holographs. He wordlessly selected one, then handed it to Corran. "Perhaps this will enlighten you."

Corran held the static holograph so Gavin could see it. The image showed two Issori, one male and a smaller, lighter-colored female. He was pouring a liquid from a pitcher onto an egg and she was brushing the liquid over the egg. To Corran, it looked similar to what he'd seen chefs do in basting a roast, but he decided to keep *that* observation to himself.

Gavin's brown-eyed gaze flicked up. "You're the egg?"

"I was, yes. The Issori have a caste-based society. The caste of the egglayer determines the caste into which the child will be born. The caste of the fertilizer determines rank within that caste and political alliances between the families involved. Breedings are negotiated, sometimes with eggs or packets traveling great distances to be used in a fertilization ceremony such as this. This image is of a *Whoon-cha*. It is an intra-caste breeding of the nobility, meant to strengthen the standing of two families within the ruling caste. A *Whoon-li* would be an inter-caste breeding within one realm involving a noble and a more common caste. A *Vuin-cha* would be a breeding between nobles from different realms."

Corran nodded. "And a *Vuin-li* would be a noble breeding with a common caste from outside the realm."

The Issori stiffened. "Such a thing would never happen."

Corran frowned. "Wait, you're telling me that no two Issori from different castes and different nations would ever breed together? What if they are in love?"

Khe-Jeen allowed himself a little laugh. "These displays of emotion that so often rule other sapients are taken in perspective by the Issori. We consider love much like a rainstorm. It can be light or hard, long or short, mild or tempestuous. It can also end. To tie the life of a child to the mercurial emotional attachments of its parents is cruel. Families agree on breedings, families raise the children. My name, for example, has three elements. Khe indicates I am of a single breeding which my father's family negotiated. It is not his family name, but instead comes from the character of our alphabet that my father's family uses to mark such a union. My mother was of the Jeen family. I am known as Slee. Both the Khe and Slee parts of my name were chosen based on a formula that allowed the numerical values of the letters of my name to add up to an auspicious number."

Corran shot Gavin a glance. "Get your hands on that formula and you'll have no problems naming the kids you adopt."

Khe-Jeen crackled the rest of the bone to splinters in his mouth. "Our point is this: On Issor there are no unwanted children, and even those orphaned are the responsibility of the families of those who were bred to create them."

Corran scratched at his forehead. "But if eggs and packets can travel, isn't it possible that children are actually born after the parents are dead? And isn't it possible that someone could breed a rival to a leader by stealing eggs and packets from people closer to a throne than he is?"

"Indeed, we have often bred using packets of dead heroes or leaders—we have used the eggs of their sisters or wives or daughters similarly to preserve the bloodline. The families always care for these newborns." The Issori shrugged his broad shoulders. "As for unsanctioned breedings, they are known as *vrecje*. The closest Basic word is stranger, but it runs deeper since not only do we not know them, but they have not been raised by a family, so they are not really considered Issori. They are wretched, tortured creatures and are slain as wild beasts are slain."

"Having families raise kids sounds right by me." Gavin smiled, then wiped his mouth with a napkin. "Asyr has said that family means a lot to the Bothans, and I've agreed that any children we adopt should have a full understanding of their own culture."

Corran raised an eyebrow. "You're going to adopt Bothan children?"

"At least one, yes." Gavin reached out and rested his right hand on Corran's left forearm. "Look, after we're married, a lot of people are going to come around asking about Asyr and me, and whether or not we're suitable for raising kids and everything like that. I want to use you and Mirax as references, if that's okay with you."

Corran raked a hank of dark brown hair out of his eyes, then nodded, dropping it back down again. "Sure. I'll run it by Mirax, but I'm sure she'll agree. We'd be happy to help you."

"Great, I'll tell Asyr. She'll be excited."

"Where is she?"

Gavin shrugged his shoulders and chewed a mouthful of beans. He glanced around the room, then shook his head. "I thought she was going to try to join me for lunch. She got a message right when our briefing let out. She said she would try to be back."

Corran glanced at his chronometer and stood. "Speaking of back, we've got fifteen minutes before we're due in the simulators. I'm going to get come caf, then find Whistler. Anyone else need caf?"

Khe-Jeen Slee shook his head once, sharply, as if tearing a hunk of flesh from an invisible beast. "Our digestive system is too refined for your caf. If there is chokolate, I would take that."

"Got it. Gavin?"

"I'm good to go, Corran." Gavin fished some credits from his pocket and held them out. "Let me buy for you two, though. For the help with this adoption thing."

Corran waved the money away. "Save it, Gavin. When you finally get kids, there will never be enough of it. Somehow, though, I think the two of you—and your family— will do just fine."

Borsk Fey'lya turned slowly from the window looking out over Coruscant. He found Asyr Sei'lar standing just inside the door to his office, with the sunlight streaming past him making the white fur on her face and hands glow with a dazzling intensity. Her violet eyes still had the fire he'd seen in them years ago, and her expression had a determination to it that matched the fire. *Good, she is prepared to fight, which means she is prepared to deal.*

"You sent for me, Councilor Fey'lya?"

Borsk opened his hands slowly and let a little hurt tone play into his voice. "You feel the need to be so formal, *Captain* Sei'lar? I thought, between us, between Bothans, we could be more familiar."

Asyr's eyes tightened, as did her fists. "I merely wished you to know that I am aware of where the power resides, Councilor."

"I see." Borsk smiled carefully, then stroked his creamy chin-fur. "Congratulations on your promotion, by the way. Well deserved and long overdue. Just like a human to keep your rank artificially low."

The black fur rose at the back of Asyr's neck. "Rogue Squadron has never been overly worried about rank, Councilor. Getting our jobs done has been our paramount concern. The reward of rank has been more than justified by our actions. In fact, I would say that the New Republic has been quite penurious in rewarding heroes such as Wedge Antilles."

Very good, Asyr. Borsk nodded and moved from the window toward his desk. *You suggest that Antilles has been insufficiently rewarded, and allow the implication that we have been similarly neglectful of the rest of the Rogues to chastise me. You play the game well.*

Borsk waved a hand toward the chair before his desk. "Please, be seated. I want you to be comfortable."

Asyr moved forward, but stood behind the chair. "I've been sitting all day during briefings. It feels good to stretch my muscles, but do not let me stop you. Please, be seated."

And let you look down upon me? Borsk nodded and seated himself in a massive chair. He tapped a datacard—the only datacard—on his desk with his index finger. He let the sound of his nail clicking on the datacard's casing fill the room, then he scooped up the card into his hand and slowly turned it over. "You know what this is."

Asyr stiffened, then gathered her hands at the small of her back. "I assume it is my application to adopt a Bothan orphan."

"You do know, of course, that a hero of your stature would never be denied such an honor. There are doubtless Bothan families that would gladly give up one of their children to you, knowing their child would be raised in a home where power does not trickle, but flows and *floods*." Borsk tapped the datacard against his muzzle, then lowered it and smiled. "After the second Death Star was destroyed and the role of the Martyrs was revealed, their families were overwhelmed with claims that children had been fathered by the Martyrs. Claiming a piece of the grand Bothan tradition is so important to our people that we would give our own flesh and blood away so they can be part of it."

Her chin came up. "Then you called me here to tell me the application has been approved?"

"No, and you know that is not true." Borsk slid the datacard across the desk toward her. "I want you to withdraw the application."

"What?"

"Please, Asyr, you know how impossible this is. You are involved in a liaison with a human—you want to marry him. It might add a bit of exotic luster to your image on Bothawui, but the vast majority of Bothans consider it something of a perversion. He's all but furless and his face is so squashed it's, well, hideous. That you have found something in him that attracts you, this I can understand, but you cannot allow this infatuation with him to last."

"It's not an infatuation. We love each other."

Borsk Fey'lya raised his hands and waved away her declaration. "Infatuation, love, lust, whatever you call it, it doesn't matter. What matters is this: We were prepared to indulge your dalliance, but no more. You cannot be permitted to marry him and create a family with him."

"His name is Gavin Darklighter, and he's every bit as much a hero as I am." Asyr's clawed hands came around and gripped the back of the nerf-hide chair. "I cannot believe you have the impudence to sit there and tell me what I can and cannot do with my life."

"No?" Borsk kept his voice low and even, meeting her hot stare with a cold one of his own. "And I do not believe you can stand there and have the impudence to totally abrogate your responsibility to your people."

"What?"

Borsk spread his arms, resting his hands flat on the desk. "I have told you before that you have become a role model for young Bothans. The Martyrs represent what we all hope we could achieve, what we hope we would be willing to do when called upon. They are shining examples of what we are at our best. Their greatest virtue is that they are dead. They are defined by the moment of their death, and nothing that went before matters. All their weaknesses, their frailties and vices were washed away when the Empire spilled their blood.

"You, my dear, are different. You have accomplished much and you still live. You provide an ongoing example to our people. When a young female faces a decision, she might ask herself, 'What would Asyr Sei'lar do?' You defied your parents and entered the Bothan Martial Academy. You've taken up with a human. You have no interest, apparently, in bearing children of your own, but are content to raise a mongrel pack of children salvaged from the ruins of the Empire. Yes, humans certainly see that as charitable and enviable, but it is not the Bothan way. By following your example, others will destroy the Bothan way of life."

Asyr shook her head. "No, it is not fair to put the blame for change on me. Bothan society was repressed by the Empire and by turning inward, by maintaining our strength, we survived that oppression. Now things are different, change is happening and there is no way to stop it."

"I don't want to stop it, Asyr, but I do need to direct it." Borsk paused for a second, less for dramatic effect than for a genuine need to gather his thoughts. *If I cannot convince you of your part in the salvation of the Bothan people, other steps may have to be taken.* He admired the steel in her spine, the energy blazing from her eyes, but if he could not control her and the direction she took, the disaster he saw looming on the horizon would swallow the Bothan people.

Desperation fueled inspiration.

He sighed heavily. "The Empire put forward the idea that any species that was not human was inferior. Humans were held up as the absolute acme of accomplishment. If we were to aspire to greatness, we had to aspire to be human or more than human. That is a message we had beaten into us during the Imperial period. Children of your generation have been raised in a world where that is the reality. Humans are the measure against which we compare ourselves.

"Now you, a Bothan, are a hero who has attained parity with human heroes. They accept you, and you accept them, and this is very good. The same is true for Ooryl Qyrgg or Chewbacca. You are shining examples to humans of what nonhumans can do. In this capacity you serve every nonhuman species in the New Republic very well."

Borsk drew his hands together, rubbing one over the other. "You, however, have a romantic relationship with a human. The message that sends is not one of equality. It suggests that, somehow, a nonhuman is not sufficiently worthy of your affections. This relationship was tolerable and manageable when it could be dismissed as a dalliance. Settling down for a life with Gavin Darklighter will confirm what the Empire has been telling us all along: We are inferior to humans, and even our heroes know that, which is why you, Asyr Sei'lar, take as your life companion a human."

"No, that's not right." Asyr shook her head, but the earlier vehemence in her voice had lost something. "By choosing Gavin, it says there are a galaxy of possibilities out there."

Borsk slowly shook his head and allowed a kindly note to enter his voice. "Possibilities, yes, but sterile ones, unfruitful ones. You're telling everyone that you would rather turn your back on the family traditions of the Bothans to marry a human than accept your responsibilities in our community. That may not be the message you intend to send, but that is the one everyone is hearing."

Asyr leaned forward, bending over the back of the chair. "You're telling me that by exercising my freedom of choice, a freedom I fought for and helped win from the Empire, I will be perpetuating the Empire's influence?"

"It is not as grave as that, but essentially you are correct. You have the misfortune to be a Bothan hero in a time when we desperately need Bothan heroes to be very Bothan. It's not fair. It's even cruel. But it is your lot in life, and your responsibility to deal with it."

She looked up at him. "What would my future be? What do I have to do to be more *Bothan*?"

"I have not thought along those lines."

Asyr snarled, curling a lip to show some teeth. "You can badger me, you can hurt me, but do not treat me like some stupid child. The second you saw my application you plotted out the course you would like my life to take. You would have me break off my relationship with Gavin and then what? Resign from the squadron, return to Bothawui to command my own squadron? Then, after a time and suitable negotiations I would be wed to a nephew of yours? Perhaps a son?"

Borsk narrowed his eyes. "That would be an acceptable course, yes. Your family is desirous of your return to our world, and there are many Houses that would welcome you into them."

She nodded. "And the alternative is what, to be ostracized, cut off from my people? I would get no Bothan child to raise, and you would use your power to see to it that Gavin and I never adopted any other child? You would make my life miserable because if I am unwilling to serve as the sort of example you want, you can make me into a negative example that will serve your purpose just as easily."

Borsk nodded a brief salute to her. "You are *very* Bothan at the moment, Asyr. This is good. Your choices are clearly laid out for you."

"You would have me break Gavin's heart." Asyr hesitated for a second. "You'll let our people break mine for me."

"Better one heart broken than the culture of a people lost forever."

Asyr straightened up. "I will need time to think on this."

"It is understandable." Borsk Fey'lya smiled easily. "Rogue Squadron's current mission should redouble your fame. At its conclusion your decision would be expected."

She nodded once. "You'll see how truly Bothan I am, Councilor Fey'lya. As power flows are warped and twisted, just remember it is *you* who made me remember, and made me live up to my heritage."

12

Adjusting his blaster belt, Corran Horn sprinted across the *Swift Liberty*'s launch bay and leaped halfway up the ladder connected to his X-wing's cockpit. The X-wing had been repainted the green, black, and white color scheme it had sported when he'd been with CorSec. The techs had even dutifully painted on his kill markers again and stenciled his name, CAPTAIN CORRAN HORN, on the side. He let his fingers brush over his rank, then he climbed into the cockpit and waved at the techs pulling the ladder away.

Whistler blatted harshly at him as he pulled on his helmet.

"Yes, Whistler, I heard the call, but I was finishing up a message to Mirax in case we don't make it back. Of course, I figure she'll miss you more than me."

The droid warbled in a very self-satisfactory manner.

"Good to know we're in agreement." Corran strapped himself into his seat and hit the switch that lowered the canopy and locked it into position. He punched the ignition sequence into the command console. The engines caught on the first try, sending a gentle thrum through the fighter.

"Whistler, set my inertial compensator at point-nine-five gravities and load fleet, squadron, and Three Flight comm channels into switches one through three respectively." As the droid did that, Corran ran power from the engines into the weapons system. One by one the X-wing's lasers all came online and began charging. The proton torpedo launcher's computer reported the device was set to go, and the magazine was loaded with six torpedoes. The diagnostics screens showed that the X-wing sported an auxiliary belly tank with enough fuel to allow them to fight both in space and down in atmosphere for an extended period of time.

I hope this belly tank works better than the one I had on Borleias.

Wedge's voice crackled through Corran's headset. "Good to have you with us, Captain Horn."

"Sorry about that, General Antilles. I was recording a message for my wife and there was a bit of a line to use the equipment." Corran looked over at the mission chronometer on the command console. "We've still got two minutes to reversion. Besides, with General Salm's B-wings out there, we won't be needed at all."

"Then they'll release us to hit ground targets." Wedge's voice carried with it a hint of amusement. "The B-wings are tough and will take a lot of damage, but they're still slower and less maneuverable than the eyeballs and squints we'll be facing. Salm may only leave crumbs behind, but they're *our* crumbs."

"I copy, Rogue Leader." Corran switched his comm unit over to Three Flight's channel. "Okay, Rogues, we're under two minutes to reversion. All systems should be green. I don't know exactly what there will be out there for us to light up, but whatever it is, I want us shining really bright."

Commander Vict Darron strode onto the *Direption*'s bridge and was pleased with the fact that his crew kept hard at work. *When I was Krennel's executive officer, if the crew didn't immediately fawn all over him when he appeared, he'd start working up insubordination charges for the lot of them*. Darron knew any distraction for a crew on a warship was an invitation to disaster, and disasters are never good on a warship.

Krennel had given him command of the Imperial Star Destroyer, Mark II, after its previous commander, a Captain Rensen, had been executed for failing to raze a village that had been home to someone who tried to assassinate Krennel. Darron immediately set about locating those crewmen who Krennel had cited for being insubordinate and asked for them to be assigned to his ship. He promised Krennel they would no longer be a problem, and Krennel gladly gave them up.

But Krennel also demanded he raze the same village his predecessor had refused to destroy.

Being well aware that Krennel's mechanical hand could crush his throat as easily as it had Rensen's, Darron had immediately agreed to carry out the mission. From the second he left Krennel's presence he sought for a way to preserve his life without engaging in the wholesale slaughter of villagers. His search took him back over old territory, for every Imperial officer in any position of authority had long since wrestled with his piece of responsibility for the destruction of Alderaan and the policies of the Empire.

Many simply laid the blame on Grand Moff Tarkin and said, had they been in charge, they never would have used an inhabited planet as a target. That, of course, overlooked the fact that the Empire had created a weapon that could destroy planets, then built another one after the first was destroyed. Clearly the Emperor intended to be vaping worlds, and any officer who didn't do something to stop that madness bore some guilt for it.

Darron himself acknowledged that there were cruel and even evil policies carried out under the Emperor. Still, he saw the anarchy promulgated by the New Republic as even worse. His role in the galaxy was to preserve order and allow people to live in peace. He and the *Direption*'s crew were the bulwark behind which those whom the New Republic's forces would devour could hide.

When Krennel had made himself into a warlord, Darron had followed and brought his family with him. While Krennel's mental stability—or lack thereof—did bother him, Darron feared more a world in which his children would be forced to cohabit with aliens. Such things went against the natural order of life, and he couldn't consider himself true to his responsibilities as a father if he did not fight against such things.

But wholesale murder did not make him comfortable, either, so he found a creative solution to the village problem. With the *Direption* in orbit above Liinade III, Darron took a shuttle down to the village and addressed the people there. He told them that because an assassin had arisen from their ranks, their village had to be destroyed. In exquisite detail he laid out how the village would be destroyed, grid coordinate by grid coordinate. He told them that when he returned to his ship, the assault would begin, and that it would not end until every building in the whole place had been slagged.

Then he returned to his shuttle, but before it lifted off, he discussed his plans with his weapons-officers. He had them run full checks on their heavy turbolaser batteries, targeting arrays, and planetary survey data. He demanded that everything be perfect for his demonstration against these people, and when he was satisfied that all was ready, nearly three hours after he had spoken to the villagers, his shuttle returned to the *Direption*.

The village was razed, but no one died in the attack. Darron filed a full report that Krennel had not liked, but Darron pointed out that the homeless refugees were taken into other communities on Liinade III and carried with them their tale of Krennel's swift retribution. The implication was that future rebellion would bring quick and probably more dire attacks. Krennel reluctantly agreed to how the situation had been handled, but had warned Darron never to fail him again.

At the front of the bridge, Darron looked out at the green-blue, cloud-streaked ball of Liinade III spinning below him. *To me falls the duty of preventing the New Republic from taking this world.* He sighed. Liinade III was clearly the most viable target for the New Republic. Darron had made a strong case for that point to Krennel, but the Prince-Admiral had refused to allot any more troops to its defense. *At least he gave me full control of deployment. When they come, we'll be ready.*

A warning klaxon began to sound, and the blond-haired man spun around. "Lieutenant Harsis, report!"

A small, slender, dark-skinned man looked up from the sensor station. "I have two contacts, Commander. They came out of hyperspace two klicks to our aft. Looks like an Imperial Star Destroyer and a *Victory*-class Destroyer. Broadcast codes make them New Republic. They're deploying fighters, X-wings, and B-wings."

"Helm, roll us to port and bring us about. Flight Command, have our TIEs deploy while we're turning so they can't see them coming. Shields, I want full power now." Darron smiled. "The mongrels have arrived, people. They aren't welcome and we'd best let them know that."

Admiral Areta Bell watched the holograph of the *Direption* roll and begin its turn from her Combat Command Center deep in the heart of the *Swift Liberty*. She stood there, arms folded across her chest, her booted feet firmly planted on the deck, and narrowed her blue eyes. "Helm, give me three-quarters full, heading zero-seven degrees, mark twenty. Roll me forty-five degrees to starboard.

"As ordered, Admiral."

"Guns, give me firing solutions for the starboard guns. Pick a point and have everything hit it." She raised her left hand to her mouth and gnawed on the flesh of her index finger for a moment. "Flight Control, get the Rogues out there. Tell them *Direption* is launching something while we're blind."

"Relaying the order now, Admiral."

Areta nodded slowly. Given her angle of attack, she'd exchange broadsides with *Direption*, which would hurt her ship badly. Still, the way *Moonshadow* would be coming in meant that the attention paid to *Swift Liberty* by Krennel's ship would leave it open to a devastating broadside from *Moon-shadow*. And if *Direption's Captain deals with* Moonshadow, *I get to hammer him. His turning to attack both of us makes no sense. He should be remaining at range and fighting a delaying action until he can get reinforcements here.*

"Sensors, be sharp. Someone else is coming in, or something is going to intervene. Watch for dirtside action, or something popping into our aft."

"As ordered, Admiral. Scopes clear at the moment."

"Sing out when they're not." She stared hard at the holograph of the unfolding battle. "The only surprises I want here are the ones we bring to the fight."

Wedge jammed his throttle forward as the X-wing cleared the *Victory*-class Destroyer's belly. He rolled out to port, getting himself well away from *Swift Liberty* as the capital ship started to maneuver in toward *Direption*. Further starboard, driving in at a sharper angle but still level, *Moonshadow* disgorged its B-wings, which formed up and flew toward the *Direption*. Already Wedge could see TIE starfighters and Interceptors coming up around the enemy Deuce's hull.

Looks like they launched a whole wing. With seventy-two TIEs in the battle up against an equal number of B-wings, it looked like Corran's comment was accurate. *Then again, just because B-wings have shields and TIEs don't, there's no guarantee our side will prevail.*

Wedge opened his comm channel. "Rogues, on me. Come up over the top of *Swift Liberty* and down on the squints. They'll be outdistancing the slower TIEs. We'll pounce, break them up, then let Salm and the others pick up *our* crumbs."

He rolled his X-wing up onto its right S-foil, then pulled back on the stick. He pointed the nose up over the *Swift Liberty*'s knife-edge, then inverted as he came over the top. The X-wing flashed over the capital ship's white hull, then rolled to starboard to bring the *Direption* into view.

The Hegemony Impstar had already leveled out to

match *Moonshadow*'s profile. *He'll accept what Bell's ship can do just to pound* Moonshadow. Wedge shook his head. *I don't understand those tactics, which is why I'm better in this cockpit than I will ever be on the bridge of a capital ship.*

Wedge nudged his stick around and, with the flick of a thumb, switched his weapons over to proton torpedo control. He centered the box on his heads-up display over the distant spark that was the lead Interceptor speeding toward the B-wings. The box started green, but quickly went yellow and, when Gate started piping in a constant tone, the box went red. Wedge pulled the trigger on his stick and launched a proton torpedo.

His target immediately rolled and broke toward the planet. There wasn't much of a chance that he could outrun the torpedo, but Wedge knew what he was trying to do. If the Interceptor pilot could get the torpedo pointed at Liinade III, then break sharply at the last second, the missile would slam into the planet's atmosphere and would be reduced to so much space junk.

Three other squints broke off their run on the B-wings to follow their flight leader, which suggested to Wedge that the pilots were a lot more green than they should be. Switching his weapons back to lasers and quading them up, he dropped the aiming reticle over another squint's outline. When the crosshairs pulsed green, he tightened up on the trigger.

The four laser bolts converged on the Interceptor's starboard wing, slicing down through it. Sparks exploded from the blaster cannons and the panel disintegrated. The squint flew on, slowly rolling over and over, functionally out of the fight.

Asyr's X-wing flashed past Wedge's, so he dropped in behind and starboard of her fighter. She rolled onto her port S-foil as she dove at a climbing Interceptor. The two fighters twisted around, each one's energy weapons firing above and below the target. Then Asyr's X-wing snaprolled ninety degrees and clipped off a quad burst before she began to climb up and out of the way.

Her four bolts hit. Two burst through the inside of the starboard wing, melting long gashes in it. The other two pierced the transparisteel bubble between the pilot and the vacuum of space. Something burned red and hot in the cockpit for a second, then a roiling gold explosion ripped the dead craft apart.

Wedge rolled out to the right to avoid the explosion and pulled the stick back to his chest. He brought his X-wing around, ready for another pass up through the Interceptor formation. Liinade III loomed above him for a moment, then a trio of daggerlike ships filled his vision of the sky. All three had moved into range and cut loose.

Moonshadow's gunners concentrated their fire along *Direption*'s port edge, seeking to destroy the other ship's weaponry. Heavy turbolasers, heavy turbolaser cannons, and ion beams all played out, splashing red and blue energy across the *Direption*'s shields. The weapons' energy bled into the sphere of the shields, nibbling away at it, shrinking it like a balloon with a slow leak. Then suddenly the shields collapsed and beams played along the hull. Turbolaser batteries exploded and hull plates evaporated. Fire jetted into space as shots burned through the hull and consumed the atmosphere within.

Direption's return salvo proved no less deadly to *Moonshadow*. The Hegemony's gunners concentrated their fire on several points, driving energy wedges deep into the shields. Breaches opened and beams ripped long, jagged scars over *Moonshadow*'s surface. Sensor towers exploded and ion cannons melted beneath the withering assault.

Swift Liberty had swung down and around beneath *Direption* on a sharply angled course that took the ship across the Hegemony ship's line of flight. When the gunners cut loose, half of them pounded on the pristine ventral shields, while the forward gunners hit bits of the ship left naked after *Moonshadow*'s assault. The *Victory*-class Destroyer's weaponry was neither as extensive nor as powerful as that of the larger ships, but the turbolasers and double turbolaser batteries still ate away at the Hegemony Deuce. Liquefied weapons congealed into metal threads, and at least one secondary explosion blasted a small chunk of *Direption* into space.

The joyful spike that sent Wedge's spirits soaring as he watched the damage inflicted on the enemy crashed back down as another ship materialized in the system. Smaller and blocky, it appeared slashing across *Swift Liberty*'s aft. *That's a Dreadnaught. It's not that powerful, but in that close, in Bell's aft, it can cripple her.*

Tycho's voice filled the comm channel. "*Direption* has a friend. Shall we introduce ourselves?"

"Squints and eyeballs first, Rogues. The big ships play with the big ships." Wedge felt a knot tightening in his stomach. "When it comes to the point where they depend on *us* for a rescue, we're *all* in worse shape than we ever wanted to be."

13

Admiral Bell staggered for a second when the Dreadnaught's attack blasted into *Swift Liberty*'s aft. "Did their attack breach the shields?"

"Negative, Admiral." The Twi'lek sensor officer, Commander Tal'kina, looked up from his sensor array. "We lost gravity for a second because I had to shunt power to reinforce them."

"Well done, Commander." Bell flicked long locks of red hair back over her shoulder. "Helm, heading zero-four-five and level us out."

The helmsman looked up, surprise on his face. "That will leave the Dreadnaught in our aft, Admiral."

"Thought occurred to you, too, did it, Lieutenant Cyslo? We can weather another of their shots, and we want them watching us." She gave the man a quick nod. "Do it, now!"

"As ordered, Admiral."

"Good. And Guns, pour more fire into the *Direption*. I want it hurt and hurt now."

·   ·   ·

Wedge snaprolled his X-wing onto the port S-foils and followed Asyr through a quick split-S maneuver that let the squints that had been on their tails overshoot them. They leveled out again and broke to starboard, applying rudder to get their noses around, then cruised in on the Hegemony fighters. Wedge chopped his throttle back a bit as he made his approach, but Asyr shot ahead and closed fast with her target.

The Bothan pilot fired off a quad burst of lasers that converged on the squint's cockpit. The scarlet beams burned the top off the cockpit, instantly liquefying the Quadanium steel. It condensed into tiny round pellets that sparked off Asyr's forward shields, but that was as much of a threat as the Interceptor posed to her. Fire flared in the engines, and the ship started a slow spiral down toward Liinade III.

Wedge settled in on his target and dropped his aiming reticle over it much too easily. Part of him wanted the pilot to juke and move the ship, to make the shot tough for him. He realized instantly that his desire did not come because he wanted to prove himself the superior. *It's just that I'd rather not slaughter some kid on his first mission.*

Wedge immediately pushed that thought aside and tightened up on his trigger. The quad burst of laserfire drilled the Interceptor in its twin ion engines. The engine housing began to melt, warping out of shape, which compressed the reaction chamber. The engine exploded with a great gout of golden flame, jetting the Interceptor forward. The fire at the squint's aft winked out, snuffed by the vacuum of space, leaving the fighter to fly on powerlessly.

Wedge felt a moment of remorse for the pilot's death—whether it had come with the engine explosion or would come from exposure and suffocation as the squint's life-support systems failed. He didn't let himself dwell on the enemy's fate, though. The other pilot had accepted the same risks Wedge did when he entered a cockpit and flew into combat. *Dead is dead, no matter how you go.* Wedge's brown eyes narrowed. *And the object of this exercise for me is to avoid getting dead at all.*

Wedge glanced at his sensor scopes, and aside from

some fighters tied up in a dogfight with the B-wings, the Rogue Squadron area of operations appeared clear. "Rogue Lead to Flight Control. We are negative for targets. Do you want us on the Dreadnaught?"

"Negative, Rogue Squadron. Prepare for targeting run on Alpha target dirtside."

"I copy, Control." Wedge punched up the squadron's tactical frequency. "Form up on me, we're being cleared to go to ground."

"There's more targets up here, Lead."

"Really?" Wedge smiled. "You mean Asyr left a few?"

The Bothan's voice came on the comm channel. "I didn't think I had."

No, you were on a crusade, Asyr. I wonder why? Wedge shook his head. "Punch up your ground attack data. We need to be ready to go as soon as it comes time to ferry troops down."

Tycho asked a question. "*Swift Liberty* doesn't want help with the Dreadnaught?"

"They seem to think they have that situation under control, Tycho."

Even as Wedge made that observation, he looked up through his canopy and saw the capital ship battle still under way. The *Direption* had begun to come about to starboard, swinging its shieldless port side away from *Moonshadow*. *Moonshadow* was coming up and turning to port, its port-side batteries firing against *Direption*'s aft shields. Red and blue laser and ion cannon fire pumped terajoules of energy into the shields, but somehow they stayed up.

Probably shunting energy from the port side shield projectors into the aft shields. Wedge watched as *Swift Liberty* cut inside *Moonshadow*'s maneuver and cruised beneath *Direption*. As *Swift Liberty*'s gunners got target locks, they blazed away at the larger ship's naked left side, further compounding the damage done by the *Moonshadow*'s assault.

In *Swift Liberty*'s wake came the Dreadnaught. It continued to target the *Victory*-class ship's aft shields, finally collapsing them. Red-gold turbolaser blasts scored armor around the *Swift Liberty*'s engines, but Wedge saw no secondary explosions. *Even so, that sort of pounding will eat a ship up if it continues.*

But continue it won't.

Captain Sair Yonka's *Freedom* knifed its way from hyperspace and into the battle on a course that drove it beneath *Direption* and straight at the Dreadnaught. Yonka's ship had come in perpendicular to *Direption*'s keel and raked it with shots from all its starboard guns, running from bow to stern as it passed. Heavy turbolaser batteries played shots over the Hegemony ship's unprotected port side, burning great black pits in the ship's white hull. Flames exploded and curled away as superheated atmosphere blew out through weakened hull plates. Ion cannons sent blue lightning skittering and leaping across the ship's hull, with several bolts joining like ivy to grow up over the bridge. In yet more spots more laserfire burned straight through the hull. Wedge could see space through the stricken ship.

Freedom's port gunners had no intention of being cheated of their chance to wreak havoc on the enemy. As *Freedom* drove forward, guns started firing on the Dreadnaught as they came into range. The sheer volume of fire filled the smaller ship's shields with color and seemed to stop the Dreadnaught in mid-flight. Then the shields collapsed and *Freedom*'s precision fire started burrowing in on the Dreadnaught, right beyond the forward superstructure of the bridge. Hull plates, all twisted and half melted, flew off as secondary explosions racked the vessel. What started with fire-blackened armor became a glowing metal pit that drilled deep into the ship's interior. Finally one huge explosion shook the ship, and all the lights in the forward section winked out.

Seconds later Wedge watched as the Dreadnaught broke into two at the point of the assault. In the cold silence of space, the bridge began to drift away from the aft, one piece twisting toward the planet and the other toward space. Fires burned at the point of the break, but quickly died as they exhausted the available oxygen.

Direption pulled its nose up and began to make a run deeper into the system. *Moonshadow* and *Swift Liberty* both fired full salvos at it and collapsed both the aft and starboard shields. Outgunned and already weakened, *Direption* didn't stand a chance of escaping. Despite its troubles, it could still inflict a great deal of damage, so *Freedom* maneuvered into position to slag it if necessary.

Direption's running lights blinked on and off four times in rapid succession, then stayed off. "Control, this is Rogue Leader. What is the status up there?"

"Standing by, Rogue Leader. Looks like *Direption*'s commander may be reasonable. New orders just flashed for you, Rogue Lead. *Freedom* is deploying troop carriers and assault shuttles. Head to your assigned ground targets. May the Force be with you."

Corran nodded and punched up his target zone. "Three Flight copies, Lead. We're on blue sector." He switched over to the flight's tactical frequency. "We're clear to blue sector. Think you can stay with us, this time, Eleven?"

Asyr answered in a voice that wasn't quite as subdued as Corran wanted to hear. "I copy, Nine. I'll work on it."

"Stay sharp down there. We don't know what they have, but it could be decidedly nasty." Corran rolled out to port and started the atmospheric insertion. He felt a slight bump as they entered Liinade III's atmosphere and he had to keep his hand steady on the controls. Despite the more difficult flying, he felt a bit of tension flow from him. *At least we can breathe this atmosphere, which makes survival here more likely than out in space.*

As the X-wing broke through cloud cover he saw a lush green planet spread out before him. Three Flight was coming in over the southern continent, which featured a prominent spine of mountains dusted with snow running up the west side. The target for Three Flight was a hydroelectric powerplant that supplied most of the electricity for the large city on the plains to the east of the mountains. The mission goal was for the X-wings to eliminate any fighter cover around the powerplant and suppress opposition as a shuttle full of commandos came in and secured the place.

Corran caught the flash of sunlight off a slender ribbon of water running through a canyon and dropped down toward it. "This should be the outflow from the dam, right, Whistler?" White water churned through the canyon and a small flotilla of boats made its way down through the perilous watercourse.

They have to be freezing down there—there's snow on the ground. What some folks think of as fun I just don't understand. He shook his head, then keyed his comm unit. "Target is two klicks out. Ten, with me. Eleven and Twelve, fly high cover."

Corran brought his fighter down on the deck and Ooryl's X-wing came in behind him. Corran kicked the X-wing up on its starboard S-foil and tugged back on the stick to curve to the right, then rolled back to port and sailed around to the left. The inertial compensator's adjustment allowed him to feel the twists and turns he put the fighter through and just for a second he felt the absolute joy and freedom flying had always given him.

Then he came around a bend and saw the dam.

In the simulations they'd run on this mission the dam had always been tall, but seeing the solid edifice of ferrocrete, with spots where moss had grown along seep lines, and seeing the great rush of water pouring from the sluicegates, that he'd not expected. Evergreen trees and bushes grew thickly through the riparian area along the riverbanks, but thinned a bit up on the hillsides in the canyon. Everything, save the twin Atgar 1.4 FD P-tower units built atop the dam, looked peaceful and sedate.

The antivehicular artillery units, with a laser cannon centered in a round dish, looked decidedly hostile, but they came as no surprise. A single stormtrooper crewed each weapon and the Rogues had known about them going in. Corran tugged back on his stick a bit and ran his throttle down as he dropped the aiming reticle over the outline of the leftmost weapon. "I've got port. Ten, you take starboard."

"As ordered, Nine."

With the flick of a thumb Corran shunted power from his rear shields to his forward ones. Staggered red bolts from the P-tower hissed as they splashed harmlessly over his reinforced shields. Corran stroked his trigger once, sending a quad burst of laserfire to burn through the P-tower, but even before it exploded, an overwhelming sense of dread pounded him.

Unthinking, he jerked the X-wing stick to the left and saw a small projectile sizzle past him from behind at an angle in from the right. It flew on and impacted to the left of the dam. The warhead exploded, spraying dirty snow and launching a tall evergreen into the air. Other trees sagged and fell on the forested hillside.

"Abort, they've got missiles. Ten, pull out."

Before Corran could punch the throttle forward, something hit his low port stabilizer and detonated. Whistler's high-pitched shrilling matched the warning buzzers in the cockpit. Corran saw a whole bank of red lights start to burn amid curls of smoke. Power level indicators showed a quarter of the X-wing's power lost immediately, and the fighter's nose began to swing around to the right.

Corran stomped on the left rudder to stop the flat spin, then dove toward the river to pick up some airspeed. Pulling back on the stick, he started a climb, then inverted and flew toward the small fire the other missile had started. Rolling again, he righted his craft and carried it over the canyon's ridge.

"Ten, I've been hit. I've lost port-two engine."

"Nine, that S-foil is gone."

"What was it?"

"Ooryl doesn't know. Ground-launched and didn't scan."

Corran nodded. "Probably stormies with Merr-Sonn PLX-2Ms."

"A chip shouldn't have taken off an S-foil. Shouldn't have gotten through your shields."

"I shifted power forward and they caught me in an engine." Another warning light started to burn on his command console. "Ten, I'm losing engine coolant and will lose my other engines if I don't do something soon. I've got to set down. You've got the flight. Warn Control about the chips here. There must be something else of value here, too, otherwise they wouldn't have guarded it that way."

"I copy. We'll fly cover for you until they pull you out."

"No, get out of here, all of you. They might have other weapons to take an X-wing down. Leave, but promise me you'll be back with help."

"As fast as Ooryl is able." The faint clicking of the Gand's mandibles came through the comm channel. "May the Force be with you."

"Thanks, I'm going to need it. Nine out."

Corran rolled the X-wing once to give himself a quick look at the terrain below, then pushed his fighter over another ridge about three kilometers away from the dam. He would have liked to have gotten further away, but the heat indicators on his engines were spiking enough that the computer reported the numbers in blinking red numbers.

Gotta get down now. "Hang on, Whistler, this isn't going to be much fun."

He picked a spot uphill of a rocky outcropping and clipped off a series of laser shots at it. The red bolts scythed through the underbrush, melted snow, and exploded venerable evergreens. Smoke from a small fire obscured the landing zone, but he nosed the craft toward it nonetheless. He shifted power into his repulsorlift coils, lowered the landing gear, and slowly, awkwardly settled the fighter into place. The aft port landing gear ended up planted on the stump of a tree, making the craft list heavily to starboard, but Corran shut down the engines rather than risk a total meltdown to shift the X-wing to another position.

A chill settled over Corran as he hit the release on his restraining straps. "Think it's over for this fighter, Whistler? We've seen a lot of action together."

The droid mewed weakly.

Corran cracked the cockpit canopy, then swung himself out and under the cockpit lip. He moved up to the fuselage and crouched on the back end of the canopy. The chip missile's blast had peppered the left side of the fighter with engine shrapnel and Whistler had caught a chunk in his left shoulder joint. Corran reached out to touch it, but Whistler squawked sharply at him.

"Okay, okay, I won't touch it. No, I don't want to do more damage." He shook his head slowly and felt his stomach begin to knot up. "I'll get you out of here somehow, Whistler. Not a problem."

The R2 unit piped bravely.

"Thanks." Corran returned to the cockpit and pulled the small survival kit from the compartment beneath his seat. He opened it and transferred a couple of spare powerpacks for his blaster to the gunbelt pouch over his right hip. He stuffed some survival ration bars into his green flight suit's pockets, though he thought of them as fairly lethal weapons. *If only I could get stormies to eat them.*

He looked up and was going to share that thought with Whistler, but he saw the little droid's lights blinking painfully slowly. His throat immediately thickened.

"I will get you out of here, my friend." Corran brandished the lightsaber he pulled from the survival kit. "We'll teach these Imp-wannabes that by grounding me they haven't made me switch from hunter to hunted, just switched the direction I'll be coming at them from."

14

General Wedge Antilles leveled his X-wing out and glanced at the range indicator to his target. *Fifty kilometers, we'll be on it in no time. I wonder what they've got waiting for us there.*

He punched up the flight's tactical channel. "Okay, Rogues, Three Flight ran into trouble in blue sector. Ground fire damaged one. They think it was from chip missiles, so keep your shields strong and eyes open."

The rest of the flight acknowledged his message, then followed Wedge down onto the deck for the final run at the Valleyport spaceport facility. Located in a river valley to the east of the mountains where Corran had gone down, Valleyport was by no means the largest city on the continent. In fact, it was relatively small, but it sat astride the main ground transportation route through the mountains and likewise was a communications nexus. The spaceport facility, while underutilized by local traffic, was more than sufficient for bringing in ground troops who would take the planet.

Below him the landscape changed. Forests gave way to vast tracts of treeless land covered by a thin blanket of snow that let the stubble of harvested grain stalks poke up through it. Houses dotted the landscape and, since it was midmorning, some people were out and about in the fields, directing the droids tending to livestock. Wedge knew that any of them could use a comlink to alert Valleyport officials that fighters were incoming, but by the time the report got through, the Rogues would be over their target.

The city of Valleyport came into view, obscured by a brown haze. A few tall buildings rose above the haze, but most sprawled within it. The haze covered both sides of the river and spread out onto the plains above. The spaceport's towers showed up clearly on the northern side of the river, against a mountain backdrop toward the west. Wedge let his X-wing sideslip to port, then flashed across the river and set his lasers for single fire.

Already E-webs and a couple of P-towers started filling the early morning air with sizzling bolts of coherent light, but tracking an X-wing running in at full throttle proved more difficult than the gunners would have liked. A stray bolt hissed against Wedge's shields and in return he clipped off a cycle of four shots—one from each of the X-wing's laser cannons—then pulled his fighter's nose off onto another target.

His laserfire tracked bolts across icy ferrocrete decking and up the sides of buildings. Misses left little black stains centered on a guttering flame. Hits blew chunks out of the enemy's mounted blasters and antivehicular weapons. One bolt caught a stormtrooper in the chest, ablating his armor away in an eyeblink and continuing on unabated. The man's burning corpse slammed into a wall, then rebounded and pitched forward over the balcony railing he had tried to take cover behind.

"Lead, I'm getting fire from the west, coming from within those hangars."

"On it, Hobbie." Wedge hit some right rudder and chopped back his throttle, shortening a turn to port. A line of large hangars formed the western perimeter of the spaceport and the red-gold bolts from a pair of heavy laser cannons sprayed out at the X-wings. Seeing a line of fire begin to track his fighter, Wedge goosed the throttle back to full and began a port spiral to get some altitude.

Out of the hangars trotted a quartet of AT-ATs, the Imperial walker units that had wrought so much havoc at Hoth. They moved quickly, not looking as cumbersome and slow in the light snow as they had on Hoth's icefields. *Back then we were in airspeeders—undergunned and overmatched.* A smile slowly twisted his lips. *Not the case this time.*

"On them, Rogues. The groundpounders are incoming and we need to get rid of the walkers. Be careful."

"Starting a run on the first one." Lyyr Zatoq, the Quarren, rolled her X-wing out to port, then let it swoop down in a glide that brought it in on a diagonal slashing course on the last of the walkers. The machine's head slowly swung to the left to try to track her fighter, but she blasted away at it with her lasers at point-blank range, then climbed hard and pulled out to the left, too fast and too tight for the walker to target her.

Hobbie, her wingman, came in on a crossing path that gave him a clean shot at the tail. Lyyr's shots had slagged armor on the mechanical beast's flank, but hadn't done any serious damage. Hobbie's attack ran from below the AT-AT's body on up the back, and at least one shot holed the fuel tank. Flaming fluid streamed down like a tail, then an explosion ripped the walker's back end open. The blast pitched the walker up into the air and through a somersault that landed it on its back. The massive legs telescoped down into the body, then tore free. The walker's armored head slammed into the snow-covered ground, cracking armor plates, and started leaking smoke.

Tycho growled over the comm channel. "Running on the next one. Decap shot."

Wedge nodded. "On your tail."

Tycho brought his X-wing down in a dive, then leveled out ten meters. Coming in at shoulder height on the walker, Tycho banked right to run from tail toward the head, then snaprolled his ship level and hit right rudder. The X-wing's tail skidded toward the left, bringing its nose in line with the walker. Tycho's first cycle of shots vaporized armor on the walker's body, but the second quartet blasted away at the joint of the flexible neck and the body itself.

Wedge marveled at Tycho's soft hand on the X-wing's stick. He followed him into the dive, but rolled out right and cut his throttle back. The walker had begun to turn to its right, so Wedge's roll put him on a direct line with the AT-AT's head. He nudged the aiming reticle over the walker's head and pulled the trigger.

A stuttered quartet of bolts hit the walker. Two glanced off, leaving long scars on its forehead, but the other two pierced the transparisteel viewports on the pilot's compartment. Fire exploded back out, and the walker slowly started to sag forward. Its chin slammed into the ground, then the body's weight snapped its neck.

"Easier ways to decap it, Wedge."

Wedge throttled up and banked starboard into a climb. "Sorry, didn't have time to consult with Ewoks to find out how they'd handle the situation." He glanced down at his chronometer. "No time to be fancy on the other two, just swarm them."

Coming back in and down, Wedge kept his X-wing very low, cruising in at a sharp angle. Tipping his fighter up onto its port S-foil, he banked in toward the walker and switched over to dual fire. One double burst missed, but the second caught the walker in the hip. Tycho's shots on the same one hit the body above the drive motor, then the two of them climbed out, pulled a half-loop, inverted, and dove back down at their target.

"Port rear leg is scraping the ferrocrete, Two."

"I caught that, Lead." Tycho swooped his fighter through a run that pumped more hot light into the walker's hip. Black smoke began to issue from the joint. Wedge's attack followed Tycho's line and drilled four more bolts into the leg.

Superheated metal sprayed out, and the walker began to list badly to the left. The AT-AT's leg bent, then snapped off at the hip. The forward feet shuffled as the rear leg fell away, but the walker had already been seriously overbalanced.

The rear end started to fall to the left, spinning the AT-AT around and pulling the front legs from the ground. The walker's body pounded the ferrocrete, pulverizing both it and the armor plates on which it landed. Black smoke started to issue from the walker's body, and escape hatches opened up and stormtroopers began to run, walk, or limp their way away from the broken machine.

Lyyr and Hobbie made short work of the remaining walker. Several runs on it had left the armor in ruins, and Hobbie cruised up along its spine and triggered a quad burst at the head from point-blank range. The red bolts burned through the neck and dropped the head to the ground. The body, leaking smoke, froze in place, leaving the soldiers contained inside stranded ten meters from the ferrocrete.

"Nice shot, Hobbie."

"Thanks, Lead." Hobbie sighed. "We could have taken them with four proton torps. Would have been easier, you know."

"Sure, but what if Krennel showed up with ships and we had to go hunting in the void again." Wedge shrugged. "Doing it the hard way worked."

Wedge brought his X-wing down and routed power to the repulsorlift coils. He hovered a couple of meters above the ground and guided the ship over to position it between the burning walkers and the landing zone for the assault shuttles coming in. The stormtroopers on the snowy ferrocrete slowed and raised their hands. Those who had escaped with weapons dropped them and a few of the more injured individuals just collapsed.

"Lead, I have a question for you."

Wedge glanced over at where Tycho hovered his X-wing. "Go ahead, Two."

"Wouldn't the AT-AT assault been more effective if they'd waited to launch it until the shuttles landed? Walkers are death on ground troops."

"True, and stationing the stormies around the spaceport instead of inside those monsters would have been better, too." Wedge frowned. "These guys might look like stormtroopers, but they certainly aren't thinking that way."

"And yet Intel said there were crack units here, but if not *here*, where?"

Wedge's mouth soured. "The sector where Three Flight ran into trouble. You think Krennel is hiding something there? Save for the dam, that's a pretty remote area."

"Where better to hide something you want to remain hidden?"

The first of the assault shuttles landed and started to disgorge troops. A couple of squads moved forward to deal with the captured stormtroopers. The others fanned out, found cover, and established a perimeter on the ferrocrete. The second shuttle landed its troops closer to the hangars and a third dropped its troops near the main spaceport facility.

A light blinked on Wedge's communications console. He punched it. "Rogue Leader here."

"Commando One here." Kapp Dendo's voice came through strongly. "Thanks for vaping the stalkers. I wouldn't mind it if you want to strafe the approaches to the spaceport, just in case some local militia decides to hop a hoverbus here."

"I copy, Commando One. I help you, you help me?"

"What do you need, Wedge?"

"I have a flier down at the dam in blue sector. Lots more activity there than here."

"Search and rescue ops are a bit down in priority, Lead. I'll see what I can do." A grave tone ran through Kapp's words. "How hard did your boy go down?"

"Under control, I'm told." Wedge smiled. "He can probably take care of himself, but if the stormies we were expecting to be here are actually *there*, for just how long I don't know."

15

I don't like the looks of this at all. Corran crouched in some brush overlooking a ravine with a small, ice-crusted streambed at the bottom of it. The ravine showed signs of flooding with seasonal runoff, but had a high-water mark far higher than he would have expected. Just north of his position lay the reason for the extraordinary high-water mark: A tunnel had been bored through the granite hillside and clearly, once upon a time, had been used to divert river water around the site of the dam.

The tunnel mouth had been plugged with ferrocrete and two sets of durasteel security doors. The larger pair of doors would admit vehicles; the other was for personnel. Four stormtroopers stood guard outside the doors, but had moved from beneath the shadow cast by an outcropping to soak up the direct morning sun.

Corran ran a hand over his mouth. *This has to be what they were protecting with those chips—and a lucky shot meant they did more than just chip my hull. This place wasn't on any of the survey maps of the area, which means it's very new, or very secret or, worse, both. Getting in there and getting out again is clearly a job for a Jedi Knight.*

He fingered the lightsaber clipped to the left side of his belt. *Unfortunately, there isn't one here.*

For an instant Corran regretted having rejected Luke Skywalker's generous invitation to train to be a Jedi Knight. Had he accepted it, he could have used Jedi powers to walk right past the stormtroopers without their noticing. He could use his lightsaber to deflect blaster bolts. He could find out what the facility was all about and likely neutralize it as well.

That sense of regret died quickly, however, as Corran thought about what he'd have had to give up to become a Jedi Knight. He admired Luke Skywalker and wished him the best in his quest to reestablish the Jedi Order, but he also knew Luke was paying quite a cost. Corran had Mirax to spend the rest of his life with, but Luke had no one. Moreover, the fact that he was needed to solve problems all over the galaxy, and his never-ending quest for information about the Jedi, meant that he had become a wanderer. His quest killed any chance for a normal life, and a normal life wasn't something Corran wanted to surrender.

My father would probably think me terribly selfish in making that decision. He sighed and blew on his hands to warm them. He knew Whistler carried with him an encrypted message from Hal Horn about his Jedi heritage, but he couldn't bring himself to listen to it. He didn't want to be torn between his father's urging him to become a Jedi and his responsibilities to Mirax and their life together. He wished he had the courage to face that dilemma, but knowing he didn't, he sidestepped it entirely.

Well, I may not be a Jedi, but I am *a Rogue, and figuring out what's going on in there is going to be important. Getting in will be a trick, though.* Corran backed away from the edge of the ravine and began to work his way to the west. He wanted the sun at his back as he moved, and once again was pleased that he wore a dark green flight suit, not the bright orange most of the squadron's other pilots wore. *I'd stand out like a Hutt at an Ewok celebration. Of course, white stormtrooper armor isn't much better in a forest.*

The undergrowth made his passage very slow. Though he'd been raised in Coronet City on Corellia, he wasn't hopelessly unfamiliar with forests and how to move through them. He used the thick-boled trees to his advantage, and watched out for icy patches of ground that would bring him down. Moving from point to point, he avoided skylining himself at the crest of a hill, carefully surveyed the next leg of his journey before moving out, and listened for signs of the enemy, knowing he'd hear them before he ever saw them.

Crouched in the shadow of a snow-capped fallen tree, he scouted his way along a little depression that headed to the southwest. It ran for approximately thirty meters and gradually sloped up into a thicket of thorny *zureber* bushes. He was looking for a way around them when two stormtroopers came over the depression's northern lip. They paused and looked around, sweeping the area with their blaster carbines, then one started his way down into the depression.

The lead stormtrooper caught his left toe on a root that had been hidden by snow and pitched forward. He landed flat on his face, bounced once, then rolled to a stop at the bottom of the depression. His blaster carbine flew further south and landed on the depression's south slope. The other stormtrooper watched his comrade fall, then came down the slope in a high-step gallop that sprayed snow and frozen leaves into the air.

The second man bent over his partner and started laughing. The first stormtrooper rolled onto his back. "Huttspit! If the designer of these helmets ever had to use them in the field . . ."

"Very funny. Maybe you should just learn to walk."

"Oh, shut up." The fallen man sat up, then pressed his right hand against the edge of his helmet. Corran heard a click and a buzz from a comlink. "No, Control, no problem. Just had an equipment failure. I'm going offline to fix it. Seven Six One out."

The standing man cocked his head. "Equipment failure?"

Seven Six One extended his left leg and ran his foot around in a little circle. "Twisted the ankle."

"I can use the rest." The second man sat down and removed his helmet. The first stormtrooper did the same. Steam rose from both of their heads as the second one reached for the canteen on his equipment belt.

Corran's first blue stunbolt dropped the canteen from the stormtrooper's hand. The second one hit the same man again, tensing his body for a second, then slackening it. Two more bolts caught the first man as he made a dive for his blaster carbine. It took a third before he stayed down.

Corran came up over the fallen log and slid down into the depression. He quickly crossed to the stormtroopers and stripped them of their weapons and equipment belts. He also removed their torso armor, then dragged them through the snow to a tree at the southern edge of the depression. He tied them to the tree with the cord from their equipment belts. Using more of the cord, he fastened one of the carbines and his own blaster to a tree, then ran cord from the triggers, back around another small tree, to the stormies' bound feet. He set both blasters for stun and aimed them to catch the men in the stomach. *If they move their legs, they get stunned again. Great way to keep them out.*

He decided against killing them for a couple of very good reasons. First and foremost, he didn't need to kill them. He knew of other New Republic soldiers who wouldn't have blinked an eye at killing helpless stormtroopers, but he considered doing that murder. As he'd learned in CorSec, no matter how much a criminal might deserve killing, it wasn't necessarily his place to pull the trigger.

Second, and more important, the two downed stormtroopers were intelligence resources. While forensics might allow a dead man to tell some sort of tale—*like Urlor*—interrogating live stormies would be a lot more productive. Since no one in New Republic Intelligence even knew the installation near the dam existed, he assumed these men would have a wealth of information General Cracken would be very grateful for.

Corran stripped his flight suit down to his waist and pulled on one of the stormtrooper's torso armor. He managed to get the flight suit on over the bulky armor, and zipped the flight suit back up nearly all the way, but not quickly enough to avoid getting chilled. He knew he looked ridiculous, but having something that would slow down blaster bolts meant he could live with his embarrassment and laugh about it later.

He pulled the comlinks from the stormtroopers' helmets. Lowering the volume and input gain on one, he listened for a bit to the chatter going back and forth. He couldn't make much sense of the call signs, but he heard a number of people reporting on that comm channel. Station checks seemed to come on a regular schedule, but he had no idea when the two guards he'd put down would be seen as missing.

He shut the comlinks off, then looked at them and smiled. Using a last bit of the stormtroopers' cord, he swapped one of the comlinks end for end, putting the mike near the speaker on each, turned the volume and gain up to full on both, then tied them tightly together. With a nod he hefted the remaining blaster carbine, took it off safe, and started north again.

Not the best plan in the world, but one that will work. He got to the edge of the ravine and found himself twenty meters from the doors, at the top of a ten-meter-high scree slope from which the snow had long since melted. The quartet of stormtroopers he'd have to take out were another ten meters beyond the doors, putting them a fair distance away as far as a blaster shot went. *Not going to be easy at all.*

He took a deep breath and let it flow out, taking his anxiety with it. In the calm clarity that followed, he realized two things. First, by taking down all the stormtroopers he could and causing as much trouble as he could, he would cut down the odds of another New Republic soldier getting killed. Second, he knew it was his responsibility to take care of the site. No one else was in position to take care of it—*no one else knows it's even here*—and hitting the Imperials before they prepared for any New Republic ground action was vital.

With his right hand firmly around the blaster carbine's grip, he flicked the comlinks on with his left thumb. Because of the way they'd been tied together, an earsplitting feedback loop immediately built and injected itself into the comm channel. The four stormtroopers below clapped hands to their helmets and wrestled to pull them off as Corran ran, slid, and leaped down the scree slope.

Once he hit the area outside the doors, he sprayed red blaster bolts over the distracted stormtroopers. His first shot took one man through the stomach, folding him up and pitching him back into a second man. Another shot spun a third man around, having caught him in a hip. A subsequent shot snapped his head back. The fourth stormtrooper tried to return fire, but before he could bring his carbine around to target Corran, a shot to his left thigh dropped him to the ground. A final spray of shots killed him and also slew the stormtrooper who had been knocked to the ground.

Without pausing to check them for signs of life, Corran brought his grandfather's lightsaber to hand and thumbed the silvery blade to life. With one swipe he carved a line down through the man-sized door, then kicked it in. He triggered a quick burst of blaster fire through the opening, then ducked inside and dove to the right.

A woman in a green Imperial army uniform had gone down with a smoking hole in her uniform over her stomach. She thrashed, clawing for a dropped blaster. Corran shot her twice more, then rolled onto his back and slashed his lightsaber around in an arc through the doorway to his left. The silver blade slashed through the legs of a stormtrooper, toppling the man backward. The stormtrooper's carbine tracked a line of fire just past Corran's head and up toward the ceiling as he fell.

Corran laid his own blaster carbine across his stomach and triggered off a burst that caught another stormtrooper in the chest. The trio of shots lifted the stormtrooper up and sent him tumbling back over a desk, scattering a glowlamp and a holoprojector plate.

Corran hit the powerpack release with his right thumb, dumping the spent duraplast packet to the ground. Letting the lightsaber rest on the ground for a second, he slapped a new powerpack into the carbine and rolled to his knees. He recovered the lightsaber, turned it off, and clipped it again to his belt. Then he got to his feet and moved deeper into the installation.

To the left, just beyond the vehicle doors, a ramp led down to a garage area. Off the foyer two corridors led away, one north and one south, going deeper into the facility. From the southern one, off to his right, two more stormtroopers came running. Corran's initial burst caught the second one on the left flank, punching through his thigh and chest armor. That man slammed against the foyer's back wall and bounced down to the floor.

The lead stormtrooper twisted and dove, extending his right arm toward Corran. The blaster carbine he was carrying spat hot light. One bolt burned through the flight suit over Corran's right hip, but the pilot had already begun to move to his own right, so the rest of the stormtrooper's bolts passed wide.

Corran's return fire scythed across the man's midsection. The armor did a good job of deflecting a couple of shots and ablating even more, but one drilled in through the gap between codpiece and thigh. The stormtrooper screamed and clutched at his leg. Corran stroked the trigger twice more as the man came up into a sitting position, dropping him to his back forever.

Something hot and hard caught Corran in the left flank, spinning him around. As he came about he saw a smallish man in an olive uniform holding a blaster in a double-handed grip. Corran staggered a bit, then dropped to his knees and flopped onto his back.

A grin slowly started to spread over the man's face.

He was deliberately aiming *at my back and only caught my flank?* Corran groaned aloud. *And he only shot once? Has to be a clerk.*

The Lieutenant's expression changed from one of joy to one of wide-eyed horror as Corran sat up. The Rogue's carbine came around and the burst Corran triggered tracked blasterfire up through the doorway of the office with the two dead stormtroopers. A trio of bolts lifted the clerk from his feet and spun his body back deep into the office.

Corran slowly regained his feet and jogged over to the office. He peeked in quickly, didn't get shot, then moved in past the dead stormtrooper and clerk. He checked the second stormtrooper to make sure he was well and truly dead, then searched the rest of the office for anyone hiding in desk legwells.

He was alone and slumped back against a wall for a second. He could have used more of a rest, but as he pressed his back to the wall, the wound complained. Reaching back with his left hand, he probed it and found a nice neat hole burned through his flight suit and the armor about the level of his floating ribs. Luckily for him it had come in at an angle and most of the energy had been ablated by the armor. When he poked a finger all the way through, it came back wet and red, but the blood hadn't begun to soak his flight suit, so he was fairly certain the wound wasn't that serious.

Looking around at the room again, he realized he was standing in what passed for the small installation's communications and security office. A dozen monitors showed shifting views of locations within the facility and he took heart that only a couple of the monitors showed folks moving around. Those individuals were not stormtroopers and looked like technicians working on some sort of research project.

Appropriating a datapad, Corran called up a site map and located one of the labs in the north wing. He tried to call for a general security lockdown of the facility, but the computer refused, indicating the user didn't have the authority to do so. He shifted to another desk—one that looked like it had belonged to the female Major who had died as he broke in—and repeated the request.

The clanging shut of blast doors echoed through the base.

Corran slipped from the office and stopped at the Major's corpse. He pulled the rank cylinder from her breast pocket, then headed off through the north corridor. It extended twenty meters into the rock and ended in a durasteel security door. He pressed the rank cylinder into the locking mechanism and the door slid open.

The assembled workers, all in long white coats, barely glanced at him at first. When he produced and ignited the lightsaber, they paused and looked at him. He got the distinct impression they were more fascinated by the weapon than they were threatened by it. *It's as if they see it as technology, pure and simple, with no regard for what it could possibly do.*

Corran slashed the blade to the left and bisected a duraplast chair. The clatter of both halves toppling to the floor seemed to drill some reality into the techs' consciousnesses. They returned their attention to Corran and he was pleased to note that a number of them were decidedly pale.

"I'm Captain Corran Horn of the New Republic. Either I'm here liberating you or capturing you, your choice." He smiled quickly. "One note: I hate taking prisoners."

He nodded toward a holoprojector on a table in the center of the lab. "Show me what you're working on and you'd be cooperative, which prisoners never are."

A small blond woman moved to the datapad connected to the holoprojector and started to punch in a request for data. A man moved to stop her, but Corran waved the lightsaber through the air and its hum seemed to drive the man back. "*Cooperative.* You want to be *very* cooperative."

The woman finished typing her request and an image

flashed to life above the holoprojector pad, just hanging there in the air.

"Oh, you have been cooperative with someone, big-time cooperative." Corran felt his guts tightening into a knot. "Correct me if I'm wrong, but it looks as if you were going to help someone build himself a Death Star."

16

The briefing room felt hot and close to Wedge, even though it dwarfed the X-wing cockpit he'd ridden in on his return to Coruscant. Corran had flown on his wing in a borrowed X-wing and now stood with him at the far end of the briefing table. Mon Mothma sat stone-faced at its head, with Leia Organa Solo at her right hand and Borsk Fey'lya at her left. In the middle of the table a holoprojector displayed a schematic of a Death Star.

The New Republic's Chief Councilor looked through the holograph and Wedge felt energy sizzle through her pale, aquamarine eyes. "I am certain that General Cracken and your own experience have made it abundantly clear to you that what you know in this matter is highly classified. You will not speak of it outside this room, neither between yourselves nor to others."

Wedge nodded. "Understood."

"As ordered."

Corran's voice carried with it the weariness that Wedge felt. The Rogues had brought Kapp Dendo's Team One in to secure the lab, then New Republic Intelligence operatives had pounced on it, hustling off the workers and dismantling the equipment and carting it all away. In the meantime the Rogues had returned to active duty, engaging in support missions that lasted another three weeks until no Hegemony hostiles were present on Liinade III. Immediately following the planet's conquest and reinforcement, Corran and Wedge had been recalled to Coruscant.

Borsk Fey'lya's claws scraped along the table's matte black surface. "It is hard to believe that someone even as cruel as Krennel would resurrect Death Stars."

Leia shook her head. "Since we have not found the original shipyard that created the Death Stars, the possibility that one or more are under construction is something we can't ignore."

Wedge pointed at the holograph. "You're also wrong in calling this a Death Star. It looks like one, but this is a decidedly scaled down version. It looks to be inspired by how the Emperor used the Death Star at Endor, targeting capital ships. That was a gross underutilization of its power, but it was very effective.

"What Krennel was creating here is a system domination weapon. It pops out of hyperspace, cranks up gravity well generators—that's what those blisters around the center are—and all traffic in or out stops cold. The planet-splitting beam from the original Death Star has also been scaled back and multiple sites for it have been created. Those are all the dimples on the thing. With each of those beams capable of killing a Super Star Destroyer, it's a decidedly lethal ship. It also bristles with smaller antiship weapons and can support a half-dozen TIE wings, which gives it plenty of defensive capabilities."

Corran folded his arms over his chest. "We've taken to calling it a Pulsar Station."

Mon Mothma calmly pressed her hands together. "Does Krennel have an operational version of the device?"

Wedge shrugged his shoulders. "Unknown, but unlikely."

The Bothan Councilor's eyes narrowed. "Explain."

Wedge raised an eyebrow. "I would have thought it

would be obvious to you, Councilor. Creating a ship this size would require an incredible amount of resources. Just the durasteel alone would necessitate the mining of a planetoid and its total conversion into metal. The factories needed to turn out the finished pieces don't exist in Krennel's Hegemony—or, as Captain Horn would point out, we don't know of their existence."

The Bothan waved a hand graciously in Corran's direction. "Would you care to explain?"

Corran shrugged his shoulders. "Data on some of the Hegemony worlds is thinner than the cushions on a Hutt's reclining platform. Krennel is clamping down on information sources, so getting any data out is going to be tough. Some worlds we can eliminate as candidates: Ciutric, for example, is a well-charted and traveled system. Others, like Corvis Minor, are hardly known at all. The shipyards could be there, perhaps positioned to always be opposite the main world in orbit, so the sun blocks any sensor readings of the construction on that world."

Leia sat back, her brows knitted with concentration. "The only way to confirm this would be to scout the systems."

"That's the quickest way." Wedge nodded. "We can run a T-Six-Five-R through the system and have it pull all the intel it can gather."

Leia frowned. "The X-wing recon version has no weapons, so such a run would be risky."

Wedge laughed. "I wasn't thinking of taking it in all alone, even though an accompanied ship will be easier to spot. Still, we pick the right location to come into the system, make a quick hit, and go, and we might be unnoticed."

"Fact is, though, we might need to be noticed." Corran nodded toward the holograph. "The facility we found was relatively new, with the team there assembled only over the last couple of months. As nearly as we can determine they're not part of a design team per se, but are analyzing the data being produced by the actual designers. They're trying to look for flaws in the thing the way you did at Yavin."

The fur rose on the back of Borsk Fey'lya's neck. "I fail to follow the significance of this information."

"Two main points really. The first is that we don't have an exhaust port to dump proton torps into." Corran ticked points off on his fingers. "Second, their simulated assaults are run against the Pulsar in various stages of construction. Within a year of construction starts, the hyperdrives should be operational. Two months after that, one of the big beams will work, as will shields, gravity well generators, and two of the TIE wing bays."

"So it can defend itself."

"Right, but its primary mode of defense will be to run." Corran opened his hands. "If we can make it run, we stop construction. We can harry it until supplies run out and then take it at our leisure."

The Bothan Councilor drew himself up tall in his seat. "You mean to suggest that a squadron of X-wings might be enough to scare this Pulsar Station into running?"

Wedge let mock surprise wash across his face. "Well, we *are* Rogue Squadron."

"And we were going to let Asyr lead the raid." Corran smiled. "The fact that they've been discovered is going to make them jittery, especially with the New Republic fleet so close by."

"You overestimate the effect of your reputation, I think."

"Maybe, but we might be able to enhance it a bunch."

Mon Mothma sat forward. "What is it you are thinking, General?"

It took Wedge a moment or two to realize she was speaking to him. "You selected Prince-Admiral Krennel as the target of our operations because we had the pretense of murder to justify what we're doing."

Fey'lya snorted. "It's more than pretense. You were there."

"I was, but that's not my point. Krennel's murder of Pestage is not clearly an evil. As you say, I was there, and I was tempted to murder him myself. The other warlords out there have seen us destroy Zsinj because he was an aggressor and attacking the New Republic. Our going after Krennel makes us the aggressor, and something as simple as this murder charge doesn't carry with it the moral authority that defending yourself does."

Wedge leaned forward on the briefing table, holding himself up on his arms. "Revealing the fact that Krennel is working on a new and improved Death Star–style weapon *does*."

Fey'lya shook his head. "Impossible. We can't let that news out."

Leia held a hand up. "Let Wedge finish. He has his reasons, I'm certain."

"I do, both political and practical. Let's start with practical: We're going to have troops hunting for this thing and it would be utterly immoral not to advise them of the threat they face. Moreover, it would be stupid. If they don't know what they're up against, they'll get hammered. And the fact is that no matter how good our security, once word goes out to the troops, it will spread.

"The key thing here, however, is that this news could be very divisive and hurt Krennel a lot. Talk to anyone who ever served the Empire and came over to the Rebellion, and the Death Star resonates in their memory. It's the embodiment of evil and, sure, lots of folks died when we blew it up, but lots more died on Alderaan and no one doubts the evil of the destruction of Alderaan. Even the most strident supporter of the Emperor—save perhaps Isard—would allow that destroying a moon could have made the point just as clearly as Alderaan's death."

Leia stared at the projected Pulsar Station image. "The Emperor's construction of a second Death Star put a lie to the claim that the first one had been Tarkin's folly; but the Emperor's death allowed everyone to shove the blame off onto him. His death absolved their consciences, and they believed that such a station would never appear again."

Wedge nodded. "Until now. And remember that Krennel has been waging a propaganda war against the New Republic, offering his Hegemony as a refuge for those we'd mistreat. If we reveal this project, folks who are inclined kindly toward him will reconsider. And the other warlords will have to wonder what this station would do to their holdings. If we make this public, we will force a lot of people to ask a lot of questions of Krennel."

The Bothan looked to Mon Mothma. "If we reveal this information, we could start a panic."

"Councilor Fey'lya has a point."

"Revealing the nature of the mission to those who will fight the thing will start news leaking that could start a panic. Coming from the government, this becomes a security advisory that ought to generate support for what we're doing against Krennel." Wedge straightened up. "It's important that we get this Pulsar Station now, while it can't do much more than run, and explanations about the situation should make that clear."

Mon Mothma nodded slowly. "This is an intriguing strategy you suggest, General Antilles. The Council shall consider it. You'll likely be on station again in the Hegemony before you learn of our decision."

"I understand, Chief Councilor Mothma." Wedge gave her a smile. "As long as the information is going to get out, I think we should make it work for us. Make Krennel's allies and the station's people uneasy. It might even get us the station without a shot being fired."

Borsk Fey'lya barked a short laugh. "Do you actually believe that, General?"

Wedge shrugged. "No, but I hope it all the same."

Prince-Admiral Delak Krennel slowly extended his mechanical index finger, letting it uncurl from his fist, and pointed it at Ysanne Isard as she entered his office. "This is your doing, is it not?"

Isard graced him with the hint of a smile. "I admire the way you keep your rage from your voice. A good skill to have." She turned away from him and looked at the holo-projector unit in the corner of the room. "As for *that*, no, I had nothing to do with it."

Krennel shifted his finger to point at the projector, then brought his thumb up to hit one of the buttons on his index finger. The projector's volume came up as General Cracken moved into the center of the image. He smiled briefly as the holocam pulled back to reveal a smaller holoprojector and a Death Star image behind him. Bitter bile bubbled up into the back of Krennel's throat as Cracken began to speak.

"One month ago, as New Republic forces liberated the world of Liinade Three, we uncovered a secret research and development base in which scientists were engaged in studies devoted to creating the next generation of weapons based on Death Star technology . . ."

Isard turned back and waved her left hand dismissively at Krennel. "You may shut it off. I've seen it too many times in the last day. I know his boring monologue by heart."

Krennel's chin came up. "Ah, you were so entranced by all this that you could not come when I summoned you after my first viewing of this message?"

"Hardly." She shrugged effortlessly and remained standing in the center of his office as if she owned it. "I was not on Ciutric. I traveled away from here to obtain reports from agents about this lab the New Republic *says* it found."

The Prince-Admiral heard something in her voice that sounded like a mixture of boredom and disgust. "'*Says* it found'? You don't believe the report?"

"You do? You believe this transparent and pathetic charade?" Isard's eyes narrowed with disbelief. "Please, Prince-Admiral, do not allow yourself to sink in my estimation. This is an obvious sham, meant to take in those who are a neuron shy of being able to form a synapse."

Krennel pounded his metal fist against his desk. "It's not a matter of belief. I *know* I had no such lab and no such project under way."

She nodded, slowly crossing her arms over her chest. "I know. You could not have hidden such a thing away from me."

The Prince-Admiral leaned forward, his teeth set in a feral grin. "But you, Ysanne Isard, *you* could conceal such a base from me, couldn't you? You could carry on such researches, couldn't you?"

"Indeed, Prince-Admiral, I could, but the New Republic's analysis shows I did not. Certainly, I could have put that lab in place, moved those people in, covered the tracks so you couldn't find them. That would be child's play, really—indeed, such projects *were* my childhood amusements." Her eyes focused distantly and she chuckled for a moment. "That's not what you wanted to hear."

Krennel sat back in his chair. She was right, that wasn't what he wanted to hear, but it was also what he expected out of her. He had assumed from the beginning she would have any number of little projects going on that he would not know about. His only control over her activities came through the resources he allotted to her. Her budgets, while not tiny, certainly were not overly generous. He expected that she supplemented what he gave her from other sources, but even doubling or tripling her funds would not allow for huge projects.

He smiled. "Ah, I see your point. The New Republic says this base was involved in researches, which you could have financed, but the construction would be beyond your reach." He held a hand up to forestall her protest. "Or, rather, if you had such resources, you would not have allied yourself with me."

Isard gave him a respectful nod. "Your Academy education does you proud. This report by the New Republic is clearly a hoax designed to provide them the moral high ground in its struggle with you. Your championing of freedom and personal choice, as well as our painting Pestage as an Imperial butcher on a scale that cried out for his elimination, had pretty well eroded support for their war against you. Their desperation shows in their use of this tactic."

"So there is no evidence for this lab?"

"There is a hole in the ground where they indicate there should be one, yes. It's gutted, with all useful material long since gone. How long it was there, none of my agents can estimate. The place has been there for a long time, but any refits were fairly recent. One agent remembers having gone fishing in that area two years ago and he saw nothing. None of your resources were used in guarding it and no traces of transactions regarding it can be found in local records."

"Were they sliced out?"

Isard blinked her eyes in an uncharacteristic way that Krennel took as a sign of confusion. "It *is* conceivable that they were, but a completely successful codeslice job leaves exactly the same trace as no slice job at all. I suppose you could conclude the evidence on this point is inconclusive or incomplete."

"But you don't think so?"

"No. I think this is all a put-up job by the New Republic to get at you." Isard began to pace. "We will have to fight this, of course."

"I have a more immediate concern, which is fighting the New Republic's armed forces."

Isard's features sharpened and a razor's edge entered her voice. "Be aware of one thing and never forget it, Prince-Admiral: This war against you is a *political* war. They have forged this moral imperative to get at you because they do not have the belly to exert the force they should. Perhaps they cannot—perhaps Thrawn's assault hurt them more than we can imagine. They are taking things gradually because slow is the only speed they can hit. Our counterassault will involve three steps that will cause them to seriously re-evaluate their chosen course."

"Three steps?" Krennel opened his metal hand and ran his fingers across the indentation he'd made when he pounded his fist into the desk. "And they are?"

"First, you will issue a statement concerning this charge against you. You will be distraught and angry. Do you remember Wynt Kepporra?"

Krennel closed his eyes for a second and saw the face of an eager young man, head shaved, blue eyes bright, in a cadet's uniform from the Imperial Academy. "He was in my class from Prefsbelt Four. We were in the same company because our last names began with the same letter. I recall him, vaguely."

"Well, now he was your best friend there. He was from Alderaan—this is true—and died when the planet was destroyed. He was home on leave, visiting his family. His death hurt you terribly, so much so that you volunteered for service in the Unknown Regions. Later you reconsidered and returned to try to exert influence to make sure there would be no more Alderaans. For the New Republic to suggest you would have anything to do with a project that would re-create the weapon that destroyed your friend, well, those are tactics that are painfully Imperial in nature."

The Prince-Admiral pursed his lips, then nodded. "I can deliver that message."

"And shed a tear?"

"I was a fighter at the Academy, not in the Thespian Union like Kepporra."

"No matter, we will slice in suitably altered material." Isard turned quickly and paced back the way she had come. "The second thing we will do is release a series of files that will show that you do not have the resources in the Hegemony to build such a project. One of them, the Corvis Minor file, will have been tampered with."

Krennel smiled. "Ah, yes, your little trap for Rogue Squadron. Perhaps this new bait will be more to their liking."

"Indeed, I hope so. When they are gone, of course, the New Republic will hit Corvis Minor rather hard. At that point, the third step goes into play. You will attack Liinade Three, hammering their garrison forces. We will insert insurgents who will undertake a covert war against the New Republic forces and, if we are fortunate, will inspire a popular uprising that will force them to devote more troops to holding the place than they ever intended."

"Their moral justification is undercut, a storied unit is dead, and I show I have steel to back the political integrity of my realm." Krennel slowly nodded. "It could work. It *must* work."

Isard smiled very coldly. "It *will* work. And once you've shown the galaxy that it is possible to oppose the New Republic, you will be seen as the Emperor's rightful heir. At that point we will both attain what we most desire."

17

Though Gavin Darklighter's eyes burned with fatigue, the image of Delak Krennel coming in over the recreation room's holoprojector held his attention and kept him awake. The projector rendered Krennel three-fourths his real height, but because Gavin was seated on a couch next to Asyr, he had to look up at the man's image. Krennel had abandoned a military uniform and instead had adopted well-made civilian clothes, but stayed away from the robes long associated with the Emperor's intimates.

"So now I am faced with the onerous task of rebutting the charges Mon Mothma and the New Republic have made against me. To many of you it would be inconceivable that such researches were taking place on a world under my control without my knowledge of it." Krennel's expression remained open, his eyes guileless. "I concur, and I tell you that I had no knowledge of these researches. I would point out that the New Republic has offered no proof that I knew of them and, in fact, has offered no proof that anyone knew of these researches *prior* to the New Republic's conquest of Liinade Three."

Gavin frowned. "What reason in the galaxy would the

New Republic have for faking a lab and accusing you of d[o]ing Death Star research?"

The other pilots in the rec center nodded in agreeme[n]t with Gavin's question.

Hobbie laughed. "Not like we didn't have better thing[s] to do when pacifying the planet."

"It wasn't that hard, Hobbie." Myn Donos stretche[d] his arms and rolled his wrists around. "I mean, we did hav[e] some spare time—an hour or two—in which to plan an[d] execute such deception."

Krennel's flesh and blood hand rose innocently. "[If] suggesting the New Republic fabricated this eviden[ce] against me, I would be as remiss as they are if I did not offe[r] you proof of their perfidy. Why would they want to di[s]credit me so? By accusing me of Sate Pestage's murde[r] they've already provided themselves with as much justific[a]tion as they needed to launch an invasion of my Hegemon[y.] These charges against me serve only to unite the New R[e]public by making the Emperor's ghost haunt my activities— a New Republic that apparently was not united behind th[e] attack in the first place. In fact, there was much more div[i]sion in the New Republic than anyone could have ima[g]ined, and that very division is what prompted this move."

Krennel's chin came up. "In keeping with my pledg[e] to provide land and shelter and a future to any beleaguere[d] population within the galaxy, I have been involved i[n] negotiations with the leadership of the Alderaanian re[fugee population. I was prepared to offer them Liinad[e] Three's southern continent—one known for its parallels t[o] Alderaan—as a haven. By fabricating evidence implicatin[g] me in furthering the sort of researches that resulted i[n] Alderaan's tragic destruction, the New Republic has scu[t]tled this effort that would have provided peace for the pe[o]ples of Alderaan, and for the peoples of the Hegemony."

Gavin glanced over at Tycho Celchu and watched th[e] other pilot's arms cross tightly over his chest. "Colonel, what he's saying true?"

Tycho shook his head slowly, as if barely registering th[e] question. "I don't know. I don't pay much attention to th[e]

Alderaanian refugee groups and they leave me alone for the most part. They'd see me as linked to the New Republic anyway, so if they were negotiating with Krennel, telling me about it would interfere with their plans."

Krennel bowed his head for a moment. "What pains me the most about the New Republic's tactics is that Mon Mothma has accused me of perpetuating the sort of terror weapons that destroyed Alderaan. She has painted me as an inhuman monster in doing so and has suggested that those who forget the horror of Alderaan will again allow such atrocities to be committed.

"The plain fact of the matter is that I have *not* forgotten the lessons of Alderaan. Captain Wynt Kepporra was from Alderaan and went to the Imperial Academy at Prefsbelt Four at the same time I did. We were friends, good and close friends. He had returned to Alderaan to see his family and was there when Grand Moff Tarkin . . ."

Krennel's voice failed him and he brushed away a tear with his left hand. He set his face again, then nodded and continued. "Wynt was on Alderaan when it was destroyed. I've been to Alderaan. I've been to the Graveyard and I've left my offerings to him and his memory. It was in his name that I chose to negotiate with the Alderaanian refugees. It was in his memory that I sought a suitable world to give them. Now, to be accused of such cruel duplicity as to be negotiating with them on one hand and scheming to create a Death Star on the other, well, the Emperor was never so vicious in dealing with his enemies."

"Besmirch their reputations, no." Asyr snarled. "Blow up their planet, sure. I'm not certain I like Krennel's definition of vicious."

Gavin draped an arm around her shoulders and gave her a hug. "You're reading my mind again."

The Prince-Admiral raised his chin. "It is a sad fact that brutality often begets brutality. The New Republic, which in its infancy desired freedom from oppression for all, now has grown into a monster that oppresses those who oppose it, just as the Empire tried to do to them. To the New Republic there is no place for neutrality, there is no chance for others to find their own path to freedom. This has always been my desire.

"We have been through a savage civil war in this galaxy, with its horrors all fresh in our memories. There is not one of us who has not looked back and in perfect hindsight suggested that if I had acted here or there, perhaps, just perhaps, the pain and suffering of billions could have been averted. The brave act of standing up to tyranny could have smothered it at its birth instead of requiring its execution at the height of its power."

The holocam closed in on Krennel's face. "The New Republic's tyranny is in its infancy. Oppose it now and we need not shed the blood of billions. The people of the Hegemony will fight to preserve our freedom. We invite all those who pledge themselves to liberty to make a stand and join with us, so the sacrifices made in overthrowing the Empire will not be tarnished by the rapacious predation of the New Republic."

The image slowly faded and Gavin found his flesh puckering. He shook his head, then frowned. "Anyone else get the feeling, even for a second, that we're on the wrong end of this war?"

"Sure," offered Inyri Forge, "for about as long as it took me to remember the locals trying to shoot my X-wing down."

The round-faced Myn Donos raked his fingers through his black hair. "I think Krennel would argue that they were just trying to defend their planet against our attack. We *were* the aggressors."

"And well we should have been." Inyri gestured toward where Krennel had been standing. "If we had not come here and someone hadn't tried to kill Corran, we would not have found that lab. A year from now, or two, Krennel could show up over Coruscant with his Death Star and cause a lot of trouble."

Myn held up his hands. "Hey, I'm not saying Krennel is right, but I do think there will be plenty of folks who will be given cause to wonder."

Asyr shifted from beneath Gavin's arm and sat forward on the couch. "Humans, you mean, Myn."

"Not necessarily. Take the Bothans, for example." Myn nodded in her direction. "You're a sophisticated people who have sacrificed much to help the Rebellion. You're politically astute, have colony worlds and a thriving economy. What if an indigenous people of one of those colony worlds decides it wants the Bothans gone and the New Republic decides to back this independence movement—largely because of a vote organized among species who don't care for Bothan politics? You Bothans would immediately be put into the same situation some humans might be feeling squeezed by right now.

"And there are humans who saw the blacker depths of the Emperor's heart, too. One of the Wraiths came from Toprawa. The Imps reduced them to puling animals. Folks might wonder why we're not liberating them instead of fighting over worlds that haven't asked for our help. I mean, I have no more love for Krennel than the rest of you, and I do think he has to go down, but using the idea of Pestage's murder as justification is rather thin."

Gavin shook his head. "Myn, if I hear you right, you're suggesting that because the New Republic says one thing, and Krennel says the exact opposite, most people will wonder if the truth isn't really somewhere in the middle?"

"Right. They have cause to wonder who's right."

Tycho stood. "It's called the gray fallacy. One person says white, another says black, and outside observers assume gray is the truth. The assumption of gray is sloppy, lazy thinking. The fact that one person takes a position that is diametrically opposed to the truth does not then skew reality so the truth is no longer the truth. The truth is still the truth."

He nodded slowly. "The truth in this case is simple: Krennel is an unreconstructed Imperial who has been shown in the past to have a penchant for cruelty and murder. We've found a lab that indicates he might be trying to build a new Death Star–type station, and maybe that's as far as it's gone. The fact that we don't know means we have to keep checking, keep pursuing. Even if Krennel's right, he didn't have anything to do with this lab, I don't doubt for an Imperial minute that he'd use such a station."

Inyri raised an eyebrow. "Even after what he said about his friend from Alderaan?"

Tycho snorted lightly. "I attended the Academy at Prefsbelt Four well after the two of them. Krennel's name appeared on a few trophies for unarmed combat. Kepporra was supposed to have been some engineering whiz. I don't see them being the best of friends, but even assuming they were, it would take more than a tear to make me believe Kepporra's death had that much effect on Krennel."

Inyri folded her arms across her chest. "Do you really think you can judge what went on in Krennel's heart based on one holocast?"

"Nope, just going by what I know of him in the past. He strafed a crowd at Axxila and murdered Pestage on Ciutric." Tycho's eyes narrowed. "More telling, though, is the fact that he didn't leave the Imperial service until four and a half years after the death of his friend. Alderaan's destruction caused me to defect immediately, but you'd expect that because I'm from Alderaan. Others took longer to come over, a month, a year, a couple of years, but eventually they did. Krennel remained with the Empire even after the second Death Star's destruction and only left when he was able to usurp Pestage's Hegemony. Someone with that track record only cares for himself."

Gavin let Tycho's words sink in and in them found a truth. In the whole of his three and a half years with Rogue Squadron, the emphasis had always been on helping others. It didn't matter how difficult the mission was, they went out and did it because they were making life better for someone, somewhere. *Sacrificing our futures so a bunch of other folks had their own futures secured always seemed like a solid bargain.* Krennel and people like him never would see it that way because they saw themselves as more important than anyone else.

Which is why we have to stop him.

Gavin ran his hand down over the fur on Asyr's spine. "I don't know about the rest of you, but it seems to me that Mon Mothma's announcement and Krennel's answer means that having evidence of this station's existence is going to be very important. I figure we've got a bunch of snoop-and-scoot missions in our future."

He stood and stretched. "It's about time for me to run some brush-ups on piloting a T-Six-Five-R, so I'm heading down to the simcenter. Anyone else wants to join me, I'd love the company."

18

Iella Wessiri shifted the toolbelt on her waist so the hydrospanner banged along her right thigh instead of against the back of her leg. The toolbelt, duraplast helmet, and gray-and-blue striped coveralls completed a disguise that started with her dyeing her hair jet black and putting in bright blue contact lenses. Everything worked together perfectly to make it appear as if she were a worker for Commenor Holocom, which was a common enough sight to let her pass unnoticed.

Mirax, on the other hand, had colored her hair a bright red and had donned a red business suit with black blouse beneath it, which attracted a lot of stares. She carried a datapad in her left hand and used a stylus in her right to point Iella this way and that, giving anyone watching the impression that she was Iella's supervisor making a quality-assurance run with her. The situation clearly pleased neither of them, as was evidenced by muttering on the part of both parties.

Various and sundry sapient characters on the street gave both of them a wide berth.

Iella had wanted to head out to Commenor within three weeks of her conversation with Mirax, but Corran's discovery on Liinade III had given New Republic Intelligence a brand-new focus. She'd spent the better part of a month pouring over data on Krennel's Hegemony worlds, looking for a possible shipyard for the Pulsar Station. She hadn't been able to pinpoint one, and sincerely doubted one existed, but the lack of data on some of Krennel's worlds disturbed her.

The world's pacification gave her a bit of a break, so she and Mirax headed out for their mission to Commenor. Their first stop had been the *Errant Venture*, the Imperial Star Destroyer Mirax's father had won from the New Republic for his role in the liberation of Thyferra. There Mirax had talked Booster Terrik into using the ship's facilities to manufacture fraudulent documents to get them into Commenor, and Booster had even managed to find them passage to the world with another ship. Iella had reluctantly agreed with Booster that the *Pulsar Skate* was too well known a ship to get them onto Commenor unnoticed.

They entered the lobby of a large office building and paused at the holodirectory. With the air of a bored executive, Mirax punched up the data for the offices of Wooter, Rimki, and Vass, Attorneys at Law. The directory noted the offices were on the eighteenth floor and closed for the weekend, but Mirax punched a button to summon a turbolift to carry them upward.

"The offices are closed, Supervisor. They're not working on the weekend, as we shouldn't be."

Mirax spitted Iella with a hard stare and poked her in the shoulder with the stylus. "If you had not cross-melded two lines, we wouldn't be working on the weekend and they *could be*."

One member of the janitorial staff, a Trandoshan, winced, while two insectoid Verpines just waggled antennae at each other. Iella trailed after Mirax rather dejectedly, keeping her eyes cast down at the ground. Wordlessly she entered the turbolift and the doors closed behind her.

Mirax ran her hand over the wooden wall paneling. "Genuine, not some fiberplast substitute. Very stylish and very expensive."

"Easy to do when you're on an Imperial expense account." Iella slowly shook her head. "If Mem Wooter hadn't decided to get greedy, he could have been in the clear."

Mirax smiled and curled a scarlet lock of hair behind her left ear. "I thought you were the one telling my father that snatching Wooter and sweating facts out of him couldn't be done because we weren't sure he was involved. I thought you were reserving judgment."

"Well, I was." Iella shrugged uneasily. "Fact is I'm as bad as Corran in resisting suggestions your father makes."

"No, you're not."

"Okay, maybe I'm not that bad." She laughed lightly. "After spending years hearing horror stories about him, though, I'm not comfortable doing what he suggests. This is especially true when it comes to the realm of crimes against a person."

"And what we're going to be doing is different?"

"Crimes against property, big difference." Iella hooked her thumbs through her toolbelt as the lift stopped and the doors parted. "I tell you, Supervisor, they made unauthorized repairs to their own line that caused the problem."

"The problem was unauthorized lum consumption, Splicist." Mirax led Iella down the hallway to the double doors with the firm's name emblazoned on them in gold Aurebesh lettering. She knocked firmly on the door, then waited. Under her breath she commented, "Looks like a Kambis Ninety-Four-Hundred lock. Not bad."

"You're kidding, right?" Iella fished a square packet from a toolbelt pouch. The device fit neatly in the palm of her hand. With a flick of her thumb she turned it on and a slender tab the thickness of a keycard snapped out on one of the long sides. She flashed it down through the keycard slot once quickly, then twice more. On the third try the door clicked open.

Mirax blinked. "How did you . . . ?"

Iella shrugged. "Whistler could have opened this door."

"So could I, but folks would have heard the blaster whine."

Iella ushered Mirax into the office foyer and closed the door behind them. "Intel has some interesting toys. Set it for the lock type, flash through once to blank the current code, a second time to set a new one, and a third to open the door."

Mirax smiled. "Know where Cracken gets those things?"

"I doubt he'd want you having one."

"Hmmm, then I guess a brisk trade in them would be out, too." Mirax looked into the office. "Then again, if this office is any indication, working for the Imps might be far more lucrative."

Iella couldn't argue with Mirax there. The office entryway had halfwalls topped with turned wooden pillars that upheld a reflective silver ceiling. A massive desk crossed the foyer. Off to the right a number of very comfortable-looking chairs surrounded a table in a small waiting area. Off to the left an open doorway led back into what, on the blueprints for the office, had been the research center, file room, utility closets, and small food prep station. Back behind the desk stood three doors to the partners' offices.

Iella inclined her head toward the open doorway. "File room first, then Wooter's office. If there is evidence here, we'll find it."

In reviewing the evidence collected from the raid on the Xenovet facility, Iella had realized there was very little at the actual site that hadn't been gone over. She stepped back from the physical evidence and began to examine the environment in which the facility had been located. The presence of the Xenovet site was indeed a physical fact, but the circumstances surrounding its use were not. The prisoners had said that they thought they had been in that facility for years, but that conflicted with the history of the site according to area residents.

Or, if the prisoners had been there during that time, the Imps also ran the breeding business as a cover.

In widening her search for details concerning the

Xenovet facility, Iella ran across a local attorney named Mem Wooter. Wooter had made a living during the Imperial era by acting as counsel for thieves, glitbiters, and other lowlifes being prosecuted by Imperial officials. The cases were unremarkable and Wooter got them assigned to him under the Imperial pretense of having a defense representative for all prisoners. He seemed good at making deals for clients and not pushing things where the Empire's evidence in the case was especially weak.

While Wooter's experience had been in minor criminal cases, when Xenovet went into receivership, Wooter had been appointed a trustee for the firm. He paid the site's expenses out of his own pocket, looking to recoup his losses when the site was sold. The bankruptcy records Iella had pulled from Commenor computers appeared to be very tidy and perfectly in order, which was a marked contrast to Wooter's filings in criminal cases. Still the bankruptcy court had no problem with him since he made no unreasonable demands on them and documented all his expenses. The case judge had even made a note in a file to the effect that if Wooter spent as much as the site cost, the court might just award him the property and close the file.

Mirax flipped on the glow panels in the file room and looked around at an endless array of shelves filled with datacard boxes. "Well, this won't be an easy search."

"No, but we'll have plenty of time to do it." The building's blueprints had been cross-checked against utility records, showing that Wooter's security precautions began and ended with the Kambis 9400. "No alarms, no surveillance equipment. We're in the clear."

Mirax frowned as she pulled one box of datacards from a shelf and set it on the long table running down the center of the rectangular room. "Wooter's certainly a contradiction. Smart enough to have a good lock, too dumb to have a security system. Smart enough to handle the Xenovet facility for the Imps, dumb enough to display his wealth by taking this sort of office."

"Makes things seem kind of obvious, doesn't it?" Iella

set her duraplast helmet down on the table. "But that's what brought us here anyway, right?"

"True." Mirax plucked a datacard from the box. "Look at this one. It's the Xenovet accounts."

Iella took Mirax's datapad from her and slipped the card into it. "Encrypted, but I'll make a copy of the data and we can slice it elsewhere."

A shiver shook Mirax. "It's too easy. There's something about this I don't like."

Iella handed back the datacard and slipped the datapad into her coverall's left thigh pocket. "You're beginning to sound like Corran. Don't tell me you have Jedi blood in you, too."

"Worse, my father raised me to be suspicious."

"Then he didn't do a good enough job." A man standing in the file room doorway slipped a blaster carbine from beneath his long nerf-hide coat and leveled it at them. "You'll be coming with us." He stepped into the room and to the right, allowing them to see another man similarly armed standing in the office foyer.

Iella slowly raised her hands and Mirax followed suit. Long years of training, first with CorSec and later with the Rebellion, told Iella that to make any sort of move would be suicidal. While she knew that going with the two of them meant the chances of her living through the encounter were slender, in the file room they had no place to run. *Shooting us here would be easier than blasting a bantha in a turbolift box.*

Mirax exited the room first with her hands held high. Iella followed close on her heels and was impressed that the man coming after her didn't poke her in the back with the muzzle of his blaster carbine. *Doing that would let me know where the weapon is, which might give me a chance to knock it out of the way and attack him.* His caution showed he wasn't some streetlurker out to prove how tough he was. *He's a professional, which means he's not going to panic. That's good.*

In the hallway outside the office two more men joined

the first two. They came out of the next office over—the legend on the door proclaimed them to be accountants. Iella smiled. "You ran surveillance gear in through air ducts so the power hookups would be billed through the other office, not Wooter's. Nice."

The first man directed them down the hallway to a doorway allowing access to the maintenance lifts.

Mirax nodded. "Very nice. I bet Wooter didn't even know he was being watched. Just like Isard to think of that sort of thing."

The lead man let the comment pass, but one of the others hitched for a second. The leader caught the hesitation as quickly as Iella did and stopped. "You two can keep quiet, or we stun you and carry you out of here in trash bins. Your choice."

Another of the men summoned the freight lift as they assembled in the little tiled room that looked all the more dingy and cheap because of the contrast with the rest of the building. All four of the men were tall and strongly built— Iella guessed they trained on a high gravity world—but they were different enough that she didn't figure them to be clones. They could have passed for stormtroopers had they been wearing armor, which made Iella think they were probably Special Intelligence operatives, which were just the sort of people Isard had employed on Coruscant and elsewhere to do her dirty work.

All six of them piled into the freight lift and it descended. The blaster carbines all retreated inside jackets for appearance's sake, but Iella knew that making any sort of a move in the crowded lift would be insane. *Crossfire might get some of them, but we'd be in the middle of it, which would hurt a lot.*

The freight lift opened onto a freight dock area at the rear of the building. The scent of rotting garbage assaulted Iella's nostrils, and a hand in the middle of her back propelled her forward. As she stepped from the turbolift she saw one of the Verpine maintenance workers from the lobby. One of their kidnappers flashed his carbine at the Verpine and the creature chittered and bowed his way into a retreat while the others led Iella and Mirax out into the alley behind the building.

A trio of wheeled trash bins along the right side of the alley narrowed it appreciably, and a pair of twitching legs sticking up out of the nearest open one brought a smile to several faces. Beyond the trash bins Iella saw a pair of black hovercars and assumed they were their destination. The doors on the hovercars opened and two more individuals exited each vehicle. She looked around and saw another alley leading off to the left about halfway down to the vehicles. The main street lay behind them, with two of the kidnappers between her and it. Another street capped the alley back beyond the hovercars.

If they get us into the hovercars, they can take us wherever they want to, interrogate us, and kill us. As desperate as she knew the situation to be, there wasn't anything she could do about it. One kidnapper led the group, followed by Mirax and a second guard. Iella came next with the last two kidnappers following her. *And in this narrow alley, shooting us down would be easy. Still, if I had a diversion...*

They'd moved past the first trash bin when the diversion came. The grubby figure of a man who had been digging in the bin skipped and capered his way past them, then asked each of them for money. "I'm not a glitbiter, just something to see me by." He tugged on the sleeve of the first man in line, then swept on down, grabbing at Iella's right hand. A snarled command from the man behind her brought a shocked look to the derelict's face, then he backed off, pressing his spine against the middle trash bin.

"Wish I could help," Iella said slowly.

"You will, kind lady." The man lunged for the last kidnapper in line, slamming him across the alley and into the ferrocrete wall on the other side.

The kidnappers all turned as their comrade yelped and the men by the vehicles pointed down the alley toward them. Iella brought her right hand up and slid her index finger onto the trigger of the holdout blaster the derelict had slipped her. She shot the third kidnapper in the middle of his back, pitching him forward into the derelict and last kidnapper. She spun to shoot the second kidnapper, but Mirax had already scythed a booted foot through the man's knee, dropping him to the ground. Iella shot the first kidnapper in the face, then grabbed Mirax's hand and sprinted with her toward the hovercars.

The men at the vehicles didn't fire at the running women—whether from surprise or out of fear of hitting their confederates Iella didn't know and didn't care. She cut into the alley with Mirax and started running full out. The alley broke to the right and they raced around the corner, then stopped.

"*Sithspawn!* Dead end." Mirax slapped her hand against a ferrocrete wall. "Don't have anything to blow a hole through it on that toolbelt, do you?"

"Sorry."

"Never a husband around with a lightsaber when you need one, you know?"

"Yeah, having him or Wedge or all of Rogue Squadron here right now would be rather handy." Iella slid back behind a fiberplast crate and hunkered down. She aimed her blaster twenty meters back at the alley mouth. "They're going to be coming and they're going to be angry."

"I gathered that might be happening." Mirax shifted another fiberplast crate around and started piling broken chunks of ferrocrete on the top. Smaller pieces she kept closer at hand.

Iella raised an eyebrow. "You're going to throw ferrocrete at them?"

"Might not work well, but it will make me feel much better." Mirax shrugged. "Besides, to hear Wedge tell it, rocks worked for the Ewoks."

"Well, I'd be happy to see a battalion of those furry little critters right now."

Down at the far end of the alley the white crescent of a face poked its way around the corner, then drew back quickly. The muzzle of a blaster carbine followed and sprayed lethal red energy darts through the narrow, ferrocrete alley. The bolts left guttering flames burning on the walls.

"I'd rather take you alive," someone called around the corner.

Iella sighted in on the corner, dropped her aim point thirty centimeters, and moved it a meter out. "Don't expect us to make this easy for you."

"I didn't think that was in the plan."

Iella watched, waiting for them to make a move. A muffled thump rolled down the alley, but she couldn't place the sound. The stuttered whine of blaster carbines going off followed, with a hail of red darts tattooing the end of the alley. Two men came rolling and stumbling past the alley mouth, driven forward and picked apart by concentrated blasterfire. They rolled to a stop in the middle of the alley, their clothes smoldering and their bodies limp.

Iella glanced at Mirax. "What's going on?"

Mirax shook her head. "I have no idea, but I think I like it."

The two of them remained down behind cover until a chittering filled the alley and two blaster-toting Verpines crouched over the dead men. They poked at one of the bodies, then waved someone else along. They remained over the bodies, looking at Mirax and Iella, but they made no move toward them, nor did they point their weapons in their direction.

An older man with a fringe of white hair on his head and a flowing white mustache ducked his head into the alley and pulled it back again. "Don't shoot, I'm a friend."

Iella set her blaster down. "We believe you."

"Good." The man stepped into the alley, letting his blaster dangle by a shoulder strap from his right shoulder. "You're both unhurt?"

"We are." Iella stood and folded her arms across her chest. "Who are you?"

The man smiled. "Baz Korral. Mirax's father saved my life in the mines on Kessel, and he asked me to keep an eye on you. When one of my Verpines reported you'd been taken, we moved. Meant to be here sooner, but we came as fast as we could."

Iella nodded. Verpines were able to communicate via

energy waves produced and received by their antennae. They were the perfect species for creating a net of watchers. "Don't worry, the guy you had in the alley had us covered." She pointed at the holdout blaster. "He gave me this and got things moving."

"Someone gave you a holdout blaster?" Korral's white brows arrowed in at each other. "I had no one in the alley, no one with a blaster."

Mirax frowned. "The derelict, he wasn't yours?"

"Derelict?" Korral looked at his Verpines. Their antennae twitched, then one shook his head. Korral looked back at the two women. "The Verps in the main alley say there's no one there but the guys who took you and their friends."

Mirax looked at Iella. "Remember when I said this was too easy?"

Iella nodded. "I do."

"Well, I was wrong." Mirax shivered. "And I don't think I like it at all."

19

Wedge Antilles waited until the last of Rogue Squadron's pilots sat down, then nodded to Nawara Ven to lower the lights in the briefing room. Wedge hit some keys on his datapad and the holoprojector it had been linked to served up the image of a solar system. At its heart lay a yellow star; seven planets orbited it, three outside an asteroid ring that marked the halfway point between the system's outer edges and the star at its hub.

"This is the Corvis Minor system. The third and fourth planets are inhabited. The third is a semi-arid world with temperate zones at the poles, and the fourth is a water-rich tropical world. Both produce some exotic xenobiological products that sell as luxury commodities within the Hegemony and outside, though all trade outside the Hegemony flows through Liinade Three or Ciutric. The populations on these worlds are small and benign. A *Victory*-class Star Destroyer is on station around the fourth planet. It's called *Aspiration*, came into the Imperial Fleet right after Endor, and joined Krennel when he installed himself as the Hegemony's leader."

Wedge hit another button and the image shifted. The focus moved past the asteroid belt to the fifth planet. Then it zoomed in, revealing a gas giant with a half-dozen moons in orbit. "This is the planet we're concerned with, or, rather, one of its moons. Astronomical data on this section of the system is sketchy at best, but computer simulations indicate that this moon, Distna, named after the discoverer's wife, may be hollow. It has half-standard gravity, a bit of an atmosphere, and could be the equivalent of a spacedock. It is possible that Krennel is building his Pulsar Station inside it, or even building the station *into* it."

Tycho ran a hand over his jaw. "If the station is actually being built into that moon, the crust will act as far more effective armor than the Death Star ever had."

Hobbie groaned. "How come *we* never have these superweapons that could eliminate a problem like that?"

Wedge smiled. "Because, Hobbie, we rely on pluck, courage, and skill instead of capital expenditure."

"I guess, then, that the rumors of a raise are not true?"

Wedge joined the others in laughter, then cleared his throat to settle them down. "Our mission is going to be a simple one. We're guiding a T-Six-Five-R into the system. We'll do fly-bys on Distna to collect what data we can, then we get back out. Because of the gas giant, the various moons, and the asteroid belt, jumping into that area is going to be difficult. We have a limited number of entrance and exit vectors, and they will change, so we need to work up a variety of exit solutions."

Corran raised a hand. "Two questions."

"Go ahead."

"First, who gets stuck driving the snoopscoot?"

Wedge pointed to the Quarren pilot sitting next to Tycho. "For those of you who don't know him, this is Nrin Vakil. He flew with the Rogues back before most of you joined the squadron. The New Republic has had him on other duties for a while, but he's good with the recon ship. He'll be Rogue Alpha for this run."

Nrin raised a hand and Hobbie reached over to slap him on the shoulder. The other pilots nodded and murmured hellos. Wedge assumed Nrin would be interrogated by the others once the briefing was ended. *Given Nrin's penchant for being a bit dour, they'll learn that whatever hardships they've faced, they were nothing compared to the earlier days of the squadron.*

"Your second question, Corran?"

"The Vic around the fourth planet, it's not going to be a problem?"

"*Aspiration* isn't likely to come off-station because of the difficulty of navigating in and out of hyperspace for that sort of micro-jump. Thrawn may have used that sort of jumping to tactical advantage, but landing in here would mean the Vic couldn't jump back out to defend the inhabited worlds without some very difficult maneuvering. Using sub-light drives to get out there would eliminate the problem, but it would also take far longer for transit than we'll be in the system. If it *does* jump in, we use Distna to shield us from its guns, run to the asteroid belt, and hit an exit vector."

"Other questions?"

Khe-Jeen raised a hand. "No reports of fighters being stationed on Distna?"

"None, but intel is weak on that point." Wedge sighed. "Look, people, we could run into anything out there, and the sims you'll be running over the next two days will point that out. We're not expecting heroics, we're just there to get some data. Clearly, because we're going in with a full squadron instead of just a flight for cover on the snoop-scoot, we're prepared for trouble. Regardless, this is a recon mission, not a raid. We'll fight what we have to fight and roll on out of there."

He looked around the room and let the gravity of his words sink in for a moment. "Okay, two days from now we'll be in the Corvis Minor system at approximately twenty-one hundred hours local time. Within six hours you should be back here, safe and sound."

Janson laughed. "And in another forty-eight hours we'll be back at Corvis Minor finishing the job by splashing that station."

"Probably right, Wes, probably right." Wedge hit a key on his datapad. "Okay, you all have the briefing details in your datapads. Sims commence in an hour. Let's work hard at this here, people, so we don't have to work hard over Distna."

Corran slumped down outside the simulator cockpit and closed his eyes against the sting of sweat. This last run, the squadron's third, had been the most grueling. The first recon run at Distna had showed minimal electromagnetic radiation, but occasional spikes above normal background readings demanded a closer look. As Nrin came in on a tighter pass, Interceptors and TIEs boiled out of Distna to tangle with the Rogues. The sim pitted them against a full flight group—half a wing—which left them outnumbered three to one. The faster Interceptors broke runs for exit vectors and herded the Rogues back toward the waiting TIEs.

He opened his eyes as Gavin grunted and slid to the floor. "Nice work there, Corran. You got, what, five of the eyeballs?"

"Yeah, but you vaped two squints and let us make a break for it."

Asyr dropped down beside Gavin and rested a hand on his thigh. "You shouldn't have waited around for me, Gavin. You should have just gotten out when you could."

The young man shrugged. "The scenario was done, we'd gotten hammered. I had nothing to lose."

Asyr's claws snagged in the orange fabric of Gavin's flight suit. "Listen to me, Gavin Darklighter, you cannot treat these sims as games. If my ship is disabled out there, I don't want you disobeying orders and hanging around to protect me against impossible odds. If I have to die, I want to do so knowing that you continue to live. You have to promise me that's what you'll do."

The Quarren, Nrin Vakil, approached, his boots clicking against the tile. "Do not, Captain Sei'lar, ask of Captain Darklighter such a sacrifice. Do not make him give such an oath."

Intense pain rolled off Nrin in waves that sliced through Corran. "Voice of experience, Major Vakil?"

Nrin nodded slowly, his mouth tentacles knotting and

unknotting slowly. "When I was with the squadron we had another pilot, a Mon Calamari, named Ibtisam. She died on Ciutric. Krennel's pilots killed her. I killed many of them, but she did not make it." His shoulders slumped forward a bit, and he leaned against Corran's simulator. "She and I, we had been friends, close friends."

Nrin crouched, resting his forearms on his knees, and looked at Asyr. "Had Ibtisam demanded of me such a promise, I would have been destroyed. I could not have left her alone, but I would have hated to violate my promise to her. In your heart, in all of our hearts, we know what the right thing to do is. We have to trust each other that we will do it, keeping faith with each other, and with our mission."

Corran nodded slowly. Even more daunting than the idea of dying was the idea of surviving the death of others. The death of a friend slashed the spirit and made it that much harder to continue living and fighting. The Rebellion had united everyone in the pursuit of a future that would be bright for all, but the deaths accumulated along the way dimmed that future.

"Speaking of the mission, you're a pretty hot hand with the recon ship." Corran patted Nrin on the shoulder. "You spend a lot of time driving these things?"

"Some, but mostly on training exercises." Nrin looked down at his hands. "After Ciutric I took a leave from the squadron, to think about things. I realized I couldn't quit the Rebellion since it was too important a cause. I also realized that I had no desire to fly in combat anymore. That doesn't mean I didn't, but I did get a transfer into a training squadron. Training pilots and then sending them away to die meant I didn't have to deal with the pain of their deaths."

Gavin settled his hand over Asyr's. "But you're back flying missions now."

"Indeed, I am. The Thrawn threat caused the New Republic to reshuffle their assets . . ."

"Which landed your asset in a cockpit." Corran rolled his head around to loosen his neck muscles. "Is this your first recent combat mission? Because you sure didn't fly like it in sim."

"I flew in a few battles against Thrawn." The Quarren shrugged. "I don't have the desire for bloodletting that I once had. I also know I'm better suited to some missions than others might be. I accept my responsibility."

"Do you like being back with the Rogues?"

Nrin hesitated before he responded to Asyr's question. "Yes, I think I do. There is a proud tradition here and I enjoyed being part of it. Getting a second chance to be part of it is rare. Now I can view Ibtisam's death with some perspective, which allows me to deal with the pain more easily."

Corran's eyes narrowed. "And coming back to deal with Krennel, that has to be satisfying as well."

The Quarren's tentacles parted enough to display two needle-sharp fangs. "Yes, that aspect was not lost upon me." Nrin stood, then offered Corran his hand and pulled him to his feet. "In the old Rogue Squadron we'd often discuss these runs over a mug of lum. Is that behavior still suitable?"

Corran stretched. "Drinking? Rogues?"

Nrin blinked. "Have things changed that much?"

Gavin laughed. "He meant to ask 'Drinking lum?' Nope. More lomin-ale these days." He climbed to his feet and gave Asyr a hand up. "Lead the way, Major, and you'll see that some Rogue traditions live on very strong."

Wedge glanced through the numbers hovering above the holoprojector pad. "I don't know, Tycho. I don't like the losses we took in that last run. Five pilots lost."

Tycho, who wore his black flight suit unzipped to his navel, scratched at his throat. "They jumped us with thirty-six fighters and we blasted twenty-five of them apart. Nice kill ratio, *and* Nrin's snoopscoot got away with its data intact. I don't like the results of the exercise, but the performance wasn't bad."

Wedge sat back and tapped a stylus against his right cheekbone. "You're right, we performed better than a computer projection would have had us doing; which means we're capable of performing the mission within acceptable parameters for a worst-case scenario."

"'Within acceptable parameters for a worst-case scenario'? Feeling a bit feverish there, Wedge?"

"Would it get this mission scrubbed?"

"Probably not." Tycho frowned. "What's with the phrasing?"

Wedge tossed the stylus at his datapad. "Missions are being evaluated on a risk basis to determine if we go or don't go. We're only allowed casualties within acceptable limits lest folks in the New Republic think too much blood is being shed for too little gain."

Tycho's jaw dropped open, then he snapped it shut again. "Um, for us pilots, the acceptable level of blood being shed is zero, right? Especially if it's *our* blood."

"That's my thinking, yes. As nearly as I can tell, losing Rogue Squadron would be a negative for the New Republic, and I'm certainly in favor of them doing everything to preserve our lives. Balancing our lives, though, against the discovery of a superweapon I think is rather short-sighted of them." He shook his head. "I mean, you and I have survived Death Star runs before, but we had a bit more help than just the other Rogues."

"Right, but this is just a recon run. We're not being asked to take the thing out, just to see if it's there."

"And if Janson's prediction is correct, that mission will be next."

"And when was Janson ever right with one of his predictions?"

"Well, I can't argue with you on that point." Wedge hit a couple more keys on his datapad and the numbers hovering in the air collapsed in on themselves. "There we go, that's it, I've just sent Command confirmation of our orders and mission specs. Unless we uncover some serious problems in future sims, we're locked in. We pull a quick swing through Corvis Minor, get out again, and await orders from our masters."

Tycho stood and stretched. "Back to the simulators, then?"

"Yeah. That worst-case scenario, I want to run it again." Wedge nodded solemnly. "I want to run it until it becomes Krennel's worst case, not ours."

The order confirmation memo that Wedge fed into the Rogues' computer on Liinade III was shoved through an encryption program and then dropped into the queue for routing through the HoloNet. Once into the HoloNet, the message traveled all but instantaneously to its desired destination, then was decoded and sent on to Admiral Ackbar.

During that process, as the message entered the queue and as it worked its way through the computer network on Coruscant, copies of it were created and appended to other information transmissions. They shot off through the HoloNet to a different destination where the masking messages were discarded and the Rogues' message was decoded, compared to the New Republic's decoded version, and transmitted to a holoprojector for display.

Shrouded by the shadows of her sanctum, Ysanne Isard sat back and steepled her fingers as she reread the simple text message glowing green in the air above her holoprojector. "'Corvis Minor, the moon Distna, 2100 hours local, two days time.' Splendid, better than I could have hoped. Now I have Rogue Squadron exactly where I want them."

20

Mirax waited at the base of the shuttle's gangway and gave Baz Korral a warm hug. "Thank you for everything you've done for us. Getting us out of that bind, and finding me that deal on those Alderaanian statuettes. They're exquisite. If you find more, I have a number of clients who will take them off your hands."

"I'll see what I can do to get more." Korral smiled broadly, then looked past her. "Booster, you look more fit than ever. Running this ship must agree with you."

Mirax's father, who towered over Korral and outmassed him by being fit rather than fat, boomed a hearty laugh. His left eye, a mechanical replacement, burned red, while his brown eye reflected his joy at welcoming the shuttle to the *Errant Venture*. "The profit margin agrees with me, though the overhead does not. Good to see you again, Baz; and you, Iella."

He held his arms wide open for Mirax, but she poked a finger into his breastbone. "I don't think I'm talking to you, *Father*."

Booster winced. "That formal, and that tone? What did I do?"

Mirax narrowed her brown eyes and folded her arms over her chest. "You had Baz watching us, that's what."

Her father looked confused for a moment. "But having the Verpine watch you and report on what was happening saved you from being taken away and killed."

Iella shook her head. "Booster, just leave it alone."

"No, just wait a minute there, Iella. Mirax is *my* daughter and I feel some responsibility for her safety."

Mirax looked at Iella. "He's following the script, isn't he?"

Booster's head came up and his eyes slitted. "Script? You two discussed how this chat would go?"

Iella nodded and tried to pull Booster away, deeper into the Imperial Star Destroyer's aft docking space. "We did, and you're following it too closely for my comfort."

He slipped his arm from her grip and posted his fists on his hips. "You have a problem with my having Baz watch you, Mirax?"

She studied her father for a moment, all tall and defiant, and felt years slip away. When she was a child he'd been her hero. He told great stories and lived large, talking to her of places she'd only visited in dreams. After her mother died, Booster used to take Mirax with him in the *Pulsar Skate* on any runs that he deemed safe. When she couldn't go with him, he left her with friends—including Wedge Antilles's family prior to the death of Wedge's folks. As a child she had worshiped her father and felt safe because he had been there to take care of her and protect her.

Then Hal Horn caught up with him and Booster was sent to the spice mines of Kessel for five years. Though not yet legally an adult, Mirax took command of the *Pulsar Skate* and built her own business. Instead of hauling highly illegal cargoes for next-to-no profit margin, she specialized in exotics for which people paid a great deal. Her father's reputation, and a certain amount of sympathy for his current situation, had given her a legitimacy and entrée into the shadowy side of the Empire's economy, but she quickly made marks for herself and earned respect in her own right.

In short, while her father was on Kessel, she grew up from being his daughter into her own person. *But he never saw that. I don't know if* any *father would, but I know mine didn't.* Even after leaving Kessel he hadn't gotten in touch with her, and only a chance meeting a couple of years earlier on Tatooine had reunited them.

She purposely kept her voice soft, but she met his hard stare without flinching. "You're going to want to think a lot about what I'm going to say, Father, and that means you're going to want to listen, then walk away to *think*. If you don't, you're going to get into a discussion you won't like and one you *will* lose. And you'll lose more than just the argument."

Booster slid his hands around to the small of his back. He glanced serenely around the *Errant Venture*'s bay, nodding to a few people, waiting for the pace of activity to pick up again. He then nodded to his daughter. "Go ahead."

"I've never had any complaints about having you as my father. Your getting tossed into the spice mines didn't bother me. Your gruff bluster about Corran did grate a bit, but I understood. I have been overjoyed that you've come back into my life, and I'm very proud that you have the *Errant Venture* and are making it work. I'm proud to be your daughter, but I'm also *more* than your daughter."

Mirax turned back and patted Baz Korral on the arm. "Yes, having your friend keep an eye out for us *did* get us out of trouble. By the same token, for all we know, the presence of his Verpines in the building alerted the bad guys to something unusual going on. They might have been thinking Baz here was planning some sort of raid of his own, so they set a trap and we fell into it. While he did pull us out of trouble, it could very well be your meddling that got us into trouble.

"And, look, I know this isn't a male-female thing—though I do know you wouldn't have alerted Baz if Corran were going to Commenor on the same mission we were."

"True enough." Booster's expression tightened. "I'd have tipped the enemy he was coming."

"And break my heart? Thank you, *Father*."

"Mirax, you know I don't mean anything by that . . ."

"No, *Father,* you don't see that by making such cracks

you show you don't trust my judgment. You don't trust my choice of husband, and you didn't think Iella and I could handle ourselves on Commenor."

Booster frowned. "But you came here first, looking for help to get in."

"Right, and if we needed any more help, we would have asked." Mirax took a deep breath, then let it out in a sigh. "Father, I've grown up. I'll always be your daughter, but I'm not your little girl. I'll accept your help when I need it, seek your counsel when I need it, and even listen to you when I don't, but I don't want you sneaking around behind my back to do things that you think need to be done. What would have happened if Iella and I spotted Baz's Verpines, decided they were part of the enemy, and killed them? If you have concerns about what I'm doing, let me know, and I'll decide what to do about them. And if I need you to help me, I'll ask, no problem. Do you understand?"

Booster's face remained a hard mask for a moment and Mirax knew she'd hurt him. Her heart ached and her stomach collapsed in on itself, but another part of her felt buoyed and free. *The only problem with growing up in someone's shadow is that when you grow beyond it, everyone but the person casting the shadow can see how much you have changed.* She reached a hand out toward her father and fought to control its trembling.

Booster cleared his throat, but kept his hands at the small of his back. "I can think a little bit faster than you probably imagine possible, Mirax, and I do know how to listen. I could tell you what billions of parents have told their kids: You'll always be my child, and I'll always worry about you. Thing is, you know that. How I deal with it may not always be right, from your point of view. But, in this case, you *are* right, I could have gotten you and Baz and Iella in trouble by asking him to do what I did. *That* won't happen again."

He reached out with his right hand and took hers into it. "You have grown up, and I know that. I'm proud of you. You can't know how it pleases me when people come here and identify me as 'Mirax Terrik's father.' It hurts a little, sure, and too much of it can be irritating, but I'll get used to it. And it will make me work harder to earn back my infamy.

"Thing of it is, Mirax, the five years I spent on Kessel were years I can't get back. You went from being my little girl to the woman you are now, and I never got a chance to get used to that idea. Don't know if I ever will. Don't know if I would ever want to. I figured I'd delay trying until I had no choice. Delay's over."

Mirax let Booster draw her into a hug, and she clung to him tightly. She said nothing and took refuge in his warmth and familiar scent, then let the vibrations of his low chuckle run through her. She rubbed her hands along his back, then slipped from his arms and looked up at him. "What's so funny?"

"I was just thinking that I knew a heck of a lot less about parenting than I did smuggling, but did better at parenting than I would have ever imagined."

Mirax smiled. "Just like you to take credit for the quality of the cargo when all you did was haul it around."

Booster withdrew, a mock look of shock on his face. "Surly children are never pleasant."

"That's all well and good, Booster, but we have other problems to deal with." Iella held up a datacard. "Before we got taken we copied an encrypted file onto this datacard. I need to slice it open and run it down, now. In addition, we have the identification cards for all the men Baz burned down. We need to check them to see if we can determine who they were and who they worked for."

Booster nodded. "Not a problem, we can get started after I treat all of you to dinner here on the Diamond level. After all you've been through, you must want something to eat."

"We're hungry, yes, Father." Mirax nodded, then moved over beside Iella and headed toward her father's office. "We also have work to do, important work. That datacard will confirm for us whether or not someone is setting a big trap for Rogue Squadron. No matter how good the meal, I'm not interested in delaying our work."

Booster turned, flung his arms wide, and settled around the shoulders of both women. "No, no indeed, no delay will be acceptable. Come, ladies, the resources of the *Errant Venture* are at your disposal, and I am at your service. Whatever you want or need you shall have, and anyone looking to ambush Wedge and his friends will have more trouble than they could ever expect."

Mirax stared at the data readout hovering in the air above the desk Iella had been given. Her father had provided them a suite of rooms on the level *above* the Diamond level. It was not as opulent as the luxury level below it, but it was quiet and traffic was restricted. *I didn't even know it existed, but most of the other times I've been here I've been passing through or with Corran.* That her father would keep a level hidden from her husband rather amused her.

The data did not. "Okay, let me see if I have all of this stuff straight. The financial records from Wooter's office indicate that payments were made through financial institutions located in the Corvis Minor system."

Iella swept a lock of golden brown hair behind an ear. "That's what it comes down to. The files your father has on this ship—both old Imp intel files and new stuff that he buys—make it look like the payments were part of an intel op, which would make sense. The money was being paid to house prisoners from the *Lusankya*, so it must have come from some resources Isard had hidden away."

"Okay, I'm with you there." Mirax pointed at a second set of data. "Now here you've matched dust samples laminated on the identification cards of the men in the alley with traces of mineral content from the bones of the prisoners dug up on Commenor."

"Not exactly. The forensics tech worked up a profile of soil composition needed to accomplish the decay and leave the correct trace elements on the bones. It matches the dust on the ID cards. Those two samples also match a planetoid in the Corvis Minor system: Distna, a moon orbiting the fifth planet in that system."

"Which is where you think the *Lusankya* prisoners are being housed."

Iella shook her head. "That's where I think someone— Isard—wants us to believe they're being housed. I think they're bait to get Rogue Squadron there and into a trap."

Mirax stood, a chill running through her. "We have to tell them."

"I tried. I tried the direct route and sending information through New Republic Intelligence. No reply." Iella hit a key on her datapad, killing the holographic datafeed. "I also spoke with your father, and that's why we entered hyperspace."

Mirax's comlink squawked. "Mirax, this is your father. Please join me on the bridge."

"On my way. Iella is coming, too."

"Good."

The two of them raced to the turbolift and ascended to the bridge. The lift opened and they stalked out to join Booster where he stood before the large viewport. Below the catwalk a variety of ship's officers carried out their duties. Beyond Booster the *Errant Venture*'s bow sailed through a white tunnel of light.

Booster's expression appeared as grave as Mirax could ever remember seeing it. "Getting into Corvis Minor around the fifth planet will be difficult for a ship our size. Had we not been coming from Commenor, the trip would have taken another twelve hours. As it is, we will arrive at twenty-two hundred hours local time in a pole-to-pole orbit over the gas giant. My helmsman, Hassla'tak, says Distna will be in our forward arc for fifteen minutes if we do nothing."

Iella glanced at one of the duty stations down below. "Are all your guns operational?"

"Enough are. I have a squadron of uglies and two assault gunboats to keep us safe, and we do have an exit vector within five minutes of our arrival. I'm not worried."

I am. Mirax reached out with both hands, grabbing her father's shoulder and Iella's hand. "The fact that we got here so easily from Commenor, does that suggest even more strongly we're looking at a trap?"

Booster snorted. "Sure, but the sort of trap that would catch a squadron isn't the kind that will get the *Errant Venture*."

"Ten seconds to reversion." The Twi'lek, Hassla'tak, twitched his *lekku* in time with his countdown. "Three, two, one . . ."

The white tunnel shattered into white needles that quickly resolved themselves into stars. Above the ship appeared the big gray-orange ball that was Corvis Minor V. Lightning played through the clouds in long jagged strings. Directly ahead lay Distna, a dark, rocky ball that looked completely devoid of life.

"*Sithspawn!*" Mirax stumbled forward to the transparisteel viewport and pressed her hands against it. "We're too late."

Some pieces spinning fast, others floating placidly, debris filled the space between the *Errant Venture* and Distna. Mirax recognized the blown-out ball cockpits of TIE fighters, and their octagonal wings. Melted and twisted twin hulls of TIE Bombers and fragments of Interceptors' canted wings also hung there. Among them drifted black-clad bodies, some intact, others in pieces, of the pilots who had flown those craft.

She also spotted the shattered hulks of at least two X-wings, and two bodies in the orange flight suits the Rogues wore. As she scanned space for other pieces, she saw debris flare in the distance as it slipped into the gas giant's atmosphere.

Then one piece of debris slowly tumbled toward the *Errant Venture*. When she caught sight of it her knees buckled and she slid to the decking. "No, Emperor's Black Bones, no!"

The S-foil had been painted green, and bore the distinctive markings that left little doubt it belonged to her husband's X-wing.

She felt Iella's hands on her shoulders and heard her father's gruff voice fill the bridge.

"Get recovery teams out there, now!" Booster snapped at his crew. "I want every piece of debris, every body, every thing. If there's a survivor he's worth a hundred thousand credits. Get it all, *now.* Reports come to me alone."

Above Mirax's outline, Booster's reflection filled the viewport. "I want to know what happened, who was responsible, *then* we make them pay."

21

As his newly repaired X-wing reverted to realspace and the white tunnel of light came apart all around him, Corran Horn finally recalled the first mention he'd ever seen of the Corvis Minor system. It had taken him a while, but he'd had good reason to remember that little detail. Back when escaping from the *Lusankya*, he'd found a small holdout blaster in a box that was supposed to hold the datacards for a history of the system. *I remember thinking then that if a blaster represented the system's history, it wasn't a vacation spot.*

The uneasiness that memory brought him did not drain away. He checked his sensors and found Three Flight formed up around him. Wedge's One Flight had the lead and Janson's Two Flight had swung slow toward Distna. Nrin Vakil's snoopscoot flew to the rear of Two Flight.

The recon X-wing slowly started to play out a pair of sensor pods connected to the ship by thick cables. They gathered up data to be sorted and stored in computer equipment that occupied all the space that normally would have housed an X-wing's proton torpedo launchers. The recon ship also did without lasers because the charging coils leaked enough energy to overpower the sensitive probes the ship trailed.

If Nrin gets into trouble he can jettison the pods and run, but that's about it. Corran keyed his comm unit. "Nine here. Three Flight in and running. Rear scopes clear."

"Alpha operational. Pods locked in position. Commencing initial run now. Range to target, one thousand kilometers."

Nrin cruised the snoopscoot past Two Flight and flew it with a very gentle hand on the stick. Corran marveled at how the Quarren pilot put the ship through gentle turns and slow rolls that kept the pods spaced evenly apart. Though the pods were not that large—not much larger than spare fuel pods, in fact—trailing them out behind the fighter like that created all sorts of problems by altering the flight characteristics of the X-wing. While fighter jocks considered themselves the elite—and Nrin had ample kills in his history qualifying him as such—his adept handling of the recon ship showed how skilled a pilot he truly was.

"Alpha here, Lead."

"Go ahead, Alpha."

"I am negative for activity from Distna on first pass." Nrin hesitated for a moment. "I would like permission to come in at five hundred klicks. Storm activity in the gas giant may be masking energy readings from the moon's interior."

Tycho's voice came on the comm channel. "Lead, that close a run will move Alpha and escorts out of quick escape range."

"I copy, Two. Nine, please take Three Flight up to guarantee our exit vector."

"As ordered, Lead." Corran rolled starboard and pointed his fighter toward the gas giant. "Three Flight, we're holding the door open."

A series of double clicks on the comm channel confirmed his pilots' understanding of his orders. They spread out a bit and locked their S-foils into attack position. Ooryl remained in Corran's port rear quarter, while Inyri dropped into Asyr's starboard rear quarter.

"Whistler, get me some readings on the storms on that gas giant." As he gave the order Corran tried to tell himself it was because the information would be useful upon their return to Corvis Minor to destroy the Pulsar Station. The logic of that explanation faded both in the light of the data Nrin would be collecting and the fear beginning to trickle into Corran's guts. He stared up at the orange ball streaked with gray and shot through with lightning, fearing a vision of the Pulsar Station rising from the planet's misty depths.

He saw nothing and tried to relax.

Then Whistler hooted anxiously.

Corran glanced at his sensors, then up at the gas giant. Black specs rose up through the clouds, looking for a moment like insects trapped between two panes of transparisteel. Though kilometers distant, he knew what they were: TIE fighters, Interceptors, and Bombers. He keyed his comm unit. "Lead, I have multiple contacts coming up out of CM-Five. Eyeballs, squints, and dupes, enough for a squadron of each."

"I copy, Nine. We've got contacts coming from Distna. Similar numbers."

Corran's mouth went dry. *Six squadrons!* Krennel had deployed a full fighter wing against the Rogues and their positioning meant two things. The first was that the whole Pulsar Station lab was nothing more than bait to lure the Rogues to this place and slaughter them. Corran realized such a conclusion was the height of paranoia, but that didn't shake his conviction that it was right. Everything he'd seen suggested that Krennel was the sort of commander who would stop at nothing to kill his enemies, and Rogue Squadron had made an enemy of Krennel long before Corran had ever joined it.

The second conclusion he came to was that Krennel had sources inside the New Republic that told him when the Rogue operation was going off. Spies had often plagued Rogue Squadron in the past. Corran had vaped one, Erisi Dlarit, but vaping everyone feeding information to Imperials and warlords would be a difficult task. *And a task that would take far more time than we have left to us.*

Because of the vast distances in space, the Rogues and their counterparts could see each other long before they could engage each other. Minutes would pass before they would close to effective fighting ranges. Having time to think about what was coming seldom did a warrior any good—and training was meant to take over when thought wasn't possible. *You're leading Three Flight, Corran. Prep them for what's coming.*

Corran reached out and switched his comm unit to Three Flight's tactical channel. "Okay, Rogues, this is how we do this. Whistler, designate each of the incoming Interceptors with a unique ID number and squirt three of them to each of us. We've got six proton torpedoes and we use them to burn the squints, got it? We engage them at range and pop them, hard. They're likely to be a bit out in front of the others because they'll be wanting kills."

He glanced at his monitor. "Next wave will be the eye-balls. We blow through them and go after the dupes. We want to pull the eyeballs away from our exit vector so Wedge and the others can get out, got it? We mix it up with the dupes and create a lot of targets out there. Call for help when you need it, and let's slag them."

"I copy, Nine." Ooryl's voice came through calm and strong.

"As ordered, Nine." Inyri's voice betrayed no anxiety, but came through a bit subdued.

"Targets logged and firing solutions being prepped, Nine." Asyr's reply carried with it a hint of anger at the audacity of Krennel plotting the ambush. "After we finish our targets, we help the rest of the squadron, right?"

"Right, Eleven." Corran smiled, then punched up the squadron tactical frequency. "Lead, Nine here. We're prepped to hold the door open."

"I copy, Nine. May the Force be with you. We're engaging now."

Corran glanced at his main monitor. "I copy, Lead. We have contact in two minutes."

Out in the distance, the flashes of light from the X-wings boiling into a dogfight could be seen as the flickerings of debris sparking against his shields. He punched up a request for data on Nrin's snoopscoot and saw that it had jettisoned

its pods. Shields looked solid and the changing vector data
on the ship suggested Nrin was dancing it in and out
through the dogfight, offering himself as an elusive target
for the enemy.

Whistler beeped as the last fifteen seconds to target
scrolled down. Corran dropped his aiming reticle over the
distant form of an Interceptor and watched the torpedo targeting box turn yellow. Whistler's beeping increased in intensity and frequency, then became a solid tone as the box
went red. Corran hit his trigger and launched a torpedo.

He immediately punched up his second target Interceptor, but that ship began juking fiercely. He tried to get a lock
on the third, but it bounced around too much as well. *Either they have early warning systems, or they're just being
cautious.*

Other proton torpedoes streaked out from Three Flight
and headed toward the incoming TIEs. Two Interceptors
winked out of existence, but the rest boiled on undaunted.
Corran rolled to port, then pulled back on his stick for a
climb that would take him perpendicular to their line of attack. He inverted, presenting his cockpit canopy to them,
then pulled back on the stick again and rolled onto a course
that brought him in above their flight plane.

The squints began a climb to come up after him, so
he barrel-rolled to port and cruised down toward them.
He nudged his stick right, boxing one of the Interceptors.
The box went red immediately, so Corran pulled the trigger. The proton torpedo shot out and slammed into the
squint at point-blank range. It pierced the ball cockpit, then
exploded, blasting the Interceptor into a microfine hail of
metal, flesh, and fabric.

Corran flew straight through the explosion, then pulled
his X-wing up into a tight loop. He chopped his throttle back
to tighten the loop even more, then targeted his last squint.
The aiming reticle went red and he launched another torpedo. It jetted away on blue flame, then curved up sharply after the Interceptor. The pilot twisted away at the last second,
but the proximity fuse made the torpedo detonate.

As fast as the squint was, it wasn't faster than the

torpedo's shrapnel. A metal storm shredded the starboard solar panels and continued on to hole the cockpit. The ship didn't explode, but it did begin a slow spiral that aimed it toward the gas giant. *Its gravity well is so deep it will swallow that ship whole and pretty much anything else that's left out here.*

An explosion shook Corran's X-wing and he immediately knew he was in serious trouble. One of the TIE Bombers had nailed him with a concussion missile. The fact that he actually felt the residual effects of the blast meant that his inertial compensator wasn't functioning right. His rear shield also showed damage, but before he could shift power around to reinforce it, a squint laced his rear shield with fire, collapsing the shield and pouring energy into his upper starboard S-foil.

Corran felt a weird vibration and heard a corresponding whine for a half second before the engine exploded. The squint's laserfire had melted part of the centrifugal debris extractor, which threw it out of balance and ripped it free of its supports. Parts of it sprayed back through the engine, shattering it and breaking that S-foil clean off. More debris shot out and peppered the starboard side of the fuselage. One huge chunk slammed into the fighter's transparisteel canopy, spalling off fragments. One of them lashed Corran's right cheek, cutting him along the bone, then the atmospheric pressure within the cockpit blew the transparisteel panel and all debris out into space.

The personal magnetic containment bubble projector each pilot was issued clicked on immediately, cocooning Corran in a thin layer of breathable air. Even with a full power charge, Corran knew he'd only have a hour or so of breathable air, and the cold of space would kill him sooner than that. He would have expected such a realization would fill him with fear, but he found a calm inside that surprised him.

And allowed him to act.

He slapped his throttle down to zero, which stopped the port engines from pushing him around in a flat spin. Using the etheric rudder he managed to counter the spin. He got himself oriented, with the gas giant below him and the dogfight above, then keyed his comm device.

"Nine is hit, two engines gone. I have power, so if you bring someone in front of me, I'll shoot them."

No one acknowledged his call, but he knew all of them had more important things to do. *As do I.*

"Whistler, are you okay back there?"

The droid blatted harshly.

"No, I didn't think they would have gotten you. Keep me informed if I have more missiles coming. I'm shifting power to shields now." A glance at his monitors showed the shields greening up nicely, which meant he could survive two or three more runs by a squint before it took him down. It wasn't much, but it was much better than being dead outright.

He reached beneath his command chair and pulled out a small metal box. He unlatched it and, from a compartment built into the lid, pulled out a thick duraplast panel. He brushed away the last traces of transparisteel from the broken panel, then slid the duraplast panel into place. It rattled around a bit, but a tube of sealant from the same kit provided a bead of foam that hardened to hold the panel in place.

Corran closed the box and returned it to its place beneath the seat. *I don't think those repairs were ever supposed to be managed in combat, but I've got nothing else to do at the moment.* The duraplast panel was nowhere near as strong as the transparisteel one it replaced, but it was only meant to hold a single atmosphere in and make the cockpit airtight. It would never deal with laserfire as well as the transparisteel would, but having atmosphere and heat was an immediate concern for Corran.

"Whistler, give me more atmosphere and push the heat."

When life-support indicators rose enough, Corran turned off the magcon device. Heat hit him solidly, but a shiver ran through his body anyway. "Two engines gone, I'm dead."

Whistler's keening tone sliced through his self-pity.

Corran glanced at his monitor and smiled. "You're ght, I still have torps and some lasers. Might be dead, but I an also be a nasty corpse. Get me a readout on the battle."

The data dump Whistler provided stunned Corran. hree Flight had faced thirty-six TIEs, but that number had lready been pared down to twenty-one. Corran had three onfirmed kills. The same went for Ooryl and Inyri had our. Asyr had accounted for five and even as he studied the ata, another one was toted up as a kill.

Corran ruddered the X-wing around to find her. Her -wing flashed through the dogfight with a pair of TIEs hot n her tail. She had the X-wing dancing up and down and de to side, letting their lasers slash green bolts wide. In the istance some of the bolts hit other TIEs, and somewhere long her line of flight an eyeball or dupe would catch her uad laserfire. Asyr was flying as he'd never seen her fly efore.

Asyr's X-wing broke hard to port, then immediately lled up onto its starboard S-foil and cut back along the ay it had come. A roll back to port brought her ship back n the tails of the TIEs that had been following her and anaged to overshoot her as she pulled the tight turns. A uartet of red laser bolts burned through one eyeball, let-ng loose a seething golden cloud of energy that devoured e ship.

A little rudder reoriented her ship and let her blast her cond TIE. The shots evaporated the fighter's starboard so-r panel. It began a roll that took it high and out toward e gas giant. Asyr made no attempt to follow it or fire gain. She rolled right and started a climb right back into e fight.

Which was when her X-wing collided with a dupe. At e speeds the two ships were traveling, there was no chance r avoidance. The shields in front of the X-wing sparked as ey hit the dupe first, crumpling the starboard solar panel. hey drove it back against the ball cockpit, and shattered e transparisteel viewport. At that point the X-wing's for-ard shield flashed opaquely, then imploded.

The X-wing's nose stabbed into the dupe's cockpit and

lodged deeply. The slender fighter's nose snapped off about a meter in front of the cockpit. Unspent proton torpedoes spilled out as the aft end of the fighter tumbled up and away from the Bomber. The broken Imp craft continued its flight toward the gas giant, while the remains of Asyr's rapidly disintegrating X-wing launched themselves up and away from the planet.

"Asyr, do you copy?" Corran dialed up the gain on his comm unit. "Asyr, repeat, do you copy?"

He got no reply from her, but another message blared loud through his comm channel. "Rogues, Interloper and Stranger squadrons are friendlies. Don't make us defend ourselves."

"What in the shadows of Coruscant?" Corran looked down at his main monitor. It showed a dozen new contacts which appeared as red specs on his monitor, indicating they were using Imperial ID codes. He selected one of them as a target and an image of the ship presented itself on his screen.

The fighter had a TIE's ball cockpit and an Interceptor's canted wings, but all in a very unusual configuration. The wings had been turned so they canted out, not in as they did on the Interceptor. There were also three of the wings, one mounted above the cockpit and the other two at angles that allowed them to cover low port and starboard. More important, the sensors indicated the ships were sporting shields and had enough power output to support hyperspace drives.

Whoever the new arrivals were, they fell on the remains of Krennel's pilots with a vengeance. Three Flight had all but evened the odds for the new fighters, which Corran choose to designate as "trips" for their triple wings. The trips let off a volley of proton torpedoes that savaged the remaining Bombers, then they swooped in on the eyeballs. Quad bursts of green lasers melted TIEs ruthlessly. Within five minutes of their intervention, the trips had destroyed all of Krennel's forces.

·　　　·　　　·

Rogue Squadron regrouped on the exit vector, with Corran's ship limping along. Wedge's voice filled the comm channel. "I appreciate the fact that you saved us, and I'm willing to accompany you out of here. I even understand the need for comm silence, but I can't leave without seeing to the pilots who are extra-vehicular."

"General Antilles, I understand your protest and have logged it." Colonel Vessery, the commander of what had been identified as two squadrons of TIE Defenders, spoke in strong, even tones. "We've made runs looking for survivors, but we find no traces. We have to leave now. Krennel will be sending reinforcements and you're in no shape to survive another fight."

The comm channel remained dead for a moment, then Wedge replied, his voice weary. "You're right. It's just . . ."

"I know, General. It's always been said you were an honorable man." Vessery's voice carried compassion with it. "Eight and Twelve, if you will tractor your charges, we can head home."

A little shudder ran through Corran's fighter. A Defender latched on to his ship with a tractor beam and would accelerate him to the appropriate speed to make the jump to lightspeed. On only two engines Corran's ship wouldn't have made it, though those engines were enough to power his hyperdrive. He slaved his navigation to that of Interloper Eight.

It's just as well. I don't think I want to be flying right now. He sat back and shivered. Three Flight had lost Asyr, but the rest of the squadron lost three other pilots. Khe-Jeen Slee had been the first to die, followed by Lyyr Zatoq and then Wes Janson. Corran had a hard time believing Janson was dead, but a concussion missile had blown the back off his fighter and left his body floating in space. All three of the pilots had been people he thought of as friends, but already his memories of them were beginning to fade.

Corran punched up One Flight's tactical channel. "Lead, is it safe to be going with these guys?"

"I don't know, Nine. They *invited* us to travel, but they could compel it, too." Wedge sighed. "Still, they came along at the right time to keep us alive. Whoever they work for doesn't want us dead."

"Yet."

"Good point, Nine." Wedge grunted a chuckle out. "Let's hope we're in better shape to deal with them when they change their minds."

22

Prince-Admiral Delak Krennel reveled in the pain evident on Mon Mothma's face. The New Republic's leader stood only a meter and a half tall in holo and was being rebroadcast to him by Isard, but he could still see how much the woman ached as she spoke. The interviewing journalist's question had clearly caught her off guard, but the answer she gave spoke to her quick wits and the depth of her personal knowledge.

"The question asked was if the rumors of the destruction of Rogue Squadron in the Hegemony theater are correct. As you know, we are prosecuting a war against Delak Krennel and his Hegemony and any comments about ongoing operations stand to jeopardize personnel involved in those operations. I'm certain that none of us here would like to cost the brave men and women of Rogue Squadron their lives, nor put into jeopardy the lives of anyone supporting them in their missions.

"Warfare, as all of us know, is seldom a clean business with crisp, clear results. Rogue Squadron and its leader, General Antilles, are well aware of this fact. Pending further investigation all I am willing to say is that Rogue Squadron was involved in a mission that resulted in an unforeseen set of circumstances. I know you all hope for the best for these brave fighters, and we will provide updates as information is forthcoming."

Mon Mothma's figure froze and the holocam on the other side of the connection panned up to frame Isard's head and shoulders. "There you have it, Prince-Admiral. Rogue Squadron is no more."

Krennel nodded slowly. Two days previously Isard had given him word that Rogue Squadron was about to fall into her trap. Information from Corvis Minor had indicated that there was an engagement and no word was received from the Hegemony fighter wing that had been hidden in the Distna area to spring the trap. Observers on the *Aspiration* had little to report and only after Krennel insisted had they sent a shuttle out to the area of the battle. The shuttle found virtually nothing in the way of debris and the *Aspiration* did report, well after the fact, that another Imperial Star Destroyer had visited the battleground before they sent their shuttle out. The Captain said he had assumed the Star Destroyer was one of Krennel's on a mission connected with the ambush, so he had done nothing to hail it or interfere with it.

"So, Isard, you do not find it disturbing that we have heard nothing from the fighters you had stationed at Distna?"

The slender woman stroked her sharp chin with a hand, then trailed her fingers down her throat. "A matter of concern, yes. Their silence, and the fact we could find no trace of any ships at the ambush site, means the mystery Destroyer likely scooped up whatever there was left over. What I find intriguing about that is very simple: Aside from the New Republic, the only people running around with Imperial Star Destroyers are other warlords, a pirate or two, and Booster Terrik. Terrik has a son-in-law in the squadron. Since no other warlord or pirate has claimed to have smashed Rogue Squadron, I assume Terrik did the recovery. Anything he learned he would have passed to the New Republic. Since the Rogues faced a foe that outnumbered them six to one, the survival of *any* of the Rogues would have been broadcast immediately."

"So you are suggesting that no news from the New Republic indicates that your ambush was wholly successful?"

"I think that conclusion is warranted."

"What of the pilots of ours who survived?"

Isard shrugged. "I would guess there were fewer survivors than either of us would care to imagine. While your Hegemony troops have heart and a desire to protect their homeworlds, their level of training is hardly up to Imperial standards. Those who did survive probably found themselves under the guns of the *Errant Venture* and chose to surrender. Terrik probably promised them freedom and money in return for their ships and stories."

"When you find them, have them slain." Krennel rose from the command chair in his ready room on the *Reckoning* and stared out the viewport at the black expanse studded with a rainbow of stars. "The loss of six squadrons of fighters is annoying, even if they did destroy Rogue Squadron. Replacing them will not be easy."

"Your fighters, or Rogue Squadron?"

"My fighters."

Isard smiled. "Actually, you will find that replacing them might not be so difficult. Thrawn showed that the New Republic was not invulnerable, and you are proving that they are not as mighty as once had been believed. We have already begun to get inquiries—careful, guarded inquiries—from a variety of groups who realize the Empire is waning and cannot bring themselves to support the warlords. Your battle against the New Republic seems to them to be the last chance to preserve life as they knew it."

Krennel's head came up. "Have you had word from Pellaeon?"

"None, my lord, but he will come around. Soon. After your victory."

"Indeed, after my victory." Krennel chuckled. "I expect you to keep digging into the New Republic's affairs and determine if Rogue Squadron is truly gone or not."

"I shall, Prince-Admiral." Isard nodded slowly. "I suspect, however, what you accomplish now will occupy more of their time and consideration."

"It shall." Krennel waved a hand dismissively at her. "Krennel out."

Isard's image faded, but not before a momentary flash of anger arced through her eyes. Krennel knew that dismissing her would anger her, but he wanted her distracted. When she came to him originally, she said her agenda was the destruction of Rogue Squadron. That had been accomplished, which left her needing a new goal. He expected it would be supplanting him. Knowing that, he wanted her to be angry enough to plan a vicious downfall for him—which he would prevent by eliminating her the moment she outlived her usefulness.

Krennel did have to admit she had been very useful. Isard had an understanding of politics that he did not possess. The idea of negotiating with the homeless pacifists of Alderaan had been enough to turn his stomach, but the pressure they put on the New Republic when the world he said he had been intending to give turned out to be Liinade III had been terrific. A variety of sources suggested that a second series of attacks had been delayed by the internecine squabbling within the Provisional Council.

Likewise her handling of the Pulsar Station controversy had been masterful. It sowed distrust between the government and the people. The loss of Rogue Squadron—and Krennel had no doubt that the journalist who asked the question about them was on Isard's payroll—would further undermine the New Republic's war effort. Isard had been very effective in fighting the New Republic on the political front.

War may be seen by some as political action carried to the extreme, but I know there is a difference. Krennel turned to watch the Interdictor Cruiser *Binder* drift up alongside his Imperial Star Destroyer *Reckoning*. *Warfare is a different beast, where power is displayed in its raw and naked form and there is no running or hiding from it. In politics one seeks to bend another to his will. In war the object is to shatter another completely, so neither he nor his will offers further resistance.*

"Warfare is what I do best." Krennel pulled a comlink from his pocket. "Communications, get me Captain Phulik of the *Binder*."

"As ordered, Prince-Admiral."

Phulik's holograph flashed to life. "At your service, Prince-Admiral."

Krennel looked down at the image of the portly man. "It is time for you to power up your gravity wells, Captain Phulik. Your gunners will concentrate on vectors five and six. We will cover the rest."

"Gunnery solutions are already locked in, Prince-Admiral. My people await your command to fire." Phulik looked off cam for a moment. "Gravity wells coming up, *now*."

A slight tremor ran through the *Reckoning* as the Interdictor's gravity wells powered up. Their power was sufficient to momentarily override the inertial compensators built into the larger ship. With all four gravity wells online, the *Binder* now projected a hyperspace mass shadow roughly equivalent to a good-sized planet. Any ships moving through hyperspace in the area would automatically revert to realspace, since the alternative was to smash into whatever was creating the shadow.

Interdictor cruisers often accompanied larger ships on missions because they prevented enemy ships from escaping into hyperspace. Any course laid through hyperspace had to avoid gravitic anomalies, so transit routes were plotted out with precision and, depending upon where bodies were in their orbits around a star, a system could be wide open, or only have a narrowly defined route through it. The advantages of flying through or near systems came if a ship suffered damage, since out in deep space the chance of being rescued was slender. An Interdictor's presence in a system changed the system profile, requiring new escape routes to be plotted and ships to head far enough away from the Interdictor to escape its gravity well and make it into hyperspace.

Krennel was not interested in the escape of ships in the system, but with the transit through it. The routes that connected Liinade III with worlds outside the Hegemony were few in number. The system in which he waited sat astride one of the routes and didn't even rate a name: Imperial surveyors had only designated it M2934738. While it did not provide the most direct path from the New Republic to Liinade III, it did allow for a quicker transit than many of the other routes.

The only problem the New Republic had with taking Liinade III was in supplying it and the troops on it. Even before hostilities had ceased, New Republic supply ships began ferrying in a variety of necessities, from medicine to munitions, spare parts to food. The New Republic clearly intended to use Liinade III as a staging area for further operations in the Hegemony, so the buildup continued.

Continued until now. Isard had been correct in noting that a victory against the New Republic would create even more opposition to the war against the Hegemony. A direct assault on Liinade III would prove very costly in men and materials. Cutting the supply line to Liinade III would weaken the garrison *and* provide him his victory, so, using information from Isard's sources within the New Republic, Krennel laid his ambush.

The New Republic supply convoy came out of hyperspace in the middle of M2934738. It consisted of a dozen freighters, a *Nebulon-B*–class Frigate, and two Corellian Corvettes. The two smaller warships drove hard toward the *Reckoning*, their double turbolaser cannons blazing away, but the Imperial Star Destroyer Mark II's shields and hull absorbed the damage without significant difficulty. The Nebulon-B Frigate made a run at the Interdictor, with the freighters scattering in its wake.

Krennel's forward gunners targeted the lead Corvette, a ship called *Pride of Selonia*. Heavy turbolaser fire crushed the ship's forward shields, then burned tattered, black furrows along the ship's hull. Debris and bodies vented into space, expelled by flaming gouts of superheated atmosphere. Heavy turbolaser cannons scattered shots over the bridge and back along the ship's spine, destroying its communications array. In one terrible swift salvo, the *Pride of Selonia* went from being a warship crewed by brave individuals to a floating charnel ship trailing webs of congealed metal.

The Frigate *Intrepid* fired its turbolaser batteries and laser cannons at *Binder*, but the Interdictor's shields deflected their fury. Instead of firing back at the *Intrepid*, *Binder*'s gunners shot at two freighters, each one making a run toward one of the exit vectors the Interdictor had been told to control. Quad laser cannon fire linked the Interdictor to the fleeing freighters with a stream of red-gold bolts. The laserfire pierced the freighters' shields and burned through them, leaving each ship a burning hulk floating in an escape lane.

Another salvo melted the front half of the second Corvette, leaving it to tumble out into space. The *Reckoning*'s ion cannons laced fleeing freighters with blue bolts that sank each in a lightning storm. Shields imploded and components exploded, rendering the small supply ships helpless. Escape pods burst forth from their hulls and Krennel chuckled. *Either we pick them up or they die out here. There is no escape for them.*

Intrepid again fired on *Binder*, and with its second salvo managed to punch through a shield and score the Interdictor's hull. Krennel immediately flicked his comlink on. "Gunners, this is Prince-Admiral Krennel. Break *Intrepid*'s back."

The *Reckoning*'s turbolaser fire concentrated itself on the Frigate's slender neck, which connected the bridge with the aft drive portion of the ship. Red-gold energy lances stabbed through the shields and drilled deep into the ship's structure. Hull plates bubbled up into vapor and drifted away while energy bolts disintegrated bulkheads and deck. Crew members caught at the point of assault exploded into flames and died before they were even aware of their danger.

All the energy being poured into *Intrepid* gnawed at the durasteel support structures, weakening them and making some run like ice under a welding torch. The drive portion of the ship still pushed the massive craft forward, causing the ship's narrow hull to buckle and begin to telescope. More structures gave way, allowing the drive portion to sheer off the bottom of the neck, which started to pitch the bridge portion higher. The bridge began a long, lazy somersault and—like a flower spilling pollen—escape pods erupted from it and flew away.

Krennel watched and nodded, then even allowed himself a smile. Grand Admiral Thrawn had always maintained that studying the art of a people would give an insight into how to deal with them. What Krennel saw floating in system M2934738 appeared to him to be art, and he very much enjoyed the fact that he had created it. *How better to be the artist than to be the one studying the art.*

He flicked his comlink over to a channel that would address the *Reckoning*'s crew. "This is Prince-Admiral Krennel. You have all done very well today. I want recovery crews out there to pick up the freighters we have disabled and bring their supplies to us." He hesitated for a moment, mulling a point over, then decided to address it in a way he thought Isard would approve of. "I want shuttles to go out to see to the escape pods. Inform the people in them that we are fighting the New Republic, not them. We will take them aboard and return them to the New Republic, asking only their parole. As long as they agree not to fly or fight for the New Republic for the duration of its war with the Hegemony, they will be free to go. Otherwise we will treat them as prisoners of war and house them in accord with all civilized regulations concerning such prisoners. Krennel out."

He allowed himself a smile, and imagined the praise Isard would heap upon him for his decision concerning the prisoners. *She may know politics, but I am learning. When I know enough, I will no longer need her. That day will come sooner than she can imagine, to her regret and my great joy.*

23

Wedge Antilles was glad Colonel Vessery remained silent as they walked through the interloper's base. Wedge didn't know where they were and respected Vessery's being tight-lipped about their location. The base looked relatively new and decidedly Imperial, with personnel being almost entirely human, mostly male, and outfitted with Imperial uniforms.

Broak Vessery could have stepped from a recruiting poster. He stood a bit taller than Wedge, with black hair that was beginning to lighten at the temples and sharp, no-ble features. His grip was firm when they met face-to-face for the first time and shook hands. He chose his words care-fully, it seemed to Wedge, and had a nervous habit of pick-ing all-but-invisible pieces of lint from the sleeves of his black jumpsuit.

Wedge walked beside him and realized that he ought to be drinking in more of the base's details. The two squadrons that had come to rescue the Rogues had more TIE Defend-ers in them than Wedge thought had ever been manufac-tured. He wouldn't have been surprised to find out that the base belonged to High Admiral Teradoc or even had been set up by Grand Admiral Thrawn. *And if that's the case, I should be gathering all sorts of intelligence here.*

The industrious portion of his mind couldn't shift the weight of his emotions and the numbness he felt inside. He'd lost four pilots in the Distna ambush. While part of him acknowledged that survival rate was miraculous considering the odds they faced, the pilots resisted becoming statistics. Lyyr and Slee had been relatively new to the squadron, but the fact that he identified them by their first names meant they'd gotten past the defenses he usually raised against getting to know new pilots.

Asyr's loss sent a chill through him. He'd liked her and admired how she had defied the Bothan hierarchy in continuing her membership in the squadron and her relationship with Gavin. Asyr never compromised or backed down from a fight. Her spirit and determination had always pushed everyone in the squadron to perform at their highest level. The pride that the Bothans felt in her exploits meant Borsk Fey'lya and other politicians left the squadron largely alone.

Wes Janson's death—Wedge couldn't even begin to think about it without feeling an invisible hand squeeze his heart. He'd known Wes for what seemed like forever. They'd been through everything together since just after Yavin to when the squadron had been re-formed. After the overthrow of Isard's regime on Thyferra, Janson had joined Wedge in running Wraith Squadron, then had stuck with him during the Thrawn crisis. Though Janson's sense of humor rankled from time to time, Wedge would have given his right arm to have Janson pop up with a quick "Yub, yub, Commander."

Vessery looked over at Wedge. "I don't wish to intrude on your thoughts, but I have two things to say to you."

Wedge sniffed and blinked. "Please, Colonel."

"First, I wish my people and I had gotten there sooner. I count the deaths of your people as failures on my part. Traveling through hyperspace seldom allows one to get split-second rescues right, but I should have. If I had trimmed some margins on some of the courses, we'd have been there on time."

Vessery's voice came low and sincere, bringing a solemn nod from Wedge. "Thank you, Colonel. You couldn't know exactly when they would strike, so it's not your fault. The fact that you *did* arrive means we lived, and for that I'll be eternally grateful."

"You are too kind, General." Vessery paused before a door. "The second thing I would like to say to you is this: The person you'll meet in here is responsible for our arrival. Without orders originating from this office, Rogue Squadron would be dead. Try to remember that."

Wedge frowned. "You shouldn't believe Imperial propaganda, Colonel. New Republic officers can be very grateful and gracious."

"Good." Vessery punched a code into the keypad on the lockplate and the door slid open. He waved Wedge into the darkened room. "After you."

Wedge entered the darkness boldly, striding ahead for the full length of the patch of light streaming in through the door. When the door closed and cut off the illumination, he stopped and clasped his hands at the small of his back. He heard the scrape of Vessery's boots on the floor as the other pilot joined him.

The lights in the room came slowly up, infusing an orange glow into the wooden strips that formed the walls, floor, and ceiling of the oval room. The woods had been fitted together with such precision and artistry that the growth rings and grain formed exquisite patterns in which the casual observer could easily become lost. Cabinets built into the walls were faced with great slabs of golden brown wood featuring wonderful grain markings into and out of which the wall designs flowed. While everything remained static, the eye was drawn through an intricate tracery of lines that made the room seem alive.

The desk across from the door had likewise been fashioned of heavily patterned wood and seemed as if it had grown up out of the floor. The back of the chair behind it rose above the head of the person seated in it and matched the wood designs of the wall. It took Wedge a moment to recognize who he was looking at, then that realization tightened his guts and threatened to drop him to his knees.

He couldn't remember ever having seen her in the flesh, but her image had been burned into his brain during the years after Endor. She still wore the scarlet uniform that had been her trademark, though her hair had gone completely white and her face and figure had thickened slightly. She was still a handsome woman, but had slipped beyond middle age toward becoming a matron.

Any thought that she might have softened was banished by her eyes. One, a bright, icy blue, reminded him of the coldest day on Hoth, when ice screamed and cracked. The other, a fiery red, burned into him, searing his spirit. He'd thought her dead at Thyferra and even though the Commenor prisoners had said they'd seen her, he'd refused to believe she lived until he saw her now.

Wedge's brown eyes narrowed. "General Wedge Antilles reporting."

Ysanne Isard stood slowly behind her desk. "You know who I am. It is interesting that we have not met before, you and I, having been foes for so long. I expected you to be taller."

"I expected you to be dead."

She nodded. "Defiant, I like that. It makes you an interesting enemy and, I trust, a more interesting ally."

Wedge blinked. "Me, an ally? After what you did with the prisoners on Commenor, leaving them to starve like that?" He turned to Colonel Vessery. "You can take me away from here now."

Isard raised her hand. "If you will indulge me, General, I will explain a great many things to you. You owe me at least that much, since I sent Colonel Vessery to save you."

That remark brought Wedge's chin up. "After all you have done, the debt I feel to you for saving us is still very small."

"Of this I have no doubt." Isard leaned forward on her desk. "After I had taken control of Thyferra and you began your campaign to oust me, I realized that *if* you succeeded, I wished to rob you of the goal you truly sought: the prisoners from my *Lusankya*. I decided to scatter them. This was a mission I felt I could entrust to no one—it was one I wanted to handle myself, but I was needed on Thyferra. What I did was activate a clone of myself, lead her to believe she *was* me, and charge her with the task of scattering the *Lusankya* prisoners. When she returned to Thyferra with her task complete, I had her killed—or so I thought."

Isard's face hardened as scorn entered her voice. "Your assault on Thyferra meant the job was not completed and the clone survived. How and why she was not recognized as me, I have no idea, but she believes she truly *is* me. She spent the time during the Thrawn crisis gathering the *Lusankya* prisoners back up and now has them ensconced on Ciutric."

Wedge shook his head. "Explain the prisoners on Commenor."

"Bait, for a trap." Isard shook her head. "She wanted to lure Rogue Squadron to Distna so you could be ambushed, but she did a poor job of layering her clues into the site. She was trying to be too smart and too clever. Mirax Terrik and Iella Wessiri returned to Commenor and discovered the clues she'd left there, but you were already in the Hegemony and involved in the war against Krennel, so the *Lusankya* rescue became of secondary importance. She never saw that."

"But we went to Distna because of the Pulsar Station problem."

Isard smiled and Wedge decided that her smile was not a pleasant thing to see. "Yes, and Krennel's protestations of innocence sounded genuine because they were. The lab you discovered on Liinade Three was one I had constructed there. I wanted you to go to Distna because I wanted Colonel Vessery to help you defeat Krennel's people. Without rendering that sort of direct aid to you, you never would believe that I could be your ally."

"I don't believe it now." Wedge's eyes became slits. "You could have sent an embassy to the New Republic if you sought an alliance."

She snorted a laugh. "They'd no more have believed it than you do, but you already know things that point to my sincerity."

"Such as?"

"Such as my ability to build the lab on Liinade Three. That means I have thoroughly compromised Krennel's security. How? My clone is using the procedures and codes I would have used. In this same way I knew she wanted to ambush you at Distna, so I arranged for you to be saved. As far as the New Republic and Krennel are concerned, however, both forces wiped each other out. This means no one knows you are alive, which is something I also desired."

Wedge thought for a moment. Isard's point about having compromised Krennel's security was right, and she *had* sent Vessery and his people to spoil the clone's ambush. *Granted, Isard got us there, too, with the Pulsar Station decoy, but the clone's clues would have been found and led us there in any event.* Isard had put together an elaborate charade that had Rogue Squadron dead, and therefore, she had an ulterior motive in mind.

"What is it you want, Isard?"

She sighed heavily and let her head slump forward. "My battle with you, my ouster from Thyferra, and even Thrawn's unsuccessful campaign to reestablish the Empire has shown me that the cause I held dear is dead. This does not mean I like the New Republic or consider it an improvement over the Empire. I just no longer have the will to oppose it. I want peace. I want to be left alone."

She heaved her torso up and opened her arms. "After escaping Thyferra I made my way to this place, one of many hidden facilities within the Empire. A General Arnothian was in charge here. This facility is capable of producing TIE Defenders, and Arnothian saw himself as a warlord in training. He refused to relinquish control of the station to me, so he was dealt with. I watched events unfold throughout the Thrawn crisis but chose not to intervene. I realized this place could be a base from which I could continue a campaign of terror against the New Republic, but to do so would be to sully the commitment to the Empire made by Colonel Vessery and his men.

"I realized that for us to be sanctioned by the New Republic, I would have to offer them a grand prize, and offer it in a manner that would not cost them a lot of blood. I decided that prize would be Delak Krennel and his Hegemony. I decided I would put into position the forces that would allow the New Republic to take Ciutric and shatter his power, and I decided Rogue Squadron would be the key to that operation."

Wedge frowned. "I don't understand."

"You will." Isard smiled and touched a button on a datapad on her desk. An image of a man with a metal prosthesis covering the right side of his face, replacing that eye, and an artificial right forearm and hand burned to life in the middle of the room. "You will recall your posing as Colonel Antar Roat?"

A trickle of ice ran through Wedge's guts. "I assumed the Roat identity when slipping onto Coruscant to liberate it."

"I have taken the liberty of updating Roat's profile to reflect his being in charge of an experimental unit—two full flights—of TIE Defenders. You are in the process of negotiating a deal with Krennel that will bring your force in as part of his troops. You are one of many Imperials offering their services to him. You'll be able to slip into Ciutric and wreak havoc there. What you did on Imperial Center to free it, you can do on Ciutric."

Wedge ran a hand over his stubbly chin. "You'll give us Krennel to get the New Republic to leave you alone?"

"I do not expect public rehabilitation, just a quiet retirement." Isard smiled coldly. "As for *why* Krennel, you know as well as I do that he defied my orders in the Pestage matter. I also want my clone eliminated. One of me is enough."

"I heartily concur."

"I thought you might." Isard opened her hands. "You and your people will begin training in Defenders immediately. We will work up a plan of attack that will involve a New Republic fleet. When the attack is set, you will communicate with the New Republic to let them know when to strike. We can't communicate with them too early because my clone still has some intelligence resources in the New Republic. If there is a leak, the mission will be doomed."

Wedge nodded, then looked up. "If we refuse to help you?"

Isard arched an eyebrow at him. "Refuse?"

Vessery cleared his throat. "If you refuse, General, then my men will go into Ciutric in your place. Krennel will fall, but not quite so bloodlessly. He has to." The Imperial pilot rested a hand on Wedge's shoulder. "Despite our differences, you and I are united in the knowledge that Krennel is a scourge on the Hegemony's people. He must be dealt with, and with your help, his disposition will bring other warlords in line."

Wedge felt a shiver run down his spine. *I know I can't trust you, Isard, but I also know that if I don't go along with your plan, you can kill me and my people, and no one will know you're out here until too late. I don't know what your plan is, but I know you have one, and that, for now, is enough.*

He nodded slowly. "I hate to think you and I are of like mind in anything, Isard, but the desire to see Krennel taken down seems to qualify. Rogue Squadron is at your disposal. Let's get started."

24

Corran Horn rested a hand on Gavin Darklighter's shoulder, noticing how the dark green of his own flight suit contrasted with the bright orange of Gavin's. He felt the younger man stiffen, so he gave Gavin's shoulder a squeeze and slowly lowered himself to a spot on the concussion missile storage crate. "I hope you don't mind my sitting here, Gavin."

The younger pilot looked at him with red-rimmed brown eyes. "I'd really rather be alone."

"I know you would, Gavin, which is why I'm sitting here." Corran's left hand slipped from Gavin's right shoulder and patted the man's knee. "I remember, back when we were first on Coruscant, you came to me to ask me about Asyr and if things could work between you. You wanted some perspective then, and you *need* some perspective now."

"No, Corran, what I need now is grieving."

"I know." The bleak pain in Gavin's voice stabbed deep into Corran's heart and threatened to reopen the wound left there by his own father's death. *No, now's not the time for self-pity.* "Look, Gavin, there's all kinds of trite things I could tell you. I could tell you that I've been where you are, when my father died. I could tell you the same things that folks told me at that time, that I had to buck up, I had to be tough, because that's what my father would have wanted of me. And you and I both know, that's what Asyr would have wanted of you."

Gavin sniffed and glanced over at him. "You're right. That's pretty trite and doesn't help at all."

Corran nodded and glanced around the hangar area into which the surviving Rogues had been conducted. The site itself appeared to be vintage Imperial—the Rogues had been in enough captured facilities to know the architectural style. The main difference here was that Imperials were in full force, and three squadrons of TIE Defenders filled the launching racks above the scattered X-wings. The R2 and R5 units milled about together, while the pilots had broken up into small groups, each one dealing with the loss of his comrades and wondering what news General Antilles would bring on his return.

"I know that, Gavin, which is why I'm going to share something with you that I've not shared with another living being—except Iella. Even Mirax doesn't know this." He took a deep breath and hesitated until Gavin nodded slightly. "You've heard how my father died, but not my mother. In CorSec, given what my father and I were doing for a living, we figured that we were more likely to die than she ever was, but she went first. It was a stupid landspeeder accident. A truck was blocking the other lane, some lum-dumb whipped around it and smashed head-on into her. It busted her up badly, too badly for bacta to help.

"My father and I arrived at the hospital as fast as we could, and we were allowed to visit her. We'd been told she had no chance, there'd just been too much damage. She knew that, but she lay there in bed just talking to us about what we'd be doing the next week and month. She wasn't regretting the fact that she'd not be there with us, but pretty much letting us know that she would be, in our memories and in our hearts. The whole time she was dying, she just went on living. And when she finally closed her eyes, it came as a surprise to everyone, her included."

Corran brushed a hand across his face, smearing tears away to nothingness. "Understand this, Gavin, the pain you're feeling right now, it never really goes away. It will always be there, and you can find it whenever you want to, but, in time, the amount it dominates your life will shrink. It will become a small part of the memories you'll have of Asyr, and the good memories will dominate. You can't see that now, and telling you this now doesn't mean much, but you need to hear it to know the sphere of pain you're in isn't inescapable."

Gavin rested his head on his hands, with the heels of his palms grinding into his eye sockets. "It was in the squadron that the first person I actually knew died: Lujayne Forge."

"I remember."

"And I remember wondering if I could have saved her. I wonder the same thing about Asyr."

"You're not alone. But let me tell you, Asyr was wondering what she could do to save us. She was magnificent out there, Gavin, flying beyond herself." Corran rubbed his left hand over Gavin's back. "All of us knew we were in a hopeless situation, but she understood it and rejected it. It was as though she stopped being a flesh and blood pilot and became flight and fight and death all rolled into one. We didn't fail her, nor she us, but some obscure rule of the universe broke her ship and grounded her back in reality. She was truly stellar and, after that performance, I don't know that there was any way for her to return to just being mortal."

Gavin sighed and sat back, raising his face toward the dim ceiling of the cavernous room. "That's it, though, now, isn't it? She's no longer mortal. She joins my cousin Biggs and Lujayne Forge and Wes Janson and Dack and the others on the Rogue Squadron roll of the dead. The Bothans will have another Martyr to celebrate."

Corran's eyes narrowed. "And you're afraid that they'll take her away from you, right? You're afraid the Asyr you knew will be forgotten as she's memorialized?"

Gavin's lips pressed together tightly, his goatee bristling. His larynx bobbed up and down once, then he nodded, splashing tears down his cheeks. His voice failed him as he first tried to speak. He rubbed his throat, then nodded. "I think I knew her better than anyone and that, with me, in private moments, she could relax. She didn't have to be a Bothan hero. She didn't have to be a pilot. She could just be herself. When we talked about getting married, adopting kids, she came alive."

His voice trailed off and Corran sensed a flash of anger like lightning run through Gavin. "What is it, Gavin?"

He frowned. "She met with Borsk Fey'lya. She didn't tell me what happened, but I think he tried to make trouble for her about adopting. I think she may have fought as well as she did at Distna in the hopes that no one, not Fey'lya, not anyone, could deny a hero of her stature what she wanted. She would have gotten her way, but now she's dead, so the point is moot."

"Maybe your chance to adopt kids with her is gone, but remember what was behind that whole plan: the fact that you'd make great parents. I'm not going to tell you that you owe it to her to continue on and prove her right, but you can bet the Emperor's Black Bones that I'd rather see you teaching a child right from wrong than any of a billion ex-Imp bureaucrats."

"Maybe it's a plan for the future." Gavin shook his head slowly. "Admitting there's a future at all is the tough part right now. I don't really care and I hurt enough that if there isn't one, it's all the same to me."

A fearful bleating from Whistler and the droid's sudden appearance as he raced around from behind Corran stopped the pilot's response to his friend. "What's the matter?"

Clattering after the droid came an Imperial tech with a restraining bolt and a welding rod. "Gotta put a restraining bolt on him. All droids get them."

Corran shot to his feet. "I can tell you where you can affix that restraining bolt, Huttpuss-for-brains."

The tech raised a hand and two armor-clad storm-troopers came jogging over, blasters in hand. "You want to get out of the way, Captain Horn."

"You've no idea what I want." Corran dropped a hand

to the lightsaber hanging at his left hip. "You're putting a restraining bolt on Whistler over my dead body."

The tech raised an eyebrow. "Over your *stunned* body, perhaps. I have my orders."

"Back off, Captain Horn." Wedge Antilles entered the hangar area and headed toward the confrontation, drawing the rest of the squadron in his wake. "Let's not make things more complicated than they need to be."

Corran turned to Wedge, and was pleased to notice that Gavin had risen to his feet and was shielding Whistler with his own body. "General, they want to put a restraining bolt on Whistler."

Wedge nodded solemnly. "I know, all our droids get them, even Gate." He held up a hand to forestall comment. "The situation here is complicated, but it's working in our favor. We're going to be trained to fly these Defenders, then we'll be given a back door into Krennel's capital. We're dead right now and if we can stay that way—as far as Krennel is concerned—until we're ready to strike, he will fall and fall hard. What that means, though, is that our droids have to be stored away for the time being."

Tycho arched an eyebrow. "Hostages?"

Wedge shook his head. "Just more variables than can be controlled right now. They'll be locked away, safe, out of trouble."

Corran frowned. "I don't like it, but if you say that's the way it has to be . . ." He walked over to the tech and snatched the restraining bolt and welding rod from the man's hands, then dropped to one knee in front of Whistler. "Sorry to do this, pal, but it's not the first time. You'll get through it."

He pressed the bolt to the droid's chest panel, then turned to the tech. "Okay with you?"

"A little to the left."

Corran made the adjustment, then used the welding rod to fix the bolt in place with a shower of sparks.

The tech pointed a remote at Whistler, hit a button, and the droid shut down. Another button and Whistler was back on, moaning mournfully.

Corran rose in one swift motion and gently tapped the tech under the chin with his dormant lightsaber. "Hey, just because you have the power, don't abuse it."

Wedge laid his hand on Corran's forearm. "Put it away, Captain. The tech here will take good care of all the droids, won't you?"

"Lock 'em up snug and tight." He glanced at Corran. "I may not understand your attachment to the droids, but I'll respect it. We aren't all heartless monsters."

"Good." Corran smiled coldly and tapped the man on his chest with the lightsaber. "Something happens to Whistler and you will be. You have my promise on that."

Borsk Fey'lya was not accustomed to being kept waiting, but he understood Booster Terrik's game and decided to humor him. The Bothan Councilor had never before been on the *Errant Venture*, and he occupied his time studying the ship. He recalled his ire when General Cracken reported that an intact though largely disarmed Imperial Star Destroyer had been turned over to a smuggler who had served five years on Kessel. The idea that a private citizen—an outlaw even—could bully the government into tolerating his possession of a war engine seemed the first sign of impending anarchy. Fey'lya wanted to demote Cracken for his failure to secure the *Errant Venture* for the New Republic, but the rest of the Council disagreed.

He'd let memory of the ship slip from his mind until the Thrawn crisis. Fey'lya had advocated the immediate nationalization of the ship, but New Republic Intelligence had a hard time locating it. Through Terrik's daughter, the Council had been informed that Booster would welcome the ship's rearming and his own commissioning as an Admiral. That idea had been rejected outright. Fey'lya got a degree of satisfaction when Cracken suggested leaking intelligence that would have Thrawn looking over his shoulder for the *Errant Venture*, but Terrik's failure to rally to the cause of the New Republic still infuriated him.

And now I am here, but now I have the measure of the

man, and a mission for which he is well suited. A quick message from the *Errant Venture* had alerted the Council to Rogue Squadron's destruction. Terrik had returned immediately to Coruscant from Distna, bringing with him the debris which was all that was left of Rogue Squadron and those who had killed them. The ship also brought back a sole survivor: Wes Janson, and the body of one other pilot, the Quarren, Lyyr Zatoq. Save for ship scraps, there was no trace of anyone else.

Fey'lya looked out over the docking bay at the variety of ships occupying deck space. Aside from his own *Lambda*-class shuttle, with two Bothan warriors standing guard at the base of the gangway, the ships present all could easily have been described as salvage. While Fey'lya was fairly certain the *Errant Venture*'s aft docking bay was reserved for customers who patronized the Diamond deck, the level of deterioration in the forward bay marked how difficult it was for Terrik to keep his ship operational. At least one of the turbolifts didn't work, and several of the winches that lifted small ships into storage racks were frozen. Terrik's dream of a ship that would pay for itself clearly had become a nightmare.

"Welcome, Councilor Fey'lya. How good of you to grace my humble ship with your presence." Booster appeared in the doorway of an office on the main deck and waved Fey'lya into its dim interior. "How may I be of service to you?"

Fey'lya flicked a finger toward his shuttle in a subtle gesture meant to tell his bodyguards to stay where they were. He strode past Booster and into the interior of a small office choked with datacards, cargo crates, enough parts to construct a half-dozen droids, and sufficient personal weapons to hold off an Imperial boarding team. The cloying scent of human habitation caused Fey'lya to wrinkle his nose, but he sat in the one chair that had been cleared of debris.

Fey'lya waited for Booster to take his place behind his desk, but the smuggler vexed him by perching himself on the corner of his desk and folding his arms over his chest. The Bothan smoothed the fur at the back of his head, then glanced up at the man's face. "I have come to thank you for bringing back to Coruscant as much of Asyr Sei'lar's ship as you did. The images recovered from her battlerooms have confirmed her great skill and bravery in this, her final fight. Bothans everywhere will take pride in what she did."

Booster nodded solemnly. " 'Pears she even scraped a TIE or two off my daughter's dead husband."

Fey'lya noted that Booster did not refer to Corran Horn as his "son-in-law" and catalogued that fact away for possible use. "Her devotion to her squadron-mates was quite clear. Likewise her devotion to the highest of Bothan ideals. She is an example to the younger generation."

"Indeed, appears you have another Martyr to hold up."

"It is a pity you were unable to recover her body."

Booster leaned back, pressing his hands behind him against the surface of the desk. "When we got there I sent recovery teams out. We found Captain Janson still alive— just barely. Got him into bacta. All the bacta on Thyferra wouldn't have helped the Quarren. Your Asyr and the rest, I suspect they burned up in the gas giant. Kind of fitting for Rogue pilots—blaze of glory and all."

"True, but this presents something of a problem because I had a different glory in mind for one of them." Fey'lya shifted in his chair and studied the talons on his left hand. "I was wondering if you had considered going back to look for more bodies."

The eyebrow above Booster's mechanical eye shot up. "Go back into a war zone to a system guarded by a ship better armed than this, to look for bodies that long since have been sucked into a gas giant? I've no reason to do that."

"But your daughter's husband—"

Booster's voice dropped into a bass growl. "He's dead and I'm helping her deal with that."

"And I want to help the Bothan people deal with their grief, too." Fey'lya looked up. "The Bothan people hold dear the memory of the Martyrs, but the Imperial troops who killed them also destroyed their bodies. The monument on Bothawui is empty and, because of that, it is diminished somewhat. I wish to see Asyr interred there, and I am willing to cover the costs of an expedition to find her. I really think, if you went back, you would find Asyr's body."

Booster frowned. "Did you miss what I said? It's not there."

"And I think you missed what I said. I need a body as a symbol." Fey'lya smiled. "I think a man who is as resourceful as you could find a suitable body, and you would be well rewarded for that search."

Booster's mouth slowly opened as he sat forward. "You think I could just find a Bothan body out there?"

"I have the utmost respect for your ability to get things done discreetly."

"Even if it meant the death of a Bothan?"

"There are bandits and others whose lives will come to no useful end. This could redeem them." The Bothan smiled. "I would be most generous and grateful. You would find my gratitude very useful."

"Perhaps I would." Booster slid from the desk and peered past Fey'lya for a second, then snatched him up by the front of his tunic and hauled him out of his chair. The Councilor struck at Booster's arms and felt the chair go tumbling behind him. As surprised as he was, it took him a moment to remember his claws could open the man's arms in seconds.

Booster slammed Fey'lya into a bulkhead with tooth-rattling force. All reason evaporated from Fey'lya's brain as stars exploded before his eyes. The man hammered him into the wall again, then drove his forehead into the Bothan's sensitive snout. Fey'lya raised his hands to protect his nose, then felt a heavy fist pound his stomach. Air *whoofed* from him and he wanted to vomit.

The dim closeness of the office vanished as the man carried him out to the docking bay and tossed him to the deck. Booster towered over him, his fists doubled, and Fey'lya shrank back, pulling himself along the decking for a moment. Then he remembered who he was. He stopped, but still flinched as Booster feinted with a fist.

Booster straightened up and posted his fists on his hips. "I don't know how your Bothan Martyrs got their hands on Death Star plans, but I'll bet it wasn't by asking others to do their wet work for them. It's pretty evident you don't think highly of me, my species, or my ship. I won't say I can't be bought, but I can't be bought by the likes of you."

He lowered his voice. "How you could even dream of sealing some glitbiter away in Asyr's tomb, I don't know."

Borsk Fey'lya felt the hot lash of the man's words and almost, for a nanosecond, let shame ruffle the fur on the back of his head. *I never had Asyr's compliance with my wishes, and I would have had it from the grave. It would have been for the glory of Bothans. Could that be wrong?* Yet before he could frame an answer, his bodyguards arrived at his side and were helping him up. His embarrassment at needing their aid swallowed any shame he might have felt.

Borsk coughed and rubbed at his nose. "You have misunderstood . . ."

Booster waved away his words. "Oh, I understood you. You didn't understand *me*. When I smack someone into a bulkhead and toss him on the deck, that's me saying he should get his carcass off my ship. The other things, the head butt and the stomach punch, that was just because I don't like you."

"Then our business is concluded." Borsk Fey'lya freed his arms from his bodyguards' grips and straightened his tunic. "I shall not forget this, Booster Terrik."

"Never did think you were stupid enough to let this lesson get away from you." Booster pointed at his shuttle. "Get off my ship, now!"

Booster watched as the shuttle descended from the *Errant Venture*'s belly and unfolded its wings. "That was a nasty piece of business."

"That's one way of describing it." Iella Wessiri's heels clicked against the decking as she walked over to him. "Borsk Fey'lya is not the sort of enemy I'd want to make."

"I've made worse."

"Have you?" She shook her head. "Fey'lya's the kind who will go after you, after your friends, after your friends' friends. He knows you know Karrde, so any of Karrde's associates will be on his enemies list. Through Corran anyone connected with CorSec will be an enemy."

Booster smiled. "And the downside to that is?"

"You don't mean that."

"For the most part you're right." Booster frowned. "How is she?"

"Last bacta treatment now. Mirax is with her. Should be there for another two hours."

Booster sighed. "No improvement in her memory?"

"Of the events at Distna, no. Everything else, including her last meeting with Fey'lya, that's all fine." Iella shrugged. "She's not going to be very helpful in letting us know what happened at Distna, but when we figure it out and go after the folks responsible, she'll be ready to go with us."

"And willing to do her own wet work." Booster watched Fey'lya's shuttle become a dim speck. "It's a start, and I bet there will be plenty of wet work by the time we're done."

25

Corran Horn saw the Imperial flight instructor vectoring in on him as he entered the simulation chamber, but he didn't slow or alter his course. He snapped the comlink into place inside the TIE pilot's helmet and headed toward where the rest of the Rogues stood, dressed in black flight suits. Only Tycho looked natural in it—mainly because he'd always worn black and still had his Rebel battle tabs sewn on the flight suit.

That big, bright Coruscant one really has to gall the Imps.

The flight instructor planted himself in front of Corran. "You'll do well to be on time, Captain Horn."

Corran shrugged, sweeping a lanky lock of brown hair out of his eyes. "I knew what time it was."

"And you weren't here because?"

He lifted the helmet and showed the comlink to the instructor. "I was checking out my equipment."

The instructor's eyes narrowed to brown slits. "There is nothing wrong with the comlinks in those helmets. They're all preset to the training frequency. You had no cause to adjust it."

Corran leaned forward, leaving his nose barely three

centimeters from the instructor's nose. "Ysanne Isard is running your operation, which means I have every reason I need to check out every little detail of what's going on here. Got it?" He'd discovered, among other things, that the comlinks had restricted power so they couldn't get much outside the Imperial compound. He was fairly certain that the folks in the surrounding city really didn't have any idea what was going on there, and that they were discouraged from paying too much attention.

The instructor lifted his head and sniffed the air officiously. "Your suspicions are unwarranted, given the objective of your mission and ours. We're prepping you to be an Imperial squadron that will get in past Krennel's defenses. We're giving you the most advanced starfighter in the galaxy to do so. The secret of your death is being maintained so Krennel will relax his guard. Do anything to upset that delicate balance and you could destroy the last best chance at ending Krennel's reign of terror over the Hegemony."

"I'll remember that." Corran winked at the man, then stepped around him. "Let's see what these things have."

The instructor's voice rose, but Corran didn't turn around to look at him. "Your attitude, Captain Horn, is not really conducive to learning."

Corran shrugged, then turned and dropped into a crouch beside Gavin. "Go on."

The Imp sighed. "This first exercise will be a simple one. You'll find the Sienar Fleet Systems TIE Defender is the fastest, best-equipped starfighter in the galaxy. Unlike other TIE designs, it incorporates shields, which provide the pilot with an improved survival profile. It has four lasers that can be fired singly, linked, or quadded, as well as two ion cannons. It carries eight concussion missiles or proton torpedoes depending upon mission profile, and has a tractor beam. It is very fast and highly maneuverable, both in space and atmosphere. Finally, it has hyperspace drive, which allows the ship to accomplish deep space missions without requiring a larger ship to deliver it to the target."

Corran shifted his shoulders uneasily while Hobbie coughed into his hand. Had the Imperials managed to de-

ver the TIE Defenders in sufficient quantities before the
mperor's death, the Rebellion could have foundered. The
hields alone would have allowed pilots to survive errors
nd learn from their mistakes, which would have made the
mperial Navy's fighter corps much deadlier. While it still
ook a good pilot to get a fighter through combat in one
iece, pilots only got good if they didn't die; and the De-
ender would keep a lot more of them alive.

The instructor pointed a remote toward the dozen
all cockpit simulators and pressed a button. The round
gress hatches on the tops hissed open and rose slowly.
Get into your fighters, seal up your flight suits, and initi-
te the engine start sequence. Once everyone is ready to
o, we'll begin."

Corran climbed up on the cockpit. He pulled the hatch
losed behind him, locked it down, and flipped the safety
witches on the explosive release bolts. Dropping down
nto the seat, he strapped himself in, then pulled on his hel-
net and sealed it against the flight suit's high collar. He con-
ected the hoses to the environmental control unit he wore
n his chest, then stuck out his tongue and activated the
omlink via a tongue switch.

"Red Nine online with communications." Corran
hook his head. He didn't like the Rogues having to shift
way from the Rogue designator. Wedge hadn't liked it, ei-
her, which is why he'd chosen Red. As he'd explained out
f earshot of the Imps, Red Squadron had been the designa-
ion for the group that destroyed the first Death Star, and
hat made the choice a bit more palatable to Corran.

He shrugged. *We'll just have to use the Red designator*
s inspiration, I guess. Corran punched up the ignition sequence and got console lights showing his engines were
oth running at 100 percent efficiency. He hit two other
uttons that shunted energy into the shields and energy
veapons. He brought his heads-up display to life, then
eached out with his gloved hands and took hold of the
ighter's controls.

As with other TIEs, the Defender worked with a wheel
nd yoke control system. Pulling back and pushing forward

would make the fighter climb and dive respectively, just a
the X-wing stick would do the same on that fighter. To ge
the ship to bank and turn, however, the pilot twisted th
blocky panel mounted to the top of the yoke. As with
landspeeder's controls, turning to the left would send th
ship left and vice versa. The grips on either end of the pane
had trigger switches to fire weapons, and between them la
an array of buttons and switches that controlled the throt
tle, weapon selection, target acquisition, data streaming t
the primary monitor, and a variety of lesser functions. Each
was manipulable with a flick of a thumb, and though Cor
ran preferred the X-wing's stick, he didn't find this system
that tough to work with.

Rudder pedals contracted and expanded maneuvering
planes that vectored engine thrust, swinging the fighter'
tail around for quick course alterations. This contributed t
the fighter's added maneuverability which, along with th
shields, would make the ship very hard to kill.

"Red Nine is good to go." He glanced low left at th
auxiliary monitor showing the status of his shields, then up
at the lines of lights representing his weapons. Dead cente
in the weapons display bar were two counters indicating he
was carrying eight concussion missiles. *This is a lot of fire
power for a fighter—more than enough to fight a B-wing to
a standstill.*

The instructor's voice filled his helmet. "The mission i
simple: You will engage your hyperdrive on your curren
heading and drop out of hyperspace in thirty seconds. You
will find a small space station and some freighter traffi
around it. Approach the freighter and station closely enough
to scan their cargoes. Expect possible Reb . . . *pirate* activi
ties in the area and deal with them as warranted."

"Red Lead copies. Hyperdrive on my mark. Three
two, one, mark."

The computer-generated display in the fighter's various
viewpoints became a shifting tunnel of light. Corran began
to yawn and lifted his hand to cover it, but his hand
bounced off his helmet. He growled mildly. *Having to wea*

*these helmets is reason enough for any Imp pilot to come
over to the Rebellion.*

He watched the chronometer on his main display
trickle down to zero, then his ship reverted to realspace. A
space station with three wedge-shaped platforms grafted at
regular angles to the middle of its long central spindle came
into view. He dropped his crosshairs on it and called up a
sensor scan. The computer designated it Yag-prime and a
chill ran through Corran. *It's the station at Yag'Dhul, the
one we used as our base for ending Isard's rule of Thyferra.
Someone here is being very cute.*

Corran brushed his right thumb over a targeting selection switch, toggling his way through the variety of ships in
the system. One freighter came up as the *Pulsar Skate*, another as the *Last Chance*, and yet another as the *Millen-
nium Falcon. They even have the* Star's Delight *here, the
freighter that took me off Garqi and brought me to the Rebellion. Isard's tossing up here all the freighters I mentioned
in my* Lusankya *interrogations, reminding me how much
she'd gotten out of me.*

He keyed his comlink. "They're playing some games
with us, Lead. Not a problem for me, but we need to stay
sharp."

"My thoughts, too, Nine." Wedge's voice faded for a
moment. "Five, take Two Flight and head along two-four
mark two-seven-three to check the two bulk freighters, then
take a run by the station."

"As ordered, Lead." Tycho's voice crackled along the
comm frequency. "Two Flight on me."

Corran rolled his trip to starboard, then leveled out and
swooped in behind Tycho's fighter. Inyri brought Red Six
up on Tycho's port side and Ooryl dropped Seven aft right
of Corran's fighter. Nrin cruised Eight into a high cover position to the formation's aft. Their course brought them in
below the *Falcon* and sensors reported it was hauling droids
and weapons. Corran snorted, half expecting Isard to have
filled the imaginary freighter's hold with spice.

Next came the *Pulsar Skate*, but sensors showed it as

carrying passengers. Neither of the freighters reacted in any way to the fighter fly-by, but Corran kept watching them on his aft scope. *If the shields come up, they could be the backstop for an ambush.* He ruddered his fighter around to starboard, following the course correction Tycho made to bring the flight in on a long loop toward the station. Way out to port he could see flashes of One Flight lining up to do the same thing.

"Six has readings of ships powering up in the station."

"Seven confirms. Profile is that of Defenders."

Corran frowned as a dozen TIE Defenders came up out of the station. A red light began blinking on his HUD, indicating that something had a target lock on him, then a second burned to let him know a missile had been launched at him. "Nine has incoming missiles."

"Evasive, all, now!"

Tycho's fighter rolled hard to port, while Corran went starboard. He hesitated for a second, then began to thumb his way through the various threats in the system. He found the missile heading his way and turned his ship until it was coming straight in at his tail. He watched its range scroll down on the main display, and when it hit a hundred meters, he snaprolled to port, inverting his fighter, then he dove for a second.

The missile shot past and its momentum took it well beyond his ship. Reversing his roll, Corran brought the Defender's nose back up and targeted the missile. He ruddered his ship around, keeping his fighter facing the missile as it cruised through the arc that would bring it back on target to him. When it oriented on him again, he hit the trigger under his right index finger. Two pairs of green laser bolts hissed out. The second pair hit the missile, melting it. The propellant combusted into a big ball of flame, and an explosion by the warhead a second later snuffed it.

Something inside of Corran kind of gave way as he glanced at his scopes. The Yag'Dhul station bristled with turbolaser batteries and was filling the space around it with lots of cohesive light. A dozen enemy trips twisted and spun through the system, while the Rogues scattered via evasive maneuvers. Part of him realized it was only an exercise, and the fact that the Imps would ambush them just to show the cocky Rebels how good they were didn't surprise him. He even allowed as how, in their boots, he'd have seriously contemplated the same thing. It probably was good for both groups of pilots.

Another part of him disagreed though. For these Imps, this simulator battle was redemption and justification. If they could beat the Rogues, then the Empire for which they worked, the Empire that had been their mentor and provider, *that* Empire suddenly had been lost only because *they* had not been employed in its defense. The frustration they felt at not having been present at Endor could be erased. In their minds the Emperor could have lived, his Empire could have continued, and Coruscant would never have fallen, if only they had been there to defeat the Rebels, to defeat Rogue Squadron.

But they weren't there. Corran snorted angrily. *Time to show them why it was just as well they weren't.*

Hitting switches on his control panel, he flipped his weapons over to concussion missiles and doubled them up. Then he dialed his throttle back to two-thirds of maximum. By hitting another switch, he shunted the energy stored in the energy weapon capacitors into the engines, bringing his speed back up to the maximum the fighter could do while fully recharging weapons and shields. Rolling to port and starting to climb, he oriented himself toward a pair of trips that were cruising in on Ooryl's fighter. The Gand had his Defender dancing, making it tough for the Imps to do more than hit him with grazing shots.

"Seven, this is Nine. Move to two-four-oh mark ten, now. Break port on my mark."

A double-click came back on the frequency to let him know Ooryl heard the order and would comply. The Defender leveled out and started off on the vector Corran had indicated. The Imps made course corrections to keep coming on Ooryl's tail. Corran pointed his Defender at an intercept point, then kicked the throttle in at full.

His speed climbed, as did his closure rate with the two trips following Ooryl. "Seven, mark."

Ooryl's Defender rolled hard to port and the Imp trips trailed after him like hatchlings after a mother mynock. They cruised right across Corran's crosshairs and his target acquisition system gave him a hard lock fast, since he'd closed to point-blank range faster than the Imps expected. He hit his trigger, drilling two concussion missiles into the first trip, then ruddered around and launched two more at the second one.

The first pair of missiles hit the Defender's aft shield simultaneously and collapsed it, only expending half the energy released by their detonations. The rest of the burning plasma ball they created melted away the top fin and took with it the top of the cockpit. It also fused thrust louvers, whirling the Defender into a spin that sent it back toward the Yag'Dhul station.

The next pair of missiles hit their target in sequence. The first missile blast took down the aft shield, while the second missile flew straight into one of the two ion engines. Ion thrust flared into a silver-white cone, then the missile's explosion blew the cockpit's forward viewport out. The Defender ripped itself into huge pieces and Corran flew through the middle of the dying explosion.

He nodded grimly. Given the Defenders' warning systems for target locks, any long-distance shots would give his prey the same chance to destroy the missile or begin to evade that he would have. Only by refusing to aim at them until the last second could he take them by surprise. The only true surprise he had to work with was the enemy's failure to realize that he could manufacture strategies that would work with their equipment as well as they could, if not better.

Two of the enemy Defenders vectored in on his aft, so he rolled to starboard and began a weaving run in at the space station. Green laser bolts flashed past him from the rear, while curling lines of red bolts rose toward him from the station. Course correcting a bit to the right, he raced in at the station's central spire. His flight path set him up to run a bit starboard of it, and on his rear scope he saw the Defenders split to pursue him as he came around.

As he came in tight he chopped his throttle back, then activated the Defender's tractor beam. It latched hold of the space station, but since it massed far more than the starfighter, it didn't go anywhere. Instead the tractor beam acted like a line that shortened the arc of Corran's turn. The pilot flicked the beam off again, then throttled up and hauled back on the yoke to climb.

His HUD went red as his crosshairs swept over one of the Defenders coming after him. He launched another pair of concussion missiles, which drilled into the trip and ripped it apart. Then the missile-lock warning light flashed on his display, prompting him to invert and dive. The concussion missile that had been coming at him shot past, but his dive carried him straight into a turbolaser salvo from the station.

The simulator screens went black, then the egress hatch's emergency release triggers snapped back into the safe position and the hatch opened. Corran pulled off his helmet, released his restraining belts, and hauled himself up out of the simulator. Sweat poured down his face and stung his eyes. He licked salt from his lips and sat perched on the hatch, luxuriating in the cool air of the simulator chamber.

Looking around he saw some of the Rogues chatting with Imperial pilots. That surprised him, but as he watched the men and women weave their hands through simple pantomimes of the battles they'd fought, he began to smile. *They ambushed us, but they ended up being as surprised as we were by it.* Toward the back of the room he saw Wedge and the Imperial leader, Colonel Vessery, smiling as they conversed closely.

Corran nodded slowly. Both leaders had clearly seen that their pilots would be suspicious and defensive, ready to take offense at whatever the other group might say or do; yet both groups needed to work together. This little exercise pointed out that each side had good pilots, and that the pilots had more in common than they might have otherwise expected. *Mutual respect will bring us closer faster, and let us compete as equals. That's good.*

He swung his legs up over the edge of the hatch, and

slid down to the deck. He stumbled as he landed, but an Imperial pilot helped steady him. "Thanks."

"Not a problem." The Imp smiled at him. "You were the guy who tractored the station?"

"Guilty as charged."

The Imp nodded. "Very impressive. I'll have to keep my eye on you."

Corran laughed lightly. "Use both of them. I am a Rogue, after all."

26

Whistler's lights popped on and the little R2 droid began surveying the room in which he found himself. Aside from the light he produced, he detected no other source of light energy. His scan did reveal power conduits, computer cable conduits, and a fairly large system of air duct-work behind the walls. The room had only one door, which appeared to be quite dense, and he found no thermal bleed-through from any living creatures standing guard near it or against the wall.

All of this data filtered into a simple program that assessed his situation and made available different options for his future actions. In the past the program had recommended returning to a dormant state, with lights off, monitoring local comm frequencies for any communication from Corran. He had been in that passive wait state from the moment the Imperials had placed him in the room with the rest of Rogue Squadron's astromech droids. Corran *had* managed to communicate with him via comlink and gave Whistler access to the scramble codes the Imperials used, as well as a way to tap the comm traffic during the training sessions they went through.

Corran had also informed him of the Rogues' status.

The circumstances they found themselves in were indeed alarming. Whistler's awareness of this fact was based on his analysis of Corran's speech patterns and the signs of stress in his voice. He catalogued those signs of anxiety along with the key words that seemed to trigger them: Isard [status alive], Imperial Base [secret], TIE Defenders [secret], and mission [secret, dangerous].

Whistler began a passive scan of comlink frequencies. He catalogued the vocabulary being used on each, then ran a correlation between them. First he determined that the Rogues and their Imperial counterparts were running yet another simulation that pitted the rival pilots against each other. Over the past two weeks this sort of training mission had become common. On the other frequencies he began picking up comments that indicated Corran's hunch about the base had been correct. The pilot had guessed that in such a small facility, with no serious threats to deal with, watching the simulator battles between the Rogues and the Imps would attract a lot of attention. Whistler's correlations indicated voyeur traffic on 65 percent of the local frequencies and, more importantly, 85 percent of the security frequencies.

That percentage flipped a bit in a program. A line of code called up Whistler's evasion and escape programming. Such programming was not common in an astromech droid, but few astromech droids had been refitted for work in the Corellian Security Force. Not only had his preparation for that work equipped him with special circuitry that allowed for surveillance and analysis, escape and evasion, and an array of code-slicing programs, but it had even shifted internal components around such that when a restraining bolt was fastened to him it did little more than communicate the result of commands sent by a remote. When the Imperial tech had used the remote on him, Whistler feigned shutting down and starting up again. More than once criminals had assumed a security droid was disabled by a restraining bolt and had learned to regret that assumption.

Regardless of the fact that the cylindrical device afixed to his torso did nothing to restrain him, Whistler rolled over to the corner of a shelving unit, lodged the cylinder next to the edge, and quickly spun his body. The restraining bolt snapped off and clattered to the floor.

Whistler allowed himself a low, barely audible whistle. Whirling his head about he spotted Gate and rolled over to the red and white R5 astromech. Whistler reached out with his pincer arm, sent a blue trickle of energy over the restraining bolt on Gate's torso, then pulled it free.

Gate's lights flashed on and the droid began to shudder, bouncing from foot to foot.

Whistler tootled at him to calm down, then quickly answered the taller droid's inquiries about location and status. Whistler reassured him that the mission they were being sent on had official sanction. He also informed Gate of the highly risky nature of their mission with a low tone.

Gate countered sharply that his microprocessing time was too valuable to waste analyzing meaningless odds. In the final analysis, he suggested, they were droids who had been entrusted with a mission and they would accomplish it. All non-vital calculations would only waste time and power.

Whistler hooted happily and rolled over to the large air intake vent mounted in the wall. He brought out his cutting attachment and sliced through one of the screws holding it in place. Gate joined him, cutting the grate free. Whistler slowly backed away, letting the grate lean into the room, then he caught hold of one edge with his pincer and pulled it away from the dark cavity beyond.

Gate entered the ductwork with no difficulty at all. The maintenance and construction droids used to create and repair the environmental system in the base were slightly taller and decidedly broader than the astromech droids. Gate caught hold of the other edge of the grate, allowing Whistler to come around to the opening. The smaller droid took hold of the grate and pulled it into place, while Gate extended his pincer and crimped ductwork around the edge of the grate to hold it in place.

The astromech droids rolled into the ducts and paused at an intersection. Whistler extended his communications probe and jabbed it into a communications port. The metal ductwork distorted comm frequencies enough that the repair droids regularly hooked into the base's communications and computer system for position updates, repair requests, and other data. During his time passively surveying the comm frequencies on the base, Whistler had picked up enough transmissions from repair droids coming online and hooking into the communications network that he easily mimicked one and got into the system in nanoseconds.

First he calibrated his internal clock with local and Imperial standard times. Second he sliced his way into the local spaceport scheduling and control system to download a complete schedule of arrivals and departures for the next week. He found several ships that were leaving within the next day, most of which could easily find space for a pair of astromech droids. The spaceport computer system even provided a link to a number of cargo brokers. Once in their systems, he could obtain passage for himself and Gate.

Paying for their passage faced him with a quandary. Corran had explained that Isard wanted Rogue Squadron to seem dead. If Krennel was unaware of their continued survival, they could be used against him. The very fact that Rogue Squadron had been ambushed at Distna indicated that Krennel had some intelligence resources in the New Republic, and the intervention of Isard's forces meant she had intelligence sources within Krennel's Hegemony—and possibly within the New Republic as well. Paying for the passage from the various accounts Corran held—accounts Whistler could embezzle from without too much trouble since he knew all the relevant passwords and numbers—might suggest Corran lived. That word would get back to Krennel and Isard, placing the Rogues in danger from whatever Isard's angry reaction might be.

From his communications with the *Pulsar Skate*'s computer, Whistler had drawn a list of accounts that Mirax maintained for her business dealings. Using one of them seemed most effective, since she often authorized shipments between points so she could pick them up at some waystation. Still, unauthorized use of one of her accounts would likely attract too much attention and might suggest to her that the Rogues had survived. While Whistler had no evidence to suggest Mirax was anything but smart, her reaction in absence of solid evidence might also jeopardize things.

The *Skate* had yielded yet older accounts, ones that Mirax had not tapped in a long time. All the data concerning them indicated they had been established by Booster Terrik well before he'd been sentenced to Kessel, and had not been touched since. Whistler analyzed the account activity and balances, and picked one of them to finance their escape.

Whistler ran through a quick threat analysis of their escape route, cross-correlating reports of crimes, percentages of Jawas and Ugnaughts in the local populations, and the fluctuating resale prices on droids along the course to their destination. Most of the risks seemed minor but there were a couple of points where the potential for interference seemed high. That assessment clicked in another piece of program that sent off a message setting up a rendezvous with someone who would be able to get them past the dangerous part of their journey and to their final destination.

If he showed up.

Whistler went over the text of the message again, edited it more closely, and sent it.

He would show up.

Whistler quickly established their primary connections, then created four separate and alternate routes to get where they needed to go. With a high-frequency series of squeals and whistles meant to register above the level of human hearing, he communicated full details to Gate. Then the two of them rolled off together to the maintenance egress hatch near the atmospheric control plant at the rear of the building. Once it grew dark outside, they'd escape the base and world, to get Rogue Squadron the help it was sure to need.

27

Corran Horn wiped the sweat from his face and let his torso sag forward over the padded bar of the abdominal muscle weight machine. Though only driving sixty-five kilos on one gravity per repetition, the weight added up, and his sore stomach muscles were beginning to burn. Something about the dull pain felt good, as if it were reminding him he was alive.

"Flat abdominals? I suppose your wife likes them?"

Corran's head snapped around. Ysanne Isard, clad in a skintight workout uniform that covered her from knees to elbow and throat, stood in the doorway. Black stripes running down the sides of the arms, flanks, and legs of the red bodystocking matched the fingerless black gloves she wore. She clung to each end of the black towel she had looped around her neck, making her appear almost casual, as if their meeting in the base weight room had been by accident.

Nothing she does is by accident. The pilot narrowed his eyes. "You want something?"

Isard shrugged and moved into the room to seat herself at a leg-curl machine. "I thought I would tell you that your latest attempt to get a message out to your wife has failed. Using her designator code as the origin code for a message destined to be rejected by our system was an interesting idea, but an old one. Our systems here are quite secure."

"So far, you mean." Corran gritted his teeth and curled his body forward, hoisting the machine's weight with his stomach muscles. He forced himself to breathe with each repetition, focusing on the burning sensation in his muscles and using it to drive Isard from his mind.

She waited until he finished. "Your persistence is admirable, as is the passion you express for your wife in the messages."

"Enjoyed them, did you?" He shook his head, spraying sweat around the room. "I'll continue to send them."

"Why? You know I'll intercept them all."

"Nice to know you'll have something to do with your time." Corran unwrapped his body from the machine and slowly stood. "As for why, it's because I love her and I know she'll be hurt thinking I'm dead."

Isard raised an eyebrow. "You'll be reunited with her once you've destroyed Krennel."

"So that's what, another month of pain? No good." Corran frowned at her. "Haven't you ever loved anyone?"

The question seemed to catch her off-guard and Corran felt a wave of surprise roll off her. Once again Corran regretted not having gone with Luke Skywalker to train himself to be a Jedi, because he could have used that moment of vulnerability to open her up. *I could find out what she's really planning and prevent her from accomplishing it.*

Isard brushed her hands down the tops of her thighs. "I have loved, yes, but I trusted that he would know if I lived or died."

"That's asking a lot. No one can possibly know . . ." He stopped in mid-sentence as he recalled a rumor about her. "The Emperor? You loved the Emperor?"

"Captain Horn, the surprise in your voice is hardly appropriate. Is it any surprise that I would find myself

attracted to the brightest star in the galaxy? I was raised on
Imperial Center, I came of age during Palpatine's time. He
was immensely charismatic. He could look you in the
eyes and touch the person you were. He lived for his dream
of a stable galaxy." Her voice took on an edge. "And he
died for it."

"I hope you're not expecting an apology."

"From you? For that? No." Isard set the weight machine for forty kilos, then began bending her legs, lifting the
weight. Her voice remained even though the strain began to
flush her skin. "You do owe me an apology, though."

"Oh, really? For what?" Corran folded his arms across
his chest. "Not the destruction of *Lusankya*, I hope, because I'm not at all sorry about that."

"No, no, not that." Isard finished the last rep and
smiled up at him. "Actually I'm pleased the ship is gone.
Until you escaped from it, the ship had been pristine, even
virginal. Your escape . . . violated it and soiled it. While I
used it to escape Imperial Center, I had little to do with it after that. I couldn't think of it in the same way. In many ways
I was glad it died."

"So were we." He shook his head. "I've heard from
Wedge how you scattered the other prisoners, which an-
swers one of the two questions I had concerning the ship."

"And the other was?"

"How you got it buried beneath the surface of
Coruscant?"

Her nose wrinkled with his use of the pre- and post-
Imperial name for the world, but it took a moment or two
beyond that for her to provide her response. "I wish I knew.
I know where and when *Lusankya* was created, and I know
when it was given to me, so I have narrowed down the possible dates for its insertion into the world, but even as director of Imperial Intelligence I could find no clue as to how
the insertion happened."

"But it had to have taken hundreds of construction
droids and weeks of time. A project that size could not have
gone unnoticed."

"I would agree, unless . . . the Force is something I do not understand and cannot touch, but the Emperor could. Is it possible he drew the ship down and buried it using the Force? I suppose. Is it possible that he merely stretched his mind out and prevented anyone from noticing the ship's descent? Also possible." She shook her head. "All I know is that the Emperor confided its location to me at roughly the same time its sister ship, the *Executor*, became operational."

A chill ran down Corran's spine. Even unschooled as he was in the Force, he'd managed to blank the mind of a stormtrooper looking for him. *If the Emperor could manage to do that for billions of people, the miracle of the Rebellion is that it succeeded at all.*

"So, the Emperor never really reckoned with the threat the Rebellion represented to him, did he?"

She began pumping her legs again. "I always thought you were more trouble than he did. He exerted great energies suppressing the internecine warfare between species in the Empire. He underestimated his enemy. This makes him much like you, Corran Horn."

"Me? How does that follow?"

"The apology you owe me. It's for underestimating me." Isard gave him a smile that puckered his flesh. "You thought you'd killed me, but you hadn't. You didn't push, you didn't pursue. I had thought you would have been more diligent than that. Your father certainly would have been."

Corran stiffened, then spitted her with a harsh glare. "What you know of my father you stripped from my brain when you had me on *Lusankya*. I'm not going to let you use my own memories against me."

"Oh, it's not your memories I'm using, but my own." Her smile tightened slightly as she began a third set of repetitions. "I met your father once. Spent some time with him. He was most annoying and prevented me from accomplishing my mission."

"Like father, like son."

"Indeed." Isard crawled out of the weight machine and stood slightly taller than Corran. "The annoyance factor with you is getting to be too much. I want you to stop trying to send messages out of here. You'll jeopardize the mission."

Corran shook his head, then walked over to a triceps extension machine and sat down. He glanced over at her. "You don't fool me, Isard. You don't fall in love with someone like the Emperor because you like the way he laughs or the cute dimples he has. You fall in love with him because you feel a kinship to him. You wanted what he wanted, which was power; and that lust for power won't go away. Just the way you brought us here and keep us here reflects your need for control. You have a goal and everything else will be subordinate to it."

She dabbed with her towel at a droplet of sweat running down from her left temple. "General Antilles knows what I want. He knows what the price for my cooperation is. What I want from you is your cooperation so that I have my best chance at success."

"And if I don't agree?"

Her eyes narrowed. "I know, Corran Horn, you are capable of fierce loves and loyalties. If you persist in sending messages out, I will have your astromech taken apart, and I will scatter those parts further than my clone ever scattered the *Lusankya* prisoners. With a thousand years and a thousand Jedi you would not be able to reconstruct Whistler. His fate is in your hands."

Corran let his jaw drop open to cover his surprise. Her bald-faced threat to Whistler didn't surprise him. He'd considered the droids hostages from the second the restraining bolts had been placed on them. What her threat *did* mean, however, was that no one had noticed Whistler was missing yet. As nearly as Corran could determine the droid had vanished a week previously, which meant he was fairly well along on the mission Corran had given him.

He scrubbed his hands over his face, then hung his head. "You know, the only problem with you is that while you might have loved, you never were loved back. You know how much your threat hurts, but only because you've seen such threats hurt others. You don't know firsthand the pain you're inflicting."

"I don't have a problem with being saved that sort of pain."

"No, I don't suppose you do." Corran looked up at her and met her bicolored stare openly. "You know, the real pity in that is this: You also don't know that the best balm for that pain is having a friend, a true friend, someone you can trust no matter what. But, I imagine, to you that sort of blind trust is simply a tool that can be used against someone."

"Very effectively, too."

"I'm sure." Corran reach back behind his head for the weight bar. "Well, the one thing I trust about you is that you'll be true to your nature. And that nature, Madam Director, is what will kill you in the end."

Wedge Antilles raked his fingers through his brown beard. He didn't think the beard made him look any different, and his mental image of himself still hadn't adjusted to include it. Even so, it changed the outline of his jaw enough to fuzz recognition and, combined with the prosthetic he'd wear to become Antar Roat again, it should enable him to get past any security screening Krennel put him through.

Colonel Vessery looked over at him from across the holoprojector's sector map of Ciutric. "Do you have reservations about this plan?"

Wedge shrugged. "Same I have about every plan before it goes off. We get slipped into Ciutric as an Imperial unit looking for sanctuary. We fit in, then I send out a message that gets to you and in twelve hours you show up with the commandos we'll need to break open the prison holding the *Lusankya* prisoners. At the same time the New Republic shows up with a fleet that will pound Krennel and liberate Ciutric. A lot of things can go wrong there."

Vessery smiled. "True enough, but most of them come in along the lines of command and control. With the Director controlling communications and making sure messages go where they're meant to go, everyone should show up on time. Your flight missions are fairly straightforward. One flight will eliminate the shields over Ciutric while the other neutralizes the defensive positions around the prison. Both units will then suppress ground defenses and air support. As you have seen in the simulations, the Defenders are well suited to these tasks and more than capable of standing up to the punishment."

"Nice machines. I still prefer my X-wing, but I'll take a trip in a pinch."

"Flying one in combat will convince you." Vessery looked over at the doorway as a silhouette filled it. "Come in, Major. This is General Antilles, Major Telik. Major Telik will be leading the commandos on the operation."

Wedge took the slender man in with a glance. His high cheekbones and sharp nose gave his face an angular cast. Dark brows, which matched the close-cropped hair on his head, shadowed deep brown eyes. Not terribly muscled, Telik took Wedge's proffered hand and shook it with a surprisingly strong grip.

"Glad to have you with us, Major."

"My pleasure, General." He turned to Vessery. "I've studied and annotated the plan for hitting the prison. I like the basic setup, but I've got a few changes in mind. I don't want to lock them in until I can run through a sim with my people, but I think they will streamline the operation and minimize casualties."

Vessery nodded. "That's to be desired."

Telik turned back toward Wedge. "I would have preferred to be in on the planning from the start, but I was on Commenor and have only recently returned. While I was there I saw two acquaintances of yours: Mirax Terrik and ʹella Wessiri."

Wedge blinked. "What were they doing on Commenor?"

"Following up on the leads planted by Krennel's people to lure Rogue Squadron to Distna."

"Interesting." Wedge scratched at his throat. He'd noticed that Telik had referred to "Krennel's people" and not "Isard's clone" as the one who had been planting those clues. Either he didn't know, or didn't feel he could pass that information on to Wedge if he did. Wedge expected no less in the way of informational security by Isard's people, which was why the whole mention of Commenor struck him as odd.

Telik smiled. "The Wessiri woman impressed me a great deal. She was in a difficult situation and I managed to slip her a blaster, which she used to effect her escape. Terrik went with her and, later, I saw they were fine. Not but one out of a dozen people could have done what she did."

"For as long as I've known her, she's been very good." Wedge pasted a smile on his face. There was no way Telik would have mentioned his run to Commenor, his having helped Iella and Mirax, and their escape, if Isard had not told him to do so. Hearing what he'd heard certainly put Wedge in Telik's debt, which would help inspire the sort of trust that would make the mission work more smoothly.

By the same token, I've just been told that Isard has a line on two friends of mine. If things do not go the way she wants them to go, Iella and Mirax could be killed, or worse. The sorry plight of the *Lusankya* prisoners had not escaped Wedge's mind. *Just because Isard wants me to trust Telik isn't a reason not to trust him, but I will guard against problems, somehow.*

Wedge sighed. "Well, we'll be going back and forth over these plans for a long while, I guess, since we don't have someone as good as Iella here to tell us how to fix them. It strikes me that the only remaining part of the plan to put into place is for me to record a message for Admiral Ackbar that will get him to bring a New Republic fleet with him to destroy Krennel."

Vessery nodded. "Two messages, actually. One will outline the plan and prepare the New Republic to move. The second will contain the order for them to go. Moving forces around a galaxy seldom allows for split-second timing—as we have all learned—but it can be closely simulated and we'll have to settle for that."

"Worked when we took Coruscant." Wedge suppressed a smile. "Well, let us cook up the text of the first message I'll send, so the Director can approve it. Then we can set about ending Delak Krennel's long reign."

28

Whistler dodged around workers stacking crates on binary load lifters and shot down the ramp from the *Worldhopper*'s cargo hold. The captain, an older man with two twin sons who crewed for him, glanced in his direction but did nothing to stop him. Rennik had been paid to get Whistler and Gate to Oradin, on the planet Brentaal, and no further. He'd done his job and turned his attention back to adjudicating a dispute between his sons.

Whistler whirled his head around and piped a call to Gate to join him. The R5 droid whistled back mournfully, then slowly rolled down the ramp. His previously pristine red and white exterior was stippled with a series of black and brown burn marks. More galling than that, however, Gate had been fitted with a conical scrap-metal cap that trailed a long ribbon of bright blue fabric. A few spot welds held it in place and, despite their best efforts, neither droid had been able to free Gate from the cap.

Whistler fixed his visual lens on the Rennik brothers and digitized their exact likenesses. He had no program in place at the moment to exact revenge for what they had done to Gate, but when time allowed he would pull up one of the many practical joke programs he'd picked up at

CorSec and in his time with the squadron, and implement it with the Rennik twins as the target.

He communicated his intention to Gate.

Gate replied that it would be suitable for the two boys to be made targets.

Whistler agreed. To relieve the boredom of the trip, the two boys had welded the cap to Gate's head, then used powered-down blasters to try to shoot the ribbon that trailed after Gate as the droid ducked and dodged through the cargo hold. The ribbon quickly proved to be too tough a target for them, so they settled for shooting the droid. The number of crates being unloaded from the ship bearing burn marks gave testimony to how bad the brothers were at marksmanship, but in the confines of the hold Gate couldn't dodge forever.

Whistler swiveled his head around, taking in a full view of the hangar area where the *Worldhopper* had landed. Oradin boasted an *Imperial*-class spaceport, but the *Worldhopper* had put down at one of the older portions of it. The center of the landing bay area was open to the night sky and, once ships touched down, a small tractor beam in each unloading bay would pull the ship into its own little niche. A dozen ships could be serviced at this one area, making it a hive of activity.

For a living creature, the chaos might have been overwhelming, but Whistler remained focused. Large holographic projectors filled the air with all sorts of advertisements for everything from upscale resorts like the Grand Oradin Hotel to places that offered tiny coffinlike spaces for sleep. Restaurants displayed endless assortments of dishes, all glistening, some still moving, to temp spacers tired of prepackaged fare. Machines large and small darted about, shifting crates from ship to ship, or ship to storage, with customs officials and transit agents all screaming at each other in loud voices. All manner of creatures and droids wandered around, some with clear intent, others moving furtively—causing Whistler to classify them as possible threats. Everything else he ignored because none of it was important to accomplishing his mission.

He asked Gate to keep watch on some of the threats, then moved over to a communications station and inserted his probe into the appropriate jack. He entered the MESTOP system with ease and fed into it the communications address he'd fabricated for any messages. The "Messages to Spacers" system took a little while to retrieve the single message that had been sent to him while in transit, and the message itself consisted of nothing more than a room number at the Grand Oradin Hotel and a span of dates.

Whistler confirmed that the present date was within the span and hooted with joy. He spun his head around to let Gate know they were in time to make their next leg of the trip, but only managed to get out a low moan. Gate echoed the tone and slowly rolled back toward Whistler.

In knots of two and three, some Ugnaughts slowly sauntered toward them. The little creatures avoided looking at them directly, but some carried restraining bolts and others the flash-welders needed to fix them to the droids. Lurking further back, a hooded Twi'lek flicked *lekku* impatiently at the Ugnaughts, encouraging them to be bolder.

Whistler hooted at Gate and the larger droid brought out his pincer. Blue sparks arced between the forks, widening the Ugnaughts' eyes. They slowed their approach, which drew the Twi'lek in close enough for Whistler to get a good look at his face.

In seconds, using codes he'd employed many times with CorSec, Whistler sliced into the Spaceport Security Authority. He married the Twi'lek's image to a fugitive warrant template, added charges of smuggling, slavery, and several other unsavory crimes, tacked on a reward of 25,000 credits, and pumped it into the system. He flipped a bit that noted the suspect was armed and extremely dangerous and a moment later the Twi'lek's image burned to life in the air over the hangar, accompanied by the blaring of a dozen loud sirens.

The Twi'lek, the Ugnaughts, and just about everyone else in the hangar looked upward. The Twi'lek's *lekku* twitched furiously and he began to run in the direction of the *Worldhopper*. The Rennik twins immediately shouted at him and, with blasters in hand, started scattering shots in his general direction. People screamed and ran, more blaster-fire erupted, and scarlet energy bolts filled the air.

Into the maelstrom Whistler charged, with Gate at his side, ribbon snapping and popping. Rolling at full speed they blasted into a trio of Ugnaughts, toppling them and sending their tools flying. Other Ugnaughts gave chase, but an errant burst of blasterfire cut one down and sent the rest diving for ferrocrete.

Howling like wounded banthas in the Jundland Wastes, the droids cut to the left and into a small corridor. Whistler took the turn a bit wide and crashed into the wall, with sparks trailing from his right flank. Spinning his head about he saw the smear of green paint he left behind on the wall, but two blaster bolts burned into it, leaving guttering little fires to consume it. Cutting to the left to see past Gate and his ribbon, Whistler just missed toppling a customs official. The droids raced past her, ignoring her calls to stop and sped out into the shadowy Oradin streets.

Finding the Grand Oradin Hotel did not present much of a problem for the droids. A quick scan of the facade revealed hints of old lettering that had once graced the building. The owners had simply replaced the word "Imperial" with the word "Oradin" to reflect the planet's changing loyalties. Inside the lobby the Aurebesh letter Isk still appeared in decorations, but all the new signs had the Osk for Oradin in the appropriate place.

The main turbolifts steadfastly refused to admit two unescorted droids, informing Whistler that the hotel had standards. Whistler matched Gate's sulking tone, then headed off around the corner and through a door marked STAFF ONLY. At the rear of the main lifts lay the freight lift, which was quite happy to help the droids out. It turned out that the freight lift's main processing unit had once oper-ated one of the passenger turbolifts until it had been replaced during an upgrade cycle. The lift indicated its processor had been deemed too "Old Republic" to work during the Imperial regime.

Whistler and Gate patiently exchanged glances as the turbolift went on about the various individuals he'd lifted and lowered during his time. The lift rose to the fourteenth floor and opened slowly, spinning out a tale of the battle for Brentaal that Gate actually wanted to hear, since it involved Wedge, but from a time well before Gate flew with him. Whistler suggested they could get the download on their return trip and the lift promised them a smooth ride.

The droids rolled down the hallway to the room 1428. Whistler played out a series of tones meant to announce them, but the door did not open. He tried again, but the door remained closed. Gate rolled forward and played the tones out, too, getting a result neither of them expected.

Behind them, the door to 1429 opened. Whistler swiveled his head about and looked up at the dark-haired man staring down at him. The man stroked his goatee, then smiled slowly. "Well, I knew Booster hadn't sent that message to me, but I didn't expect a droid, much less two."

"You should be careful, Karrde, they could be bait for a trap."

Talon Karrde glanced back into the room and tossed the datapad he'd been holding to the man standing there. "They didn't scan for explosives or weapons, though that hat looks somewhat lethal."

Gate moaned.

Whistler turned his body around and projected a message identifying himself.

Karrde squatted down to read it. "Whistler, yes, the droid partnered with Booster's son-in-law. Now that's curious, since you've both been reported dead at Distna. What is it I can do for you?"

Whistler spelled out his request.

"Take you to Booster's *Errant Venture*?" He turned in the doorway and looked at the other man. "Mind if we take a side trip on our way to picking up your ship, Aves?"

"I've waited this long for my own command, Karrde, another week or so won't hurt." The man smiled broadly. "Besides, seeing Booster and the *Venture* is always amusing."

Whistler hooted and flashed another message in the air.

Karrde laughed and patted Whistler on the head as he straightened up. "Yes, Whistler, I do demand payment for my services. I suspect there are things you can tell me that will more than pay for your passage. If you negotiate with me as well as you negotiated your way here, I'm certain we'll reach a deal that will work for all concerned."

Waiting beside her father for the Skipray Blastboat to come to rest on the deck of the *Errant Venture*'s forward landing bay, Mirax wished she could be anywhere else. Just thinking about meeting Talon Karrde again took her back to the time when they'd worked together closely to bring Ysanne Isard down. And thinking of those times made her remember when Corran asked her to marry him, and her father's reaction when he discovered they were married.

Those memories ripped open the wound in her spirit caused by Corran's death. In it she found echoes of the pain she'd felt when Corran was believed to have died on Coruscant, but that pain seemed dull and distant. She realized that part of the reason she felt things more keenly now was because previously Wedge had helped her through the trouble, but he was gone, too. Wedge's death also hurt Iella and conjured up for her the pain of having lost her husband, Diric, on Coruscant.

The fact that the *Errant Venture* had visited Distna and found evidence of Rogue Squadron's demise made it impossible to believe they had not all died. When Corran went missing on Coruscant, the lack of a body meant she hadn't fully accepted his death as being real. While they found no body at Distna, they had found part of his X-wing, and some of the battlerooms recovered from other ships showed Corran's fighter had been hit and out of the battle fairly early on. *He would have been helpless to defend himself.*

She looked over at her father as the Blastboat's gangway extended itself and Booster started forward. "I really don't want to be here, Father."

"I know, Mirax, but Karrde requested your presence." Her father reached out with his right hand and drew her in under his arm. "Karrde might not be as smart as he thinks he is, but he's not a cruel man. If he wanted you here, it's not to hurt you."

She sighed and wrapped her left arm around her father's waist as they walked toward the ship. Booster had always bristled around Corran and found fault with him, but since his death Booster had been very kind and understanding. She was certain he would never admit to liking Corran, but he clearly understood how important Corran had been to her and refrained from disparaging him in front of her since their discovery at Distna.

She smiled. *Part of his desire to avenge Rogue Squadron doubtlessly comes from his love for Wedge, but I'll bet he wants to take a piece out of whoever killed Corran for having deprived him of something he planned to do himself someday.* She looked up at her father, then laid her head against his chest as he looked down at her. "Thank you."

Booster gave her shoulder a squeeze, then brought his arm up over her head and extended it to Talon Karrde. "You're looking smug as always, Karrde."

"I'm pleased to see you again, too, Booster." Karrde smoothed his mustache with his left hand. "You remember my associate, Aves?"

Booster shook the other man's hand. "This is the one you're turning the *Last Resort* over to? Congratulations on getting that command, Captain Aves."

Aves blinked with surprise, then looked over at Karrde. "I'm getting the *Last Resort*? How come Booster knew before I did? Either our security is slipping . . ."

"Or I'm just as brilliant as ever." Booster beamed and Mirax found his smile infectious. "I deduced it, actually."

Karrde arched an eyebrow at Booster. "Deduced it? This sounds very good."

"It was simple, really. You'll recall that because you're now 'retired,' I suggested obtaining the services of some of your people and ships."

Aves frowned. "You were going to sell him the *Last Resort*?"

"I only wanted to lease it from Karrde, provide him some retirement income."

Karrde laughed. "As I recall, you don't have any money."

Booster's head came up. "I'm not as liquid right now as I would like to be, but that is beside the point. Karrde told me the *Last Resort* was not available, but that the new commander might consider some sort of an arrangement. That's why you brought Aves here, isn't it, Karrde?"

"Oh, you thought . . . ?" Karrde shook his head. "It's the right answer for all the wrong reasons. This is what makes you dangerous, Booster."

Mirax's father nodded. "Don't forget it."

"Not likely." Karrde reached out and took Mirax's right hand in both of his. "I actually came to see you. I would never intrude on your grief, but I think I have some good news for you."

Mirax rested her left hand on top of his and smiled. "Thank you."

Karrde freed a hand and waved back at the Blastboat's hatchway. Mirax heard a triumphant squeal, then tore her hands from Karrde's and ran up the gangway. Dropping to her knees, she wrapped her arms around Whistler's cylindrical body. She clung tightly to the droid, feeling the breeze caused by his dome spinning around.

She eased her hug open, then sat back on her haunches. "Whistler, you're okay!" Another droid behind him hooted and she smiled at him, too. "Gate, you've survived!"

Karrde rested a hand on her shoulder. "Both of them are brimming with data, but a fair amount of operational secrecy is involved here. We might want to move to your father's office."

"Good idea." Mirax stood and walked down the gangplank with Whistler. She kept her hand on his dome, relish ing the coldness of his metal flesh. Even without word of Corran's survival, she knew he lived. If he were dead, Whistler would have been destroyed along with him. If he were injured, Whistler never would have left him. *The only way Whistler could be here is if Corran sent him, which means Corran's alive. Same thing goes for Wedge and Gate, so I have to imagine that most of Rogue Squadron survived and is elsewhere.*

The two droids, Booster, Aves, Karrde, and Mirax crowded into Booster's small office. Booster took the chair behind the desk, leaving Aves and Karrde to shift debris from other chairs to the floor. Booster slid the holoprojector plate on his desk toward the forward edge and Whistler approached it with his datajack extended. Yet before he could plug himself in, a light on the projector's comlink console blinked and Booster hit it.

"Booster here, this better be good."

Iella's head and shoulders appeared above the device. "Very good, Booster. I just had a message from General Cracken. He wants us on Coruscant as fast as possible. He didn't say much, but I gather he has news about Wedge. I can't believe it, but I gather Wedge and the others might be alive."

Booster smiled. "I think you can believe it, Iella. Come down to my office and you'll have more proof than you ever needed."

29

General Airen Cracken pointed the remote at the holo-projector set up in the center of the New Republic Ruling Council's private briefing room. The Councilors' tables made a three-sided square and the projector had been set up at the open end of the formation. It had been oriented toward Chief Councilor Mon Mothma, so when Wedge Antilles's image appeared, it looked straight at her.

"Admiral Ackbar, General Cracken, you have my sincere welcome. I apologize for any shock you feel at seeing me again. I *am* alive and on the day I recorded this message, Sienar Fleet Systems stock hit sixty-seven and seven-eighths on the Coruscant market, with twenty-three billion shares traded.

"Rogue Squadron survived the battle at Distna through the intervention of a group that has as much reason to hate Krennel as we do. They have offered their aid in destroying him and his Hegemony. Toward this end they have been training Rogue Squadron for a mission that will leave Ciutric open for conquest and allow us to rescue the *Lusankya* prisoners, including General Jan Dodonna. When Rogue Squadron is in place, you will be sent another message. You will have ten hours from that point to deliver a

leet to Ciutric. Details on Krennel's defenses are appended
to this message.

"I regret there is no way for you to reply to this message. You'll have four weeks to gather your fleet at the staging area and, within a week after that, the order to go will
be given. If you do not come, I have no doubt that Rogue
Squadron will truly die. I mention that not as motivation,
but as fact. Since we are already believed dead, you may not
want to confuse issues by announcing our survival just to
let people know we've died again."

Wedge raised his right hand and touched it to his brow
in a salute. "I look forward to speaking with both of you on
Ciutric. Antilles out."

The image faded to the Rogue Squadron crest, then
Cracken used the remote to shut off the projector. He raised
a hand as the Council members began to speak among
themselves and quieted them. "That message came in three
days ago, and was recorded four days before that. The delay in bringing it to your attention is my responsibility because I wanted my best people to look it over and they were
unavailable until yesterday. They concur that, despite the
beard, the speaker is Wedge Antilles."

Mon Mothma pressed her hands together and rested
her forearms on the table before her. "Did the datafiles shed
any more light on who else might have survived Distna?"

"It is clear from the files that Wedge thinks Janson is
missing. Their file also lists Asyr Sei'lar, Lyyr Zatoq, and
Khe-Jeen Slee as missing in action—none of them were
listed as being dead. Everyone else is alive, but only one person's immediate family has been notified of the squadron's
survival. I would not have let anyone know, save for the fact
that Corran Horn's wife was one of the people I used to ver-
ify the message was from Wedge Antilles."

Leia Organa Solo nodded. "Understandable, General.
It looked to be Wedge to me, too. How do we know he was
not under duress delivering this message?"

"Indeed, it could be bait for a trap." Sian Tevv, the Sullustan Councilor, looked around at the others. "Krennel
could have taken him in and be using him to trap our fleet."

Ackbar waved a webbed hand to dismiss that notion. "First, we have a code system in place to provide warning if one of our people is being forced under duress to make a message, and General Antilles used none of the code words that would have alerted us to trouble. More importantly the plan appended to the message calls for a fleet of sufficient force to smash Krennel's fleet. We have not employed such a large force against Krennel so far because we could not be certain we would catch him in one place. If we deployed that force against him and he struck outside the Hegemony, he would seriously damage the people's belief in our ability to free worlds of tyranny."

"As he continues to do by ambushing supply fleets headed for Liinade Three?" Borsk Fey'lya stroked the creamy fur on his throat. "That concerns me less, however than the fact that Antilles is coyly silent about the identity of the individuals who rescued Rogue Squadron at Distna. I would bet they are old-line Imperial in nature."

Cracken frowned at the Bothan Councilor. "Why would you suppose that, Councilor?"

"Do you not find it curious that out of the thirteen X-wing pilots flying that day, the three confirmed kills we have were nonhuman? Over three-quarters of those rescued were human. It strikes me that the Imperial bias is at play here."

Ackbar shook his head. "Ridiculous."

Cracken said nothing, and hoped he kept his surprise at Fey'lya's comments hidden. When Iella had arrived at Coruscant, she asked Cracken to come to the *Errant Venture* and there revealed to him Whistler's evidence of Ysanne Isard's survival and leadership of the group that was helping Rogue Squadron. The way the ambush at Distna had been set up certainly proved that the real Isard had intelligence assets in the New Republic still, and the fact that she'd not been mentioned by Wedge meant she wanted her role in things hidden. Since her help eliminating Krennel could be the basis for an amnesty, keeping her identity hidden seemed like a good ploy; but Cracken had sparred with her for too many years to let himself underestimate her or her penchant for duplicity.

Leia glanced over at the Bothan. "I would remind my learned colleague that the Hegemony worlds—despite Krennel's attempts to make them into a haven for humans—are only fifty-six percent human in population, and several worlds have a strong nonhuman majority."

"Who are ruled by a human minority, yes, Leia, I recall those worlds well." Fey'lya looked around the room at the other members of the Council. "I believe we have an unsavory situation here. I suspect very strongly that Krennel's subordinates are using Rogue Squadron to stage an uprising that will unseat Krennel, and they expect us to put them in his place. While they will say they are joining the New Republic, the reality of human oppression in the Hegemony will not be changed. I think we should reject this plan because of the obligations it will place on us."

Ackbar stood to disagree. "With all due respect, Councilor, I believe you are dreading a poor harvest and the first algae cloud has yet to appear. The plan appended to the message is decidedly sound and I see much of General Antilles's direction in it. This will be a stunning opportunity to smash Krennel. Even if he were to escape, we would still possess Ciutric, which is the political and economic hub of the Hegemony. We have always known a strike at Ciutric would shatter the Hegemony, and here is a plan that will allow us to do it."

"That is all well and good, Admiral Ackbar, but it still says nothing about the shadowy partners in this enterprise." Fey'lya stood and opened his arms. "What do we do if we discover that Grand Moff Tarkin didn't die on the Death Star, but has been lurking, waiting for this opportunity to ask for sanctuary? What do we do when he asks to be repaid for his role in this conquest of Ciutric? What if General Derricote, the architect of the Krytos virus, is not dead, but instead is behind this move? Do we welcome him? Perhaps this is Thrawn's ploy, or even one masterminded by Ysanne Isard. Don't look so surprised, Admiral, I have my sources that have told me what your *Lusankya* prisoners from Commenor have told you. No matter how beneficial their contribution to the New Republic is in this operation, could we reward them?"

Mon Mothma raised a hand. "If you will permit me, I must say that Councilor Fey'lya raises some interesting points. The question of when and how someone who has worked for the Empire may make a transition from enemy to friend is one we have not sufficiently addressed. We have accepted people like General Dodonna and General Madine without question. Even after the Emperor's death, we allowed Imperials who had seen the folly of their allegiance come over to us without penalty. General Garm Bel Iblis presents a different sort of example, one of someone who, while he was one of the Rebellion's founders, left us for a while because of differences with how things were being done. In choosing to rejoin us at an important moment, he contributed greatly to the New Republic's survival. We've accepted him, but there have been those who have grumbled over that fact."

Borsk Fey'lya smiled, bowed his head toward Mon Mothma, and seated himself.

She continued. "These questions, however important, really have little bearing on the issue at hand. We started a war with the Hegemony and, so far, have failed to achieve a satisfactory outcome. Wedge Antilles offers us a perfectly good plan that will allow us to end this conflict quickly. The only reason I can see for rejecting it is if it is unmilitarily sound. Admiral Ackbar says it is not, and we have trusted his judgment before in similar matters. I see no reason to doubt him now."

Ackbar lowered himself to his chair. "I believe I can assemble the taskforce required to take the world within the two weeks. We will be ready to go then."

Sian Tevv's large ears curled forward. "You should take the full month. If you do, if the reports from the Bilbringi shipyards are correct, the *Lusankya* will be operational. I would think adding a Super Star Destroyer's firepower to any taskforce would be worth the delay."

"The *Lusankya* will take longer to be combat ready. We have not finished training a crew, and several more shakedown runs will be needed before the techs turn it over to a crew that can fight from her." Admiral Ackbar's barabels twitched. "Still, your point about firepower is a good one. To be on the safe side I will bring in more ships than called for, to provide me with a reaction force in case Krennel finds new allies."

Cracken pointed a finger and swung it around to include everyone in the room. "The most important point concerning this operation is simple: No word of it may leave this room. We suspect Krennel has some intelligence assets within the government here—ex-Imperials, speciesist crazies, whomever. If any word of this leaks, the whole operation will fail horribly."

Mon Mothma nodded solemnly. "I'm certain all the Council members understand this. No leak of this affair will come from Coruscant."

Ackbar stood again. "Then, if I may have your leave, we have planning to do."

Outside the chamber, Ackbar rested a heavy hand on Cracken's shoulder. "Did I cover it well?"

"Yes, Admiral, better than most of my operatives would have." Cracken smiled. The message from Wedge Antilles had come in two forms. One, which they had played for the Council, specified five weeks before an attack. The other, which they kept secret, chopped two weeks off the staging time. The inevitable leak from Coruscant would have Krennel waiting for an attack that would take place two weeks after they'd already smashed his fleet. Cracken had no real love for deceiving his bosses, but if a deception would protect the warriors who would die because of leaks, he had no problem lying as much as necessary.

"Better than your operatives? I find that hard to believe." Ackbar led the way between two guards into Cracken's office suite in the Imperial Palace. They passed through his antechamber, into his office, and into the totally secure briefing room beyond it. Cracken closed the door behind them and Ackbar seated himself at the briefing table.

Cracken smiled and took his place at the head of the table. "Admiral, I believe you know these people. Iella Wessiri was an investigator at the Celchu trial, Mirax Terrik you've met, and this is her father, Booster."

The Mon Cal nodded his head. "I know of Booster only by reputation, and quite the reputation it is."

Booster nodded to Ackbar. "It's so good to be loved."

Airen Cracken posted his arms on the end of the table to hold himself up. "Okay, this is the situation. The Council has given us the go-ahead to run with Wedge's plan. We've not told them that the real Ysanne Isard is alive. They've discovered Ysanne Isard is supposedly working for Krennel, but they don't believe it and we're not about to tell them she's a clone. The only source we have for the real Isard's survival is Whistler, which is good enough for me. News about Isard's survival can't leave this room."

Mirax leaned forward. "Isn't having the Council think Isard is working for Krennel as dangerous as letting them know the real Isard is alive?"

"No, because any rumor of Isard working for Krennel that gets back to the genuine Isard will just confirm how good her intelligence sources are. If she knows that we know she's alive, however, she'll vanish and we'll never find her until she wants to be found, and I don't like that idea at all." Cracken sighed. "Look, you're three of the shrewdest people in the galaxy, with access to intelligence resources I don't have. You're already in on the secret here, and expanding the circle of knowledge is not going to be a good thing, so you're it. The game here is this: If Isard is offering us Krennel, it's because she's after something bigger. I want to know what it is and I want to make sure she doesn't get it. That's your job. You have to figure it out without letting anyone know what you're doing, and have to stop her."

Booster laughed. "Is that all?"

Cracken snarled. "You have two weeks in which to do

it. Maybe less. If she discovers Whistler and Gate are gone, she may bolt."

Booster smiled. "Records will show the two droids were destroyed on Brentaal."

"Nice work, Booster, but this is Isard we're talking about. If anyone will see through that deception, she will." Cracken straightened up and folded his arms over his chest. "You've got to see through *her* deception and, for all our sakes, I hope your first guess is your best guess, because we won't get another shot at her."

30

Wedge Antilles looked at the datapad in his left hand and nodded when an ALL CLEAR message flashed across it. He unplugged the small surveillance device detection scanner from it and tossed the wandlike item to Corran. The ex-CorSec officer wound the cord around the wand and slipped it into his pocket. Wedge hoped he'd be able to slip it back into the base's security office before it was noted as missing. *And I hope this meeting is over before security comes in to see why the bugs Corran deactivated aren't working.*

He looked around at the other eight pilots gathered with him in the small briefing room. "I don't know how much time we'll have before someone is sent to look in on us, but we're clear for the moment. I know you've been briefed on the plan and we've run some very good sims of it, but I'm sensing some anxiety. Tell me what's going on."

Down in the front row, Gavin leaned forward in his chair and rested his elbows on his knees. "We're taking all the risk on this run. We go in first, we're there for a week before the attack comes. We have a lot of exposure, and I can't help but feel that Isard might just betray us to Krennel."

Wedge nodded. "Of course, if she wanted us dead,

she could have killed us at Distna, or at any time she's had us here. She could have even brought us to Krennel as prisoners."

"But by having us inserted into Ciutric, she shows Krennel the weakness in his security setup." Inyri Forge fingered her lower lip for a second. "Revealing that breach to him could reinforce the idea that Krennel needs her."

Tycho disagreed from his position by the square room's only door. "Allying herself with Krennel would put her in an inferior position. If we pull this off, if she's instrumental in taking Krennel down and freeing the *Lusankya* prisoners, she'll put the New Republic's government in a difficult position. They will be in her debt, but she's the one who had the Krytos virus created. How she is dealt with could create major human-nonhuman fractures in the New Republic."

"I agree with Tycho, but I think that political pressure angle is too slow for her." Corran sat back, tugging absently at one end of the long mustache he'd grown as part of his disguise. "I think we can all agree that she's going to back-stab us somehow, right?"

Wedge saw everyone's head bob in agreement with Corran's question. "Okay, so now we have to figure out how she'll do it."

Myn Donos raised a hand. "Look, I don't have the same history with her that the rest of you do, but from all I've heard I get the impression she's very pragmatic."

"Keep going, Myn."

"Okay, so if she's pragmatic, it strikes me that she's going to use the group that beat her—Rogue Squadron—to hurt Krennel badly. You did it before on Axxila and Ciutric, so you can do it one more time, putting an end to him. This suggests to me that whatever she'll do to us, she'll do *after* we take Krennel down."

Wedge felt a chill run down his spine. "Or she'll do it *before* we take him down, but have it take effect *after* we've succeeded."

Gavin frowned. "I'm not sure I follow that."

"Remember the mess she made with the Krytos virus?" Wedge, feeling weary, rubbed his eyes with his left hand.

"She gets someone into the facility where the *Lusankya* prisoners are being held and infects them with a deadly virus that takes a long time to manifest: a month, a year, maybe longer. All of them will be heroes, all of them will be paraded around through the upper crust of the New Republic. All at once this disease wipes out the New Republic's leadership, leaving the nation in turmoil while a public health crisis looms. Isard and an alliance of ex-Imperials step in to restore order, offering a cure for the disease. She blames the initial infection on her clone, comes in as a hero to save the day, and suddenly she's back in power."

The room fell silent as the pilots pondered Wedge's scenario. The surprised expressions and pale faces reflected the horror Wedge felt in his gut. What amazed him the most was that no one offered a denial of the plot he'd described. *We all know, firsthand, that she's capable of such cruelty.*

Corran spoke first. "The nastiest part of your scenario is that it would also kill off the *Lusankya* prisoners. When she and I spoke, she said she was glad the *Lusankya* had been destroyed at Thyferra because after I escaped from it, it had been soiled. The prisoners were part of that desecration and I think she would have killed them if she had been in control of them. She doesn't like keeping reminders of her failure around with her."

Wedge nodded. "That's a good point. Tycho?"

"I think we all agree she's more than capable of doing what you're suggesting. I also think there are simpler ways of causing us trouble. Perhaps the defenses for the prison are tougher than we imagine, so the guards will have a chance to kill all the prisoners. That would make us all feel horrible, and likely get Two Flight killed in its attempt to neutralize the defenses."

"Okay, so we run sims in which we toughen up the opposition." The General looked around the room. "What else?"

Nrin raised a hand. "I think it will be important for us to have a plan to quarantine the prisoners to prevent the disease from spreading. We need to let them know they're at risk. They'll need to speak with someone they know and trust, which means Tycho or Corran."

Corran shook his head. "Ah, um, the last time I was with them, I let them know that Tycho was a traitor. I can roll in and talk to them."

"Ah, Corran, General Dodonna knows me, too." Wedge smiled. "We'll both record messages to him and everyone will carry a datacard with the messages on them. If we go down, the messages still get in."

A knock at the door ended the discussion. Tycho opened the door and admitted Colonel Vessery. "Sorry to disturb you."

"Just debriefing after a sim run. We want to make some changes—a worst-case scenario thing. We want to see how bad it can get."

Vessery nodded. "Good idea, but you'll have to hurry. Negotiations are final. You'll be going in to Ciutric two days from now. Krennel believes you'll be hyperspacing for a couple of days to get there, but the trip will only take six hours or so. Once you're in place, you send the appropriate message and set things in motion."

"Thank you, Colonel. We'll be ready."

"I'm sure you will." Vessery hesitated. "I've enjoyed working with you all. I believe you have a saying for times like this: May the Force be with you. I really do hope it is. If you succeed, if *we* succeed, we can all go home again."

Popping out of hyperspace near Ciutric, Wedge tried to match his memory of the system with what he saw now. He got no sense of recognition, of having been there before, but that struck him as just as well. On Ciutric Rogue Squadron had lost one of its most beloved pilots, Ibtisam. Remembering brought a lump to his throat, which he swallowed against.

He keyed his comm unit. "How are you doing, Eight?"

Nrin's voice came back even, but a bit tight. "I am fine, Colonel Roat." His words revealed none of the pain he had to be feeling. He had been closer to Ibtisam than anyone else had—a fact made remarkable because of the traditional rivalries between the Quarren and the Mon Calamari. Her death had crushed Nrin emotionally and, after a leave of absence, he had accepted a transfer from Rogue Squadron to a training squadron.

"Good to hear, Eight." Wedge flipped the comm unit over to the Spaceport Authority channel he'd been given. "This is Colonel Antar Roat with Requiem Squadron. We are nine ships in total and wish landing clearance."

"Ciutric Spaceport Authority here. You will be switched to military control. Destination beacon at one-three-nine-three-eight coming on now. Please tune your autolanding function to that frequency and initiate autolanding programs."

"As ordered, Ciutric. Executing now." Wedge punched a red button with his left thumb and felt the control buck a bit as the Defender's computer controls locked on to the beacon and began to use the data it was sending to plot the entry and landing speed and vectors. Wedge relaxed his grip on the yoke, but didn't let it go entirely. He had a pilot's distrust of mechanical flying systems, and since he was running into a hostile environment, he wanted to take full control of the ship if anything started to go wrong.

Of course, the disguise he was wearing did make flying a bit more awkward. When he had assumed the Roat identity to get onto Imperial Center, the head prosthetic had been an extensive affair that covered the right side of his face, from forehead to cheek and back over his ear. A piece of it had wrapped down over his jaw and pressed against his voice box. Because Roat had been bound for Imperial Center for reconstructive surgery, the prosthetic had been modified and minimized to be a metal device that built up his right eye socket, with a thin line of metal that led down to the blinking device that pressed against his larynx and altered the sound of his voice. The eye construct unbalanced his face enough that, coupled with the beard, he looked nothing like the various images the Empire had circulated of Wedge Antilles.

His helmet hid the facial modifications, but his flight suit did not hide the other change. His right hand ended in a blocky construct that featured only two thick fingers and a thumb. It whirred and clicked as Wedge moved the hand around. The device slowed his hand movements somewhat, but it had a cutout switch that he could use in combat to let him have full use of his hand.

As annoying as all this stuff is, it's much better than flying with an Ewok puppet in my lap. That recollection tightened Wedge's gut. He'd been forced to fly disguised as an Ewok pilot because of one of Wes Janson's practical jokes. *Wes will be sorely missed.*

Despite his misgivings about turning control of his fighter over to Krennel's people, the automatic beacon brought the Defenders down without incident. Military control informed the pilots that they would have to land their own fighters and designated landing spots for each of them. Wedge offered his thanks. Letting his pilots land their own craft marked the respect the military controllers had for pilots.

Wedge was impressed to see Krennel waiting with other staff officers to greet his people. Wedge set his Defender down with a gentle hand, shut down all systems, and popped open the egress hatch. He thanked the tech rolling up a staircase for him, and when on the deck, doffed his helmet and handed it to the tech. He stepped to the front of his fighter, then looked to his left, down the row of pilots. When they'd all taken their places, he took one step forward and saluted Krennel.

The Prince-Admiral returned the salute, then stepped away from his advisors and approached Wedge. "Colonel Roat, I am most pleased you have chosen to bring your squadron of Defenders to me. You will be a great asset to the Hegemony."

The modulator on Wedge's throat injected a buzz into his voice. "It is our pleasure to find the single man with the courage to keep the spark of the Empire alive."

"Walk with me, Colonel. Introduce me to your me . . . people."

Wedge fell into step with Krennel. He introduced him to Gavin, Hobbie, and Myn as One Flight. Krennel spoke with each, but never offered his right hand to them. Since it was a prosthetic, this did not surprise Wedge at all. Krennel instead patted them on the shoulders with his flesh-and-blood hand, gracing each with a smile and a nod of the head.

Wedge had to admit Krennel was good. The display suggested Krennel took it as a personal compliment that the pilots had come over to join his Hegemony. He made a personal connection with each of them and Wedge had no doubt Krennel would remember and use the details he learned about them in subsequent conversations, when or if he ever saw them again. *He does have a certain charisma, which explains how he has gotten this far.*

Krennel slowed as he reached Two Flight. First in order were Tycho and Inyri. Both had dyed their hair a bright red and they looked enough alike to be brother and sister, which was exactly how Wedge introduced them. "Prince-Admiral, this is Major Teekon Fass and his sister, Inyon. While it is unusual to have a female pilot in a squadron, Requiem's mission required the best pilots we could find. Inyon tested out very highly, so I brought her into the program. It is a decision I have not had cause to regret."

"Indeed?" Krennel's smile diminished only slightly. "I shall look forward to a demonstration of her prowess. A pleasure to meet you both."

They moved on down the line to Ooryl. "This is the Gand Zukvir. He is a Findsman, much like his kinsman Zuckuss, who worked for Lord Vader. The Findsman's skill in a fighter is superior to most men, and his loyalty is absolute."

"Fascinating." Krennel pointed toward Nrin with his metal hand. "And here we have a Quarren."

"Captain Notha Dab, yes." Wedge smiled as much as his prosthetic allowed him to. "Dab has been tireless in his training and, while we were considering joining your Hegemony, he was your greatest proponent."

"Really?" Krennel lifted his chin. "And why was that, Captain Dab?"

Nrin's facial tentacles curled up to reveal two needle-sharp fangs. "Can't kill Mon Cals in the New Republic, Prince-Admiral. You will give me the best opportunity to do that."

A cold smile blossomed on Krennel's face. "You'll get that chance, Captain Dab, very soon, I'm certain." The Prince-Admiral turned to Wedge. "I commend your employment of interspecies rivalries to fuel your people's desires to fight."

"So nice of you to notice, Prince-Admiral." Wedge led him on to where Corran stood. In addition to growing the mustache, Corran had dyed his hair jet black. His pale skin and green eyes made for a sharp contrast that made him a bit difficult for Wedge to recognize. "This is Captain Pyr Hand. He is better known among us as Klick."

"'Klick,' as in slang for kilometer?"

Corran nodded.

"And why is that?"

Corran blinked his eyes once, slowly. "I'm a dead shot at that range, Prince-Admiral."

"Excellent." Krennel turned from the line and led Wedge with him toward his knot of advisors. "Well, Colonel Roat, your people impress me, for the most part. I'm pleased to have you with us."

"Thank you, Prince-Admiral." Wedge gave the man a quick smile. "I think you'll find we add a dimension to your defenses you haven't even realized you lacked until now."

31

Iella Wessiri glanced over to where Booster Terrik lay sleeping in the corner of the briefing room, then smiled at Mirax. "Nice thing about Booster's snoring is that it's likely to knock out any listening devices the scanners have missed."

"I'd begrudge him the sleep, but he's been really good at thinking like Isard." Mirax rested her chin on both hands. "Of course, realizing my father can simulate a cold-blooded mass murderer so well isn't very reassuring. If we have kids, I'm not sure how often we'll let them stay with their grandfather."

Iella hid a yawn behind a hand. "I know I should press you on this 'kids' thing, but I'm too tired. It's not that I don't care."

"Good. I've got 'Aunt Iella' first on the list for free baby-sitting services."

The briefing room doorway opened and Iella caught the scent of caf before General Cracken could make it all the way into the room. He brought with him a tray containing four large, steaming mugs and slid it onto the table. "Thought you could use some caf at this hour of the night."

"We could use some of what Booster's getting, really."

"Iella's right, but I'll settle for half my father's caf at this point."

Cracken seated himself and passed out the beverages. "Please, drink up. I wanted to tell you that I'm very pleased and grateful for your work. Hmmm, just as well Booster's asleep for that part. Admiral Ackbar and I have gone over your various scenarios and agree that several are highly probable. We're focusing in on those that involve the prisoners."

Mirax lowered her mug and jerked her head toward her father's sleeping form. "Those were largely Booster's work. He concocted what he called Isard's 'Hierarchy of Hatred,' then figured out what she could do to maximize damage to her enemies. Something as simple as denying ground support to liberate the prison would result in the deaths of the prisoners, a rough time for the Rogues and ground-based defenses that would make the New Republic's fight against Krennel much closer. Everyone gets hurt: the prisoners, the Rogues, Krennel, and the New Republic. Just the kind of mischief she'd love."

"We're taking precautions that should cover all of those eventualities. No guarantees, but we'll be doing our best." Cracken sat back in his chair, wrapping his hands around the caf mug. "The other scenarios, ones based on her repeating the Krytos virus situation, are frightening as well. We're mobilizing assets that can help us detect, isolate, and cure anyone who is infected, but for all we know Ciutric is just going to be one big sick world. It's not at all what we want to deal with, but we can't discount that possibility either."

Iella shook her head. "It doesn't seem like we've come up with much for two weeks' worth of work, but we've gone over every file that mentions her, all the rumors about her that we've heard over the years, and even had Booster trying to think like her. I know we've worked hard, but I can't help feel that we've missed something."

Mirax reached across the table to squeeze Iella's hand. "Isard is just one big ocean of evil. No real way to know if we've found all the currents running deep there."

Iella arched an eyebrow at Mirax. "We really have been speaking a lot with Admiral Ackbar, haven't we?"

"Yeah, it'll be months before I stop using ocean analogies."

"Well, you'll get your chance to begin recovering soon. Admiral Ackbar and I leave for the primary staging area in four hours." Cracken fished inside his tunic and withdrew two datacards. He slid one to Mirax and the other to Iella. "Because you won't be able to talk to us, I want you to have these."

Iella picked up the datacard and turned it over. It looked entirely normal, save for platinum triangles at each of the corners. She flipped it front again, then held it up between her left thumb and forefinger. "This contains ultra-clearance codes?"

Cracken nodded solemnly. "Army, Navy, Intelligence, Governmental from the Republic level on down to major municipal levels, and many corporate levels as well. It also has codes that will allow you to access five million credits—each. Based on the authorization in the card, you can go anywhere and do anything you need to do. If you think of something, no matter how wild, and you need to take steps to stop Isard, this will allow you to take them."

Booster rolled over onto his back. "Good, we can use it to buy more guns for my ship."

"That's why you don't have one of the cards, Booster."

The smuggler stretched. "The New Republic has no sense of gratitude at all."

"Go back to sleep, Father." Mirax slipped her card into a pocket. "I take it you want us to keep working on this until Isard is found or gives herself up?"

"That's it. Do whatever you have to do. If you have to break laws, try to be discreet, and if you have to kill anyone, well, try not to raze any planets."

Mirax blinked. "You're serious about this."

"Very." Cracken finished his caf and stood. "May the Force be with you."

Iella watched him leave the room, then looked again at

the card in her hands. "They're putting a lot of trust in us. They're giving us a lot of responsibility. We can't fail."

"We won't." Mirax got up, walked over to where her father lay, and gently nudged his ribs with her toe. "Wake up, old man, time to start working again. Come up with something brilliant."

Booster smiled as he sat up. He stretched again, then walked around and usurped Cracken's place at the table. "Okay, ladies, we've examined Isard's history of atrocities. We've gone through her Hierarchy of Hate. There's only one thing left for us to look at. We have to examine her dream ladder."

Iella shook her head and bolted another slug of caf. "I must be dreaming myself, because that made no sense. Her 'dream ladder'?"

Mirax held a hand up. "I think I know where he's going with this. Care to open the help files for us?"

"It's simplicity itself, ladies." Booster hefted the remaining full mug in a salute. "We look at her sense of greed. If control of the galaxy is her goal, we know where she'll get when she scales that ladder. Starting from the top, then, we go down, rung by rung, looking at how she'll have to plan her ascent. Eventually we'll work down to the lowest rung she has access to right now, and that's where we'll have her."

Iella exhaled slowly. "That will take forever and we have, at best, a week."

Booster flicked a finger against her card. "Let's order more caf then. If you're right that we missed something before, this is the way we'll find it. And when we do, we'll spill Ysanne Isard and her dreams into a black hole she'll never escape."

Wedge Antilles kept his gloved right hand on his thigh, beneath the level of the table at Shine Astara, one of the premiere restaurants in Ciutric's capital, Daplona. Wedge realized the place would require his best behavior, since the first word of the name was pronounced "sheen" with an

Imperial lilt that required the speaker to press his teeth together as he said it. *Given that I've already sent the message that will bring Admiral Ackbar and Isard's people down on this world inside a week, being on my best behavior is the least I can do for my host.*

Keeping teeth clenched together that way *did* make it easier to sneer, a trait that his host, Colonel Lorrir, had perfected. Lorrir struck Wedge as being an Imperial's Imperial. Tall, slender, angular, and very proper, Lorrir almost seemed to have been put together from a kit. The fact that he only had a white fringe of hair on his head indicated this wasn't true, since a full head of black hair would have made him the perfect image of an officer. Lorrir made up for that defect by being very demanding, which meant working with him had been tough for Wedge.

But shooting him down in sim wasn't that tough. Wedge suppressed a smile.

Colonel Lorrir nodded in his direction. "You are to be congratulated, Colonel, for how well your troops are trained. You are very formidable in combat." He looked around at the others gathered at the table. "If you can believe it, Colonel Roat even shot me down."

The other dinner guests gasped in astonishment, then looked at Wedge. "How ever did you manage that?" asked one officer's plump wife.

"Colonel Lorrir is too kind. He made shooting him down very difficult." Wedge nodded to his host. *His reliance on sideslipping to evade a following ship made me sure he was luring me into a trap. I was far too cautious because he's just not that great a pilot.* "Colonel, you clearly have superior flying skills. You have many combat kills under your belt, I imagine."

Lorrir's bald head glowed golden in the restaurant's muted light. "Yes, well, before I was transferred to the Prince-Admiral's ship *Reckoning*, I spent some time in the One Eighty-first Imperial Fighter Group. That was back when Baron Fel was in command. I was a mere Lieutenant, but a Lieutenant in that unit was the equal of a Major in any other."

Wedge tuned the man out as a waiter came over with two bottles of wine. "Since I am having the braised nerf, I'll have the green, if you don't mind."

The waiter hesitated and Wedge quickly caught the curling of Lorrir's lip into a sneer.

"Of course, I meant I would prefer the *emerald*." Wedge shook his head. "Back where I came from the wait-beasts were hardly discerning enough to understand the proper terms for wine. They would even opt for a ruby when consuming fish, if you can imagine it."

The voice modulator erased the slightly mocking tone in Wedge's words, though he had serious doubts that the two Hegemony officers or their wives would have caught them. Krennel's staff seemed to be largely filled with courtiers whose ability to please the Prince-Admiral out-shone their ability to fight or properly administer a unit. He had no doubt that they followed orders to the letter, which made them perfect for Krennel's purposes, but dulled the sort of initiative that would have made them a threat to the Rogue operation.

Lorrir's wife, Kandise, patted Wedge's left hand. "Now don't you be worried about that sort of thing anymore, Colonel Roat. The Hegemony is a bastion of Imperial culture, so you are safe here."

"You are too kind, Madam Lorrir." Wedge gave her a quick smile, then focused on her husband. "You were telling of your time with the One Eighty-first. You were with them at Brentaal?"

"I was." Lorrir sniffed mightily, then sipped some of the dark red wine the waiter had poured for him. "We would have held the world against the Rebels save for one man's betrayal."

"Admiral Lon Isoto."

Wedge's comment blanketed the table in silence. Lorrir set his wine glass down carefully and clasped his hands together. Kandise laid her left hand on his right forearm, but he shook it off irritably. Lorrir's dark eyes narrowed and the man clearly struggled to keep from exploding.

"Colonel Roat, I shall assume that because you have

long been involved in researches and developments that have kept you outside the mainstream of the Empire that you have said what you said. Your ignorance of the true facts will shield you at this time from my wrath, but understand that I will not allow you to slander the name of one of the finest military minds the Empire ever had."

Wedge went cold. Rogue Squadron had been part of the Rebel operation that took Brentaal IV from the Empire. Admiral Lon Isoto had been given command of the world and failed utterly to do anything that would protect it. He allowed the Rebels to take the moon that and, from there, stage and land on Brentaal. The only serious opposition had come from Fel's 181st.

"I apologize, Colonel, for angering you. I assumed . . . but that assumption was wrong. Who was it that betrayed us on Brentaal?"

"Baron Fel."

"What?!" Wedge made no attempt to cover his surprise. "I find that hard to believe. Not to question your integrity, but I understood that Fel had fought hard at Brentaal."

"Oh, he did, fought hard enough to lure us into a trap." Lorrir's voice dripped with contempt. "You probably are unaware that after we lost Brentaal Four, Fel went over to the Rebellion. He joined Rogue Squadron. Clearly Brentaal Four was the price he paid for clemency in their eyes."

Wedge nodded. "Ah, I see." After Fel's defection, the Empire had begun a disinformation campaign that clearly vilified Fel and elevated Isoto to the level of a hero. *By doing that they shielded others from facing the dilemma Fel had, and prevented them from making the same choice he did. He saw the Empire was evil and rejected it, but these others, they remain willfully blind.*

He sipped some of his emerald wine and relished the hints of berry flavor in the vintage. "I also understood Rogue Squadron was there at Brentaal Four."

"Yes, the squadron that cannot die." Lorrir laughed and his companions joined him. "Rogue Squadron is the biggest fraud perpetrated by the Rebels on their sick adherents. That squadron is constantly being rebuilt because they die so easily. We killed eight or nine at Brentaal, and would have gotten the rest of them had they not run off. We shredded the Y-wings they should have been protecting, destroying an entire wing of them. That engagement alone, around Oradin, would have made me an ace—had I not already been one, of course."

"Fascinating." Wedge frowned for a moment. "I did think, however, that some Rogue Squadron members had been around for a while."

"Indeed, and you can expect them back again. Antilles, Janson, Celchu—they will show up as a nucleus for the unit."

"But they're dead. Didn't you destroy them at Distna?"

"The Rebels claim they never found bodies. Part of the ploy to bring them back again." Lorrir lowered his voice. "Clones."

"Oh my." Wedge shivered. "I never would have thought they would do something like that."

"No, nor does anyone else. That's the pity of it, really, so many people being misled by such a dishonest group." Lorrir shook his head, then raised his glass. "A toast: to a time when such lies will die the death they deserve, and the truth will shine forth."

"I'll drink to that." Wedge touched his glass to the others. "And may that day come sooner than we might dare to hope."

32

Colonel Vessery entered the dimly lit briefing room with his helmet under his left arm. He started to sketch a salute, but neither Major Telik nor Ysanne Isard looked up at him. Instead they intently studied the small holograph of a man's head and shoulders.

The holographic figure spoke in hushed tones. "Ackbar's fleet left here ten standard minutes ago on an outbound course that will bring him to Ciutric. Ship list appended."

Telik stood back and smiled. "The message was sent two hours ago, which means Ackbar has eight hours to hit his target. We only need six to get to ours."

Isard nodded solemnly, then turned toward Vessery. "Colonel, I know you developed some affection for the Rogues while you trained them."

The cold tone of her voice sent a chill through Vessery, but he met her gaze openly. "I did. They are fine pilots. I have little doubt they will acquit their portions of the operation admirably. My feelings and respect for them aside, Madam Director, my pilots and I stand ready to execute our orders as well."

"I had no doubt of that, Colonel." Isard pursed her lips

for a second. "I have allowed a message to reach Krennel that indicated another attempt to reinforce Liinade Three is being made in two days. That will keep Krennel at Ciutric in preparation for another ambush. He may even call in additional troops and ships, which would translate into a surprise for Ackbar. It will be a glorious battle over Ciutric, I believe."

Telik shrugged. "We would not have time to watch much of it anyway."

"No, indeed you wouldn't, so it's just as well you won't be there." She laughed, but Vessery heard no mirth in it at all. "In rushing out to destroy Krennel, Ackbar has stripped the defenses from the greatest prize of all. Come with me, men, and in six hours we will be in a position of power that will make the New Republic tremble itself to pieces."

Prince-Admiral Krennel smiled predatorily as he listened to Isard's report. "Another convoy? How rich. How can they afford to be sending so many freighters on these very dangerous missions?"

Isard stalked the shadows at the fringes of his office. "I am not certain they *can* continue to do so, Prince-Admiral."

Krennel looked up from his desk. "Explain."

She stopped pacing and faced him. "The primary problem with a free society of the sort the New Republic represents itself to be is that a great deal of information is available on any and all subjects, save those they wish to keep secret. The fact remains, however, that a great deal of the publicly available information does touch on the secret. For example, in the past, when freighters have been diverted from their normal commercial duties to haul supplies, commodity prices on worlds that are experiencing a delay in shipping tend to rise and fall depending upon their import and export status. Factories that produce the sorts of materials a convoy like that will carry have to hire new workers, or offer overtime pay, all of which is data that is noted in stock advisories. These and dozens of other indicators like them can be correlated to a military operation. The plain fact is that I've not seen such indicators rise in the pattern set by the previous convoys."

"No movement at all?"

"I didn't say that." Isard frowned. "There *are* movements, but they hint more at another planetary invasion. It has been a quiet buildup and would have been unnoticed save for downward fluctuations in entertainment sectors of the economy that are tied to military bases from which the troops are drawn. As well an inordinate number of ships are being reported as being 'on maneuvers,' which usually presages action."

"And this information about a convoy, it was leaked to you through a previously reliable source?"

"Yes, though no report goes unverified." She pressed her hands together and rested her chin on her fingertips. "This is why I have noted the problems to you."

"I gathered that, thank you. I suspect, if we check the course of that convoy, there is really only one good spot for an ambush, and we would have been hit there ourselves. Two days, is it, when they expected to hit us?"

"Two days, yes."

"Good." Krennel stood and punched a button on his desktop comm unit. "Captain, have my shuttle standing by. I will be heading up to the *Reckoning*. Issue recall orders for all crew on leave. That recall applies to *Binder* as well. Have Captain Phulik meet me on *Reckoning*. Krennel out."

Isard nodded her head at him. "You'll be striking somewhere in the New Republic."

"I will. Once on *Reckoning* I will call for *Emperor's Wisdom* and *Decisive* to join me here to stage our raid. They should get here in four hours or so. From here we will be ready to launch the boldest raid yet, one that will show the New Republic as the sham it truly is. Eighteen short hours after we leave here, they will learn the folly of attacking me."

Isard's eyes glistened. "Eighteen hours. You'll strike at Coruscant?"

"Yes. It's a lesson the New Republic has never learned."

Krennel gave Isard a thin-lipped smile. "To kill an enemy, the quickest method is always to strike at the head."

Corran Horn had actually gotten to like some of the pilots in Krennel's employ. The nicest were the guys drawn from the Hegemony itself. They seemed interested in defending their homes from encroachment by the New Republic, and Corran had to respect that. Still, their motivation wasn't the main reason Corran liked them.

He looked down at his sabacc hand and stifled a smile. *These guys from the Hegemony must be the* worst *sabacc players I've ever met.* The stack of credit chits in front of him dwarfed the piles before the other three men playing. Better yet, he had the ace of flasks down on the table, in the interference field, and the flux had shifted the two cards in his hand into the ace of coins and the court card endurance, which was worth negative 8. Since each ace was worth 15, this left his hand with a total of 22, which was only one shy of the 23 total to win.

A grizzled older pilot looked at him. "Your bet, Klick."

Corran slid his other two cards facedown on top of the ace of flasks. "I'm locked. I'll bet two hundred credits."

Two of the pilots tossed their hands in, but the older man squinted at his cards, then tossed two gold credit chits onto the hand pot pile. "I call."

"Twenty-two." Corran slowly flipped his cards over so the others could read them. "Can you beat it?"

"No." The older man snarled. "Emperor's Black Bones, you are the luckiest cardplayer I've ever met."

"Not luck, skill." Corran glanced at the sabacc table's data readout. It indicated the pot contained 2,500 credits, 250 of which he skimmed off and fed into the sabacc pot, which currently stood at 15,000 credits. A two-card 23—which was known as a pure sabacc—or another three-card combination of 0, 2, and 3—the *idiot's array*—would win that pot and end the game. "My deal, I believe."

Corran gathered the cards and reached up to feed them

into the LeisureMech RH7 Cardshark dealer-droid. The dealer-droid—which hung down from the ceiling—shuffled the cards, then extended its body so its manipulator arms could drop a card before each player. It swiveled around noiselessly and the twin stun pikes—which most players called "cheater prods"—remained retracted. After a second circuit, the cylindrical body withdrew into its base. Its withdrawal triggered the flux, shifting the value of the cards.

Corran reached for his cards, but before he could get them off the table, a siren began to rise and fall in tone and volume. Yellow lights began burning over every doorway. The other players immediately looked up, scooped up their winnings, then turned away from the table.

"What's going on?"

The old man shrugged. "Report to your ship." He gestured at a holographic imaging station at the far end of the hangar. "If it's like before, the Prince-Admiral will tell us what's going on."

"What about the pot?"

"We give sabacc pots to the Survivor's Fund. You have a problem with that?"

"Not me." Corran stuffed his winnings into the pockets of his flight suit. "Get going, I'm right behind you."

They ran from the ready room and Corran split off to the right where the whole Defender squadron had been assembled in the back of the hangar. He found the rest of the Rogues already there, with Hobbie and Myn rubbing sleepsand from their eyes, and Tycho rubbing his wet hair dry with a towel from a refresher station. The only person he couldn't find was Wedge.

The imaging station at the other end of the hangar filled with bright light that resolved itself down into the face of Prince-Admiral Krennel. "Greetings loyal warriors of the Hegemony. I would apologize for summoning you so abruptly, but this is a call to war and one I imagine you will relish. Our enemies have made a mistake and have provided us an opportunity that is quite rare. With one blow we can end the tyranny of the New Republic and send their shattered forces scurrying home."

Corran glanced over at Tycho, then tapped the chronometer on his left wrist. *By my count, we've got a couple of hours yet before Isard's people and the New Republic get here.* "Any guesses?"

Tycho shook his head. "Too soon for guesses."

Krennel smiled magnificently. "All squadrons will be getting their assignments. You will be on board your appointed ships as fast as possible, and then we will depart to fulfill our destiny."

33

"Colonel Roat!" Lorrir's voice echoed through the nearl empty hangar. "Why aren't your people in the air yet?"

Wedge spun on his heel and hooked his thumb through the blaster belt he wore outside his flight suit "I believe, Colonel Lorrir, we had an understanding abou that. My Defenders are equipped with hyperdrive, w don't need to be loaded on the *Reckoning* or any othe ship to reach our destination. If we *are* to be loaded i the launching racks, it makes sense for us to be the las in and the first to be launched because of our capabilitie *and*, you noted yourself, that the loadmasters on the capi tal ships are still reviewing procedures for our ships to b loaded."

Lorrir's face tightened into a scowl. "That is no excus for you to still be here in the hangar."

"But, Colonel, your Interceptor is still here." Wedg held a hand up. "Perhaps we should be discussing this in a office, away from the troops?"

The Hegemony officer nodded. With his helmet unde his arm, he led Wedge off to a small office with a single, rec tangular window as tall as the door built into the wall be

ide it. The legend on the door proclaimed it to be the operations room.

Once inside, Lorrir perched himself on the desk and
shook his head. "This cannot be tolerated, Colonel Roat."

Wedge closed the door, then dialed down the opacity of
the window, taking it all the way to black. "No, Colonel, I
expect it cannot."

"You have been given your orders and I expect you to
follow them."

Wedge nodded solemnly and looked at his chronometer
for a second. "I am following orders, Colonel." He tugged
the gloved construct off his right hand, then flexed his fist.

"What are you doing?" Lorrir blinked with surprise.
"What is going on here?"

"You remember you told me about Brentaal the other
night at dinner. You told me how the Empire had been betrayed by Baron Fel?"

"Yes."

Wedge reached up and pulled off the prosthetic over his
eye, then peeled the piece off his throat. "Ah, much better.
And you recall mentioning that you'd killed plenty of
Rogue Squadron members on Brentaal, and that Wedge Antilles would be back."

The man's voice quaked. "Y-yes?"

"You were right. I'm Wedge Antilles. I'm back."

The couple of seconds it took for Wedge's statement to
blossom with all its import in Lorrir's brain proved to be
about a second longer than it took for Wedge to draw his
blaster and shoot the Hegemony officer. The blue stunbolt
hit Lorrir dead center in the chest, pitching him backward
over the desk. His helmet clattered against the floor and a
metal chair skidded back beneath him and bounced off the
room's rear wall.

Wedge holstered the blaster and pulled the desk back.
He stooped down, found a strong pulse in Lorrir's neck,
then yanked Lorrir's right glove free of his hand. Wedge slid
the glove on and picked up Lorrir's helmet. "I need a mask
for a moment, so I'll keep this. You won't be able to go up

without it, but then I won't have to shoot you down again. Sleep well."

Donning the helmet, Wedge slipped from the office, locked the door, and closed it behind him. He walked sedately over to the rest of the Rogues, then waggled his fingers at them.

Tycho looked surprised. "Things didn't go well?"

"Lorrir developed a new sense of irony. He found my revelations stunning." Wedge pointed to the Defenders. "Get in, get these things going. Fly in formation to the southern shield projector facility. We've got ten minutes for incoming and I want us ready to go."

Everyone split to their machines and Wedge climbed into his. He brought the power up, then locked the restraining straps in place. As the Defender cycled power to systems, his communications console lit up with positive check-ins from the rest of the squadron. The fleet frequency button flashed, so he punched it.

"Colonel Roat here."

"This is *Reckoning* Flight Control. When are your people going to report for loading?"

"I understood we were to head up after Colonel Lorrir. His Interceptor is still here. Do you want me to find him?"

"Negative, Colonel, just get your people airborne and headed this way. Someone else will deal with Lorrir."

"As ordered, Control. On our way."

The clone of Ysanne Isard did not realize she was a clone. She was possessed of all the original's memories, her entire life history up to a point just prior to the *Lusankya*'s escape from Imperial Center. Along with these memories came the original's attitudes, which included a healthy dose of skeptical contempt for things mystical, including the Force.

Yet, despite those prejudices, something struck her as very wrong about the message she'd gotten from Krennel. He asked her to dispatch someone to find Colonel Lorrir.

She would have sent a subordinate, but she actually wanted to locate Lorrir for herself and pass on the message of Krennel's displeasure. In Lorrir she had seen a grasping man who was abrasive with his inferiors, and fawningly obsequious with his betters. Because she stood outside the military establishment, he had treated her with cautious courtesy, which she knew would be stripped away and replaced with subservience once he knew how much power she commanded.

She reached the hangar in no time and saw Lorrir's interceptor still sitting on the ferrocrete deck. She knew it was his because he'd painted red stripes on each wing, just as the 181st used to do. She thought it a pity that a man's life should be so paltry that he had to cling to a hideous defeat as the high point of his existence.

The clone called a tech over and asked if he'd seen Lorrir. The man pointed toward the closed operations room door. She walked over to it, tried the handle, and found it was locked. Glancing at her chronometer, she mentally calculated the security override code for that quarter hour, punched it into the keypad, and entered the office.

She took immediate notice of the ozone stink in the air which, combined with Lorrir's body lying on the floor, told her the man had been stunned with a blaster. She squatted down and batted one of Lorrir's feet aside, then pulled a black glove from beneath it. The glove only had two fingers and had been fitted with metal parts to make it appear to be a prosthetic replacement.

"Colonel Roat." If Roat's hand had not been genuine, then neither had he. This meant he and his group of Defenders had been inserted into Ciutric, but for what purpose? They could do no good on Ciutric, she reasoned, unless . . .

Throughout the building and the entire city of Daplona, sirens began to squeal with a pulsating message of warning. Red lights strobed and out in the hangar techs began scurrying around.

She slapped Lorrir to wakefulness, then hauled him to his feet. "Come with me, I need you."

"Madam Director!" The man blinked his eyes in surprise. "It was a traitor, it was . . ."

"Yes, yes, no time for that. You're under my command now."

"What?" Lorrir straightened up and smoothed the breast of his flight suit. "I'm a pilot."

"So you are, and now you'll be flying for me."

"For you? Why?"

"Listen to the sirens, fool." The clone smiled and nodded a salute toward the sky. "There is a military operation planned. It's coming here. They don't care about Krennel, they're after me and my prisoners. We'll have to see they end up very disappointed."

The primary monitor on Wedge's Defender flashed brightly for a moment as image after image of ships filled the screen in rapid sequence. He caught a glimpse of a Mon Calamari Cruiser on the scanner screen, then an Imperial Star Destroyer Mark II, which matched the *Reckoning* in firepower. After that came three Nebulon-B Frigates, a half-dozen Corellian Corvettes, and a couple of fast little freighters. *That's pretty much the taskforce description I sent Admiral Ackbar, and it would have been more than sufficient for taking on* Reckoning *and* Binder.

The problem was that Krennel had called in *Emperor's Wisdom* and *Decisive*, giving the Hegemony forces a hideous edge in firepower. The *Victory*-class Star Destroyer, *Emperor's Wisdom*, had eighty concussion missile launch tubes on it. Any single salvo could bring down the Mon Cal cruiser's shields, leaving it open for raking fire from the ship's energy weapons. *Decisive* and *Reckoning* both could pound on *Emancipator*—an Impstar Deuce the New Republic had captured at Endor. While it could severely damage any of the opposing ships, it would be lost.

Wedge shivered, then punched up the squadron frequency. "You've all seen the scans, Rogues. It's not going to be pleasant. One Flight, we take out the shield generators down here, then we go to the spaceport and heist a freighter big enough to get the prisoners out of here. Two Flight, as planned, you neutralize prison defenses."

"As ordered, Lead. How do we take the prison? I didn't see Telik's commandos or Vessery's fighters in the mix."

"I don't know, Tycho. I hope they're just late. First things first, then we do whatever we have to do."

"On it, Lead. Two Flight on me. May the Force be with all of us."

Wedge rolled his Defender up onto the port side and peeled off toward the south. As he leveled out, Hobbie appeared on his starboard wing, Gavin and Myn on his port. The Defender cockpit gave him a great view of the cityscape over which they flew. Bulbous tan buildings alternated with green belts and parks, the tall skyscrapers of the municipal center giving way to smaller residential buildings and individual homes. Out beyond the residential areas he saw the massive edifices of the factory district and right in the middle lay the shield generation facility.

"Three and Four, you have the towers on the east, Two, take the ones on the west. I'm going straight in." Wedge thumbed his weapons-selector to concussion missiles. He set them for linked fire, then settled his crosshairs on the central dome. His rangefinder put him two kilometers out, with distance falling away fast.

The ion cannons mounted on towers around the facility had been cranked skyward. They pulsed out massive blue bolts that shot upward at the invading fleet, pouring out through momentary gaps opened in the shields by fire-control computers. Below them, on the same towers, turbo-laser cannons traversed their muzzles across the landscape. Three sets of four cannons had been stacked at twenty, forty, and sixty meters on the towers, with the ion cannons at the top. Bristling with weapons, the towers made formidable targets.

But targets nonetheless. Myn and Gavin let fly with the concussion missiles. Four incandescent rockets shot out at the eastern towers. Myn's hit a second before Gavin's, since Gavin's traveled a bit further, but all four were on target. They nailed the lowest gunnery station, demolishing the turbolaser cannons in a brilliant flash of light and heat. The force of the explosion expanded outward and up, jetting superheated plasma up through the next gunnery station. The ferrocrete slabs forming the intervening section buckled, then burst outward. The tops of the towers wavered, then began a tortured fall to the ground. To the west the first tower Hobbie targeted likewise crumbled in flame and smoke.

Wedge's targeting reticle went red, so he pulled the trigger and sent two concussion missiles flying toward the shield generator. The pink missiles bored through the ferrocrete dome, then detonated. Twin gouts of argent fire shot back out of the holes the missiles had made. The fire expanded and linked them into a single, larger hole, then proceeded to gnaw up into the dome until it collapsed in on itself. Windows and doors on the shield facility blew out and flaming debris rode a shockwave out to be scattered over the well-manicured landscape.

"Break port, Lead."

Wedge immediately rolled his craft left and saw an ion bolt the size of a small freighter sizzle past. The only intact tower's ion cannon had tracked him on his approach and had almost gotten him. Before he could apply some rudder and correct for an attack run, Gavin and Myn came in on a strafing run that pumped a pair of quaded-up laser bursts into the ion cannon.

The cannon exploded like an overripe fruit hit with a gaffi stick. A huge chunk of its armored shell fell away like a rind and collapsed a corner of the burning shield facility. Secondary explosions in the facility itself pitched the armor off onto shrubbery, which ignited when the hot metal touched it.

Wedge punched up a sensor scan just to confirm that the southern quadrant shield over Daplona was down. The city now lay open for Telik's commandos. *If they ever get here.*

He keyed his comlink. "Lead to Five, we're clear here. What's your status?"

"Busy, Lead, and could use some help. The guys on the ground won't go away, and I've got a dozen TIEs inbound our position." Tycho hesitated for a moment. "Better get here fast, or there may be no reason to come at all."

34

Admiral Ackbar, on the bridge of the Mon Calamari cruiser *Home One*, glanced with one eye at the holographic display of the near-space sector, and with the other looked out the viewport at the array of ships Krennel had brought to the fight. Only the unconscious twitching of his barabels betrayed his surprise. *From the depths always comes amazement.*

"Weapons, shields up and concentrate all fire on *Reckoning*. Fighter Command, deploy the A-wings and have them try to pick off the missiles that will be incoming from the Vic. After that, they're free to go after the TIEs and Interceptors."

"As ordered, Admiral."

"Helm, reverse course. Start pulling us back out on our exit vector."

"Yes, Admiral."

Ackbar looked at the small brown Sullustan serving as his communications officer. "Lieutenant Quiv, tell *Emancipator* to withdraw, but concentrate fire on *Reckoning*. Tell *Peacemaker*, *Pride of Eiattu*, and *Thunderchild* to go after the Vic. Relay those same orders to all the Corvettes. I want an orderly withdrawal. Krennel has to know we didn't expect this much strength here."

The Sullustan cheebled his assent and relayed the orders. The smaller ships in the taskforce all curled out and around from the two main ships and drove hard at the *Emperor's Wisdom*. Ackbar knew that the Nebulon-B Frigates and the half-dozen Corvettes couldn't do that much damage to their target, but he wanted the Vic's gunners, especially those manning the concussion missile launchers, to have a lot of targets to deal with.

The Corvettes laced into the Vic first, taking care to come in at high and low angles that forced the Hegemony gunners to crank their weapons to their highest attitude or lowest depression to get off a good shot. The *Mantooine*, *Dantooine*, and *Ryloth* slashed in over the top of *Emperor's Wisdom*, pumping double turbolaser cannon fire into the dorsal shield. The shield glowed pink for a moment, then began to tear apart like an algae cloud ripped by fast currents.

The Frigates exploited the gap opened in the shield, hammering the Vic with fire from their turbolaser batteries and laser cannons. Red-gold energy bolts splashed over the larger ship's hull, vaporizing armor and occasionally exploding a weapons platform. Despite the fury of their attack, and of the *Chandrilla*, *Mrlsst*, and *Sullust* in taking down the port shield, the real damage done to *Emperor's Wisdom* was minimal, leaving the ship more than capable of inflicting serious damage on the New Republic taskforce.

Ackbar's attention shifted as *Reckoning* and *Decisive* split and began to move forward, their daggerish prows jutting toward the retreating fleet. *Decisive* came in high and off to port, leaving *Emancipator* between it and *Home One*. *Reckoning* hung back ever so slightly, but sought to insert itself between the two New Republic ships. *Binder* remained behind the both of them, and clouds of fighters swirled and broke like schools of fish in the void around the larger ships.

"Weapons reporting positive weapon locks on *Reckoning*, Admiral."

Ackbar nodded to his weapons officer. "Fire at will, Lieutenant Colton. Make them all count."

.   .   .

Corran banked his Defender to starboard, then ruddered around to port to line up for his run on the prison. He unlinked lasers, letting them fire in sequence, then swooped low and leveled out barely five meters above the wall he'd been assigned. His finger tightened on the trigger, pulsing out verdant energy darts. He walked the fire straight down the wall, exploding E-webs, igniting stormtroopers, and sending faster men leaping fifteen meters to the ground.

He held his ship on target on the northeast tower and sent two bolts boiling into the guardpost on top of it. The square little building exploded into a ball of flame, scattering men and equipment. Tugging back on the yoke, he brought the trip up through the fireball, banked to starboard, and started a long loop around the prison's south end.

"Nine here. North wall is clear, northeast tower is gone."

"I copy, Nine. Wall defenses seem to be down."

"Six here, I see a lot of activity on the ground. Stormies and guards."

Corran glanced down at the prison. He saw a lot of armored individuals milling around in the open area on the western edge of the rectangular compound. The main building ran from north to south, but between it and the southern wall were three smaller buildings which seemed to house plenty of guards. All four corner towers leaked black smoke, and the ruins of heavy blaster emplacements and E-webs on the walls burned, but without troops on the ground, there was nothing to prevent the guards from entering the main building and slaughtering the prisoners.

I promised Jan Dodonna I'd see him and the others freed. I've already failed Urlor. I'm not failing them.

"Five, set up strafing runs on the guards. Scatter them. I'm going in."

"Nine, you can't."

"Colonel, I have to. Isard's people are late or aren't coming. Someone's got to go in."

Tycho remained silent for a moment. "Okay, take Ooryl and Nrin with you."

"I'll take Ooryl. Nrin will be more useful up in the sky."

"You haven't seen him in a firefight, Nine. He's with you. Go!"

"Thanks, Five."

Pulling back on his fighter's yoke, he brought the Defender back around to the north wall. Swooping down to two meters above the ground, he ruddered around until the trip faced the towering metal doors in the front wall and locked his tractor beam on them. He reversed thrust, then pulsed the throttle to full. The doors bent in the middle and metal screamed as the hinges ripped loose. The doors flew at his ship until he cut the tractor beam, then they rolled across the ground, knocking over streetlamps, pulverizing ferrocrete walkways and curbs, and finally coming to rest on top of a couple of landspeeders that promptly exploded as the great weight compressed their fuel tanks.

Corran set the Defender down and switched the ship into a passworded standby mode. Freeing himself from his restraining belts, he left his command chair, then pulled up the seat, exposing the small storage compartment. He pulled out a blaster carbine and a belt of powerpacks for it, which he looped over his chest from right shoulder to left hip. He also pulled out a fire extinguisher canister, which he flipped over. He unscrewed the bottom and tipped it upright so his grandfather's lightsaber slid out. He clipped that to his blaster belt at the small of his back, then opened the fighter's egress hatch. He poked the blaster carbine out first, then pulled himself out of the fighter's cockpit.

He slid down the ship's hull and landed in a crouch. Ooryl and Nrin had landed to his left and looked over at him. He scanned the line of the wall for signs of life, saw none, and sprinted forward. He crouched again in the shadow of one of the doors for another look, then darted forward again. He wove a zigzag course to the prison wall, then waited with his back against it, just to the western edge of the doorway.

Ooryl and Nrin joined him. Ooryl carried the standard issue blaster and carbine, but Nrin hefted a blaster rifle and a spare belt of powerpacks.

"You didn't have that in your ship, did you?"

The Quarren shook his head and then pointed the gun's long barrel at a smoldering corpse on the greensward between them and their ships. "You got him on your strafing run. I just appropriated things he no longer needs."

Corran nodded, then took a peek around the corner. He drew his head back just in time as a flurry of blaster bolts chewed into the wall near him. Opening his mouth, he activated the comlink built into his helmet. "Five, you can come in at any time."

"Copy that, Nine. Keep your heads down."

Ooryl pointed to the north. "There."

Corran crouched as the Defender came screaming in. He saw blaster bolts streak up into the sky and spark off the fighter's forward shields, but they were mere droplets in comparison with the torrent of energy coming back toward the ground. Through the thick fabric of his flight suit Corran could feel the heat pouring off the Defender's shots. The roar of the fighter's passing thundered through his chest.

As Tycho's ship flew over the wall, the trio rose to their feet. They ducked again, quickly, as Inyri's fighter shot past and came up in a high loop to finish her south-to-north run. Keeping low, Corran looked around the corner, then waved the others on with him.

The main gateway had a fence-enclosed walkway that led to the main building. Looking to the right, Corran saw the western yard where stormtroopers and guards had been gathering. Thick smoke drifted over it, but not so thick that he couldn't see burning bodies and figures crawling across the ground toward fallen comrades or parts of themselves that they'd lost. Screams of pain echoed within the yard, but a rising chorus of angry shouts started to eclipse them.

With the shouts came a scattering of blaster bolts. Corran swept his carbine over the yard, firing from the hip. Red bolts pierced the fog, pitching men over backward. Sprinting forward, he dropped an empty powerpack and slapped in a new one, then resumed firing. Hegemony troopers tracked their fire after him, spattering him with hot metal from the deteriorating fence.

Ooryl came running after him, keeping his blaster covering the eastern flank. Nrin advanced ten meters into the walkway—a third of the way to the main building—then scythed fire back and forth over the yard. His bolts spun men around, twirling them to the dirt. Their weapons flew as they went down. Other men snapped forward as bolts burned tunnels from stomach to spine. With the blaster's backlight burnishing red highlights onto his black helmet and flight suit, the Quarren seemed the antithesis of the stormtroopers in their white armor. Remorselessly and deliberately Nrin fired until the enemy resistance dribbled to a few sporadic shots, then he jogged forward and took up a sheltered position at the base of the steps to the main building.

Corran dashed up the steps and pulled his lightsaber from his belt with his left hand. He thumbed it to life, letting its silver glow banish the shadows, then stroked it down either side of the front door. Hot metal glowing red on each side, the door fell forward, then surfed down the steps to strike sparks on the ferrocrete walkway.

Corran darted into the smoky foyer, dropping to one knee. He tracked the blaster across the opening, then raised it as Ooryl came in and took up a similar position on the left side of the door. Corran glanced quickly behind him to make sure there was no office at his back.

Nrin entered the building, doffed his helmet, and clipped the comlink from it to the throat of his flight suit. "Where to from here?"

Ooryl pointed at a large painted diagram of the building on the wall. "Blue level is supposed to be the isolation block. The *Lusankya* prisoners would be there, I would think. There seems to be only one stairwell allowing access up there."

"Makes sense for security reasons—prisoners get loose,

only one way out of their hole. Besides, I like to start at the top anyway." Corran snapped off his lightsaber, clipped it to his belt again, and led the way off to the right, to the stairwell that occupied the northwest corner of the building. "Eight flights up and we're there."

The stairwell had been built tightly, with each flight covering half the distance to the next floor. At the top of one an immediate right-angle turn would lead to the next flight. The metal underside of more steps formed the roof of each flight and a wall ran down between flights, preventing someone on one course from seeing what was on the next.

The steps themselves had been floored with cheap brown duraplast tiles that were already worn, chipped, and cracking from constant use. The walls themselves were covered with a glossy beige tile with a matching tan mortar. Corran had visited many prisons during his time with CorSec, and he recognized the decor and knew the materials had not been chosen for their aesthetic effect. The fact was that they could simply be hosed down to remove blood stains. *And I'd bet that more than one prisoner has slipped and fallen down a flight or two here.*

Because they didn't know if they were walking into trouble or not, they crept up the stairs slowly. At each floor landing they paused and checked the doorway, but found no one waiting for them. Finally, after five agonizing minutes, they reached the top floor and entered a small containment area.

The isolation cells themselves ran in two long blocks down the center of the fourth floor, oriented north to south. On the east and west sides two spacious galleries, easily five meters wide, separated the back walls of the cells from the tall, translucent windows along the exterior walls. A wall of heavy durasteel bars separated the containment area from the cells and galleries, but allowed Corran to see everything on the fourth floor very clearly.

And it allowed the guards who had overturned a desk and were using it for cover to see Corran. They opened fire from the western gallery, which drove him to the floor. He rolled to his right, reaching the doorway to the stairs. Nrin and Ooryl grabbed him and dragged him onto the landing.

He looked up at them. "Good news is that there's only four of them. Bad news is that they have cover and there's a metal bar wall between us and them."

Nrin shrugged. "Use the lightsaber to slash it open."

"Oh, I'd love to, but I'd be shot to pieces while getting there." Corran hesitated for a moment, then bounced the heel of his left hand off his helmet's forehead. "Sometimes I'm an idiot."

Ooryl's helmeted head canted to the side. "Sometimes?"

Corran gave his wingman a contemptuous sneer, but being hidden by the helmet drained it of its effect. "Nrin, give me your blaster rifle."

The Quarren handed it over. Corran took it, ignited the lightsaber, and laid it parallel to the blaster rifle's barrel. He walked over to the wall near the door and pressed the muzzle to the wall. He then slid the lightsaber forward until its tip poked through the wall on the far side. He retracted it to about a centimeter shy of the surface, then held it tight against the barrel.

Nrin and Ooryl both ducked down the stairs as Corran brought the weapon around and stabbed it into the wall on the south side of the stairwell's landing. Because he was using the rifle barrel as a guide, the silver blade only penetrated the wall to the depth of twenty-nine centimeters instead of piercing it completely. Corran cut across for about a meter, then ran down for a meter and a half, burning a black outline of a doorway into the wall. He shut the lightsaber off and handed the rifle back to Nrin.

"There should only be a centimeter of tile between the wall and the gallery at the cut lines. I'll draw their fire, you break through and catch them with flanking fire."

Nrin's tentacles curled up smartly. "For an idiot, you seem to think well."

"First time for everything."

"Thanks, Ooryl."

Leaving his two friends poised to act, Corran dove out

through the doorway and triggered a burst of blasterfire.
He let himself continue to slide to the left, using the security cell block corner to eclipse the guards' fire, then he
sprinted forward to the wall of bars. Peeking around the
corner he triggered another burst of red bolts, then ducked
back as a flurry of bolts burned into the walls and scorched
metal bars.

He heard a crackling sound, then heard the whine of
more blasterfire. He scooted forward and fired. His bolts
nibbled away at the desk, but Nrin's heavier bolts burned
clean through it. One guard tumbled back and another
scrambled to maintain his balance. His arms flailed, then a
bolt to the chest picked him up and sent him flying deeper
into the gallery. A third guard took a bolt in the shoulder,
and the fourth tossed his blaster out onto the floor before
raising his hands.

Corran slashed the gate in the wall of bars open while
Nrin and Ooryl kicked their way free of wall debris. As the
other two kept their weapons on their captive, Corran used
his lightsaber to cut away a corner of the stairwell wall, allowing someone to cover the lower landing and the flight up
to the door. "This should let you hold off reinforcements."

Ooryl nodded and took up a position beside the corner hole.

Corran waved the man who had surrendered over to
him. "General Dodonna, now!"

The man's jaw dropped. "But I can't open the cell. I
don't have a cardkey."

Corran worked the humming lightsaber blade through
an infinity loop. "I can handle it."

The guard led him into the isolation cell area and
pointed at a cell about a third of the way down. Corran
stabbed the lightsaber into the lock mechanism, then
worked the blade around in a spiral to sever the latch. The
door slowly swung open, the lightsaber's light seeding the
recesses with dark shadows.

In the corner, on a hard pallet that served as a bunk, an
old man raised his left hand to shield his eyes from the glare.
The white hair and beard spoke to the man's age, and the

way he straightened up in the face of what seemed to be an Imperial pilot armed with a lightsaber gave testament to his inherent courage.

"General Dodonna?"

The old man nodded. "I'm Jan Dodonna."

"It's been a long time, General." Corran removed his helmet and smiled. "Are you ready to go home?"

35

The reddish glow from the fist Prince-Admiral Delak Krennel made with his mechanical right hand painted his face in bloody highlights. Through the viewport on *Reckoning* he watched the New Republic fleet begin its withdrawal. *Yes, they're running. This is better than I could have expected.*

Krennel could not believe his good fortune. He'd been staging for a long grazing strike at Coruscant. He expected it to embarrass the New Republic while they were waiting to ambush him. In reality they struck at Ciutric, expecting him to be away waiting to ambush another convoy. Their error, which was compounded by the relative weakness of their taskforce, would allow him to crush them and *then* make his strike at Coruscant.

"Weapons, target the Mon Cal cruiser. Same orders to *Decisive* and *Emperor's Wisdom*."

"As ordered, Prince-Admiral."

A smile spread over Krennel's face as his forward gunners lashed *Home One* with heavy turbolaser battery fire. Gold-tinged scarlet energy bolts battered the New Republic ship's bow and port shields. The Mon Cal shield sphere slowly shrank as the incoming fire boiled off layers of energy. Finally the bow shield collapsed and the hull itself crisped to a blackness as paint ignited and armor ablated. Ion bolts skittered, arced, and danced over the rounded ship's surface, then a dozen concussion missiles from *Emperor's Wisdom* tracked a series of explosions over the hull. Fires raged in a couple of craters, prompting cheers from the bridge crew.

Krennel stared down at the crew pit from his catwalk. "Why isn't *Decisive* firing?"

The communications officer looked up from his station. "*Decisive* reports that *Emancipator* reinforced their port shields and soaked off the damage that had to pass them to get to *Home One*. They request leave to engage *Emancipator*."

"No! Tell *Decisive* to roll to port, then come up and over *Emancipator*." Krennel thrust a finger at the viewpoint. "I want that cruiser *dead*!"

The Mon Calamari cruiser and *Emancipator* fired. The Mon Cal's turbolaser batteries concentrated their fire on *Reckoning*'s forward shield. The invisible energy bowl protecting the ship's bow suddenly filled with a translucent pink that quickly evaporated as blue ion cannon bolts lanced through it. Blue lightning crawled from corner to corner and glided along lines over the ship's hull. Two heavy turbolaser batteries exploded and Krennel saw at least two gunners ejected into space as their stations ripped themselves apart.

Emancipator's weapons on both sides cut loose. The port gunners delivered a full broadside into *Decisive*'s port shield, shredding it. Turbolaser fire slashed black furrows along the Imperial Star Destroyer's hull, and drilled deep at several points. Ion cannon bolts sent jagged lightning whips cavorting over its hull, with a couple scurrying up the command tower as fast as Jawas after droids. The New Republic ship's starboard batteries targeted *Reckoning* and peeled away its starboard shield. Krennel felt the deck shift beneath his feet as a power surge momentarily knocked the inertial compensators offline. Turbolasers vaporized portions of the hull. Warning sirens blared and fires burned as atmosphere vented.

Krennel clutched at the catwalk railing. "Sensors, are they still withdrawing?"

"Yes, Prince-Admiral. They're pulling out on an exit vector that will allow them to go to hyperspace in thirty seconds."

"Security, damage report."

"Minimal, Prince-Admiral."

Krennel nodded solemnly. "Helm, come about to a heading of ninety degrees, but keep her level. We'll give them our port shield to shoot at and a full broadside on the Mon Cal. Weapons, port on the Mon Cal, starboard targets of opportunity."

"As ordered, Prince-Admiral."

"Prince-Admiral!" The man at the sensor station waved a hand at him. "I have the southern Daplona shield down. Two of the New Republic ships are heading to ground."

"Weapons, send a squadron of TIEs down to deal with that problem."

"Done, Prince-Admiral."

"Two are running for the ground, and the rest for space. We can't have that." Krennel flashed teeth in a cruel smile. "Communications, tell *Binder* to power up the gravity wells. Our dying enemies can't be allowed to leave. After all, the fun has just started, hasn't it?"

Recognition bloomed in the old man's eyes, bringing a smile to Corran's face. "So you *did* escape *Lusankya* after all. Isard tossed us a skull and said you didn't make it."

Corran nodded. "I did, and even had a hand in killing her. At least, I thought we killed her."

Dodonna stood. "She's still been in charge of us."

"That's a clone. The real thing is still out there, too."

Dodonna's eyes widened. "Two of her?"

"Yes, General. Now you know why we need you back." Corran tossed the General his blaster pistol, pulled the comlink from his helmet, and clipped it to his flight suit's lapel. He tossed the helmet on the General's cot, then turned and poked his blaster carbine at the guard. "Can you pop the rest of these cells?"

"Some."

"Good, get them open and I'll get the rest." Corran crossed the hallway and started slashing open cells. A motley assembly of individuals slowly shambled out. Some he recognized from his time on *Lusankya*. Forty cells produced a total of ninety prisoners.

"Is this everyone, General?"

Dodonna squinted, then nodded. "We all managed to communicate despite the guards' best efforts to the contrary. A few here weren't on the *Lusankya*, but Krennel had them imprisoned for political crimes."

"Well, you're all free, courtesy of the New Republic."

Nrin's voice rose above the husky cheering. "Corran, come here, fast."

Corran sprinted back toward the stairwell and immediately identified the reason for Nrin's yell. Both he and Ooryl stood at the corner hole in the wall, shooting down into the stairwell. Shots were coming back up at them, but they managed to dodge back before any burst could hit them.

Ooryl pointed at the hole. "Guards and stormtroopers have worked their way up the stairs. We've been keeping them back. I think they're going to get a door from below to use as a shield."

"Got it." Corran pointed two of the *Lusankya* prisoners at the dead guards. "Get their blasters and come with me."

He ran over to the stairway and dropped to one knee. He stabbed his lightsaber into the top landing and cored out a big circle. It dropped down three meters, clanging off the heads of some stormtroopers who fell back down the stairs. Thrusting his blaster into the hole, he triggered a burst that danced two guards back against the wall, then left them twitching on the landing a half a floor below.

He leaped back as a flurry of shots burned up at him. The blaster bolts chewed flaming holes in the wall and scattered hot shards of ceramic tile all over. Corran felt a sting on his right cheek and his hand came away bloody. He fired another burst down the hole, then pulled back and let the two freshly armed prisoners take over.

Halfway between that hole and the other one, he met General Dodonna. The older man studied the situation for a moment, then nodded. "One stairwell was put in to limit access of the prisoners here to any escape routes. If there was a riot, however, the guards probably would have come through the roof to deal with us. Your lightsaber can cut us an opening to get out, but what then?"

Corran shrugged, dousing his lightsaber and hooking it to his belt again. "I don't know. Let me ask." He keyed the comlink on his lapel. "Five, we have the prisoners, but can't get down the northwest stairwell. We're going to the roof. Can you get us off it?"

"Negative, Nine. Things are hot up here. We've got a dozen TIEs inbound and there is ground traffic. Looks like the local answer to CorSec coming to contest your hold on the prison."

"I'm not liking what you're saying, Five."

"I'm not terribly keen on it myself, Nine." A certain amount of strain came through Tycho's voice. "Krennel's got us outgunned up-atmosphere, so you may well be in the best position of all."

"Youch! I copy, Five. Let me know when help is available." Glancing over at General Dodonna, he shook his head. "If you have any ideas, General, I'm open to them. After all, you saved the Rebellion at Yavin. By comparison, this should be child's-play."

Wedge smiled as he keyed his comlink. "Nine, he saved the Rebellion by putting pilots in the right place at the right time. One Flight is inbound. Standby." He flicked the comm unit over to the flight frequency. "Two, Three, and Four, join Five and Six tackling those TIEs. I'll take care of the incoming ground troops."

"As ordered, Lead."

The other three Defenders peeled off, breaking starboard to intercept the TIE formation closing fast on Tycho and Inyri. The Defenders launched a concussion missile each. The projectiles streaked through the sky and hit their targets hard. Three small explosions twinkled brightly and flaming debris fell from the comets that were the burning remains of three TIEs.

Wedge flicked his targeting computer over to ground-search mode and immediately picked up flickering readings from a convoy of landspeeders, a couple of gravtrucks, and a Chariot light assault vehicle. The LAV was the most heavily armored transport in the convoy, but it might as well have been made of flimsiplast as far as its ability to deal with the Defenders' weapons was concerned. *The commanders of the convoy are likely in that thing, and it looks as though they don't mind leading from the front. Right idea, just wrong place and time.*

Wedge dialed his throttle back down and brought up the power in the repulsorlift coils. A little rudder straightened him out as his fighter drifted down into a canyon of tall ferrocrete buildings. Half a kilometer east, battering smaller landspeeders out of the way, the Chariot LAV came boiling down the center of the roadway. The wedge-shaped craft used its armored prow to push aside anything blocking the street. Given the slightly erratic path it made, sideslipping left and right down the road, the pilot clearly enjoyed tipping smaller speeders over, dumping them into sidewalks.

Wedge centered his crosshairs over the LAV's outline and waited until it reached the closer end of an enclosed block before he opened fire with his lasers. The weapons fired sequentially, punching the first two bolts through the transparisteel windscreens, which blackened, then exploded back out in a geyser of golden fire. A third bolt lanced through the starboard repulsorlift engines. They exploded, dropping the craft's right side to the ground, then slewing it around to the left. The fourth bolt hit the broadsided vehicle in the middle, melting enough of the support structure to crack the Chariot and allow flames to shoot skyward through the gap.

He kicked in a bit more throttle and brought the Defender up so he could shoot over the burning roadblock. He shifted from lasers to ion cannons and fired at the vehicle furthest back in the convoy. His initial shot fell short, but wreathed a gravtruck with blue lightning. It immediately grounded with sparks shooting from the undercarriage.

The guards who had been in the back spilled out, most of them jerking and twitching with the energy. One guard's clothes were smoldering. He stumbled into the street and the landspeeder following the gravtruck hit him when it swerved to miss the dead truck. The guard pitched up and over the speeder and landed in the road behind it, while the speeder went out of control and slammed into a storefront.

Wedge walked fire back down the convoy, hesitating a couple of times as guards leaped from their gravtrucks and sought shelter in doorways or behind ferrocrete benches or old monuments to Imperial glory. The ion blast would short out a vehicle's electronics, and wasn't much kinder to any living creature it hit. He continued to target vehicles, stopping the ones he hit, bottling up the ones he did not.

A few of the men on the ground fired blasters at the Defender. Wedge scattered them with an ion blast and searched for more vehicles to shoot, but something moving through the sky caught his attention. He brought his sensors back into air-to-air mode and directed them at the object lifting from Daplona and heading out toward the prison.

The sensors reported it was an Imperial Assault Shuttle, with shields at full, all four laser cannons charged, and concussion missile launchers in working order, with one life-form on board. Bringing his throttle up, he punched in a request for a comm frequency scan of the ship and switched his comm unit over to the unscrambled one it was using.

"This is General Wedge Antilles of the New Republic. You would be Ysanne Isard."

There was momentary silence. "General Antilles? I thought you died at Distna."

"I thought you died at Thyferra, so we're even."

Pure venom poured through her voice. "If you think to make this the tiebreaker, you'll lose."

Before Wedge could contradict her, fire blossomed in the shuttle's concussion missile firing tubes. Two missiles jetted out and began a gently curved flight toward the prison's top floor. "Corran Horn has returned to be with those he escaped," she hissed, "now it's time for all of them to die."

36

Admiral Ackbar climbed back into his command chair. "Damage Control, report."

A Twi'lek female turned in his direction. "Artificial gravity restored. Hull breaches forward, decks one and three. The *Mrlsst* is dead in space, *Sullust* and *Mantooine* are badly damaged. *Peacemaker* is also dead in space."

The human at the sensor station raised a hand. "Admiral, *Binder* has brought its gravity well projectors up. Nothing is leaving the system."

The Mon Calamari nodded slowly. "Signal the fleet. Begin the Thrawn Pincer."

In waging his war against the New Republic, Grand Admiral Thrawn had proved himself to be a masterful martial tactician. Rumor had it that he credited the study of a people's art as being the key to understanding and defeating them. Ackbar didn't know if that were true or not, but what he did understand was that Thrawn had a superior command of how to utilize the tools of his trade. Thrawn had again and again used an Interdictor cruiser as the equivalent of a magnet. He sent it into systems to pull a fleet from hyperspace with more precision than most navigators could plot.

Ackbar had learned well from him.

While Ackbar's main battle group had jumped directly into the Ciutric system, arriving to the sun side of the planet, the second part of the taskforce had exited hyperspace deeper in the solar system. When the signal from Ackbar reached them, the two *Victory*-class Star Destroyers jumped in toward Ciutric and were dragged from space by *Binder*'s presence.

This brought the two ships out of hyperspace at *Binder*'s aft. The second the crews oriented themselves, General Garm Bel Iblis issued orders to engage the enemy. They unloaded their beam weapons on the *Emperor's Wisdom* and launched their concussion missiles at *Reckoning*. They did this just after *Reckoning* completed its ninety-degree shift to starboard, presenting its undamaged side to *Home One*, and its unshielded flank to the newly arrived *Selonian Fire* and *Corusca Fire*.

A terrifyingly beautiful garland of explosions rippled down *Reckoning*'s right flank and on up the command tower. Heavy turbolaser batteries disintegrated, hull plates buckled, while even more missiles stabbed deep into the ship's interior to detonate and tear holes that breached multiple decks. Fires raged as the void of space sucked air out of the ships. Pieces of the hull broke away or twisted out of place, leaving the Impstar looking as if it had sideswiped an asteroid.

One missile shot past the front of the command tower, then course corrected and circled around to strike the forward viewport. The transparisteel resisted the impact at first, but the interior layer cracked and spalled off a hail of crystalline fragments that stormed through the bridge. They passed over the heads of those individuals at the action stations, but blew through Prince-Admiral Krennel so fast that they had exited his back without appreciably slowing down at all.

Krennel looked down to see his white uniform covered with red dots slightly lighter than the scarlet trim on his cuffs and hem. Only his right forearm sleeve remained pristine. He got as far as realizing that it had not changed color

because the arm underneath was purely mechanical, before
blood running from his forehead dripped down into his
eyes, blinding him.

Then the concussion missile detonated.

The comlink on Corran's lapel squawked loudly. "Concussion missiles incoming prison east!"

"Everyone, down! Get down!" Corran screamed at
them, waving his arms at the ground. "Down, DOWN!"

A missile slammed into the prison at the southeast corner of the fourth floor. Corran saw a brilliant light blossom
in that direction and caught a fleeting glimpse of cracks ap-
pearing in the mortar between the building blocks that
made up the isolation cells. Then the explosion's shockwave hit him, blasting him off his feet and knocking him
backward into the wall. He saw stars as his head hit, then
sputtered as dust from the tops of the hanging lights drifted
down to choke him.

He rolled to his feet and saw Nrin getting back up, too.
The Quarren fired a short burst through the hole in the
floor, then backed off to feed another clip into his blaster rifle. Ooryl took over for him, firing off a long burst that
brought weak return fire. Corran ran to the corner cut he'd
made and triggered a burst through it. He heard a scream
and a clatter, but wasn't certain who or what he'd hit. More
distant sounds of sporadic firing came to him, but no hot
light burned its way up toward his position, so he wasn't
certain what to make of it.

His comlink crackled again, this time with a voice he
could not instantly place. "Nrin, please advise as to your
situation."

The Quarren frowned, then keyed his comlink.
"Fourth floor is secure. The isolation cells shielded us from
the missile blast. We're holding off the guards, but are running low on power."

"I copy. We're incoming."

Corran keyed his comlink. "Who's 'we' and where are
you incoming from?"

"We've cleared the tower to the second floor. Team One is on the way up."

Nrin laughed aloud. "Come fast, Kapp. We promise we won't shoot any Devaronians."

"I like hearing that, Nrin." Kapp Dendo's voice pulsed confidently through the comlink. "Sit tight and we'll have you out of there in no time."

Wedge punched up the Rogue comm frequency. "Concussion missiles incoming prison east!" Even as he shouted the warning, he ruddered his fighter's front to starboard and dropped the aiming reticle over the spark that was the first missile. He tightened up on the trigger and sent an ion bolt sizzling out after it. He cursed, switched to lasers, but by the time he tracked the second missile, it was too late.

The ion bolt succeeded in hitting the first missile, surrounding it with a blue energy web. The missile corkscrewed into a spiral and climbed skyward before detonating. A skyfall of burning sparks slowly descended at the base of smoky snakes, falling among parks and homes.

The second missile slammed into the prison's top floor at the southeast corner. The resulting explosion ripped a hole in the building that extended down two floors and shot debris hundreds of meters into the air. Bodies hung from the hole, then were pitched to the ground as prisoners from the second and third floors began a dash for freedom.

Wedge punched up One Flight's tactical comm channel. "Gavin, Myn, Hobbie, give me full spectrum scans of the shuttle. Myn, Gavin, move to cut it off from the prison. Send the sensor data to me immediately, and take the shuttle with ion cannons if you can."

Without waiting for a reply, Wedge rolled his Defender to port and came up, leveling out at the same altitude as the assault shuttle. His maneuver brought him in for a deflection shot that would hit the starboard aft section of the ship. The assault shuttle ruddered around to present its aft to him, then sideslipped to port.

Wedge switched to ion cannons and dropped his cross hairs on the shuttle. It juked up, then sideslipped port again. The pilot made the ungainly craft dance with a surprisingly light hand on the stick. *There has to be a targeting warning system in there. The moment my sensors pinpoint him, he gets a light on his HUD and jinks.*

Getting the shuttle wasn't going to be easy, but the evasive maneuvers *had* moved the shuttle away from the prison. Wedge keyed his comm unit. "Myn, stay ninety degrees off my position. Gavin, get above it. He's got an early warning system so we'll have to herd it."

He then punched up the shuttle's comm channel. "Nice flying, Isard."

"Coming from you, that's a compliment."

"I appreciate my foes and their abilities." Wedge hesitated for a moment, then spoke with a cold confidence in his voice. "Then again, I would hope a clone would be an improvement over the original."

"What?"

"You didn't know you were a clone? No, of course not. Isard wouldn't trust the dispersal of her prized captives to just anyone: She gave the job to herself. With you she could actually be in two places at one time."

"That's insane."

"So was she." Wedge triggered an ion bolt that laced aquamarine fire through the shuttle's aft shield. "Corran's escape and her evacuation of Coruscant broke her, but you were imprinted before then, so your brainwelds weren't loosened. You did your job and *she* had you shot. She expected you to die, but you didn't and here you are."

The shuttle sideslipped starboard as gracefully as a hawkbat riding air currents in Coruscant's citified canyons. "No, not possible."

"It's true." Wedge laughed aloud. "In fact, I can prove it."

"It's a lie."

"Oh, then explain why, in a similar situation on Thyferra, Isard was using her shuttle to run and you, on the other hand, are still trying to deny us the *Lusankya* prisoners, *as per her orders to you*?"

He cut off her anguished scream by switching over to One Flight's tactical channel. "Myn, move into the shuttle's aft port. Gavin, set up for shots after a sideslip starboard." Wedge punched an inquiry into his tactical computer. "Take it down, now."

The other two trips moved in for the kill like teopari on the hunt. Myn's Defender curled in past Wedge's fighter and snapped off a pair of ion bolts that took the shuttle in the aft. Electricity played through the aft shield, shrinking it to a tiny sphere that imploded in a brilliant flash.

The shuttle, as predicted, sideslipped to the right. Gavin's two bolts shot down at it and caught the shuttle on the high dorsal stabilizer, gushing down as if a fluid. Sparks shot from shield projectors as they shorted out and smoke began to trail from the concussion missile launchers. The light in the engines died out as the ship's electrical system failed and a ship that had once been elegant in flight became a heavy construct of metal and ceramics suddenly unable to defy gravity.

The left wing tip hit the ground first, gouging a furrow in a bridge roadway. Scattered speeders whirled, spun, and flipped away as huge chunks of ferrocrete decking dropped twenty meters to the shallow river below. Portions of the wing whipped through the air as it hit the durasteel supports at the bridge's edge.

The shuttle's flattening spin would have slammed it into the ground, crushing the pilot's compartment completely, but the river valley meant there was no ground for it to hit. The ship continued to spin and the right wing tip came down to splash through the water and strike riverbed. The wing lodged as firmly as if the riverbed were solid stone.

Metal screamed and ferroceramic armor tiles snapped along the wing's joint with the ship's hull. Because the wings were meant to fold up for ease of storage in the belly of a ship, the joint was not nearly as strong as it would have been were the wings part of the basic hull. Hydraulic fluid sprayed out as the hinges parted and the wing tore completely off.

The hull whirled through the air, the nose almost kissing the water after the first revolution. It came up again, sparing the pilot's life, then the shuttle hit on the right rear quarter. The section of the boxy hull crumpled, splashing out great torrents of the river water it displaced. The ship bounced up, then landed hard on the aft. The impact jolted the drive units, tearing them free of their mountings and slamming them forward into the passenger compartment.

The shuttle wavered there for a second, then the last bit of its momentum pitched it over onto its port side. Water splashed up on both sides, then the craft settled back, resting on its blackened dorsal stabilizer. Water washed up around the ship's hull and steam rose from the drive units.

After ten seconds, though, aside from the splashing of debris falling from the bridge, the lazy Daplona River had absorbed the violence of the shuttle's crash and wended on its way.

Wedge glanced at his secondary screen and the answer to his computer inquiry. He punched up Isard's comm frequency again. "I know you won't reply since you're busy playing dead. Just to let you know, there's one more way I know you're a clone. Isard tried the same trick to escape us on Thyferra. Won't work this time. It's over."

He ruddered his Defender around on a course that directed it toward the Daplona base training center. When he'd asked the others in One Flight for a full scan of the shuttle, it had included data on the comm frequencies being used, including their strength and the direction from which they were coming. By having his computer compare the vectors, he triangulated Isard's location and the place from which she was directing the shuttle.

"Oh, one more thing," Wedge added. "Tell Colonel Lorrir he sideslips too much. That's why I got him. And you."

Switching over to concussion missiles, Wedge targeted the building and tightened his finger on the trigger. A pair of concussion missiles jetted out on azure fire and another pair quickly followed it. All four hit it in sequence, blowing into the squat building's lower two floors. Brilliant explosions ripped through the building, blasting out transparisteel windows and cutting through support structures. The comm dish on the roof tipped and broke off as the upper two floors twisted, then descended into the dust cloud below them. Smoke, both black and white, rolled through the surrounding area like surf breaking. In its wake lay a mountain of rubble leaking thin vapors.

Wedge got nothing but static on Isard's comm frequency.

With a smile blossoming on his face, Wedge brought his Defender around and headed it toward the prison. Isard had betrayed them, and the individual that was a slice of her tried to deny them the prize for which they had worked so hard. Both Isards had been thwarted and, no matter what else happened, that made it a very good day.

Corran and Jan Dodonna were the last two people to come down the stairs. Because of the hole at the top of the stairs, Corran had used the lightsaber to widen the door and let folks mount the stairs from the side instead of the landing. Nrin and Ooryl led the way down and the former prisoners filed out without incident.

Corran felt an odd chill as they made their way to the lower floors. Stormtrooper and guard corpses clogged the stairwell save for the narrow path that wormed its way between their bodies. It struck Corran as very odd that very few of the bodies showed signs of having been killed with blaster bolts. Blood leaked from most of them, with knife wounds in the chest, or armpits, or any other location where a blade could easily sever a major blood vessel. Broken arms and legs appeared on some of the corpses, along with spinal dislocations. A couple of guards had broken necks, with the damage so severe that it appeared someone had tried to twist their heads right off.

They came out into the sunlight and Kapp snapped to

attention. He tossed a salute to Jan Dodonna, which Dodonna returned with a crisp grace. The Devaronian extended his hand to the older man. "It is a pleasure to meet you, General."

"My thanks to you and your men." Dodonna smiled broadly and handed the borrowed blaster to Corran. "I never doubted you'd make good on your promise, Corran. You even got around to it faster than I expected."

"Not as fast as I wanted to, but Warlord Zsinj and Grand Admiral Thrawn took up a fair amount of our time." Corran turned to Kapp, shifting his recovered helmet beneath his left arm so he could shake hands with Team One's leader. As he did so he glanced from the line of freed men making their way to the two freighters parked beyond the twisted prison doors to Kapp. "Speaking of your men, where are they?"

Kapp smiled and opened his arms. "They're all here."

Corran looked around and only saw a half-dozen bipeds he didn't instantly recognize. The small, gray-skinned bipeds' exposed legs and arms rippled with muscles and their large dark eyes watched each passing individual with the closeness of a predator seeking prey. They smiled at men who nodded thanks to them, exposing mouths full of sharp teeth. Gathering their homespun robes at the waist, they wore a belt that bore a holstered blaster on one hip, a sheathed knife at the other, and a couple smaller throwing blades sheathed at the small of their backs.

Corran frowned. "*Those* are all the men you brought?"

Kapp laughed aloud. "They're Noghri, Corran, a half dozen is all I needed."

"*Those* are Noghri?! I'm glad they're on our side." Corran glanced more closely at one and got a broad, tooth-studded smile in return. "They *are* on our side, right?"

"They worked for the Empire because Vader had tricked them. Princess Leia managed to turn them to our side. They're a peaceful people, but they're willing to act for us to atone for some of the things the Empire had them do."

Kapp offered Dodonna his arm and the older man took it to steady himself. "General, if you'll come with me, we'll get you off this rock."

Corran pointed to the sky. "What happened up there?"

"Bel Iblis's battle group blasted *Reckoning* and *Emperor's Wisdom*. *Reckoning*'s bridge is gone, and Krennel along with it. The crews of *Binder* and *Decisive* found themselves outgunned and decided accepting a New Republic amnesty was preferable to being reduced to scrap." Kapp shrugged easily. "I think the pols intend for the Hegemony to enter the New Republic as a unit, and these guys would get stationed here to maintain order. They still protect their homes and we don't have to kill them."

"Win, win." Corran nodded, then waved Kapp on toward the freighters. "I'll catch up with you—I need to get air between me and dirt."

Corran jogged over to where he'd landed his Defender and smiled as Wedge's ship set down easily. He waited for Wedge to exit the ball cockpit and offered him his hand. "Thanks for the warning, Wedge. Air got a tad warm there, but no serious damage done."

"Good." Wedge surveyed the prison and the line of men heading toward the freighters. "Got them all?"

"As nearly as we can tell, yes. Did you get Isard's clone?"

Wedge smiled. "She had Colonel Lorrir flying a shuttle by remote—I recognized his love of sideslips. Myn and Gavin brought the shuttle down, I triangulated back to the point of origin of the control and comm broadcasts and laced it with two concussion missiles. Brought the whole training center down."

Corran arched an eyebrow at him. "Great, now I'll never get my deposit back for locker rental in the recreation area."

"Don't worry about it, Corran. If the New Republic ever comes through with our pay, I'll cover it."

"Works for me." The younger man looked around, then shifted his shoulders uneasily. "Kapp says our fleet took Krennel down and, without their leader, the others surrendered. Everything turned out very nicely."

"It did, so why the shiver there?"

"We did better than expected, muddling through without Isard's help." Corran's green eyes narrowed. "So, where is she, and just how good a day is she having?"

37

The daggerish hull of the *Lusankya* hung in the middle of the Bilbringi shipyard like a vibroblade waiting to be plucked up and used to kill an enemy. The eight kilometers of its length had been restored fully, with running lights burning around its edges, the prow returned to needle-sharpness, the armor restored, and the ship painted an even gray tone. Two bloody Rebel crests graced the ship toward the aft, both on top and bottom—marred it really—and destroyed any chance of the gray hull vanishing against the backdrop of space.

But then, she thought, *hiding a Super Star Destroyer has always been impossible.* Isard laughed lightly. The New Republic had tried to hide *Lusankya* from her. They had circulated rumors that it had been taken apart for scrap or cannibalized to repair countless smaller ships, but she had known from the start that all such stories were deceptions. The *Lusankya* was a prize they had sought to deny her. Such a ship could lay waste to fleets and project political power to the furthest reaches of the galaxy.

She pressed her right hand against the transparisteel viewport on the incoming freighter *Swift*. Behind her she heard the communications officer play out the watch code that allowed their freighter to approach the larger ship. Her spies in the New Republic had managed to produce it, as well as a copy of the program used to determine watch codes. Nothing the New Republic could do would deny her a return to her ship.

"This is Bilbringi Control. *Swift,* you are approved for docking on the command tower. Proceed on vector three-three-two mark three-four-five, steady as she goes."

"*Swift* acknowledges three-three-two mark three-four-five, Control. *Swift* out."

Isard stared at the reflection of the bridge behind her. "Sensors, data please."

"Only thirty percent of the ship has gravity and atmosphere, all along the central spine and up into the command tower. Only essential systems are engaged, with no power to weapons. Engines are in station-keeping mode only." The sensor officer's reflection ducked its head toward the screen he was studying. "I have nearly five hundred mixed lifeform readings on board, human and other. They are largely confined near the bow, working on the restoration of areas that were severely damaged at Thyferra."

"Very good. Captain, take us in."

Isard watched, her eyes widening hungrily as the *Lusankya* loomed larger. She had not lied when she told Corran Horn that his escape from *Lusankya* had soiled the ship, disgraced it and tainted it. She really didn't want anything more to do with it and had been pleased when the New Republic had pounded it mercilessly. In fact, her command to Captain Drysso, telling him to flee before the New Republic killed him and *Lusankya,* had been calculated to have just the opposite effect. As she intended, Drysso had remained at Thyferra and had been killed in the battle.

Now, with years of hindsight, Isard realized how Horn's escape and her forced evacuation of Imperial Center had affected her. It had worn her down. She had not been thinking clearly during her time as ruler of Thyferra. She made mistakes that now she could see were clearly preventable. The loss of Imperial Center through her narrow escape from Thyferra had been a crucible in which her desperation and insanity had been burned from her. During the time of Thrawn's campaign she had pulled herself together, tapped into still existing sources of information, and had taken over one of the many hidden Imperial installations, from which she plotted her renewed rise to power.

Crucial to that rise had been the repossession of *Lusankya*. At Thyferra *Lusankya* had likewise been in a crucible. Its defects, the taint Horn had left on it, had been burned out of it. The New Republic had taken it away from Thyferra; first to a hidden Rebel installation where the basic refits had been done, then to Bilbringi where the final work could be completed. The New Republic had fully restored *Lusankya*.

And now I shall use Lusankya *to restore me to power.* With the Super Star Destroyer under her command, bringing the various warlords to heel would be simple. As powerful as they were, she would threaten them with destruction unless they allied themselves with her. Teradoc and Harssk might pose a problem at first, but people like Tavira, with her *Invidious*, would flock to Isard's banner. With a new Imperial force she would be able to negotiate with whoever succeeded Thrawn and even unite the disparate worlds that still claimed allegiance to the Empire. In a very short time she would forge a new Empire and press in on the New Republic, shattering them. *I will have a realm which will make the Emperor proud.*

The *Swift* slowed as the command tower loomed up over it. The freighter rotated ninety degrees to orient its docking collar with the docking point at the base of the tower. Below her, booted feet clanked along grating as Major Telik's commandos positioned themselves to move forward and take possession of the ship. They would make immediately for the bridge along with a hand-picked crew of Naval officers who had been training for months on how to run a Super Star Destroyer.

Her ears popped as a small pressure wave pulsed through *Swift*. Isard turned from the viewport and descended a ladder to the lower deck. Commandos in dark gray armor poured through the docking collar and into *Lusankya*. The black-clad sailors jogged after them and soon were lost in the bowels of the larger ship.

Isard started toward the docking collar, but the *Swift*'s Captain stopped her. "Colonel Vessery's squadrons have made the jump in-system and have taken up patrolling in case garrison troops from Bilbringi come up. I've told him you'll issue a recall for his fighters to dock with *Lusankya* or that Helm will send him coordinates for a jump when we leave the system."

"Very good." Isard eyed the man up and down. "Perhaps it is time for you to move up and command something larger than this freighter."

The man smiled. "It would be my pleasure."

"Report to the bridge and let me know when you get there."

The Captain straightened up to his full height. "It would be my honor to escort you to the bridge, Madam Director."

"I'm certain, but I am headed elsewhere."

"We only have fifty commandos on the ship. Not all areas are secure."

Isard drew back her left sleeve to reveal a holdout blaster concealed there. "I am not without resources to defend myself, Captain Wintle. Contact me when you reach the bridge."

"As you command." Wintle took off running into *Lusankya*, as eager as a little boy being given his first airspeeder.

Isard allowed herself to smile at that, less taking joy in his display of enthusiasm than in her realization that allowing someone to attain a dream, or think a dream is within grasping distance, creates a vulnerable period during which striking at and destroying them is easy. *In their joy they let their guard down, and that is when they die.*

The solitary echo of her footfalls as she entered *Lusankya* reminded her of the first time she set foot on the ship. The Emperor had brought her to one of his hidden sanctums, one of the various satellite palace complexes he maintained on Imperial Center. He let her enter *Lusankya* all alone, being the first person to touch it, the first person to see it. If it was true that the very act of observing and experiencing something changed the thing being observed, then Isard had been the agent of change in *Lusankya*, and it had changed her as well. It became her source of power, hidden, lurking, much as she hid and lurked and worked to preserve the Emperor's power.

She entered a turbolift and ascended to a midway point in the command tower. She exited the lift and paced down a half-lit hallway. A couple of twists and turns later she stood before a pair of red doors. She pressed her hand to the center of them and they opened at her touch. She smiled. The ship's ability to recognize her had been hard-coded into the basic systems and clearly the New Republic had not found all of them.

She entered a room that was small by planetary standards, but huge when compared to the cabins on a ship—even a ship the size of a small city. The Emperor had ordered it finished in fine exotic woods—something he knew would please her—and the New Republic had not stripped away his handiwork. The dimmed lights glowed golden off the strips of paneling, imparting a warmth to the room that made her realize that for the longest time she had felt terribly cold and disconnected from the world.

Stepping deeper into the room, she did notice one change. There, on the back wall, between the hatchways to the rest of her suite and a small storage closet, the wood-workers had once used ebony to create the Imperial crest. The whole of that inlay had been pulled out and, in its place, natural reddish woods had been employed to display the Rebel crest.

She hated the Rebel crest's soft curves and languid angles. To her it had no strength, no ability to stir the spirit. The Imperial crest, all hard and angular, sharp and dark, radiated strength and commanded fealty. *The Rebels, they never could appreciate that fact. I will give them another chance to learn that lesson.*

Isard strode to the high-backed chair set in the middle of the forward part of the room. She sank into the thick nerf-hide cushions, letting the raw, wild scent of them take her back to more pleasant times. She unclipped her comlink from her belt and snapped it into the circular jack on one of the blocky chair's arms. "Captain Wintle, report, if you please."

A holoprojector mounted in the floor conveyed a three-quarters tall image of a winded Wintle to her, placing it at her feet. "Forgive me, Madam Director, but I only just got here. The atmosphere here is a bit lighter than expected—the equivalent of a mountaintop. We are working with environmental controls to change that now. The atmosphere would be appropriate for Verpine technicians, and there is some indication the creatures have been working here."

"I see." Isard's eyes narrowed. "Is there a problem adjusting the atmosphere? That should be a simple matter."

"It should, yes, but environmental and helm controls seem to be locked out up here. They are routed into the auxiliary bridge. We're preparing a team to go down there and shift control back up here."

Isard's frown deepened. "Dispatch your team, and send commandos with them. Do it at once. I will meet them at the auxiliary bridge."

"As ordered, Madam Director."

"Be quick about it, Captain Wintle. Isard out."

She plucked her comlink from the chair slot and stood, for the first time noticing the open door to the rest of the suite and the woman standing there with a drawn blaster. Isard thought for a second, then nodded slowly. "Yes, you are the Wessiri woman. You work for Cracken. You were married to one of my people."

Iella Wessiri's brown eyes hardened. "Diric was never one of your people. Even at the end he defied you."

"Ah, then the reports I read of his killing Kirtan Loor and your killing him were incorrect?" Isard allowed herself a smile. "I can tell you about your Diric. He broke almost immediately. We'd barely gotten him strapped into the interrogation unit when he started babbling on about all manner of things. I know more about you and the intimate details of your life with him than anyone should have been forced to listen to. Why . . ."

"Shut up."

What surprised Isard was not what Iella said, but how she said it. Isard expected a shrill, snapped answer, uttered as censure and meant to inflict pain. Instead it came as a matter-of-fact comment, devoid of emotion. Isard couldn't believe Iella could be so calm in the face of what she had been saying. *And she will not remain so forever.*

Iella shook her head. "You're not in control here, Isard. I have three people in the auxiliary bridge. Your people left on the bridge will suddenly find themselves with too little oxygen to function and they'll drop into a deep sleep. Those heading down to the auxiliary bridge will find themselves trapped in a section of corridor in which the atmosphere will be pumped up to five times normal pressure. Even if they have their own sources of oxygen, the pressure will prevent them from being able to breathe. They'll go out, too.

Isard twisted the bottom of her comlink, then raised it to her lips. Her words burst out over the ship's internal communications system. "Now hear this, I am Ysanne Isard. To the three people in the auxiliary bridge, I offer twenty-five million Imperial credits each to turn the ship over to my representatives. If your compatriots object, kill them and the whole amount is yours."

The holoprojector burned to life again, showing a tall, white-haired man with a mechanical left eye standing between a dark-haired woman and a black Bothan with splashes of white over her fur. "This is Booster Terrik, Acting-Captain of the *Lusankya*. My loyal bridge crew and I agree there are not enough credits in the galaxy for you to buy control of this ship from us. Iella, kill her and be done with it."

As the holograph faded, Isard looked over at Iella. "So, I forced you to murder your husband, and now you will shoot me in cold blood? Is that the plan?"

Iella shook her head. "Booster's idea of justice is a bit more direct than mine, a little less refined."

"Really? No desire for revenge?" Isard arched the eyebrow over her blue eye at Iella. "I am the one who warped your husband. I bent him to my will, shattered his mind, made him into my plaything. Don't you want me dead?"

"I'm not going to shed any tears when you die, Isard." Iella smiled easily. "Killing you would be too easy, though. It would deny you the time you'll spend agonizing over how we found you, how we knew you were coming for this ship."

A shiver ran down Isard's spine at the thought she was predictable, but she twisted a smile onto her face to hide her consternation. "Actually, I wonder how you even knew I was alive. Deducing the rest from that fact I can imagine. None of Horn's messages got out."

"No? And when was the last time you checked on the droids you had put into storage?"

Isard's head came up and an unfamiliar sensation of dread crawled through her belly on sharp, icy claws. "The droids were restrained and used as hostages, but no one checked on them. So, one got away."

"Two, actually."

"Base security will be purged for that." Isard nodded a salute to the other woman. "Next time, no such mistake will be made."

"There won't be a next time."

"No? The New Republic won't dare put me on trial. Too many of the people you rely upon to administer the government could be exposed. I know all their secrets, and that includes many members of your precious Senate." Isard allowed herself to smile broadly. "I'll never come to trial in a Ministry of Justice court."

"No, you won't." Iella's smile matched her own. "You

attempted to take control of this New Republic ship. That's piracy, and that's an offense for which you can and will be tried in a military court. No public trial, no chance to stir up hysteria. You'll just be convicted and sent to a very secure prison."

The woman hesitated for a moment, then nodded. "I understand they're thinking of keeping you here, on *Lusankya*. You'll be an anonymous prisoner, cared for by droids, forgotten, locked away in the heart of the very prison you yourself created. For the rest of your natural life."

That prospect stunned Isard and, in a moment's intro-spection, was what undid her. The terror inspired by such a fate prompted her to shoot her left arm forward, letting the holdout blaster slide down into her left hand. It was a rash act, one only possible when the horror of *life entombed* out-weighed the horror of death.

Her shock also made her a bit slower than she should have been. Her first shot took Iella Wessiri in the left shoul-der, halfway twisting her around. The blaster in Iella's right hand remained steady, however, and the shot from it caught Isard square in the stomach. She felt herself snapping forward, then flying back. Pain shot down her legs as she struck the wall, then stars exploded before her eyes as her head rebounded. She heard the distant clatter of her blaster on the floor as she slid down the wall.

Peering down, she saw her red uniform jacket was smoldering. Smoke rose to her eyes, which was the only rea-son she began to shed tears. Blood soaked her jacket and be-gan to seep into her trousers. Pain, a raw, fiery sensation, pulsed through her body, and every breath came with wringing agony.

She looked up at Iella and opened her mouth to make yet one more taunt about Diric, but her lungs couldn't project as much as a squeak. Isard tried to give her a hard stare, the sort of hard stare that had broken Imperial no-bles and invoked fear in her inferiors, but her gaze swam out of focus.

Then, before she could find any other way to try to hurt another human being, the world grew dark around her. In that last moment, in the sanctum the Emperor had given her, she realized she had failed him. With that realization held solidly in her mind, she admitted to herself that death would not be so bad after all.

38

Standing in the midst of a party being held on the *Lusankya* summoned up for Corran Horn a variety of conflicting emotions. The freed prisoners and anyone who had been in contact with them had been brought to *Lusankya* and ensconced on a crew deck, being served by droids alone, for two weeks until New Republic medical officials completed their scans and decided they were disease free.

The release of the prisoners from isolation became a cause for celebration that drew officials and important people from all across the New Republic. At the far end of the large reception room, with his back to a massive transparisteel viewport that looked out over the vast expanse of the ship's prow, General Dodonna stood flanked by Admiral Ackbar and Generals Bel Iblis and Antilles. A constant stream of well-wishers moved past them, exchanging comments, glances, handshakes, and smiles. Dodonna greeted warmly those individuals he recalled from Yavin and before, exuding the warmth and wisdom that had made him the natural leader of the prisoners.

Corran smiled slowly. During his escape attempt from *Lusankya*, Jan Dodonna had killed a man who tried to stop Corran. The way to freedom was clear and Corran offered to let Dodonna accompany him. Dodonna had refused, knowing that if he escaped, Isard would have wiped out the rest of the prisoners. He traded his freedom for their lives, a sacrifice that earned him two more years of captivity.

I'm not sure I could make that choice. Corran sipped Corellian whiskey. *I hope I could, but I don't know if I'm that good a man.*

While everyone around him seemed to be very happy—with Booster's booming laughter echoing from the far corner of the room—something felt out of place for Corran. *The last party I was at, Urlor Sette died, propelling all of us down the path that brought us here.*

Friends died and countless people suffered. Through the milling crowd he caught sight of Gavin Darklighter talking with Myn Donos and a couple of other people Corran didn't recognize. Gavin had a smile on his face, but the way he moved and his short responses told Corran that Asyr's death still ate away at him. *Gavin's a good man and doesn't deserve such pain. I'm going to make sure to talk with him, help share the burden. He's strong, he just needs someone to remind him of that fact.*

Wes Janson came over and slapped Corran on the back. "We dress well for dead men, don't we?"

"Well, better for me this time than the last one." Corran smiled at him. "But making a habit of being left for dead isn't a good idea."

Wes nodded solemnly, though his smile only eroded slightly at the corners of his mouth. "When I thought you guys were all gone . . ." He shivered for a second and his voice faltered. "Then to see you again, albeit through a transparisteel wall while you were in isolation, you don't know how happy I was."

"Oh, I have a clue." Corran jerked his head toward the front of the room. "My ears are still ringing from the happy *whoop* Wedge let out. He really couldn't contain himself."

"Yeah, and that little Ewok dance of joy is pretty ugly to watch, isn't it?"

"Watch? I was trying to get my feet out from under

his." Corran and Wes both laughed, then the Corellian pilot gave his friend a nod. "Wish you'd been with us on Ciutric, and I'm very glad to have you back with us now."

"Yes, active duty beats being dead all hollow." Wes tossed him a wink, then threaded his way off in Wedge's direction.

Corran shifted his shoulders to loosen them. *Probably going to pull some Ewok prank on Wedge, and Wedge will love hating every minute of it.* Turning away from Wes's departure, Corran smiled as Iella and Mirax cut through the crowd and joined him.

Mirax looked radiant in a long, sleeveless gown worn daringly off one shoulder. The garment appeared black, but a shimmering rainbow of pinpricks channeled light over it and her. She wore her dark hair up, and two tiny diamond studs sparkled from her earlobes.

Iella wore a white gown with a short jacket over it. A single diamond on a platinum chain lay at the hollow of her throat, casting off dazzling light darts as she moved. Her hair had been gathered loosely at the back of her neck with a simple black cord. Her outfit, while not as flashy as Mirax's, had an elegance to it that matched Iella's noble bearing.

Mirax slipped her right hand through the crook of Corran's left arm. "Enjoying yourself?"

"Now I am, yes." He smiled at his wife. Her physical warmth and presence bled into him, pushing aside the sense of foreboding he'd been feeling. "How's the shoulder, Iella?"

She worked her left shoulder forward and back. "It's fine. Full range of motion and all. Nothing bacta couldn't handle. You know that—you've been wounded much worse and survived."

"True, if there's a spark of life, bacta will keep you going."

Iella nodded. "Happy to be out of isolation?"

"Very." Corran jerked his head toward General Dodonna. "It was very weird to be a prisoner of sorts on *Lusankya* again. We got the run of the deck they trapped us on, which happened to have been the deck where we were held the first time. The accommodations were a lot nicer this time around, though."

"*Lusankya* looks nothing like it did when we were married on it." Mirax took his whiskey from him and drank a sip. "I definitely think it's an improvement."

Corran nodded. "I guess a lot of refitting went on. There's a whole forward area where living creatures aren't allowed to go. It's just serviced by droids."

Iella coughed into her hand. "It's a bio-containment facility. It apparently struck some of the designers that in rebuilding the prow, they could put in scientific and medical suites that would allow *Lusankya* to be more than just a military ship. I think their sense of irony prompted them to put an area on board that, had it existed when the Krytos virus broke out, would have been useful in thwarting Isard's plan. In the heart of that area there is supposed to be a containment cell so secure that any breach in it will immediately vent the whole area to space. Nothing, no virus or germ, will be getting out of there alive."

"That's a plus." Corran smiled slightly, then looked around. "Kind of funny about Isard coming back here. I guess it makes sense, but she had me fooled. She told me she was glad the ship had been destroyed, since I ruined it for her. How did you figure out she was coming back for it?"

The two women exchanged a laugh. "Actually it was Mirax's father who figured it out."

"You're kidding."

"Nope." Iella shook her head. "The process sort of involved logic, but it was a bit twisted . . ."

Mirax sighed. "It was Booster-logic."

"I hope you had a Three-Pee-Oh there to translate."

Mirax slapped Corran on the arm. "Easy, husband. If not for him you'd be fighting this monster."

Iella smiled. "Booster started from the idea that Isard wanted to reestablish the Empire, then he started breaking it down into all the steps she'd need to succeed at to get there. Somewhere in that list was a serious need to be able to inflict heavy damage on her enemies. From there Booster got to the *Lusankya* reborn, which he'd figured the New Republic was refitting because of the prices being offered for parts on the secondary commodities markets.

"Cracken provided us with authorization to commandeer whatever we needed, so the four of us came here and took command."

"Four of you?"

Mirax and Iella exchanged a quick glance, then Corran's wife gave his arm a squeeze. "Booster, Iella, me, and a Verpine tech who did some quick rewiring. We trapped Isard's people and Iella took care of her in her own private quarters."

Corran remained silent for a moment, then nodded. "You think Diric is finally at peace?"

"I hope so. Isard had reduced Diric to something he never wanted to be. Eliminating her won't bring him back, but she'll never do that to anyone else, so that's a plus. I can live with it."

"And live much better for it." Corran shivered. "I wonder if she'll end up haunting this place."

"I have no doubt part of her will always be with the *Lusankya*."

"Right where it belongs." Corran sipped more of his whiskey. "Any word on what happened to Colonel Vessery and his people?"

Iella shook her head. "He vanished, taking his two squadrons of Defenders with him. General Cracken isn't looking forward to his return."

"I can understand that, but I don't fear it." Corran smiled. "In his own way Vessery is a very honorable man. He'll do what's right for his people."

"Let's just hope that doesn't include piracy." Iella looked up toward the front of the room. "Looks like speeches are about to begin."

Corran turned to follow her gaze. Borsk Fey'lya was moving toward a podium, with Admiral Ackbar and General Dodonna standing near him. Other officials lined up off to the right, and in the background a disk-shaped freighter lazily cruised down the Super Star Destroyer's length. "I think we can get closer."

"You two go ahead. I'm going to slip out for a moment, get something from my room." Iella patted Corran on the shoulder. "It's another adventure we've survived, Corran. Twice now you've been declared dead and come back. Impressive."

"But that's the last time for that." Mirax gave Corran a hard stare. "Anybody goes missing and next time it's me. You can do the worrying, okay?"

"Okay." He turned to Iella. "Hurry back, we'll save a spot at our table for you for dinner."

"Thanks." Iella turned and headed for the hatchway leading toward the turbolifts.

Corran took Mirax's hand in his and led her forward to where they could see the speakers. She moved around to stand in front of him and pressed her back against him. He rested his chin on her bare shoulder and snaked his arms around her waist.

Mirax turned her head and kissed him on the cheek. "It truly is wonderful to have you back. And I very much appreciate the sacrifice you made in sending Whistler to find me and let me know you were alive."

"I floated it as a plan, and Whistler insisted. He's quite fond of you, you know."

"And I am of him." Mirax smiled and kissed him again as Fey'lya began to speak. "After all, he's my ally in keeping you safe and that's a job we intend to continue for a very long time to come."

Iella slipped into her small cabin on *Lusankya* and inserted her comlink into the room's comm unit holoprojector. "This is Iella Wessiri calling *Starweb*."

The image of the disk freighter she'd seen from the reception hung above the projector pad for a second, then it shifted to Asyr Sei'lar's head and shoulders. "I left a message for you and for Mirax to let you know I'm leaving."

"You don't have to, Asyr." Iella glanced out the room's viewport and saw the freighter hanging off the starboard bow. "You can come back, we can explain things."

"No. I'm better off dead."

"But, Gavin, he's . . . you can tell he hurts inside."

The Bothan looked away from the holocam for a moment, then sniffed and turned back. "I know, Iella. I know how much he must hurt, but he will get over it. He's a strong man. He will mourn, then recover and thrive. I know it. You have to remember what I told you from the start, when you recovered me at Distna, about why you had to tell no one I lived."

"Borsk Fey'lya isn't the Emperor." Iella opened her arms wide with exasperation. "You said he told you he'd never allow the two of you to marry and adopt, and that he would make your lives miserable. That's a gross abuse of power. He can't be allowed to get away with that."

"I know that, Iella, and I won't let him." Asyr's lips peeled back in a smile that revealed sharp white teeth. "I'll go to one of our colony worlds and assume a new identity. I'll work to make changes within Bothan society that will guarantee politicians like Fey'lya cannot ruin other lives. If I come back to life now and expose what he's done, I will take one individual down. The system still fosters that sort of power, and I need to work to change it."

"Gavin would be a great help to you in all that."

"I know, but it will be a dirty battle, fought the way only Bothans can fight." She blinked her violet eyes. "It will consume my life, but I won't have it consume his. Gavin is a good enough man that he would devote himself to helping me, but I can't do that to him. He deserves better. Help him through it."

"I will, we will."

Asyr nodded. "Thank you. And I apologize for putting you and Mirax through the pressure of keeping my survival hidden. Spouses shouldn't keep secrets from each other."

Iella raised an eyebrow. "Never been married, have you?"

Surprise showed on Asyr's face, then she laughed. "No.

Perhaps someday. Well, I'm clear on a vector to hyperspace. Let Booster know this ship will be waiting for him at Commenor, as we discussed. Good-bye, Iella, and thank you."

"Bye, Asyr, until we meet again."

The Bothan's image blinked out as the freighter shot into hyperspace. Iella brushed a tear from her right cheek, then took her comlink and headed toward the door. It slid open, with a man standing there, his hand poised over the door buzzer button.

"Wedge!"

"Iella, good, I did find you." The leader of Rogue Squadron gave her a sloppy, boyish grin. "I saw Corran and Mirax. They said you'd come down here."

"And you came to find me." Iella grinned. "Looking to have me recommend to General Cracken that we make you an intelligence operative based on this tracking experience?"

"Ah, um, no." He raised his head. "I was wondering, I mean, I thought of this before, but never got a chance to ask you . . . They said they would be saving a place for you at their table, but I'm having to sit with a bunch of Senators who I don't know . . ."

"And you want someone on your wing?"

"Yeah, someone on my wing." He extended his arm to her. "Interested in the job?"

"Sounds like a dangerous assignment." She squinted at him for a moment. "Think I can handle it?"

"Definitely, Iella. You're Rogue material." Wedge smiled as she slipped her hand on his arm and laid his left hand over hers. "We both eliminated a Ysanne Isard from the galaxy and, after that, together, there's nothing that can beat us."

ABOUT THE AUTHOR

Michael A. Stackpole is a writer and game designer who wasn't born in a galaxy far, far away, but was born a long time ago. He grew up in Vermont and then moved to Arizona to pursue a career in writing. He could have pursued that career in Vermont, of course, but shoveling snow would have taken up a lot of time in the winter, cutting his output. (*Isard's Revenge* is his twenty-eighth published book since 1988.) He lives in Arizona with Liz Danforth and three Welsh Cardigan Corgis: Ruthless, Ember, and Saint. In 1998 he took up the hobby of white water rafting and lived to tell about it.

He's just completed *The Dark Glory War*, which will be available from Bantam Books in January 2000 (or, for those of you working with Windows, January 1901).

His website can be found at http://www.flyingbuffalo. com/stackpol.htm (Please note that there is no "e" on stackpole there, and the extension is .htm, not .html.)